Northern Exposure

By

Dallas White

Table of Contents

Dedication

This book is dedicated to my friend, the Gypsy Queen, an exotic, intelligent, wonderful dingbat of a woman I had the pleasure of meeting at exactly the right time in my life.

GQ, I love you for exactly who you are and thank you for the knowledge and insight I needed at that moment in my life to start this book. Shukran.

Prologue

Late Summer of 1960

Horseshoe Basin Area of the Pasayten Wilderness

Northcentral Washington State, USA

"Rory," yelled Callum Blackwood to his young son. "Go get that lamb."

Rory, who had been sitting whittling with his new friend, bolted immediately, grabbed the lasso hanging on the broken limb hanging next to him and began walking nonchalantly toward a mother and lamb that huddled at the fringe of the herd of sheep grazing lazily about one hundred feet away.

"You can go, too," Blackwood said to Mike, who was sitting next to his son and appeared around the same age as Rory.

Mike was the ten-year-old son of lead the U. S. Forest Ranger, Mark Anderson, who was stationed in the Conconully office. Anderson had recently finished his degree in range management at Washington State University a little over ten years earlier. Anderson agreed to a two-year stint in the small town of just over 100 people on the promise by the Regional Superintendent that he would be transferred to the Okanagan office some forty miles away when his daughter finished the eighth grade. If they did not make the move at that time, the girl would have to drive or be driven to school in Okanagan. Confident their move would happen in the fall, Anderson had brought his two boys, Mike and Bob, and wife Dorothy with him on an early summer assignment into Horseshoe Basin, believing this would be their last opportunity for such a trip.

His mission was to restock a remote, one-time homesteader's cabin, now owned by the Forest Service cabin, with supplies for smokejumpers regularly dropped into the wilderness area to fight lighting-started forest fires. By late fall, however, bears, often grizzlies, regularly broke into the cabin to scavenge for unused, unprotected food before they entered hibernation. Rory motioned to Mike to come along, and Mike jumped up, scurrying to catch up.

Trial and error had taught the sheep the right distance to stray from the sheep herder's camp. More than three hundred feet, the two dogs that watched them would bound to the herd's outer limits, barking advice and intentions to one another while nipping at their ewe's heels until they moved them back to an acceptable distance from the campground. Instinctively and interestingly, the sheep did not actually fear the dogs. Yes, the nips were annoying. But they knew there were dangers too far out, unfamiliar beasts in the shadows, bears, wolves, and cougars, that were far greater threats than the pesky dogs that constantly managed them. The dogs were the sheep's warning signal and gave them the luxury of not having to pay attention; even animals as dumb as sheep understood the constant presence of death lurking inside the forest's murkiness.

"Sure," said Mike, unaware of what was about to take place, and the two boys headed out to help his new friend catch a lamb.

As the boys approached the selected sacrifice, Rory pointed his index finger toward the right, signaling Mike to flank the lamb before slowly moving his arm and palm down, implying he should approach the mother and lamb carefully. As soon as the ewe and lamb looked in Mike's direction, Rory held up his hand, palm facing Mike, to stop. The two animals looked at Mike to assess his next move while Rory, holding the loop in his right hand, prepared his lasso for throwing, releasing enough rope from his left to allow him to make a ten-to-twelve-foot toss. When he was within throwing distance, Rory halted.

In the meantime, the mother-lamb duo continued to graze, occasionally glancing up in Mike's direction to monitor his presence. Rory waited patiently for a minute or so, and when the lamb raised its head to look in Mike's direction, he casually tossed the loop at the lamb's head. The loop plopped onto the lamb's neck, causing the animal to jump forward, which immediately pulled the rope snug around its neck. Rory pulled the rope with his right, and the lamb did a 1-80, turning around to face him while backing away toward Mike. The lamb quickly began bawling, and its mother stopped eating long enough to assess the two boys as 'no risk' before returning to completing garnering another mouthful of grass, not demonstrating any concern until the boys began directing the lamb, Rory pulling and Mike pushing toward the campsite. The lamb's bawling transformed into an all-out wail for help, finally catching the mother's attention, and she began following her baby. The dogs quickly directed her back towards the flock, where she watched dumbly, dazed, whimpering a sad, pitiful ditty of concern between munches of grass.

"Bring it over here," said Callum.

As soon as the lamb was in front of him, Blackwood stepped his left leg over and grabbed a handful of hair at the top of its head. Squeezing the animal between his legs while maintaining his grip with his left, he pulled his knife from its sheath on his right backside. The lamb's blood created a magically macabre bright red and white contrast. Mike, along with his mother and sister, gasped. The lamb's mother, smelling death, began a passionate cry that caused the flock to temporarily move left and right in nervous, abrupt, zig-zag motions. The lamb made no noise; Blackwood's cut deep enough to sever its larynx. The animal quickly fell to its knees, and Callum quickly began skinning and gutting it.

"You okay?" Blackwood said to Dorothy Anderson, who had begun a series of dry heaves from where she sat.

"Yes," she said. "I just wasn't prepared for this…"

"To be so fresh," Blackwood finished for her.

Dorothy smiled and nodded.

"Well, sorry to lay that on you, Mrs. Anderson. Sorry. This won't take long."

Blackwood finished prepping the animal for cooking shortly and then wrapped the head and entrails in the hide before sending Rory and Mike off to the forest's edge a half mile from the campsite, where they were to put it thirty yards or so inside the tree line. He had set up a pile of wood under a spit, which he lit, before cleaning the carcass. Once cleansed, he mounted it on the spit. Two hours later, the main course for dinner was ready to be served.

As the families sat at their respective places in a staggered circle some twenty paces to the east of the fire, Dorothy asked, "What is that dust ball, Callum?" Her point of interest looked to be about three-quarters of a mile away. The large natural meadow where Blackwood grazed his sheep every summer was about two hundred yards wide, north to south, stretching almost a mile and a half west to east.

"That?" he asked, pointing. "That's a group of new American citizens, most likely." Dorothy's face contorted in confusion. "They're Chinese, is my guess. They come from Hong Kong to Vancouver. Both in the Commonwealth and all that. So, most legally. Those who don't want to stay in Canada, though, can't get into the

U.S. legally; well, they have to wait to get a Green Card. But that can take a pretty long time, so they come in through the Pasayten instead. Mostly through Horseshoe Basin here."

"No shit," said Mark Anderson. "Where do the go from here?"

"They take the Pacific Crest Trail, I'm told, for the most part," said Blackwood, "usually down to the head of Lake Chelan, and they boat 'em out. Sometimes, they cut across to Ross Lake. That's a little more visible, so I believe the preferred route is to Lake Chelan."

"Shouldn't we stop them? Don't the cops want to stop this?" asked Ranger Anderson.

"Well, there ain't any cops out here. None to stop them or help us deal with those bringing them in, for sure. Easier to leave 'em alone. It's not a huge number. Maybe a couple hundred or less a year. A bunch of locals, though, make a lot of money. Part of the local economy and all that. No need to swat that hornet's nest. You'll just end up making enemies with otherwise pretty law-abiding folks."

Anderson considered the situation. No tourists ever came in here. Unbeknownst to him and the others, wilderness trekking would not become popular with the general population for another twenty years. He had worried for his family's safety before deciding to bring them in, but not by aliens crossing the border illegally. It was more about if they got hurt from falling off a horse or an attack from a wild animal. They could not call for help if someone got hurt, so playing sheriff only magnified the risks. "Hmm," he pondered. "Makes sense." The two men nodded their heads in unison. "I guess that answers 'where do all those Chinese restaurants in small town USA come from?'" Anderson concluded.

"There you go," said Blackwood, and the group laughed.

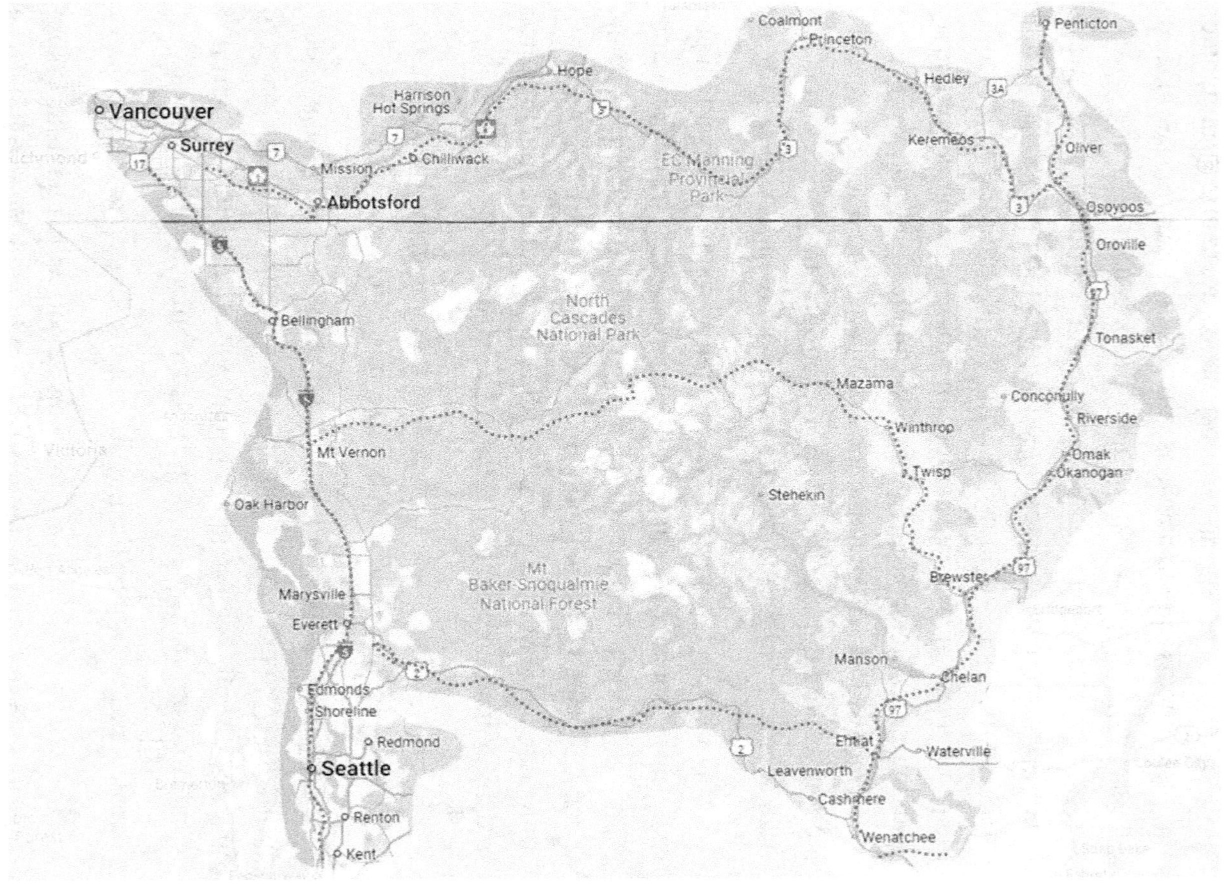

Vancouver
Surrey
Abbotsford
Mission
Chilliwack
Harrison Hot Springs
Hope
Coalmont
Princeton
Hedley
Penticton
Keremeos
Oliver
Osoyoos
Oroville
Tonasket
Conconully
Riverside
Omak
Okanogan
E.C. Manning Provincial Park
North Cascades National Park
Mazama
Winthrop
Twisp
Stehekin
Bellingham
Mt Vernon
Oak Harbor
Mt. Baker-Snoqualmie National Forest
Brewster
Manson
Chelan
Marysville
Everett
Edmonds
Shoreline
Redmond
Seattle
Renton
Kent
Entiat
Waterville
Leavenworth
Cashmere
Wenatchee

Part I –
Entanglement

Early March

2020 Vancouver, B.C.

"Balil! Balil, come back!!" yelled his father.

Balil, a small boy, stood in the boat as it slowly drifted toward the waterfall's edge.

"But I cannot," he cried out. "I have no oars," he wailed in terror. "You must come and help me."

Balil's father held up his arms, palms up at shoulder height. "I'm sorry, my son, but I cannot. You must save yourself. Get out of the river before it sweeps you away. Come back to shore where you belong."

"But I cannot turn around," Balil sobbed as the dinghy began to slip over the edge of the falls.

Just as his boat began to fall, he recalled something his high school physics instructor had said during a discussion on gravity: It's not the fall that kills you. It's the sudden stop. As he cascaded down, he also remembered what his grandmother had told him: If you die in a dream, you die in real life. He fell in 'slow motion,' the ground beckoning him as he descended. "Wake up," his grandmother called just as he smacked into the ground. Hard. It hurt.

Groggy, he steadily began to open his eyes. Was he dead? Was this heaven? Hell? He was certain it wasn't heaven. It was too dark, though it seemed to be getting lighter as his eyes adjusted. He blinked a few times and rolled onto his side.

Gradually, the surroundings became mildly familiar; it was his Uncle Ali Al-Ebadi's condo, one of the unit's two guest rooms, where he had slept for most of the past two days.

The mountains to the east of the city delayed the sun's arrival, holding it back like a car's headlights about to crest the horizon, increasing in intensity until it finally rose high enough to breach the barrier, flood the landscape, and blind the onlooker. As daybreak crept in, the sky came to life leisurely in a panoply of reds, pinks, oranges, whites, and blues, creating a tapestry of colors capable of inspiring chills in even the most hardened of hearts.

For just over an hour, Bilal lay on the floor and watched this progression as the condo's bedroom walls grew increasingly brighter before finally getting up, stretching, and walking into the living room. Ali's cornered window looked east over Stanley Park and south across the bay toward Grouse Mountain. Small patches of fog hovered over the harbor, some so close to the water that the bottoms of several ships disappeared and reappeared as if playing hide-and-seek while others seemed to float on clouds above the water. As the sun rose higher, the water began changing from a dark, bluish-green to a brilliant royal blue. 'This might not be heaven,' he thought, 'but heaven could not be more beautiful.'

Balil's real name was Abou Amin, a nickname meaning "Chosen One," given to him when the boy turned three by his father, Amir Amin, who was certain his precocious son would change the world. His two friends, Farhan and Odion, were still in bed, and as Balil absorbed the panorama, he reflected on the ordeal the three had gone through the last two months, particularly the last three weeks.

They had been smuggled into the city on a small cargo ship registered in Panama that primarily transported fresh produce from Central and South America to the American West Coast and Canada. After dropping off a small load of food supplies, the ship returned to its primary pickup port in Valparaíso, Chile. There, it loaded containers of fresh and frozen fish, avocados, various vegetables, grapes, and other seasonal fruits and nuts before continuing to Pisco, Peru, where it added to its cargo.

Just above the old ship's propeller was a door leading to a repair space that submerged below the waterline when the ship was fully loaded. The room was a cramped cubicle measuring approximately 6.5' x 8' x 8,' where mechanics could maintain and repair a section of the drivetrain between the engines and the propellers when the ship was docked and empty. The three men had boarded the ship in Pisco, Peru, while the room was still accessible, eventually allowing them to avoid a more thorough inspection by customs in Los Angeles or Vancouver. Although only approximately 5% of commercial vessels were physically examined in these ports, the men were aware of their perilous condition and took measures. Within three hours of entering the barely accessible room, the door had completely submerged as additional freight was loaded.

For the first three days of the first six-day leg of their voyage, the men had only a small amount of bread and cheese. As their provisions dwindled, they were left with just two gallons of water and one loaf of bread. Even if they had more food, it would have been difficult to keep it down. The constant pitching of the vessel in the cramped space caused severe seasickness for all three men, amplifying the nauseating stench that filled the cubicle. A small pot in the back left corner, initially used as a latrine, filled halfway through the fourth day with a grotesque, marinating mash of urine, feces, and vomit.

By the final two days, with little left to excrete except water and bile, the men endured the constant noise of the engine and propeller. They wore headphones over earplugs to protect their ears, but the cacophony of mechanical reverberations, grinding metal, and other relentless thumps was unbearable. The room was nearly pitch black, with only a small amount of light seeping in from the forward rooms around the propeller shaft. They used one of three flashlights to navigate the darkness, but with two of them burned out and the remaining one's light fading, maintaining their composure was a struggle.

Despite the deplorable conditions, the men were somewhat accustomed to such environments. In the years following the U.S. invasion of Iraq, they had all experienced periodic imprisonment or detention in cramped, torturous conditions. Loud, continuous rock music, minimal food, pitch-black rooms with no beds, solitary confinement, and inadequate sanitation had all been part of their pasts. Their captors had inadvertently prepared them for this ordeal. They were hardened, resolute, and willing to sacrifice. They would persevere.

"We can handle this," Bilal repeatedly told himself, adding, "But please, Allah, get us there quickly so I can breathe fresh air and hear nothing!"

In Los Angeles, the men enjoyed limited fresh air and food while their cabin was partially rinsed as the ship unloaded and reloaded produce before continuing to Vancouver, B.C. The men were relieved to find that their prayers had been answered as the ship remained on schedule, arriving in Vancouver six days later at the beginning of the second week of March. From there, they learned it was scheduled to unload the rest of its cargo and pick up a small load of lumber for Hong Kong before continuing to the Alang Ship Breaking Yard in India for salvage.

Upon arrival, they caught a cab to a nearby motel as directed by their sponsor. Though the trip's second leg was somewhat better than the first, the combined trip left them physically decimated and certain they would never smell the same. After two days of long showers, extensive sleep, and consuming takeout from a nearby Chinese restaurant twice a day, the men took a cab to Ali's condo, pretending they had just arrived.

Each man had been given a separate room and a set of clothes, including shirts, two pairs of pants, one sweater, casual shoes, and light boots. One pair of pants also contained a wallet with seven hundred fifty dollars Canadian. Balil had called Ali the day they arrived and told him they were driving up from Seattle and would arrive in two days. Though Ali wanted to pick up the group, Balil insisted they take a cab from the car rental dropoff to his condo. Happy to see the boy after so many years, he noticed they appeared a bit thin and traveled light, pondering how they managed to keep their clothes in such pristine condition.

Walking to the kitchen, Balil found their host reading the morning paper as usual with a cup of coffee. Bilal's training over the past two years had taught him to always walk softly and quietly.

"Salamu alaykum, Uncle."

"Ah, there you are—Al akum salaam. Good morning, good morning, my young friend," Ali said in Arabic, stroking the greying beard that framed his broad Iraqi smile. "Sit, please." He began pouring Bilal a cup of Luwak Star, adding, "Come, have a croissant and coffee with me. They're lovely," he said, gesturing toward the chair nearest Bilal. "Have you looked outside? Of course, you have. This is going to be a wonderful day. They aren't all this wonderful this time of the year. We'll have to go to the park for a walk, don't you think?" Ali asked enthusiastically. "It's probably a little chilly, but I have a nice coat for you."

Bilal said nothing at first, just sitting down stoically, getting comfortable, taking in the smell of the brew, and eyeing the golden, flaky croissant in front of him. He marveled at the transition from where the three soldiers had been such a short time earlier to where they were now, inside a plush, luxurious high-rise condominium in downtown Vancouver, British Columbia. It seemed like another lifetime. Surreal.

Now they had a toilet that made their waste disappear, faucets with endless fresh water, a shower for bathing, a refrigerator stocked with fresh foods of all kinds, and, most of all… quiet. Part of him wanted to stay here, to live in this wonderfully peaceful reality… forever.

He reached a little unsteadily for the plate, his fingers teasing several slivers from the croissant he carefully guided onto the tip of his tongue, savoring every morsel. Picking up a chunk, he dipped it into the pot of melted butter in the middle of the breakfast table, then added a mini spoonful of strawberry jam from the adjacent bowl. After carefully considering the concoction, he closed his eyes and guided it to his mouth, briefly relishing it before feeding himself three or four more pieces. He let them rest there before adding a sip of coffee, the disparate flavors melding into a splendid culinary amalgam that diffused throughout his mouth before he swallowed gratefully.

"Good, yes?" asked Ali.

Bilal simply nodded.

"You look like your father, Bilal. Do you know that?"

Bilal smiled. "Thank you, Uncle." Ali had reminded him of this regularly since his arrival, and Bilal always appreciated the comparison. He had loved his father deeply and thought of him daily since his passing almost two decades ago.

Ali was not Bilal's uncle but rather a business partner and close friend of his father, Amir Amin. Balil had adopted the term at a young age to honor the friendship and demonstrate his appreciation and respect for Ali's commitment to the Amin family over the years. Together, they developed a profitable business exporting quality Persian rugs as well as fine mohair and cashmere fabrics.

Before the Gulf War of 1991, Bilal's father and grandfather, with over forty years of experience between them, had built a successful midsized operation that served regional demand but had begun making inroads into European and North American markets.

However, after the Iraqi invasion in 1991, communications and travel were restricted, making it increasingly difficult to maintain relationships and conduct business outside the country.

To help the suddenly flailing business, Mr. Amir had recruited Ali, who had been working for a government agriculture agency. With Ali's help, the company recovered somewhat from the war's initial impacts. Balil concentrated on maintaining old relationships and creating new ones in remote areas of the country, while Ali kept communications open with their buyers. Toward the end of the 1990s, Ali and the Amir family decided that the business would benefit if one of them were outside the country. Being single, with no close family, and a Shia Muslim, Ali was the logical choice.

Though New York or Los Angeles were Ali's first choice, he was unsuccessful in obtaining an American visa. However, Canada welcomed young immigrants with money, which Ali had. While most Arabs in Canada lived in the eastern part of the country, Vancouver was booming. Besides appealing to the traditional population, his products also appealed to the appreciable number of new residents relocated from Iraq and Sudan. The business, known for its fine, hard-to-find products and superior customer service, grew in tandem. His personal image and reputation flourished within the city and the Pacific Northwest, and his retail business thrived.

"Salamu Alaykum," Balil's two compatriots, Farhan and Odion, greeted in unison as they entered the room.

After just under a week in Vancouver, all three men had regained their 'land legs,' though the conditions of their voyage still lingered in their minds. Most importantly, the pounding in their heads had nearly subsided, although the old adage, *The Silence Was Deafening*, was sometimes meaningfully unnerving.

"Al akum salaam," Bilal and Ali responded in chorus.

"Please join us," Ali invited with a welcoming wave toward the table's two remaining chairs. Ali poured coffee and laid out another plate of croissants, and the two guests eagerly dug in.

"Thank you, Uncle," said Farhan.

"Yes, thank you, Uncle Ali," added Odion.

Bilal and Farhan had only met Odion just before their deployment. The two, however, had been childhood friends in Baghdad, growing up in the same neighborhood and attending school together. They had attended Al-Mutamaizeen High School, an elite academy in Baghdad.

In the summer of 2002, fearing for their safety due to growing tensions between Iraq and the United States, Mr. Amin sent them to Hawaii Preparatory Academy on the Big Island of Hawaii. The school, recommended by an American friend working for Halliburton, had a strong international reputation and a significant number of boarders, including children of American oil executives in the Middle East. Amir hoped that sending Balil to America would ensure his safety and improve his chances of attending a good American university.

To ease his son's transition, Amir also sent Farhan, who had been like a member of the Amin family since the death of his own mother and the disappearance of his father during the first Gulf War. The boys quickly adapted, learned English, excelled academically, and led their soccer team to a state championship in their junior year. They were set to repeat their success in their senior year in 2003 when they were brought home for spring break to celebrate Bilal's eighteenth birthday on March 20. However, this date coincided with the start of the American invasion of Iraq. Scheduled to return on March 22, Mr. Amin had hoped the boys would leave before any conflict began. Instead, they found themselves trapped in Iraq, their planned two-week visit extending into a nightmarish fifteen-year ordeal.

Not long after the U.S. invasion of Iraq, they spent a brief period in Abu Ghraib prison, imprisoned at the behest of a Shia neighbor who had a long-standing feud with Balil's father over the Amin family's pet dog. The neighbor, who had become an influential civil servant after the American takeover, accused Amir of collaborating with a group that had been setting off explosives in their area. The boys were eighteen at the time they were arrested, along with Mr. Amin. The three spent nearly forty-five days in confinement before being released with no charges filed. Mr. Amin, broken by his incarceration, struggled to keep his business viable. Within two years, however, he was dead, and his wife died of breast cancer a little over a year after that. Balil had a younger sister who married an American serviceman later stationed in Germany. They maintained contact for about five years before he stopped responding. Despite her continued efforts to reach him, she eventually gave up after two years of silence.

Fate had led the boys to this point. With Ramadan approaching in a few weeks, they were focused on gaining weight and rebuilding muscle mass before the fasting period began. They knew their next directives could come at any time and needed to be prepared.

"And, Balil," Farhan said warmly, "How are you today? Do you have any plans?"

Balil smiled at Farhan. "A walk with Uncle, perhaps," he said, his gaze shifting to the television where the U.S. president spoke on CNN International, the volume muted. He glanced back at Farhan and Odion and quoted their prophet: "Mohammed, may God's blessings and peace be upon him, said, 'Do not be like the hypocrite who, when he speaks, tells lies; when he makes a promise, he breaks it; and when he is trusted, he proves dishonest.'" He paused, then added, "The best way to defend Islam is to practice Islam. Let's pray."

After Amir died, the two had not communicated for almost two years. Then Balil resurrected his father's business, and the two relied heavily on one another's support for seven or eight years. Then Balil all but disappeared for all but almost three years. Ali had thought he was probably dead. But about twelve months earlier, Balil had reached out to him again, saying he was back in the business and was building back up the supply lines his father had spent so many years developing. Balil had said he wanted, along with two associates, to expand his business contacts in the States and Canada, see Vancouver, discuss business, and simply visit with his father's longtime friend and unofficial uncle. Ali had welcomed them all, expecting to see them for ten or so days.

The Covid outbreak, however, triggered a lockdown and a cessation of virtually all international travel, with Canada closing its borders to most travelers in mid-March and the U.S. a week later. That was followed by a lockdown of local activities, offering ideal cover for the three.

Ali insisted they not return to Iraq but stay in Canada, where they would be 'safer' and where medical treatment was better and more accessible than in Iraq. Within a couple of weeks, he assisted each in getting a short-term place to stay, believing the pandemic would end in a few months. This worked out well given their last received message, a post on Twitter, directed them to 'lay low' until the extent of the pandemic and its impacts had been 'clarified.'

The three's introduction to the city via Ali's condo was nothing short of a perfect complement to their assignment. The three integrated well into the neighborhood community and ran under the radar of those traditionally looking for suspicious behavior in Arab neighborhoods. The emergency of the moment, the pandemic, was the most important security issue and where most security forces and efforts were directing their attention and resources.

The three were originally introduced to neighbors as business contacts of Ali, whose high-end Persian rug and fabric retail outlet in the Central District, just off Robson Street and a few blocks from their condo, had achieved local and international acclaim. They quickly became known to the buildings' residents as 'the three businessmen temporarily stuck in the country.'

The three stayed away from the mosques and went out only to walk and exercise in Stanley Park. When they prayed, it was once a day in private. As a successful Shia businessman and almost thirty-year resident, Ali had never been considered a threat by either Canadian officials or his neighbors. His guests, therefore, were considered both safe and welcome. One he even introduced as his godson. The limited exposure that came with the confines of Covid added to the three guests' ability to maintain a low profile and easily blend into the building and the neighborhood.

***

Early March

Winthrop, Washington

The University of Washington was one of the first universities in the country to close its classrooms due to COVID-19. The outbreak had begun in Seattle; at least, those were the first known cases reported. The governor swiftly isolated the initial cases and took aggressive precautions to stop their spread. UW closed their classes in early March as an employee of the school had tested positive. By the end of the month, other state schools had identified other students and employees who tested positive, and the state transitioned rapidly to online courses. At the same time, most of the rest of the country held their breath and waited for information on the virulency of the quickly spreading disease and clarification and guidance from their leaders on how to protect themselves from the escalating crisis.

Cody Dickson, like most of the students at the university, had mixed emotions about the news. Initially, most people felt confusion and panic, confusion around the disease, what it was exactly, where it had come from, and how serious it might be. Around the latter matter, however, most within the Seattle area quickly became extremely fearful as reports of numerous deaths began circulating from senior living facilities in the Kirkland area on the east shores of Lake Washington. Alarm, even near hysteria, around speculations of the virus' presence and virulence continued to escalate throughout the Puget Sound area.

Due to the clear connection between population density and the spread of the virus, Cody was mostly happy and very accepting of going home. The university had closed on March 7, and two days later, he was back home in Winthrop, a small, isolated community just inside the eastern slopes of the Cascades. If travel were curtailed quickly, Winthrop would be an extremely safe place to be. Regardless, Cody was looking forward to being near his friends and, to a lesser extent, his family.

The Dicksons had moved to Winthrop the summer before Cody entered the eighth grade, the fifth he had attended over the prior seven years. Comfortable with, but not liking to be 'the new kid,' Cody had settled comfortably into this town. He no longer saw himself as an alien and had finally found a place that felt like home. A three-and-half-hour drive from the edges of Seattle, Winthrop was surrounded by the Okanogan-Wenatchee Forests on the west and east and by the Pasayten Wilderness area to the north. The nearest town of any consequence was Wenatchee to the south, a hundred miles away on the banks of the Columbia River.

Cody had gotten into town around three o'clock and had driven straight to Sweetie's house. Sweetie's parents, Bill and Chirine MacManus, owned 'Lebanese If You Please,' a deli in the town center that Sweetie and a coworker ran most of the time, especially during the summer months. Usually, she would get off between 5:00 and 6:00 p.m. before her parents came and closed out for the day. But it was off-season, and she usually got off earlier in the afternoon, around 3:00 p.m. To make sure he beat her home, he had called her mom and asked her to devise an excuse to keep her a little longer, to which her mother readily agreed. Sweetie's car was nowhere to be seen as he pulled up the long driveway, so Cody immediately knew he had beaten her home.

He parked and hurried toward the front door to set up his portable Bose speaker just inside, where she could hear the music when she got home. As he approached the front door, Sweetie's dog, Pedro, began yapping annoyingly. With each yap, Pedro bounced up, her bobbing head barely clearing the aluminum bottom half of the door, trying to glimpse who was coming. On about the third jump, Pedro recognized Cody, and her yaps went up in tempo and volume.

"It's you!!" she lovingly conveyed in apparent 'dog speak.'

Pedro, a white female toy poodle, was a birthday present that Cody, then a senior in high school, had given her not long after they began dating early in her junior year. Sweetie named the dog after a friend of hers since the sixth grade, a young boy, Pedro, who visited

Sweetie regularly at her home. Pedro loved to try on Sweetie's clothes. They would put on her mother's makeup, play music, and dance like nobody was watching. For Pedro, Sweetie's was his safe house, where they could play, dance, dress up, scream like young teenagers, and be girls. Sweetie never told anyone of Pedro's inclinations, not even her parents.

In the ninth grade, Pedro moved to Wenatchee, closer to where his father worked as a warehouse manager for a regional fruit wholesaler. Two and a half years later, word came back that Pedro had been killed. The boy had orchestrated a similar relationship with a classmate whose older brother, after walking in on them during one of their after-school fashion shows, decided he did not take kindly to his sister's new friend. A group of his senior friends at the high school cornered Pedro one night after a movie in an alley off the main street not far from the theater as he was walking home and beaten him to death. Devasted by Pedro's death, Sweetie named her dog Pedro in homage to her friend. Nobody but Sweetie, her parents, and later Cody, Seth, and Chris knew the entire connection. Nobody needed to. Sweetie had often told her friend, Pedro, "Don't care what they think. Be who you are," a piece of advice she had aped to Cody on many occasions regarding his conflicts with his father.

Cody opened the door and let the dog out. Pedro kept jumping on his leg, crying warmly, happy to see her master's friend. Cody rubbed her manicured head gently as he squatted down to look her more evenly in the eye.

"Good girl. Good girl, Pedro," he said lovingly. "I missed you, too. Yes, I did," he said as scratched her butt, prompting her to walk in small circles for a few seconds before he picked her up. The dog continued to lap in the air, grinning at him, clearly hoping to land one on his face. Momentarily, he sat her back down and told her, "Go pee," knowing she had been in much of the day. As if he had flicked on another switch, the dog ran out onto the lawn several feet, sniffing along the way, before finding the right spot, squatting, and relieving her bladder. Once done, she glanced at him before continuing her sniffing quest diagonally across the lawn, crisscrossing a narrow path three or four times before squatting again and pooping. Then, she quickly hunched down on her front paws and made a couple of ferocious-looking scratches before bouncing back to Cody with a 'did you see what I just did' look on her face that only a dog can portray.

Bending down on his left knee, Cody reached out with his right hand and rewarded her with another butt scratch and a "Good girl" that he immediately dialed up in enthusiasm with another, "Good girl." As he picked her up again, he scratched her tummy as he cupped her in the bend in his arm, prompting a little yap.

"Ooops. Sorry there, tiger. Looks like a little cyst," which he flicked softly with his index finger, eliciting a muffled whine of discomfort from the dog.

"Dogs," Cody said out loud. "You gotta love 'em," and Pedro, the emotional mind reader of humans, absorbed it all and smiling like a kid at Dave and Buster's, whose dad has finally held onto one of the balls long enough with the mechanical arm to drop it in the exit hole for recovery, ran into the house as Cody dropped her with one hand and held the door open with the other.

Reaching into his hip pocket, Cody pulled out his cell phone to check the time. Sweetie would be home, errands aside, in fifteen to twenty minutes. She expected him tomorrow, so he had parked a little out of the way. Though he knew she would probably see his car, he still wanted to stage an event to match the moment.

***

Sweetie's heart raced when she saw Cody's car. Her mother had told her to leave early to clean the house before Cody's arrival the next day. Now, a whole new anticipation sat in. He's here. Has he missed me? Is he as excited as I am? What's to eat? Do we have any beer? Did Pedro make it through the day?

Sweetie had thought about going to college, but her folks did not have much money, and there was nothing she wanted to do or be badly enough to go into a decade or more of debt. Their relationship had survived since his senior year, almost four years now, and she was happy to continue to let the relationship take its course. Besides, the pickings for men were slim in Winthrop. The only other locals she would seriously consider were Seth and Chris, and Sweetie had no intention of compromising the friendships that bound the four together. Many of the younger locals and a few of the 'a-little-too-old' ones had tried to court her. But she kept any relationships in town casual, preferring to wait for Cody, who regularly made the three-hour-plus drive home to see her. And she could occasionally catch a ride with her parents to spend a day or two with him in Seattle when she could arrange a cover for her in the deli. She had not seen him since Christmas Break, almost eight weeks earlier. Now, he was home for at least five months, and she wanted to make that time count.

She parked the car in her regular spot, just off the pavement, and turned off the key. Excited, she began to take it out of the ignition, only to almost drop the entire ring before recoiling and catching them in her left hand. Tears started to pool in her eyes, but she held them back, not wanting to show 'too much' of what was welling in her heart. She paused in her seat briefly, and when she was confident that she had regained control, she threw the keys into her purse that was sitting in the passenger's seat, grabbed it and her favorite baseball hat sitting next to it, pushed the driver's door open, swung her legs to the ground, stood, slapped the hat onto her head, and bounded toward the house.

Pausing momentarily at the entrance, she pulled down on her hat's brim, trying to stare past the reflection on the glass of the screen door and into the house to see if he might be looking out from the living room. When she did not see him, she assumed he had not heard her, though she wondered why Pedro was not sounding off.

Slowing, she walked discretely the last several feet to the house, hoping to enter quietly and perhaps surprise him in the kitchen or back on the patio. As her hand touched the front doorknob, she suddenly caught the opening notes of a familiar tune, an old Joe Cocker song that popped on when they were listening to her parent's Pandora playlist several months earlier. The horn section trumpeted the intro as the accompanying piano joined in as the band began thumping out the beat, and she broke into an unfeminine guffaw before collecting herself. As she walked through the door, her head started bobbing in tempo as she began a slow, sultry, two-step, hip-shifting shuffle toward the living room, where, it turned out, Cody was seated on the couch, just out of site.

As she rounded the corner, Sweetie's blond pixie haircut and striking blue eyes took Cody's breath away, as they always did. He had missed her terribly and immediately began to rise to meet her, anxious to hold her 5'2" frame in his arms. But Sweetie had other plans. She stuck her right arm out, making a fist before pointing her index finger straight into the air, wagging it side to side while slightly shaking her head, clearly commanding him to stop. As directed, he halted, at which point her finger began wagging up and down, back toward the couch, directing him to sit back down.

It was not spring, and she wore her North Face winter coat. As Cocker began the first verse, '*Baby take off your coat, real slow,*' she dropped her arms, held them back at a slight angle, gave her shoulders a slight seductive shake, and the jacket effortlessly slid to the floor in perfect concert with the lyrics. Cody, impressed, cocked his head slightly and smiled, his wide-open eyes and his quizzical look asking if there was more.

Sweetie knew the words and what came next, "*Baby, take off your shoes; I'll take off your shoes,*' she took rapid, baby steps in Cody's direction, getting there in time to hold up each foot in tandem so that he could peel off each of the snow slippers she had worn to work. The next stanza was coming fast, '*Baby, take off your dress, yes, yes, yes.*' She was wearing a short flannel dress over fleeced-lined leggings. Crossing her left hand to her right elbow and raising her right hand with extended index finger to her right cheek, she put on an innocent-looking, 'Oh well, what do I do now?' face. Cody, remaining seated, motioned for her to turn around with a twirling right turn of his index, to which she willingly complied. Then, standing, he unzipped the dress, but rather than raising it over her head and running contrary to the song's allowance, he pulled it toward the ground. She had no bra on, only her leggings. As she stepped out of the dress, her left foot snagged it. He caught her as she staggered in that direction. Keeping time to the music and syncing with the lyrics was no longer possible. The lights were on, and there was no chair to stand on. They were both laughing, but when Cocker hit '*Raise your arms in the air,*'

Sweetie took a step back and raised them, then slid them down her side sensuously so that when Cocker got to '*Now give me reason to live,*' her hands met her leggings, and she began to push them down. By the time the Cocker had repeated the line four times, her leggings were on the floor. Then, stepping out of them, panties and hat still on, she began to walk backward toward her bedroom, her hand coaxing him to join her.

As he followed her into the bedroom, she turned and embraced him again, this time cooing, "I'm so happy to see you," before pausing momentarily and adding, "I missed you so much."

"I missed you, too," he echoed softly, holding her close. Cody loved her size, petite, wonderfully formed body, always feeling safe when he held her.

She returned his grip, holding on as if the world were about to end, and when she pulled away, tears were streaming down her cheeks. Fighting to regain control, she asked, "Where's Pedro?" as she stroked her right eye with the back of her hand.

His eyes were pooling, too, and he pinched the corner of each simultaneously with his index finger and thumb. "She's in your folks' bathroom."

Pedro, stashed in the master bedroom's bathroom toward the back corner of the house, began whimpering excitedly at hearing Sweetie's voice.

"I better get her." With that, she began walking to the bedroom, stopping momentarily to drop her panties. She looked back over her shoulder, smiling invitingly.

"Just the hat now, darlin,'" he said. "Nicely done."

"I might need some help in here," she said playfully as she sashayed toward the doorway. "You know how Pedro can be. You have such a way with her."

***

"What time are your folks coming home?" pulling Sweetie closer as they lay on her bed.

"Mmm, probably not 'til eight thirty-ish. They'll be doing some prep for tomorrow," Sweetie answered. "I don't think they plan to visit anyone after they close shop, so they'll come straight home."

Sweetie's parents had met when he was on duty in the Middle East following the invasion of Iraq in 1991. Chirine had been a Lebanese flight attendant working out of Bahrain. Bill, who was a close friend of Cody's dad, Jim Dickson, aka Big Jim, the two having had grown up together in Okanogan, forty miles east of Winthrop, had both enlisted together in the Marines shortly after Iraq invaded Kuwait in 1990 and Operation Desert Storm began to coalesce. They both served one twelve-month tour of duty, stationed in Qatar and were due to be sent stateside. Big Jim had dated Chirine first. They had both met her in Bahrain by the pool in the hotel where they were staying while on R&R. Big Jim dated her three times for a month or two but lost interest once he heard that he would be going back stateside soon to finish his tour of duty at the Oceanside base in Pendleton, California. Bill, however, stepped in quickly to fill the void, fell hard for Chirine, and signed up for another twelve-month tour of duty.

Bill was two months into his second tour when he was wounded by leg shrapnel from a roadside mine that killed an even less unlucky soldier riding in the vehicle's passenger seat. He was reassigned to

28

the Headquarters at Camp Panzer Kaserne in Böblingen, Germany, as an administrative assistant. From there, though, he could visit Chirine semi-regularly, including bringing her on one occasion to Germany and another to Paris. The two continued their long-distance romance for another two years before they successfully brought Chirine to the United States permanently.

For as long as they had known one another, Bill had told Chirine stories of the Great Northwest, its beautiful peaks, plentiful forests, and excellent business opportunities. By the time she arrived, he had completed half his business degree at Washington State University in Pullman. Chirine enrolled in the school's Food and Restaurant Management program, making it halfway through when Bill graduated. A vet, his schooling was paid for, but hers was not. Believing she had learned enough, Bill applied for and was soon granted a small business loan through the Veterans Administration to start a deli in Winthrop.

Their timing was excellent, as the little town's retail opportunities followed its growing popularity as a weekend respite and second home market for a burgeoning Seattle population of mid to high-end professionals in myriad entrepreneurial business sectors that were all just a three-hour drive away through some of the country's most beautiful mountain areas. The deli was a smash hit as Chirine introduced visitors and residents to a bevy of delectable, organic Middle Eastern dishes.

It was about five, and Cody had texted Chris and Seth earlier to drop by around six.

"I think Seth and Chris will probably come by in an hour or so," he said.

Since moving to Winthrop, Seth Johansen and Chris Ellison had been Cody's two best friends. In Cody and Rick's junior year, the trio had led the school to a state championship in football and fourth place in basketball. Seth had even turned down three football scholarships with small, out-of-state schools. Together, they had regularly explored large areas of the surrounding regions throughout high school, often taking weekend and weeklong hiking, fishing, and camping trips into some of the region's most challenging places. Collectively, the three boys were a fountain of knowledge of the area. They knew one another's favorite camping sites, had explored little-known trails with spectacular sites, and fished most of the best fishing holes in the Pasayten. Their knowledge was unique, a knowledge Cody had leveraged into an excellent summer job as a guide for one of the local outfitters.

"You told them to stop by? How unromantic." she said, giving him an accompanying pouty face before sultrily asking, "Can you handle one more?"

Cody smiled. "Come here," he replied, and their bodies intertwined again. Twenty minutes later, they got out of bed, put some beers in a small Costco cooler, moved to the living room, and set the Pandora playlist to 'Sweetie.'

***

Chris was the first to arrive. They heard him ring the front door before opening it and asking, "Is anybody here?"

"Come in," they yield in unison. "We're in the living room," added Sweetie.

Sweetie and Cody were cuddled next to one another on the sofa, hurrying to get in a couple of more kisses before Chris fully arrived. They failed to get the last one in before he rounded the corner.

"It's gonna be like that, huh?" Chris said jokingly. "I'd say get a room, but you probably already did."

Cody pivoted a quarter turn, dropped his right arm around Sweetie's shoulder, and replied, "Yeah, yeah. You're just jealous Sandy's not back. You gotta pound it for another week."

Sweetie immediately slapped Cody on the chest in mock reprimand.

"Don't make fun of him, now," she said quietly but loud enough for Chris to hear. "He's just lonely."

"I didn't know lonely started with an H," Cody prodded, smiling at Chris. Chris fist-bumped Cody before sitting in a chair near them and next to the Costco cooler they had stocked.

"Yeah. No," Chris said with a smile, "I'm lonely." Grabbing a bottle from the mini cooler, he added, "And that H thing. And thirsty. You interested?" he asked Sweetie, who didn't appear to have one.

"In a beer," she said playfully with a smile.

Chris smiled back and then feigned a pout that seemed to say, "Well, dang then."

"When's Sandy coming back, anyway?" Cody asked.

"She's not," said Chris.

"What?"

"Pandemic," said Chris. "Doesn't want to leave her grandma right now." Sandy Dobson had visited her grandmother in Denver two weeks earlier. Still, Covid had grounded many of the flights, and Sandy didn't want to leave her 85-year-old grandmother alone until the pandemic's severity became clearer and it was more evident that it was safer to travel on a plane.

"Make's sense, actually," said Sweetie. "You okay with that?"

"Yeah," replied Chris. "Whatta you going to do, right? Can't go anywhere around here anyway. We could all be held up forever from what you hear on the news and see online about this stuff."

"Yeah, Mom and Dad are really worried, actually," said Sweetie, genuinely concerned. "We're a food business, so we can probably stay open in some format, but things seem to be going from slow to nada for now. The state is still trying to figure out how to handle businesses, especially the small ones. I can't imagine what we'll do if people can't sit and eat. Take out... maybe."

"Yeah, this summer could be a real shitter," responded Cody. "I have to go see Steve in the next day or two and see what he's got going for this summer. I'm not even sure we'll be taking any groups into the backcountry." Steve was Steve Thompson, an early thirty-something who ran a guide service that took small groups of hikers or horseback riders into the surrounding wilderness areas. He had grown up in Winthrop and had dated Marie, Cody's older sister, by four years, the summer before Cody's junior year of high school. Like many from the state's east side, Steve had also gone to WSU and obtained a computer science degree. Upon graduation, he went to work for Boeing in Seattle as a surveillance design specialist but returned home to start his business after three years. Cody had worked for him as a summer assistant since the summer between his junior and senior years in high school. Two years ago, Cody had advanced to 'full guide status' from 'gopher assistant' for smaller groups. Now, he led groups of all sizes into Cathedral Pass Loop and Billi Goat Loop, forty-four and fifty-mile hikes or horseback rides, respectively. The pay was good, but the tips were great. And the job was terrific. "I don't want to' be too hungover," Cody said, adding, "I'm not sure I'll even be working this summer, but I want to let him know a.s.a.p. I'm available now."

"There he is," said Chris cheerfully.

Seth Johansen ensured they heard him coming, gunning his engine and honking his horn several times. Seeing Chris' car, Seth knew he probably was not walking in on anything private, but he liked making the announcement just the same. Grabbing his beer cooler, he headed through the house as he had done dozens of times before.

As Seth popped through the door, Chris and Cody both stood to greet their friend.

"How you been, dude?" Chris asked, offering him a hand-clasp shake.

"Good. You?" said Seth, who returned his hand warmly.

"Stellar."

Seth turned to Cody, who had extended him a fist bump. "That's it?" Seth asked playfully with a smile before putting his arm around Cody's shoulder and pulling him into an awkward hug. "We don't have Covid yet, you big pussy. Get in here."

Sweetie started to get up to greet him, but Cody, who had turned around to sit down, checked her with his eyes while shaking his head, 'No.' Sweetie rolled her eyes, shrugged her shoulders, and nodded in Cody's' direction three quick times, smiling all the while.

"Sweetie, long time no see." Seth started to walk toward her but then halted and said, "Wait, your dog is trying to hump my leg. Hey, Pedro." When Pedro heard Seth's voice, she rushed to greet him. After Sweetie and Cody, Seth, for whatever reason, was Pedro's favorite. Seth picked her up and cuddled her.

"Hey, baby. How you been? You miss me?" he said. Expecting Cody to be guarded on social greetings, Seth treated the concerns lightly. Looking at Sweetie, he nodded toward Cody and lightheartedly said, "He's just jealous because of our connection." He held up the three fingers between his thumb and pinky. "Here's the three of us. Here's Cody," he said, collapsing the outer two so that his middle finger remained.

Cody turned to her and said, "See, you've spoiled him so bad he can't count straight."

"Do you think you'll be going back?" Seth asked Cody.

"They told us we'd definitely finish this quarter online. We might have to take finals. What can they put together for a lecture that quickly, though? Finals week would have been next week. No more actual classes."

"Mellow," said Seth.

"If we want to do spring term, it'll have to be online. Not sure I'll do a spring. Depends on what Steve has for me. How about you?"

"Yeah, we're about halfway through the semester, but I'm sure it'll be an easy finish. Easy enough. I'll graduate in June." Seth had been a year ahead of Cody and Chris in high school and was due to graduate from Washington State with a degree in Animal Husbandry. As an only child, Seth was on track to inherit the 2,400-acre farm/ranch, which had been in his family, well, his mom's family, the Blackwoods, for four generations and over a hundred and fifteen years. But while Seth loved ranching and the valley's lifestyle he had experienced as a child, he also recognized the value of the real estate he would soon own and its value to the ever-growing number of outsiders buying into the area, albeit mostly part-time residents. While his grandfather, Farhan, was alive, Seth would be a rancher. "I can actually drop a couple of classes and finish anyway. I'm taking twelve credits, but I only need four. We'll see. I'm sure the old man will fill up my schedule fast enough. It's all good, as they say," said Seth. "Shit way to finish, though,"

Cody nodded in agreement. "True dat, brother."

The four spent the next two hours catching up on the latest gossip, worrying about where the world was headed, telling stories and sharing their latest escapades, kicking back, drinking, getting loose, laughing, and enjoying the certainty of their friendship and affection for one another in what was fast becoming an uncertain world.

Finally, Seth said, "Where's your folks, Sweetie?"

"They'll be coming anytime," she said.

"Well, I've missed you guys. This is like old times," Seth proclaimed softheartedly. "I gotta split. Sorry. But let's toast!" Standing, he reached into the cold pack on the ground and quickly popped off the tops of its remaining four beers, handing out the first three as he did so. Chris, Cody, and Sweetie stood as well. "TOAST! The Three… !" Seth said, then quickly added, "Sorry, Sweetie. The Four Mustyturds. I mean the Four Musketeers!"

"CHEERS!" the four yelled enthusiastically in almost unison as they clinked their bottles and began guzzling.

'The Squad,' as they were referred to by most in the community and themselves, were back and reunited.

***

Early March

The White House

POTUS bit his lower lip and pensively stared toward the room's far corner. As he unconsciously toyed with the white hair flowing backward over the top of his right ear, he pondered the previous month and what actions he had taken, well avoided, after being initially briefed on the forthcoming pandemic. "Well, that'll either be a savior or a shitstorm for the election," he had told his favored aid, Emma Grant, having added, "It's all a matter of how we see and deal with it accordingly. It's either a glass half empty or half full."

He had thought out loud about taking it public, but Emma had brought him back to earth. "Sir," she had fervently, "this is a motherfucking glass half full if you don't mind my saying so." Completely disingenuous about the 'if you don't mind my saying so,' she knew he would not mind.

Emma Grant was POTUS' closest aid and, without question, the most hardline around several conservative issues, including immigration, guns, abortion, and various welfare programs. "If you can't take care of yourself," she was fond of saying, "just go somewhere else already. It's not our job to find someone who can. That's a family matter."

Regarding her own family, her parents came to the country when Emma was four, having immigrated from Eastern Europe twenty-six years ago. Her family name was Babic, and she was tantamount in Croatia to Smith or Jones. She liked the name Emma, which was her given name, but the Croatian version was spelled Ema. In the second grade, she finally accepted the American version of E-m-m-a as how she would spell it going forward after numerous arguments with her second-grade teacher about the correct spelling. In her mid-teens, before applying for college, she changed her last name to Grant, having had a crush on Hugh Grant and believing Grant combined well with Emma into an All-American persona.

"Go, girl. Help your motherfucking self," he said, waving his palms forward, his face and tone serious. "Tell me what you see."

"Trust me, "Emma cooed, "it's a savior, sir. If we control it, you're a hero. If things so south, you can always declare a national emergency and delay the elections."

POTUS smiled at that. "Yeah," he said, nodding, "it is a bit of a win/win. I'm a hero if I stop it or a great leader if I take control." Looking out the window, he gave a serious Mussolini-style tug on his coat's lapel before adding, "This is just what we needed, Emma. This election is going to be a piece of cake. There's no way in fucking hell I'm going to let one of those liberal fucks beat me." He then hit the intercom on his phone. "Mary," he said, "can you please have the kitchen send me a piece of chocolate cake?"

"Her name's Maryanne."

“What?”

“Your assistant. Her name is Maryanne.”

“Oh,” POTUS said casually. “Pretty close. She gets it.”

“Well, we need it, sir,” Emma said. “A win. And we’ll need to have some serious Plan As and Bs,” her tone now very serious. “The virus has clearly shown up and is taking off in several places now. Everyone in the country is scared shitless, and some a little more than pissed.”

“Jesus,” POTUS said, shaking his head in disgust, “that’s what those crazy bastards get for eating bats. No wonder people say they’re batshit crazy,” he added, smiling as if he were the first to make the reference.

“Pangolins, sir.”

“What?” he asked.

“Pangolins. Well, maybe. Ant eaters. Never mind.”

“I thought they liked chicken. Chicken and pork bellies.” POTUS said, hunching his shoulders. “Anyway, what have you heard from Jack?”

Jack Hoffman, the Vice President, had been in Beijing for the last four days negotiating a trade deal and was due back within the hour. Between the fallout from the expanded tariffs and now the virus, an easy rerun for the office in November, now just seven months away, was beginning to look like a far more brutal fight than it did the same time last year. The CDC has been vocal about locking down the country to stop the virus from spreading over the previous few days.

That would spell doom, most believed, for the economy he had so vigorously and vocally orchestrated for the last three years.

Yes, the prior administration had begun a solid economic recovery eight years before his election, but his tax break for big business had dumped gas on an already burning fire. And Americans were well known for their short memories, poor understanding of economics, and fickle allegiances to politicians who might be in charge when the shit was good or who might be in the neighborhood when someone or something turned on the fan.

"Just a short email, sir," she replied. "He said he's got some very interesting news and a related offer from the Chinese. He's on your agenda for eight a.m. tomorrow."

A thoughtful look crossed the President's face. After a moment, he said, "Sounds good, but make it 10:30. I want to catch a couple of the news shows tomorrow morning. There's a new Fox poll out, and Robert Frank's doing a high-end real estate spot on CNBC. I'm thinking South Africa might be my next favorite place."

As he wandered over toward his window and gazed out, she wondered for a moment what he might do if she yelled 'squirrel.'

"Yes, sir," she said. "I'll let him know."

***

The following day, the president sulked into the Oval Office like a fourteen-year-old whose cell phone had just been taken. Hunched forward, eyes scowling, he reached his chair and fell into it like a Conor McGregor opponent who didn't duck fast enough.

"Where's Hoffman?" he yelled.

"He's not here yet, sir," Grant replied. "He's not due for another hour."

"I thought we had an eight o'clock," he wailed.

It was 9:30, but Grant had watched the Fox polls report earlier in her office. She knew he would be in one of his 'moods.' He had almost certainly exploded after the poll results were announced; the results were not good. Usually, he would have a tirade for twenty or thirty minutes before settling into a primarily silent funk for another hour or two, sometimes more. Given the gravity of today's poll, today would likely be a long one.

"You moved it to 10:30," she said, though she believed he already knew.

"Yeah, well, I'm moving it back to right now," he said, poking his index finger several times into the top of his desk to emphasize when and where 'now' was. "Call him and tell him to get his ass back down here, NOW," he yelled.

"Right away, sir," she said calmly, hustling to her office where, after fifteen minutes, she finally reached Hoffman. "Get over here quick, Jack. Code red. The polls sucked."

"Yeah," said the VP, his voice serious. "I saw them. On my way."

POTUS fidgeted at his desk, swirling around in his chair periodically, stopping randomly to look out the window for a moment before continuing his methodical revolutions, an act his staff called 'Circling Uranus.' He was worried.

Meanwhile, knowing she would likely be paged in another couple of minutes, Emma found her way to the ladies' room and found an empty stall in which to sit and think. The polls showed a drop in support around one essential and one innocuous question: 1) Do you think the country is headed in the right direction, and 2) Do you think the President is doing a good job?

She hated the first question. It was so broad it was almost meaningless. Everybody on both sides of the political fence had something to bitch about, whether it was gun rights, abortion, the cost of gas and food, their spouse, aliens… of all kinds, or global warming. The second question was far narrower and of greater importance to her; the president worried about both.

Approval ratings for both issues had dropped to the mid-thirty percent levels. Emma knew his core was around thirty-two percent, implying he was losing the middle… badly. And the problem was the virus. 'Fucking Chinks,' she thought. 'Should be billed as the Asian Contagion.' But as she had told POTUS the day before, it was all in how you framed it. Presently, the country was panicking. The worse it got, the greater the risk, but the greater the potential reward. If the White House could control the narrative and mitigate the fear, they would pull large numbers of voters from the middle into their camp. Otherwise, they might need a distraction.

Hoffman arrived in twenty minutes instead of the usual thirty. He had also seen enough of the mood swing results to understand what Grant meant by 'code red.' Nobody went into the Oval Office while POTUS waited for Hoffman.

Maryanne came on the intercom and announced, "The Vice President is here, sir."

"Send him in," POTUS ordered.

"Mr. President," Hoffman said as cheerfully as possible as he entered the room. "Good morning, sir."

"Sit down, Jack," the president commanded, pointing to the left chair that sat in front of his desk. "The polls are fucked, you know. Did you know that, Jack?"

"I heard they were not optimum," Hoffman said just audibly.

"Not optimum? What kind of fucking response is that? They're shit. It's all that batshit disease the fucking Chinese created." He paused, shaking his head in disgust. "Mother fucking fuckers."

Hoffman said nothing, unsure if the seemingly mounting tirade would escalate further. The silence finally got to POTUS. "Well, what do you think?" he bellowed.

"About what exactly, Sir?" Hoffman ventured carefully.

"About the fucking polls, Jack. Jesus."

Hoffman winced uncomfortably in his chair when POTUS said Jesus. Knowing Hoffman did not like the use of the lord's name in vain and that he was his poster boy for, and primary link with, the religious right, the president brought his voice's tenor down and carefully repeated, "The polls, Jack. This virus is killing us." Then, suddenly realizing what he had said, he added, "… no pun intended." They looked at each other momentarily before sharing a little chuckle that quickly evolved into a shared chortle. "Glad I didn't slip with that one at a press conference," he laughed. "Can't believe I said that."

"Yes," Hoffman said agreeingly. "Probably right on that."

"What did you learn in Beijing, Jack? They got a handle on it, do you think?"

"I think they may have done this on purpose, Mr. President," Hoffman said stoically.

The president's head had veered in another direction, and Hoffman's statement caught him off guard. He almost didn't hear it. It took a few moments for it to register, and Hoffman could see the look on his face morph as his mind turned from where it had been, heading back to the comment he thought he had just heard.

"What did you say, Jack?" he asked.

"There's a decent chance this got out of the lab accidentally. But I have three excellent sources that tell me the Chinese government did this intentionally," Jack replied. "Actually," he added, "one accused the Russians of doing it and planting the first batch in Wuhan."

There was more silence as POTUS processed. "Why?" he asked. "Why would the Russians do it?"

"The Chinese say to make them look bad and sow dissent between them and us."

"Putin wouldn't do that to me," said POTUS. "He likes me. We're bros, man. What would motivate the Chinese?"

"Bargaining chip," Hoffman replied tersely.

"I don't get it."

"In the trade talks." Hoffman paused momentarily as POTUS' frozen face screamed WTF. He started to say something, but the vice president cut him off. "They had nothing to respond with after that last round of tariffs. You had them in a corner. They almost certainly have a vaccine… IF they did it on purpose," he emphasized

The President's mind immediately went to the accolade rather than to the point. "I did, didn't I," he said, with more than a hint of self-admiration.

"Sir?"

"I made a great move."

"Yes, sir. Yes, you did. Excellent move, Mr. President," Hoffman continued. "They couldn't let you put that amount of tariff increases on their goods imported by us without some kind of response, though."

"Oh shit, Jack. They know the consumer pays those, not them," he said, smirking. "My voters don't know the difference. They think I've got China bent over the table."

"Probably," Hoffman agreed, "But those eventual price increases won't be received well by Walmart shoppers, for sure, when they happen, and they will. Those customers are end users for so many of their goods; of course, they're our voters. Those 'everyday low prices' for a whole bunch of goods will be going up. Those tariffs could work their way into those prices by the time the election rolls around. Almost definitely by next spring. That's gonna include TVs, cell phones, computers, you name it."

"You think?"

"Yes, sir. For sure"

"Well, we don't give a shit if they don't begin to happen until next spring. Can we slow them down some? For this year? The price increases. Maybe we can still talk them up but manipulate their implementation?"

With a thoughtful pause, Hoffman considered the question. "Possibly," he said, finally.

"Get Susan in Consumer Affairs on that," said the president.

Hoffman had no idea who he was talking about. "Well, Sir, it's actually a matter for Homeland Security, Border Patrol. They're the tariff collectors. I'll talk to John today and see what he says. The Chinese tariff matters might also cause problems with some of the farm products they've promised to buy. They could cut their orders at any time. But at the same time, as soon as they had any internal problems with any staple food product, like a pork shortage, they would probably have to come back to us. At least in the short term. They needed some other leverage." He had the president's attention. "So, they launched a Black Swan, you might say. Thought outside the box. A real disrupter," Hoffman said in a slightly admiring tone.

"Yeah, I get it," said POTUS, his tone slightly sneer-ish, not wanting to accept that he might have been outplayed, even a little.

He did an analysis of the matter quickly. Though his general instincts around negotiations were reasonable, given his, albeit narrow, business background, he regularly underestimated the stakes and the available chips to play in international politics, especially those involving trade, the military, and preparedness for natural disasters. He saw things as black and white. You have that, and I either want it or I don't. Take this out; I'll give you less money. Put this in; I'll give you more—quid pro quo, plain and simple. And if you don't pay attention, I'll screw you as far into the ground as I can, so far you'll think you're in the fracking business.

But International negotiations were far more complicated. Negotiations for power and prestige always and virtually always involve keeping the population that keeps you in power happy. POTUS got that at home. But seeing himself as the King of Kings, he underestimated its importance to other global leaders.

Hoffman proceeded to give the president an overview of the situation and a couple of possible responses. War, of course, was off the table. Neither side would be a winner. "Don't forget what happened when the U.S. set up an embargo to keep Japan from getting oil," the vice president told POTUS.

"And?" the President said, sounding vexed.

"World War II," Hoffman replied. "They bombed Pearl Harbor."

"Oh yeah," POTUS said cursively. "Right," as if he had already known.

Hoffman went on with his elucidation. He explained that a constantly sick country cannot send an army to war. Overt military alliances with countries not friendly to us, like those in the Middle East and Africa, were also off the table. Less aggressive but still strategic moves, such as meetings between heads of state, could send a message of consolidating new business relationships toward improved political solidarity, which was expected. Such discussions' impact on possible military actions was implicit and therein deniable. Each side could make myriad clever, reckless, sometimes scary gambits, whether they were terrorists or solid and functioning governments. But the actuality of putting other leaders in what you perceive to be checkmate positions was virtually always merely a 'check.'

Boxing a leader into a corner, especially a powerful one, where their only response was a military action, was dangerous. Unless, of course, you thought you could easily win, a belief that America had miscalculated numerous times in its history since WWII. On the other hand, America's position as an economic juggernaut had been used many times to successfully impact global despots and sometimes allies toward behavior favoring the United States.

However, China was now a global economic powerhouse and could respond with meaningful, impactful trump cards. The virus might simply be another move in a multidimensional, global chess game. Negotiations between countries always involve holding onto power or gaining more. Whether they cared for their people or had no genuine compassion for them was often of no consequence, though more so in nondemocratic regimes. People were sacrificed at will to achieve the real objective most leaders sought, maintaining their power base, which concomitantly required saving face.

China's population size was both a pro and a con. Indeed, their ability to scale up to manufacture anything was unparalleled globally. And the smartest fifteen percent of their population was numerically more than the entire adult population of the United States. But, if only one or two percent of the Chinese population, a fraction of the billion and a half people, became unsettled, that was a lot of people… almost fifteen to thirty million. Ten percent would be completely unruly, and any more than that, a full-on revolution. Give them a job and enough money to buy food, a decent place to live, a television, and a cell phone, and most people anywhere are happy. A functional Communist country promises full employment. Regardless of why, any real disruption to the supply chains of products being exported meant lost jobs. No jobs means no food. Disruptions to the food supply produced the same problem. If people cannot buy food, they get aggressive and demanding. Hoffman said the President of China's belief, well, it was the Vice President of China speaking for their president, was that their citizens, like Americans, love their country, are happy to be who and what they are, and will fight to maintain it, a veiled threat to 'don't box us into a corner.'

Hoffman went on to explain that POTUS' self-proclaimed excellent friend, the President of China, or POC-man as POTUS sometimes referred to him, was beginning to see losses of jobs, losses of supplies for one of their favorite foods, pork, and cries for democracy from a colony, Hong Kong, that had experienced some degree of it within the lifetimes of many of its residents. So, Beijing needed a distraction, Jack's informants had postulated. POC needed to distract his citizens from their current concerns with a major shitstorm, an epidemic. They had tested them before. Like a Malcom Gladwell example in *Tipping Point*, they implanted the product into a controlled population, likely some small rural village, watched how it spread, controlled the communications, and tested controlled responses before turning the virus loose on us via Wuhan.

Knowing it would mainly kill the elderly and those with weakened immune systems, they assumed you, in particular, might not care. They framed it as both a warning and an offering. With an average death rate of ten percent for all over the age of sixty-five or seventy, it would ultimately save the United States and the world billions in health system costs over the next decade or so. The Chinese would also get to watch in real-time how the U.S. government, its businesses, and its people would respond to such a plague relative to their own. Scourge or panacea? Is the glass half empty or half full? It's a matter of perspective, depending on your place in power. And parenthetically, the added message was 'other strains can kill far more of you than that, certainly enough to bring you to your knees.' It's business. Check.

It was an excellent strategic move IF they had intentionally done it. Plausible deniability. The president had not thought that far ahead and considered possible impacts from and reactions to his tariff impacts on China. Releasing a more virulent strain would have led to war. His security advisors had said such options are always considered and analyzed by the primary players, including the U.S., but he had minimized them. He had almost gotten the country into a war with Iran because he had underestimated the resolve of the power lords in that country and the depths to which they would go to maintain their place in the governing hierarchy. The same was true for North Korea. Being the supreme ruler of a country of dirt-eating minyans was still far more satisfying and fun than owning a couple of billion dollars of resorts. Heck, there, you really could kill people that you didn't like or got in your way and get away with it. He would have to think about his response to this pandemic carefully.

"Thoughts, sir?" asked the vice president.

"What can we get from them without looking like we caved?" he asked.

"Well, as I said, we get some ag purchases, hopefully. We need those to ensure we keep the Midwest. And they have a vaccine, they say. They understand optics. I think we can keep some token tariffs in place to appease our core. And we may have to buy some of those vaccines or at least the formulas. Otherwise, we must develop one ourselves."

"I can't see our people trusting a Chinese vaccine. That'd make our pharmacy companies look bad and make me look like a pussy," said the president. "Same with the paying for the vaccines. That ain't happening. Can we make a vaccine, Jack?"

"Well, they generally take some time, usually years. Some novel methods, like DNA sequencing, are being researched, though. Our health science is the best in the world."

"We should talk to our big pharmacy companies, don't you think, Jack?"

"Well, I can ask around, sir."

"You want to be in charge of that, Jack?"

"In charge of what exactly, sir?"

"Working with our pharmacy companies… to get a vaccine for this Covid thing. We've got great pharmacies. Right? Should be easy."

"Our pharmaceuticals are the best in the world, sir. But there's a process by which drugs are developed, tested, and approved… to make sure they're safe. That's why our industry is the best. Because we have a process. That's what the FDA oversees."

"Process, shma-cess. We're the best at this shit because we're the smartest."

He paced slowly in front of the window, back and forth in short distances. His eyes wandered to a painting of George Washington that hung to the right of the window. Extending both arms out, palms up, he asked exasperatedly, "What do you think he'd do, huh?" Before Hoffman could answer, POTUS' bellowed, "Those assholes had it so easy. THESE are tough times," he said emphatically, looking directly at the vice president. "I'll think about it, Jack. In the short term, get in touch with Homeland Security, the Commerce Department, or whoever else and see how we can slow down the implementation of our tariffs." Contradicting his just spoken lament, he added, "This virus thing is no big thing. It'll blow over in a few months. I gotta hunch. It's just a bad case of the flu. We can get a shot for it, just like the flu. Work on the tariffs. Keep me posted.

"Yes, sir. Right away."

"Wait, Jack. One more time, so I'm sure I got it. So, we slow applying the tariffs, even though we're hyping them, and they guarantee to buy more, right?" Jack nodded yes. "Okay, okay. So yeah, call Homeland Security or whoever a.s.a.p. and get those tariffs spread out. Hell, maybe we can just get rid of income taxes and pay for those with tariffs. Yeah?"

"Well, that would sound good initially to the voters, but it wouldn't be such a good idea, sir," said Hoffman.

"Why not?" POTUS asked.

"Because 47% percent of people don't pay income taxes."

"Leaches," said Emma, scornfully.

"Not really," said Hoffman. "They don't pay income taxes. That would include plenty of rich people with good accountants. It's not just poor people." Emma and POTUS said nothing, so Hoffman went on. "They pay plenty of other taxes… or related ones. Like sales taxes, gas taxes, and service charges like water and sewer if they're renting. Stuff like that." POTUS had begun looking down when Hoffman brought up some rich people not having to pay income tax and had yet to raise his head. "Actually, poor people, along with the middle class, pay the lion's share of the other related taxes."

"No way," POTUS countered, looking up.

"Way," said Hoffman. "Tariffs are just taxes nested in the price of certain products. If you use those to cover income taxes no longer collected, you've made it even harder on the poor."

"Not tracking with you," said POTUS.

"I get what he's saying," said Emma, her voice indicating displeasure at the revelation. "Yeah. So, consumers would pick up the costs of the tariff. Hoffman nodded affirmatively. "A lower income tax rate would mostly benefit the higher income bracket and maybe some upper-level mid-income. The 47% who don't pay income tax now would see the cost of most imported items go up."

Hoffman looked at her directly. "Excellent. Thanks, Emma. Yes. The items that most people use daily. Food, toys, computers and printers, gasoline, food…"

POTUS cut him off. "Okay, Jack. Enough with the economics lesson. Just get the vaccines solved. And fuck their vaccines, crazy bat fuckers? You get our pharmacies to develop a vaccine. You oversee it. You're in charge. Okay? Get a program going. Make something happen," the president said. Hoffman, looking serious, nodded. "We're good for now, Jack. You can go. The Five is coming on Fox in a minute, and I need to see what's happening in the world. Give me a ring later for an update."

"I'm on it, sir," said Hoffman as he scurried obediently out the door.

***

Early June

Vancouver

It was early March, and their arrival had been serendipitously camouflaged by fast-evolving global events. The outbreak of COVID-19 triggered a lockdown and halted nearly all international travel. Canada closed its borders in mid-March, followed by the U.S. a week later. Local lockdowns followed, providing ideal cover for the three men. Ali advised them not to return to Iraq but to stay in Canada, where they would be safer and have better and more accessible medical treatment, to which Balil had 'reluctantly' agreed.

Ali's condo initially suited their needs perfectly. They integrated well into the immediate neighborhood, staying under the radar of those typically monitoring Arab communities. The pandemic's urgency shifted most security resources and attention away from traditional surveillance. The men avoided mosques and limited their outings to walks and exercise in Stanley Park. They prayed privately at least once a day. Ali's high-end Persian rug and fabric retail outlet near Robson Street in the Central District developed strong local and international acclaim. His three guests quickly became known among the building's residents as "the three businessmen temporarily stuck in the country." As a successful Shia businessman and nearly thirty-year resident, Ali had never been considered a threat by Canadian officials or neighbors.

Consequently, his guests were seen as both safe and welcome. Ali introduced Balil as his godson and the other two as his friends and associates. The limited exposure due to COVID-19 and the men's ability to maintain a low profile allowed them to blend seamlessly into the building and neighborhood. Their fake passports and visas initially allowed them a legal six-month stay in Canada from March 1.

By late April, two of the three men had relocated to other parts of the city. Balil had told Ali that both men had intended to have gone to the east side of the country to visit relatives and business associates but did not feel safe and wished to isolate in Vancouver for a few months with him until the pandemic's restrictions and severity were more evident. On the other hand, the condo unit was too small for four men. As one with 'family ties' with Ali, it 'made sense' for Balil to stay with his uncle where the two could continue to work on business and for the other two to relocate. Ali had many friends and associates in Vancouver, and in short order, he was able to find temporary housing for the other two.

Farhan and Odion were moved to nearby apartments, Farhan just a few blocks away in the Downtown Eastside area and Odion to the suburb of Surrey a few miles away. Their stories remained consistent: they were businessmen from the Middle East in the delicate textile and garment sector who had recently arrived but then had become isolated because of the pandemic. According to their script, they had initially crossed the border from the United States by train, having completed some business in the Los Angeles, San Francisco, and Seattle areas before coming to Vancouver. Strategically, spreading themselves out in the city and remaining to themselves lessened the chances of all being watched or arrested.

Ali had arranged for both men to be in homes that were cordial to hosting Middle Eastern men stranded as they were. Farhan had been detailed to a young couple about his age, both originally from Iran, whose families had trekked out of Iran via Iraq until they arrived and received asylum in Turkey in the late 1990s. Both families then made their way to Canada and, eventually, Vancouver, where they started a successful Iranian restaurant that was later duplicated in two other neighborhoods in the city.

The couple had known each other since they were young children and had the same adventures and ordeals, so teaming up for the ordeal and adventure of marriage seemed like a natural progression in their life journey. Those experiences had morphed into a love built on a common spiritual evolution, and the couple was happy to help a wayward traveler with whom they could recount shared memories of Iraq. They both spoke Farsi and elementary Arabic, but English was now their native tongue. Communications often included pieces of all languages, as Farhan spoke some Farsi. And though Arabic was his native language, his English was quite good. Neither couple were devout Muslims, having adapted to the Western lifestyle of Canada. They neither prayed regularly nor attended services at nearby mosques, though most were closed or their attendance was limited because of COVID-19. The couple's many friendships included numerous young Arabs from the Middle East and Northern Africa who had, like themselves, located in the area at a young age but maintained aspects of their cultural heritage.

Believing he would only be around for four to six months, Farhan was offered work for the restaurant as a food deliverer for takeout orders in the neighborhoods immediately surrounding their downtown Vancouver eatery. His language capabilities were a definite plus. It was easy to pay him cash in addition to his housing, keeping him off all company employment and tax records. It's a win-win for all.

Odion's roommates were two young men, one a Somali immigrant and the other an Ethiopian, the two having come to Canada ten and eleven years earlier, respectfully. They had let him, at the request of a friend of a friend at another mosque in the city, the ultimate friend being Ali. Both worked at the international airport, the first in baggage claim for Air Canada and the other collecting fees at the airport's public parking lot exit. Though their hours had significantly reduced, they were still paid in full. They were happy to spend much of their newly found free time playing video games with their new tenant. Both were Muslim and loved living in Canada. They knew many of the people in the immediate neighborhood, several of which were young girls their age, and it was not unusual for the apartment to host weekend video game parties that included other ex-pats. As far as they knew, Odion was another recent immigrant who had not gotten dislocated due to COVID-19.

Odion's roommates had lined him up with three businesses that called him to do odd jobs or fill in for other workers, including janitors or menial laborers. He did not make a lot but could make a meaningful contribution to rent and household expenses, enough that his new friends were placated and had decided they did not mind having him around for a few months. Besides, Odion had a penchant for video games and was the one to beat in the apartment and the neighborhood.

Like his friends, he did not attend the mosque, and as far as they knew, if he prayed, which he had come to do more casually, he did it when they were not there in the privacy of his room.

Balil, in the meantime, was genuinely trying to help Ali with his business. Initially, the retail operation had closed completely. But after regulations around allowable business operations crystalized, the shop was allowed to let customers in on an appointment-only basis, and masks, of course, were required. Initially, Balil's efforts focused on handling phone calls and scheduling showings, which was more of an administrative assistant function, but expanded to working directly with the clients. He also provided input to the company's webmaster, his uncle, who had utterly neglected its maintenance for over a year. Balil ensured that communications through the channel were up-to-date around business hours and operations and that there were current photos of every rug and textile type in the store's inventory.

Under normal circumstances, he would have shared his list of providers of products in hard-to-reach places in Iraq, Iran, and Northern Turkey with his uncle. But knowing that communications of such international emails were almost certainly monitored by Canadian and U.S. agencies alike, he mentioned only a couple of reputable operations in Baghdad to his uncle that he could deal with directly that would not raise any suspicions.

Sales at the store had tanked from those of the same period the previous year for March and April, barely covering their bills and overhead. Around the end of May, Ali's business made a noticeable sales jump, mainly due to a TV commercial Balil conceptualized in late April advising viewers, 'This is the time to make home improvements.'

While many of the small businesses in the city, including those in the neighborhood, had quickly disintegrated to the brink of insolvency, local news stations' stories spoke of how the online dimension of many sectors was doing surprisingly well, particularly home improvements. They had noted that an expected crash in the real estate markets had not materialized, and experts saw continued strength in both new and existing house sales. Activity in remodels sored, as well, as work-at-homers took a keener interest in projects around their homes.

The market was hot. Balil correctly determined that if the store strengthened its website and drove people to it with a few local TV and radio ads, it could tap into the growing demand for home products. Their products were high-end, and people would pay for them if they could figure out how to get them before them while still adhering to Covid business guidelines. He and Ali identified three efforts that would be especially effective for increasing sales: a personalized home needs analysis and an in-store tour of relevant inventory, free deliveries, and installation for all purchases. The study included visits to prospective customers' homes who had called in to have someone either come or schedule an in-store visit to identify products that fit the home's decor. Ali and Balil rotated between in-store and home appointments. It was on one such store visit that Balil met Mayla.

***

Mayla, whose family owned a condo in one of the higher-end buildings just three blocks from the shop, came to the store looking for Persian rug runners for the new unit they'd recently moved into. She had made the appointment online a day before. Balil had emailed her about the matter and assured her that only she and he would be in the store while she was there. When they met, they distanced themselves from one another, and both wore masks, formalities that were at least somewhat consistent with some of his social experiences in parts of the Middle East.

They made small talk for the first thirty minutes, with Balil showing some of the most expensive rugs on the racks. For the rest of the time, they sat, drank tea, and talked about the world's troubles, life in Canada, the city's fine restaurants, beautiful sunrises, Stanley Park, the museums and universities, and their favorite music. An hour into the conversation, Mayla was very interested in knowing what the gentleman she had been talking with looked like without a mask. His yellow eyes were striking, mesmerizing even against his dark brown skin. He said she had never seen anything quite like them, a gift from his mother's side. While a little thin, he was notably fit, his arm muscles nicely toned. His English was excellent; his expressions and descriptions in his stories were articulate, sometimes eloquent.

Balil's stories of the products told of their quality and qualities, the materials involved, where they had been made, and the people who made them. His demeanor was urbane, and he had a surprising sophistication and gentleness, given some of his history over the last thirty-odd years he shared. His story about being delayed in Canada due to the pandemic while on a business trip appealed to her spirit of adventure.

The personal questions soon became the norm as they both learned the other was single. Mayla also knew, though, that Balil was thirty-two, had been married, and had lost a wife and daughter five years earlier by an exploding IED in the northeast part of the country while the family was accompanying him on a business trip to try and secure a new source of material for high-end fabrics. His father, he told her, had died in the early years following the invasion, though he did not detail the cause. Balil stated that he had struggled mainly with his father's business for many years because of the conditions in the country. Still, he had come to Vancouver to resurrect the relationship with his father's prior partner, Ali, see his business firsthand, and hopefully better assess the market and product demands better to match them to existing and potential suppliers at home.

Mayla could have stayed for the rest of the day, but she had a prior meeting that she knew she must attend. Still, at a distance, she removed her mask. "Is it possible for you to come to my condo and tell me which products you feel might be the best fit for the spaces?" she asked.

Used to seeing only parts of women's faces, Balil had known from the moment he saw her that she was beautiful, but the depth of it still took a little of his breath away. She was tall, maybe just three inches shorter than his six feet, and had a great body accented by a close-fitting white blouse, black business pants, and a black, pinstriped blue jacket. Her heels brought her lovely brown eyes almost up level with his.

"I'd be most pleased, Miss Hassan. Is Saturday after 3:30 alright?" he asked. "We don't have any appointments at this time, but we do get some phone calls on Saturdays during the day.

"Is there any way we can do it on Sunday?" she asked. "My parents have arranged a visit to the mosque and won't be there. I want this to surprise them, so I'm hoping we can take advantage of their being away."

Balil was over himself, buzzing with excitement. Typically, he would have denied such a time slot given her parents' absence, but he would not pass up this opportunity to meet her again. He hadn't spoken to any ladies in private or in depth in the last five years, not since his wife and little daughter died.

"That's fine," he replied. "What time?"

"Let's say, 10:30? That way, we can have lunch after work. How does that sound?"

"I look forward to it?"

"Great. I'll email you the address. It's not far, and it's easy to find."

"Very well."

"I very much look forward to the visit, then," she said expectantly. With that, she smiled and walked out the door.

Mayla's parents, Mohammed and Mira Hassan, left at nine that morning to go to the mosque. From there, she knew they intended to have lunch with a couple who were friends and business associates. They had moved to Vancouver thirty years earlier to attend the University of British Columbia. They had met there as students; he was a structural engineer, and she was an architect. After working for different consulting firms, they set up their own firm. While still in their late twenties, they concentrated on growth in the city, particularly those backed by relocated Middle East assets. They had initially lived in the Surrey area before moving to the very high-end community of Shaughnessy Center, around the time Mayla started school as a first grader eighteen years ago. Like her mother, she had pursued a degree in architecture, though she preferred interior design as a complementary tangent. Her project was the family's residence, where she was still living.

Mayla began preparing for her visitor as soon as her mother and father were out the door. While she fully intended to do the work the visit focused on, she was also excited to see Balil. Like a teen suddenly enamored by the new kid in school, she began to organize for the meeting. First, she tidied up the condo, making the beds in all the rooms. Her parents would like that later, she thought. She laid out a couple of books on the coffee table that she thought he might know of or find interesting, including one of the historical sites in Iraq and the surrounding region. She began putting a veggie platter together for lunch but then changed her mind, put them in a plastic container, and hid them in the back of the frig, thinking that it would be more intimate to enlist his help with the effort. After that, she focused on putting on her makeup, getting dressed, and fixing her hair.

Balil buzzed her intercom at precisely 11:00, having waited downstairs for fifteen minutes until the exact hour of his directed arrival. She buzzed him in and hurried with last-minute details.

"Hi," she said as she opened the door.

"As-salaamu Alaikum,'" he said.

"Ah," she said. "I'm sorry. Please forgive my manners. Va-alaikum As-salaam."

"Come in, come in," she invited.

"Shukran," he replied.

"You're not going to make me speak Arabic, are you?" she said with a laugh.

He raised his two hands, palms out, and said, "No, no," then laughed. "It's just that it is such a lovely residence. It makes me feel the need to be formal. Sorry."

"Well," she replied, "just relax. There are no expectations here—only celebration."

"I like that. May I use that myself sometime?"

She laughed again. "Yes, you may. It's not an original. I borrowed it from a friend. I use it often. I believe it's a good philosophy."

"I agree," he said, nodding in earnest agreement.

The small talk quickly morphed into an extension of topics they had discussed at the store, such as the state of the world, life in Vancouver, favorite foods, and travel. When Mayla turned the discussion to future life plans, Balil quickly turned the conversation to the day's work, deciding what textiles and carpets fit with the condo's architectural and current furniture motif. He brought his laptop and presented some online images he thought would work. He also tried to describe some of the store's inventory she had seen online that he thought were most suitable. She recalled most of what he was describing for the store but pretended not to, suggesting to revisit the store for a relook.

Around one o'clock, she moved them to the kitchen, where, to her liking, Balil helped her prepare lunch. He was careful and clean, which pleased her considerably. She was unsure what to expect from a man who had lived alone in Iraq and seemed to travel quite a bit.

Sometime in the middle of the afternoon, Balil said he must leave, but before he left, they scheduled an appointment in the store for that Wednesday at noon. She volunteered to bring lunch, to which he happily agreed. Before she left, she ordered approximately $35,000 of material, which he delivered to the home that Friday.

Just before the two completed the order placement, Mayla's parents returned home. They raved about the selections that had been made and the choices being considered, as well as wanting to know more about his life and how he had come to visit Vancouver. He spent the next hour talking and getting to know them, and they invited him back to dinner the following Saturday, to which he happily agreed.

Mayla walked him downstairs to the entrance and said goodbye. She wanted to hug him but thought twice about it, knowing that such an informal act would likely make him uncomfortable. Instead, she offered him a handshake and said, "See you Wednesday."

"Yes, yes," Balil said. "Wednesday. I look forward to that."

****

"The Hassan's," Ali said after Balil told him about the meeting and upcoming appointment. "Oh my. They are quite well known. And I hear their daughter is lovely."

"She is," Balil said, smiling widely. "Quite."

Balil waited excitedly for Wednesday with almost more anticipation than he could contain. When Mayla arrived, she was as stunning as the last two times he had seen her earlier. This time, she wore a white Cashmere coat that covered a tight-fitting, royal blue dress that hugged her body and ran to her knees. She knew men, and his subtle gulp when he saw her did not go unnoticed.

They immediately went to work, going through the material choices she had feigned, not remembering. By the end of the meeting, her commitment to various products had escalated from the previous estimate of $35,000 to a current one of $50,000.

When they were finally done, she said, "My parents have another place in Whistler. Have you been there?"

"No," he said. "But I hear it's very beautiful."

"I'd like to do the same thing there. The order won't be as big. Probably only about half. Can you go up there with me?" she asked thoughtfully.

"Certainly," he replied.

"Next Sunday?"

"Yes. Of course. That would be nice."

"Great. You'll love it. It… is… beautiful. Amazing. The mountains are spectacular. I'll pick you up at noon in the morning in front of the store." His mind flashed briefly about whether they would have enough time. He did not know precisely how far away Whistler was, but she quickly continued, leaving him no time to ask her for any details. "Great. Bring a set of clean clothes. We won't be back until later Monday, maybe Tuesday, so make sure you don't make any other appointments. And don't forget dinner this Saturday with my parents." Before he had time to understand what had just happened, she turned and hurried out the door.

***

Winthrop

Early June

"Hey, Dingus," someone yelled from the car that had quietly pulled up next to him. "Is that a Hemi?"

Seth turned and looked down to see who was behind the voice. Dingus? His initial, mostly contained sneer, quickly turned into a broad smile when he saw Cody.

"Hey-hey there, Dude," Seth exclaimed. "Howzit?"

"Excellent," Cody replied.

"Cool. Shit, I haven't seen you in over a month, man. You been hanging out at Sweetie's?" Seth said quizzically.

Cody smiled, then said, "Yeah, but Steve has been getting a mega number of reservations for pack trips and hikes. I've been doing six days a week. Sometimes seven. I got in last night and am leaving tomorrow for two days. This will be his best and busiest summer ever. I've been booked solid for over a month now. Making some coin."

"Nice," Seth said, nodding.

"I'd heard your old man had bought you some new wheels. Doooope, dude."

Seth's truck sat almost two feet above the ground, combining oversized tires and elevated shocks. It was mostly black with flames that started near the front tires and spread across the doors toward the back of the vehicle."

"Sweet, huh? Dad found it in Yakima."

"Man, you are up there. You must need a step ladder to help you get in," Cody barbed.

"Hey, man. This thing'll drive over logs… and boulders," countered Seth. "It's hell on wheels, trust me."

"I believe you," Cody responded, his eyes still scoping the truck. "That's a beast. Looks almost new; was it used?" Cody asked, trying to decide the model's age.

"Well, yeah," Seth said a little sheepishly. "You know, Dad. He picked it at a government auction for seized properties. Seems it was a favorite of a couple of local drug amigos."

"That explains the paint job."

"I like it!" Seth said, his voice slightly defensive.

"A chick magnet for sure in Yakima. Wasn't that a little pricey for your dad? That's not a cheap trick."

"I think Dad slipped the auctioneer a few bucks to accept his 'silent bid,'" Seth confided.

"Ever the Scotsman."

"Yep, in the blood," Seth chirped. "Just like Grandpa Callum. He never bought a new car in his life. Says it's the biggest waste of money…"

"Yeah, yeah," Cody cut in merrily, waving his hand as if to signify 'no more.'

Seth just smiled and shrugged his shoulders, then added, "Hey, Ellison," leaning his head down to try and see the driver of what he knew to be Chris' car. "That you?"

"Hey, Big Guy," Chris Ellison answered. "Nice ride. You need some oxygen while you drive that thing? Might have a can in the trunk."

"Hey, I have Friday off. Come by Sweetie's. Her parents are gone. Come by," yelled Cody, "about 6:00. I'm buying."

There was a gentle honk from the car behind Seth. A driver had come up behind the trio, signally to turn left. Seth began moving slowly forward, and Chris and Cody followed, parallel to the big Dodge. Chris waved, stuck his arm out the window, and pointed for the car to pull ahead and turn. A farmer, Mr. Adams, who lived on the east side of the Methow River between Twisp and Winthrop, pulled up on Chris' side, recognized all three, waved congenially, then peaked both ways as he pulled further ahead and turned left.

"I'll be there, then," Seth shouted back enthusiastically. "Bud?"

"Bud, it is."

"Works for me," said Seth, waving his hand as high as he could as he pulled away.

Chris and Cody went the same way but quickly moved to the right lane and pulled into Chris' dad's auto repair shop and service station, where Cody had left his car. Cody had seen him while driving by on the way to the store to run errands for his mom, but he stopped to say hello. Chris then convinced him to go with him on a short trip to a small farm nearby to check out a tractor the owner was having trouble with.

While Cody had gone to college, Chris had not, opting instead, and with intense pressure from his father, to help run the failing business. Autos and farm equipment were getting considerably more complicated, including more technology, and his dad did not have the expertise to fix the increasingly complex problems. However, there was still a market in the valley for fixing aging pickups and larger trucks that farmers and ranchers used.

"So you coming by later?" Cody asked.

"No, I'll wait 'til Friday. I gotta get up early."

"Cool. I'll get the booze, though. My treat. Don't bring anything," said Cody, knowing Chris, who still lived at home, didn't have much money.

"Nice. Thanks, bro. I'll owe you," Chris replied, smiling back. "See you then."

***

"That sounds like Seth coming," said Chris as he squinted his eyes in an apparent strain to better hear.

There was a momentary pause before Sweetie and Cody smiled as their concentration left the conversation and shifted to listening to what Chris was referring to. As Seth's truck's now-signature rumbling grew closer and louder, a vibration became more noticeable.

"Hah, there he is," Cody agreed.

Just then, Seth honked the horn, which was tweaked to play, 'I wish I were in the land of cotton.'

"O.M.G.," said Chris, "he's gone Confederate."

"He's so funny with that thing," added Sweetie. "Have you seen the bumper stickers and flags he's added?" she asked.

"Yeah," said Chris, with a hint of enthusiasm. "He's been quite committed to 'making the country a better place to live.'"

Cody's shift in his chair showed modest discomfort with that thought. "Whatever," he said quietly.

"Oh, come on, Babe," said Sweetie, "he's just being Seth. They don't come any more conservative than his dad and grandpa. He's just pleasing them."

"I don't know if he's just 'pleasing them,'" Chris said. "Seth's gotten a little redder around the collar the last couple of months. He's not too happy with what's going on in Seattle and Portland." Then he added, "I'm not either, really."

"My folks went over to Seattle just last weekend," Sweetie responded. "They went downtown and said the national news, at least some sources, have blown it a little out of proportion. They said it's mostly business as usual in most of the city, but there were more than a few tents on the sidewalks. I don't know about Portland. They're a different animal."

"I've been emailing a classmate living there," Cody said. "Kind of the same thing your folks said, somewhat overblown but still, a mess. Apparently, they have those nightly demonstrations, but they're limited to a couple of block areas around the Federal Building downtown. According to her, it's more like a sometimes-rowdy social get-together, at least most of the time. Same people mostly, sort of a cultural phenomenon, the whole 'keep Portland weird' thing. Hard to say, I guess."

"Her? You're emailing girls in Portland?" quipped Sweetie, feigning concern. "Hmp," she added with mock indignation.

Cody gave her his 'Elvis' smile' and shook his head. "Classmate," he said, adding, "We were in the same marketing class for winter term. All the news stations are loving the turmoil, so hard to separate the bull from the shit, as the old man says."

A moment later, they heard Seth enter and walk through the house before exiting the sliding glass door and joining them at the pool.

"Heeey," they all said in unison as Seth gave a friendly enough wave that seemed to hold back contrary feelings.

"Mi amigos," he said, smiling, as he opened his arms and followed it with quick fist bumps to all three.

"Hey, Sweetie." Seth did a double take on Sweetie, who was fully tanned and wearing a tight cut-off tank top over her bikini bottoms.

"Damn, dude-det. You be looking lit." Seth said with a big smile, "Where's Pedro? I missed my welcoming committee."

"Oh, she's been at the vet getting a cyst removed. Doctor says it might be cancer," she said sadly. "Mom and Dad are picking her up after work."

"Bummer," said Seth with a concerned look. "Good luck with that."

"Glad you made it, man," said Cody. "Your folks makin' you hump?"

"Working hard, man," replied Seth. "We're just getting the first hay cut in and stored. How about you two."

Chris went first. "Oh, same-oh-same-oh here. It's summer, so ranchers and farmers' crap are breaking down everywhere."

Seth nodded in agreement. "True dat."

"We're even getting some tourist action. They're everywhere. Mostly fixing and changing flat tires."

"Same for us," said Cody. "We all thought it'd be dead, but Steve is booked out 'til after Labor Day."

"Cool," said Seth earnestly. "Everybody wants to breathe our healthy fresh air, then, I guess."

"You look buff, Dude," Sweetie said encouragingly while batting her eyes in comic flirtation. "Those six packs are solid."

Of the three boys, Seth was the fittest. Chris had been gangly in high school, a six-foot three-inch bean pole, adding another two since graduation. Seth's height had ceased in his junior year, but he had continued to fill out over the next three. He was solid muscle at six foot three and two hundred fifteen pounds. He had been offered three football scholarships before graduating, two at instate community colleges and one at a small university in Northeast Oregon. He thought about trying out as a walk-on linebacker at WSU but opted instead to focus on his studies in Animal Science.

At just barely over six feet, Cody was the smallest and lightest of the three but of the same athletic caliber as Seth, at least for basketball. A star in high school, he was just too short to be competitive at a higher-level college program, and playing in a minor program, even if on scholarship, did not interest him. Despite his size, he could easily outwalk or hike his two friends.

"I'm hard all over, Baby," Seth said with a friendly wink and smile.

"Except for one muscle, right?" Sweetie prodded amusingly, holding out her drooping index finger in limp mockery.

"Oh, Snap," said Chris.

"Whoa. I thought your name was Sweetie, not Karen?" kidded Seth in return.

"WHOA. Snapback," said Chris, laughing.

"I'm not old enough to be a Karen, retard," Sweetie shot back. "You don't even know what a Karen is. You're a fucking Karen," she said, slapping his arm playfully.

Cody shook his head, familiar and comfortable with Seth's jocular, often naughty, sometimes vulgar, rarely ill-intended nature, smiled and made a face that said, 'I can't believe you just made a dick joke to my girlfriend… in front of me.'

"That means no dates for the cowboy," Chris said, to which Cody held up a clenched fist in mock solidarity to Chris' interpretation.

"Some truth there," Seth said, nodding in agreement as he grabbed the beer Chris had handed him from the cooler and sat between Cody and Chris in the lawn chair.

Cody pursued the topic. "Really, though, no hotties to chase?" Seth just shrugged.

"I'm telling you, you gotta spend more time in town, man," Cody reemphasized.

"Yeah, we're busy as heck at the deli. Tons of girls coming in," Sweetie said before taking a sip of beer. "I've had to make it off limits to Cody; there are so many."

Cody nodded in faked confirmation. "I've had to sit outside on the bench in front of the hardware store," he lied, "and wait for them to come out. No room in the deli."

"Is that why you were out there? I thought you didn't want to help me," Sweetie said, playing along. "You need to come in for lunch, Seth. Mass women."

"Kind of a long way to go for lunch, Sweetie. Besides, you guys are my only entertainment. I'm either here, on the ranch, or running up and down the road trying to find something else to fix." He paused momentarily, pondering the invitation, then said, "But I'll think about it. How's that?"

"I've got an idea," she said excitedly. "How about you come in next weekend? That gives you plenty of time to schedule it, and I'll give you lunch for free and post your picture on our Facebook page… you'll be our 'Saturday Special.' You're hot, dude."

Seth smiled. "Yeah," he said, "it's a curse. Fire Marshall will probably shut you down."

"There's a band next weekend in the park, too. Come into town, Seth; I'm not scheduled that day. Let's all go," Cody offered. Chris nodded in agreement.

"I'm hoping for a couple that want to socially un-distance," Chris said in Seth's direction. "We'll be each other's wingman."

"Ah, I've got plans," said Seth. The eyebrows of all three of his friends went up simultaneously, their facial expressions begging for more information. "I'm going to a Freedom Fighters meeting in Yakima," he shared.

Shocked, Cody asked, "You're not fucking serious, are you?"

Seth's facial and body expressions said otherwise. "As serious as genital herpes," Seth said.

Like three astronauts feeling the pull of a black hole on their spaceship, with none wanting to ask any of the others if they thought it, too, the rest studied one another silently for counsel.

"Whew. Serious, then, I guess," Cody replied, pulling his head back slightly and squinching the left side of his face as he considered Seth's metric. There were a few more moments of awkward silence, each in the group clearly hearing what everyone was thinking but afraid to verbalize. Finally, Cody said it. "Why?" he asked.

Seth thought of just saying, 'Why not?' but decided on something less flippant, something with more explanation. "I just can't take what's going on in the country anymore, man, what's happening in Seattle and Portland. BLM used to stand for the Bureau of Land Management. That's who we work with for our grazing rights on federal lands, you know," the tenor began to elevate just a little in his voice. "Now, it's something altogether different, Black Lives Matter. What's that about, anyway? Like, what the fuck, man? All lives do. Right?" he asked emphatically.

Chris stared down while listening, not looking up, nodded ever so noticeably, and added a barely audible, "Gotta' point there."

Knowing all the boys shared different real estate on the political spectrum, Sweetie waded in gently, with Cody and Seth at likely opposite extremes. "Of course, that's true, Seth," she said comfortingly. "Saying something like 'black lives matter, too' or 'just as much' would probably still have made the point... maybe even a little better. Then there'd be less to argue about... maybe. I think a sign made at that moment probably became a tagline. Just happened. Nobody thought it through, like, 'What happens if this becomes a national motto for our movement?' Seems as if it's another group or their media that asks the question and then makes a deal out of it. I don't really think blacks intended the statement to imply others don't matter. It's a little like the kid always picked last in gym class for a team. They're like, 'Hey, I want to play, too. Why are you guys always leaving me out.'"

"Yeah, maybe," said Cody thoughtfully. "Nice analogy, Sweetie. But I get your point, too, Seth. But honestly, man, you have to admit they don't seem to matter as much, at least compared to white people, don't you think?"

Usually silent, Chris looked up and said, "And I hear you, Bro. But don't you think they could have picked a better martyr than the guy the cops killed in Minneapolis?"

"Amen," chimed Seth.

"What do you mean?" asked Cody solemnly.

"Well," Chris responded, "he was a fucking felon, wasn't he? A druggie. Why is he considered a hero all of a sudden? Couldn't they have found someone better, a better person to rally around? Maybe someone without a criminal record?"

"Here, here," said Seth, his tone agreeable but slightly irritated.

"Well, it's not like there was an audition for the role," said Cody. "And he's not a hero. He was a victim. Shit, man, there are plenty of examples of blacks shot by police that were just stopped for simple traffic violations, like burnt-out brake lights. Happens on the West side way too often. They're not all criminals, for Christ's sake. I think he was just the tipping point for a problem that's been around for a long time. And just because one might be a criminal doesn't mean you don't treat them with the same respect you treat other humans of different color."

"Well, those folks shouldn't be tearing up the cities. It's criminal," Seth said emphatically as Chris, eyes wide open, slowly nodded in passive concurrence.

"'Those folks' being blacks?" Cody said.

"Oh, come on, Cody," Seth scoffed. "It's not like I used the N-word." There was a pause in the group as everyone waited to see where the conversation was going next. Seth went on. "N-word. I hate that fucking term."

"Really," Chris smirked. "What do you tell your little kid when they come home from school and ask 'What is the N-word, mommy? It's a naughty word, honey. Well, what's the word mommy?'" He looked around.

Seth answered. "That's a good question. Funny, I hadn't thought about it like that. Can't say Nigger. It's like that Harry Potter name that can't be said, Double-Dork or whatever."

Everybody laughed. "Close, well sorta," said Cody, smiling. "Very close to the wrong guy. I also have a problem with the whole PC thing about what we can or can't say. It's like 'context doesn't matter' anymore?' You're right. How can you even discuss something ugly if you can't even say what it is that's ugly? Makes no sense. Well intended, but makes no sense."

"Exactly," said Seth. "Who says you can't say something, and if you do, you're bad. Who made that fucking rule, anyway? And you're bad just because you said it? Does that make a problem go away?"

Cody was looking at Seth. "Okay, okay. No, it doesn't. But back to what we were talking about, though. And this is the problem. So, what if Sheriff Johnson pulled you over for a loud muffler and held your neck down with his knee until his deputies got there?"

"He knows me," Seth replied. "He wouldn't do that."

"That's the point, Seth," noted Sweetie gently. "Might he do that to a white guy here from Seattle? Probably not," she answered herself. "An Indian from the rez? Maybe. A black guy from Seattle, he pulled over at night. Quite likely. That's reality, Seth."

"Seth," Cody pressed, "if Johnson sees your burned-out taillight, he MIGHT stop you. He'll likely pull up next to you and yell it through the window. Either way, you won't get a ticket, you won't get handcuffed and taken in, and you won't get mistreated or, worse, shot… cause you're white. That's the point. Sweetie is right. Start doing that to white tourists here in the valley, and this place will dry up overnight."

"Well, the cops are just doing their job. I'm sure whites get just as many tickets as the blacks," said Seth. "Out-of-towners for sure."

"There may be some truth to that, but the white ones don't get a knee on the neck. That's not the case on the West side. It's all about money, and they can get a lot of it from people who can't argue about the tickets. A tourist gets one here; they pay it because it's too far to come back to and argue in court. But they'll go to court if it's near their home. Poor people of color can't afford the luxury of being able to dispute the matter. They don't have the money to go to court and argue, say, a DUI away. The poor are usually just treated more harshly, especially the ones of color. Keepin' the blacks under control. The boomers and others with money look the other way because they're told they're safer."

Seth and Chris both listened thoughtfully with pensive expressions while Cody continued. "My grandfather used to say, 'If you treat a bum like a gentleman long enough, they'll start to behave like one.' I've always wondered if the reverse is true, you know, treat a guy like a piece of shit long enough…" Cody offered. After a few moments of somber silence, he added, "So, what the hell are the Freedom Fighters gonna' do to fix any of this? They gotta plan? An agenda? An outline? Just seems like more displaced… ," he said, struggling to finish the thought before he finished with, "bullshit."

Seth shrugged his shoulders and shook his head slightly. He clasped his hands behind his head momentarily and stared up contemplatively. Then, straightening, he looked at Cody and said, "I don't know, Cody. I just know I want to stand up for my rights and way of life and make this country like it used to be."

"Like when? How? Shit, I hate that fucking slogan," Cody said frustratedly. "You want to go back to when the blacks had their previous careers? Give 'em all their old jobs back?"

"Very funny. No. How about when we were just talking about when I don't have to worry about saying the wrong thing when I'm just fucking talking? When our lives aren't under a microscope a year or twenty years from now for something I said today or three years ago. When the world respected us," he said emphatically, "and we had order. When people obeyed the law."

"And when was that? Thirties? Depression. Forties? War. Fifties? McCarthy-ism. The sixties?"

"Great music... the sixties," chimed Chris cheerfully.

"Agreed," laughed Cody. "But people our age and blacks were rioting worse than now. Way worse and way more often. Right into the mid-seventies. What else in the seventies? More Vietnam. Big recession. Eighties? Inflation and stagflation nation. Nineties? The internet bubbles. Then, war, runaway real estate prices, and then a really big recession in 2008. There's never been a 'then,' Seth, that captures a 'when' because there ain't one. There's always something off, Dude," he said, as he crossed his V-signed fingers in front of his face, like a dancing Pulp Fiction John Travolta, "changes we're not comfortable with."

"Except for Levi's," Sweetie said, trying to liven up the mood. "Gotta love stretch denim."

"I thought you are majoring in marketing," barbed Seth, "not history."

"Our high school civics class. Adams. Remember him? That was the final essay question on the term final. You took it, too." Cody toned down his volume and rhythm, which he knew were getting out of sorts. "It's about fixing what is in front of us and moving forward," he said more gently. "There is no 'again' to go back to. There never was. There was no 'perfect time.' That's just horseshit," said Cody, frustrated. Seth just kept looking, expressionless, as Cody kept talking. "Generally, the country has fixed its shit over time. The biggest conflicts have eventually brought the greatest gains." He was speaking calmly by now. "Ain't that what happened with the Civil War?"

"Might be another one of those coming, brother," said Seth, his tone a little edgy. "I hope not, but many are ready to fight, you know." His tone had a dimension of warning, like a police siren wailing from the distance.

Cody wanted to ask Seth, 'With who and for what?' but knew they were on opposite ends of this discussion and that pushing it any further at the moment would probably turn unproductively confrontational. But then it occurred to him to ask, "What would you or Chris do if you saw one of Johnson's deputies with his knee on my neck in the middle of the street?"

Seth guzzled down his beer and stood up. Not opting to let Cody retake the grandstand, he stood and said with a grin, "I'd ask him if he needs any help. Hey, I gotta' go," a hint of exasperation in his voice.

"You just got here," said Sweetie with genuine disappointment.

"Working tomorrow. Gotta get up early." Seth turned to Chris and asked, "You want to go with me next weekend… to the rally."

"I might. Ask me again in a couple of days," he said.

"Well, I've got a tractor giving me trouble. The red Ford. Come look at it this week if you can, and we can talk more about it then."

"Will do," said Chris.

"Bring your flatbed in case it has to be hauled into town." Chris nodded affirmatively. "In the meantime, check out their Facebook website for details on the rally," Chris said nothing but held up his right thumb. Seth turned to Cody, who had stood up, and grinned, "I'm assuming you don't want to go."

Cody just smiled, stood, and offered a handclasp shake. He pulled his friend to him with his left hand, and the two gave each other a warm, disarming half-embrace. "Take care, man. And don't be a stranger. Let's get together when you get back, and you can tell us how it went."

"I'll do that. Decent question, by the way," Seth said seriously. With a somewhat sad smile and nuanced shake of his head, he made for his truck. A few moments later, they heard the vehicle roar to life, fading away.

"Do you really think you'll go with him?" Sweetie asked Chris.

"Maybe. I don't know," he said. "I'm on the fence. Sounds interesting. Probably not, though."

"Go," said Cody. "Keep an eye on him. That and I'd like a second opinion of the program."

"And wear a mask," Sweetie chirped. "Don't want to have to wait two weeks to see you."

Cody had thought about saying something similar himself but had held back, worried Chris would consider him a pussy. He knew Seth would have. Sweetie could get away with giving such advice. The friends ignored the CDC recommendations when together but were mostly distanced and stayed outside, especially since the weather turned nice, practices they did not have to acknowledge or formalize.

Chris coughed a slight laugh. "Yeah, I'll watch out for him," he agreed, "but I'm not sure about the mask. I don't really want to get my ass kicked… and Seth would likely 'unfriend' me." With that, Chris stood and began making his way toward the house. "Thanks, you guys. Have fun. I'll be in touch."

Alone, Cody and Sweetie snuggled in and enjoyed the privacy in frustrated and mostly sad silence.

Sweetie finally spoke first. "You worried about Seth?"

Cody puckered his mouth a little before simply nodding an affirmative.

"He'll be okay, Baby," she said softly, putting her head on his left shoulder and rubbing his chest with his right. "Don't worry. Seth has a good head on his shoulders," she said, peering up at him.

Cody looked at her, smiled, and said, "Stop trying to make me laugh. He has a head and shoulders; I'll go along with that." He leaned back and stared at the sky momentarily before saying, "He's just changed so much since last year, and this whole pandemic has really amplified it. We just seem to keep drifting apart around these stupid issues. The whole country's gone bonkers. Holy shit. How did masks become a fucking issue about freedom and liberty?"

"I know," she answered, knowing he didn't expect one. "Mom and Dad talk about it all the time. Dad says nine-eleven has something to do with it, that the whole 'thanks for your service' thing, 'all servicepeople are heroes' has just been a national promotion effort to glorify the military so we can add respect to war efforts that nobody really likes. Learned our lesson around that with Vietnam, he said. People spit on soldiers that went there when they came home. He thinks the real security problem has become paramilitary groups like the Freedom Fighters."

"I'd agree with that. "And 'the war,'" Cody said, making quotes with his figures, "is way bigger than Iraq, Afghanistan, or even the Middle East. They've become a distraction. Our War on Terror is terrorizing the world. We're killing people all over. It sells lots of military equipment and fucks up a lot of vets who spend years learning the arts of killing before coming home and trying to get a job that lets them fit in. They're all used to 'track and attack' and the 'thrill of the kill.'"

His anxiety began to show in the tone, volume, and pitch of his voice. "Guys like Seth get to hang out with a few ex-military PTSD'ers and some posers, pretending they're protecting us all. It's way more fun than video games. Made up concerns that if you disagree with, then you're part of the concern."

Sweetie squeezed his hand harder. She had heard it all before in conversations between Cody and her parents, though these topics were rarely discussed in this detail between the group of friends. "Yeah, Dad says in the sixties and seventies, it was just cops, the National Guard, and the military. Now we have SWAT, DEA, Homeland Security, Border Patrol, Federal Marshalls, yadda-yadda. Crazy. Police forces everywhere."

"And armed to the teeth. And the vets get the jobs."

"Yeah, I'm sure bunches of the Freedom Fighters are cops."

"No doubt," said Cody. "Can't get that kind of adrenalin rush in a regular job."

"That's why Mom and Dad love to visit with you," Sweetie said comfortingly as she hooked her arm in his, pulled herself close, and put her head on his shoulder.

"And why all the hassle around wearing masks for a while? I wouldn't want to make my gramps and gramma sick."

"I thought they were dead," she said goadingly.

"They are," Cody said, smiling. "But if they weren't," he said. "I'd wear a mask to protect them. People are fucking selfish. God… I'm glad people can't smoke in most restaurants… or on planes. I hate being around that shit. People don't talk about losing their rights over that anymore because most people don't do it or like to be around it. It kills you. Can't yell 'fire' in a theater." His face, arms, and hands suddenly became animated as he spoke. "Makes sense. Can't drink and drive. Those aren't considered losses of freedom. They're accepted as public health and safety issues. The president doesn't wear one because he wants to appear as a tough guy, invincible, so all his idiot followers want to be tough, too. Fuck me hard. Crazy."

"Okay," said Sweetie with a coy grin and a squeeze to the back of his neck with her hand.

"Okay, what?" he asked, missing the offer entirely.

"I'll fuck you hard," she cooed quietly, continuing the neck massage. "I fuck you long time," she said with her best attempt at a bad Asian accent.

He said nothing, instead just turning and kissing her gently before pulling her to him in a robust and warm embrace.

Wagging his finger, he playfully admonished her imitation. "That's culturally and gender-ly unacceptable, you know. But tempting."

"I'm half Lebanese. "That's almost Eurasian, isn't it?"

"Good question. Might be. In the neighborhood, I guess. Do all Lebanese women speak that way?"

Batting her eyes rapidly, she said, "Maybe. The good ones." Then, leaning back, Sweetie added, "It'll all be better soon enough. Loosen up."

"Hope so," Cody responded. "Hopefully, they'll find a vaccine. I'm not sure everyone will believe in the old Light Speed program. I worry there'll be blood on the streets before this all ends. There are a lot of news shows that fire the conservatives up around masks—radio, especially around this part of the state. I'm sure the same people who hate masks will question any vaccine. Can't come fast enough."

"Unless it comes too fast," said Sweetie. "Seth is always quoting Rush Limbaugh or Lars Larson. He doesn't think any vaccine will be properly tested if they claim to find one. I think that's the only kind of news he listens to."

"And it's not even news," said Cody. "It's fucking angry, ugly commentary. Fox invented the TV version. The rest, CNN and the others are just as bad, though. Just a bunch of people sitting around giving their scripted opinions," Cody said, shaking his head. "I hate all of it anymore." Knowing his tone was getting negative again, Cody shifted the subject. "I'd better get home, too. I've got to get ready for an overnight camp. Leaves the day after tomorrow. Plus, your folks will be home soon. Sorry, but I'm not feeling very sociable. I'm spent," he said.

"Understood, but they'll be disappointed. They like talking with you. Go figure," she said, poking her elbow teasingly into his ribs. "Three lib-tards on the loose. Where are you going on this trip, anyway?"

"Horseshoe Basin. A family from Portland." That meant a twelve-mile, day-in hike, an overnight camp, a day for the family to knock around, see the sights, and hike out on day three.

"So, I won't see you for the next four days?"

He nodded yes. "More or less."

"Mom and Dad might be gone this next weekend. They said they might take the boat to Chelan and go camping up the lake. Come and stay with me. They'll feel better if you do. Me, too," she said invitingly. "Let's do a little Netflix and chill."

"Sounds like a plan. I'll put my mom on notice to the old man I've gone on a longer trip, so he doesn't go apeshit. He's not happy unless he's giving me shit about doing something around the house. We can discuss your offer when I get back," he said, squeezing her hand.

"Promises, promises."

"I'll stay next weekend. I'll help you in the deli if you need it."

"Sweet. Could probably use some on Saturday," she replied. "What if your dad comes in?"

"He won't. He's got a meeting in Wenatchee at the supervisor's office. I think it's a training class or something. I'll park behind the deli, but I'd guess he won't be back 'til late. Maybe not 'til Sunday. Janie is probably following him down."

"His secretary?"

"Yeah."

"How's he been at home?" Sweetie asked. Big Jim's mercurial temperament was common knowledge throughout the valley.

"Not so good. I thought he was going to pop mom the other night."

"Oh shit."

"Yeah, he was drunk again. Man, he pounds it way more than he used to. He comes home, sets up three shots of whiskey and a beer behind each shot glass, and they're all gone in less than five minutes. He's shitfaced in a matter of minutes. Then he goes and falls asleep for a couple of hours, and O.M.G. if you make any noise while he's down. God, he's up and in my or mom's face… or mine if I'm around."

"Must be terrifying. She must just be so afraid when you're not there."

"I don't know how mom does it. She can handle it when I'm around in the summer. Good thing I was here this spring. But, yeah, when I'm at school, it must be the shits for her. It's only a matter of time before he takes a swing at me again."

"Kick his ass if he does it again, baby. Don't let him hurt you or your mom anymore. Fucker is crazy," Sweetie said sincerely.

"Yeah," Cody said, pondering the possibility. He shook his head. "Yeah, maybe… probably."

Cody hugged her again, held her close, kissed her gently on the lips and forehead, and headed home.

***

Early June

The White House

"EMMA!!! EMMA!!! Where the fuck is Emma?" the president yelled down the hall from the doorway to his office.

"She went to a meeting at Management and Budget," said Maryanne.

"Well, find her skinny ass and tell her to get back here," he hollered. "And where's Jack?"

"He texted a little bit ago that he was on his way and would be here soon. Fighting a little traffic, it seems, Sir."

"Fine," he said before stepping back into his office and slamming the door. The sky seemed to be falling, and POTUS was in no mood to have it fall on him without sharing the event with those closest to him, some of whom he loved and some of whom he loathed.

He picked up the phone and called his wife. She didn't answer. Next, he tried his oldest of three children, his oldest daughter, Sophia. She picked up on the third ring.

"Hi, Daddy," said Sophia.

"Hi, Baby Doll? Where's Derek?" Derek Johansson was his son-in-law, who the president could not stand. The Johansson family specialized in low-income rentals, much like the president's father had done years ago.

However, Derek, unlike the president, had stuck with his father's focus and was now worth two times the president in net wealth, a fact that the president regularly reversed when talking about such matters.

"Derek's not here. Did you need to speak to him?"

"No. I want to see if he'd made any progress with Emirates on a land deal for a new hotel."

"I'm not sure, Daddy, but I know he's made progress with the Saudis on some apartment housing for workers. They have a bunch from Africa and Southeast Asia," she replied happily. "They're like our Mexicans that come into work, but the Saudis want to give them some okay housing."

The president wanted to say, 'I don't give a flying fuck what he's doing with the Saudis, I want the Emirates!' Instead, he said, "Great. That's just great," as enthusiastically as he could muster. "Say,

Honey, I'm having a really bad day. Could you say something nice for me?"

"Daddy, you're the best. Best dad, best president, smartest person we know."

"Thanks, Sweetheart. Tell Derek to call me when he can."

"Will do, Daddy. Bye," she said chipperly.

"Bye, Darling," he said and hung up.

POTUS began swirling in his chair again. His mind raced as his ass reached the outer limits of the solar system. He was not sure who he was supposed to see over the rest of the day. Generally, he tried to keep his appointments to a minimum. He knew he had a meeting with five or six members of the CDC later in the day for a briefing on the state of the Covid outbreak. He was dreading that one. He had gone on record early in the pandemic at more than a couple of press conferences, assuring the public that the danger was minimal. But, by the end of May, the death toll in the U.S. had hit just over a hundred thousand.

He continued to implicitly support his earlier prognostications of the disease's minimal severity by never wearing a mask despite suggestions by the CDC to do so. Too, he had hosted several general gatherings in the White House garden and had held three election rallies since the pandemic began. When a staffer on the communications team suggested he might set a better precedent by wearing one, Emma immediately fired her.

"Dumb bitch," Emma had told her staff. "We don't show weakness. We NEVER show weakness," she screamed. "NEVER." Later, she told the president, "You're untouchable. Not even that fucking virus can get you. That's the message we want to send to your base. You're not afraid. You've got this under control. You can handle this, YOU and YOU alone. That's the message we'll keep sending. You're not afraid, so they don't need to be afraid either. So, fuck the fucking masks. Masks are for fucking pussies."

And that was the message that went out to the right-wing media outlets. Emma, like POTUS, understood the value of controlling the media and was at the heart of all coordinated messaging that came out of the White House. Like all successful, nefariously directed efforts historically, their strategy focused on segments of the population that felt disenfranchised by the social structure.

Focus on them, blame other groups in society for their problems, and identify simple courses of action as solutions, the simplest being you are the only one who can solve their problem(s), so they have nothing to worry about. Constantly belittle those who oppose you, the other side(s), with outrageous characterizations and accusations, repeating them over and over in multiple media venues until people begin to believe. In short, successful companies used the same brand-building strategy to create the desired Pavlovian response when they heard 'You deserve a break today' or 'Because you deserve it.' Even the hard-to-convince can be worn down with enough repetitions… over time. History was on their side. Even in an era of ubiquitous facts and information, the key was to keep them conflated and buried in a sea of lies.

Her assets to those ends were many; collectively, they were insidiously effective. The Salem Radio Network, with over 2700 affiliates, covered Christian talk and radio and music, conservative talk radio, and Spanish-speaking Christian stations. The desired talking points were given to critical hosts and programmers by 'the party.' These stations dominated the choices for radio listeners from the eastern slopes of the Cascades and the Sierra Nevada ranges in the West to the eastern slopes of the Appalachians. 'This pandemic is overblown, a hoax in fact,' and 'the government is using it to justify taking away our freedoms and liberties' was the talking point of choice, with no action being more demonstrative of that than a mandate to wear a mask.

For added fear and sense of irreverence, these taglines were further seasoned with, 'and then they'll take your guns,' 'they'll take your bibles, too,' and 'they want to kill babies.' Who 'they' were was never really in question. What was important is wasn't you or yours.

That the liberals control the media, Emma mused, was a well-maintained, conservative fabrication when considered across all communications venues. Their problem was that they did not understand how to use radio and social media as effectively as the conservatives. Less impactful than radio but still significant were the one hundred and eighty-some odd local television stations of the conservative Sinclair Broadcast Group operating in eighty-some odd local television markets across the country. Get your followers to distrust the government and the other side. Convince them to believe you are the only source they can trust. Then they believe anything you say. And that is when you really start telling the lies.

POTUS grasped this particularly well, especially around social media and right-wing online news hubs. 'Twitter the fuck out of these dumb bastards,' he would often say. 'They'll believe whatever I fucking tell them.' And they almost always did. In all cases, except for television, one just had to plant a mistruth or a doubt, then nurture it by repeating it repeatedly in different venues, keeping the message consistent, until it grew to a constant in people's lexicon. Television programs had to worry a little more about telling mistruths, though POTUS had completely conflated which stations were reliable news sources, even when they showed videos of him. His lies rarely found their way to Fox, his core favorite, and they did not watch most other stations. If you get caught in a lie, deny it or call it Fake News. And if the truth cannot be avoided, come up with a new, more scurrilous story around a well-known liberal or construct a new threat to the nation.

Emma and a bastion of conservative venues had written a panoply of taglines that were as common to their core beliefs as Everyday Low Prices. 'They hate us for our freedoms' had moved from the Desert Storm battle cry to 'They're taking away our liberties and our freedom.' It was all working beautifully, and the conservative cabals behind it were throwing money at POTUS faster than spectators to the bet-taker at a Mexican cock fight.

***

Early August

Vancouver

Ever since Whistler, Mayla and Balil had been nearly inseparable. Sales in the store continued to do very well. Mayla had become their most effective salesperson, with further assistance from her parents. She sent emails to business associates, family, and friends throughout the city showing pictures of her condo and the new materials, extolling the owner's and his nephew's talents, and driving traffic to the site. Then, at least initially, she posted several Yelp posts with various nom de plumes. These were quickly supplanted with real ones, happy customers she had enlisted that then began submitting reviews of their own.

Sometimes, the older, less tech-savvy ones moved a little too slow for her liking, so she would write one for them with their blessing. The store was doing better than pre-pandemic sales, with most weekends being record-breaking busy. Customers were happy to have the personalized, concierge-focused service that Ali and Balil, in particular, provided. Ali received numerous calls from old and new acquaintances, lauding his business and extolling their gratitude for their exceeded expectations. And they constantly commented on the delightfully intriguing, even enchanting, eyes of his self-proclaimed nephew.

Ali had assumed from the time he arrived that Balil's visit would be short. But now he was hoping that he would stay and become his partner. "Stay here," he had said. "You can return to Iraq when needed, but this would be a fine home. You and Mayla are a wonderful match. You will become rich. You can have a family… again."

"I do not know, Uncle. I'm not sure that is possible. Iraq is my home. And I'm an illegal citizen as we speak. I'll be found out and most certainly deported."

"Ah, Iraq is a shithole country. It will never be fixed. At least not in our lifetimes or those of your children or grandchildren. It was bad under Saddam, but the Americans have fucked it up beyond repair. You would be wasting your time, your life, there," he said, then abruptly added, "Move here." Hugging Balil and laughing joyously, he said, "I am your father now… Do as I say. I have friends here, and my friends have more friends. We will fix Canada for you. They love people your age who have money and a job and want to move here. Open your eyes. You eat Turkish delight; it's true."

Fearing that the exposure he had been getting online and through the primarily Arab clientele might well expose him, as it were, he said, "I will think about it, Uncle. Thank you for that kind offer."

That evening, Balil sat at the computer to check the shop's website and email account. He first checked POTUS' Twitter account for a bland response that was, in fact, the directive for him and his two friends. It was posted by a user in the UK whose hashtag, shitstorm1920, identified them as their messenger. It said, "Yes, sir. It is time for action! We need to be ready." It was a relevant fit for a POTUS Twitter rant on BLM riots in Portland, Oregon, that had been going on for months.

Balil knew that in the next couple of days, the details of their assignment would become more apparent. He needed to reach out to Farhan and Odion immediately. They would have seen or would soon see the post as well. It was their predetermined plan to meet at a small park across the street from a McDonald's restaurant parking lot on Buckingham Street at 10 p.m., exactly four days from the posting of a directive, enough time for all to have seen the post as well as enough time to construct and story, if necessary, for whomever they might be dealing with at the time.

The day of the meeting turned out to be a Thursday. Balil had told Mayla the day before that he had to catch up on billings and research inventory needs, including emailing suppliers in the Middle East. She volunteered to help, but he insisted he would be fine and likely more efficient alone. Mayla did not argue the latter. Farhan offered a similar excuse the day before, but that evening, he said around 8 p.m. that he wanted some fresh air and would take a walk. Odion's roommates came and went so often without notice that he thought it more curious to them if he actually said anything about leaving the house, so he left when he felt it was the right time to get there.

What he had thought to be a two-mile walk turned out to be a bit over three because the restaurant was about the same distance for Balil and Farhan. They arrived within a couple of minutes of each other, with Farhan arriving first. They said nothing at first but embraced, having not talked to nor seen one another for almost five months and counting.

"I have missed you, my friend," said Balil. "How are you?"

"I'm fine. And you?"

"I'm fine as well; praise be to Allah."

"You look healthy," said Farhan with a grin. "Uncle Ali must be feeding you well."

"He has indeed."

"How is he?"

"Oh, very well, thank you. It's been a comfortable six months compared to what we went through. You do not look as though you have missed many suppers either," said Balil.

"Ramadhan was such a challenge in April, but working with a couple that owns a restaurant has its benefits. I think, however, they may want their privacy back," Farhan said.

"I would not be surprised," said Balil solemnly. "Well, for good or bad, that will no longer be a concern soon."

They were sitting on a park bench facing the street, just off the sidewalk. Balil told him about the general successes that Ali's operation had experienced but nothing about his association with Mayla and her contributions to the business. It was ideal for his pal not to get the right idea, possibly wondering if Balil's resolve could have been weakened. After ten minutes, Balil and Farhan began to get nervous about where their third friend might be. They had learned long ago in their training to be on time; if you were not, you had better have a good excuse.

"Where is he?" asked Farhan, sounding slightly annoyed. "We shouldn't be out here like this. We'll attract attention."

"I know," replied Balil, sounding equally put off. "Let's wait another ten minutes and then leave. We'll have to reschedule… somehow."

About twenty minutes later, Odion finally arrived. When Balil first saw Odion approaching, he did not recognize him. "I don't think that's him," he said. But as Odion got closer, his lips opened like a stage curtain, showing his wonderfully glowing white teeth that the streetlamps lit up like the white on an outside movie theater marquee.

"Oh my." said Farhan, "That's him," and he began laughing.

Odion's appearance had drastically changed from the last time they saw him. Like themselves, he had put on weight but had also bulked up. His body was fit, and he filled out his tight-fitting t-shirt, a black one that read Gamer in large, green letters across the chest. But it was his hair that was most noticeable. It was shaved tight around the bottom half of his scalp, starting about an inch and a half above each ear. However, the top of his head was a tight bouquet of five-inch or so two-strand braids that sprouted beautifully in all directions. He looked very fashionable.

"Salamu Alaykum," they all said individually, and then, "Al akum salaam."

"You look wonderful, so different," Farhan said excitedly, with a warm smile. "Life must have been good to you."

"I have missed you, my friends," he said, slightly bowing, "but yes, it has been good here."

"Your hair becomes you," said Balil.

"There are some hairdressers in our neighborhood," Odion replied. "They did it for free."

"Hmm. Maybe a 'special one' did it for free," needled Balil playfully.

"Mmm. Perhaps," said Odion coolly, not giving any more information away. "So, what have you learned?" he asked, wanting to get down to business, knowing they could not congregate for long.

"Only that we are to meet our contact, as directed before we left, at the designated location and time. Based on the date of the message, that will be the 25th of this month."

"Do we know the plan?" asked Farhan.

"Not yet," Balil said. "The contact will tell us and take us to where we need to go."

They were all still as they realized their old world of a lifetime ago had just collided with their new one. They looked at each other for guidance.

Farhan broke the silence. "I am ready. This is just like America, a corrupt world. It's all about money. They do this everywhere they go.

Repetition teaches donkeys. You'd think they'd learn. Nothing new to see here," he said, twirling his hand in the air and walking quickly and frustratedly in a tight circle.

Having suspected such a position, Odion had reflected on it in advance and responded quickly. "And if the camel could see his hunchback, he would fall and break his neck, my friend. Right?" Farhan stared at him contemptuously. "Actually, I find the people here quite pleasant," he said softly. "The lives of most of the immigrants that come here are certainly better than the lives they left, based on what I know of their areas and what most say. And most seem very happy," he said matter-of-factly. He paused momentarily, watching Farhan and Balil's reactions with interest. "I'm treated respectfully by my new friends. They call me brother… and dude," he added playfully.

Balil was slightly nodding in restrained agreement.

Farhan was livid. Seeing Balil's face, he almost said, too loudly, "Al harat," aka pussy, in Arabic.

Odion responded immediately with, "Telhas teeze," or lick my ass, as he stepped aggressively toward Farhan.

Balil shoved his two hands between them and spread them as strongly as he could to halt their respective advances. "Stop it," he said in English as loud as he dared without drawing the attention of anyone within earshot. They both held fast, and he repeated with a softer, "Stop," before quickly adding, "Please." They both eased their advances, then took a half step back. Now he whispered, "Brothers, brothers. Let's keep our heads."

Farhan was not giving in, though. "What you're saying is blasphemy, Odion. I'm sorry. You cannot be confused by the comforts of this world. They have them at the expense of our people."

"There is truth in that, My Brother," Odion said calmly. "Americans and others," he said, pointing to the ground when he said others, "have bestowed much damage and hardship on our people. I cannot deny that. But must we let yesterday take up all our tomorrows? For the rest of our lives? Can't we be messengers of God, sent to the world to demonstrate forgiveness and kindness of Islam and spread the word of Mohammed, peace be upon him?"

"No," said Farhan. "Today is the same as yesterday. Just separated by night. The Americans paint themselves as the victims. They are the good guys, and we are the bad. That is not the way it is. You know that. *THAT* is Fake News, my friend."

"Let's keep it down, all of us," said Balil. "Speaking for myself, it's mission on. Okay? We leave on the twenty-fifth. We all know where to meet and when, right?" The two shook their heads yes. "We are not changing our mission," he said emphatically. "We all agreed to this. Remember. What starts with rules ends in light." His two friends nodded in agreement. "Fine. Be there. And on time," he said, looking at Odion. "Anyone not there on time will be left behind, no questions asked or judgments made. Understood?" Again, they shook their heads affirmatively. "Then we're done here. It's getting too late to be out like this together. Is there anything left to say?" he asked. They shook their heads, both upset and looking at each other. Then let's go home. Get home quickly, but make sure you're not followed. Same for the twenty-fifth." He gave them each a gentle, quick embrace, turned, and left.

***

Early August

Winthrop

Though Cody and Sweetie regularly hung out at her folks' pool on Friday afternoons, Chris or Seth made it every other week. It was not uncommon, though, for either to be absent. Winthrop had remained extremely busy through the summer, and all four had felt the traffic somehow. The deli was busy, Steve's operation had record contract treks with tourists, and Chris had hauled in and returned more broken-down trackers, trucks, mowers, bailers, and scooters than he had ever imagined. Some of those tractors, trucks, and related equipment belonged to Seth's operation, and the two had spent more time together than any other time since they graduated high school.

The busy schedule of all four had kept them relatively isolated, except for Sweetie, who worked seven days a week, some days when her folks were out of town, which seemed to her to be more than usual this summer. Sweetie had a friend, Joann, who helped her some days, but her parents did not like anybody but themselves, and Sweetie closed out at night. Sweetie, though, had taught her the ropes, such as counting nightly proceeds, getting starting monies ready for the next day, restocking inventories after closing to replace sales, and opening.

Sweetie periodically checked on her at closing and opening to ensure she did not fudge on hours, but Joann proved utterly reliable. Sweetie had not found any errors or heard customer complaints about periods when Joann was alone, leaving her with more opportunities to relax comfortably with Cody or enjoy more 'me time' at home.

It was a Thursday, and Sweetie had gone home to let Pedro out. Pedro's cancer had gotten progressively worse, and the vet had made it clear toward the end of July that she would not live much longer, maybe five or six more weeks, at the most. Pedro was listless and generally unresponsive to Sweetie's attention when she got home. She took her to the doctor and left her overnight. That morning, she got a call at the deli, saying that Pedro had been given some medicine and had perked up a bit. She was available when Sweetie was ready to get her. Her folks were out of town, and Sweetie asked Joann to close and open the next day; she wanted to spend time with her dog. Later in the afternoon, before Cody arrived, Seth stopped by, and Sweetie told him about Pedro's current prognosis.

At that point, Pedro was doing her best to be cordial to one of her favorite visitors and sat in Seth's lap while he cuddled her, whimpering softly at times, her pain not entirely masked by the pills she had been given earlier at the vet's office. All the while, Sweetie mostly cried out loud, lamenting what a great dog and friend she had been and how much she would miss her. Seth just listened, occasionally offering some words of comfort and his outstretched hand for Sweetie to hold.

Cody showed up at his usual time, around six. Sweetie had texted him earlier that she was home and Seth was there, too, which delighted Cody. Sweetie was not alone. He knew Seth loved animals, and his relationship with Pedro was mutual; the dog loved him terribly. The three talked for over an hour, the boys offering solace to Sweetie, who continued to struggle with her anguish. Eventually, Seth stood to leave.

"I've got to get going. We're starting our second cutting for some pastures near the ponds and wetter areas," Seth said.

Sweetie stood up and hugged him and then started crying hard again.

"Thank you," she choked out. "I'm glad you got to see her with at least a little energy. She loves you so much."

Seth smiled warmly and said, "I love her, too." When he reached the door, he turned to Cody and said, "Can I talk to you outside for a second, man?"

"Sure," said Cody, who got up and followed him out.

"Come out to my truck for a second," said Seth. "I have something for you."

"Okay. Thanks for coming by, man. I'm really, really happy you've been here. That means a lot, Seth. Thanks."

"No worries," said Seth. As they got to the truck, Seth said, "Just a sec," jumped inside the cab, opened the console, pulled out a faded reddish tube, and handed it to Cody. "Here," he said.

"What is it?" asked Cody.

"Propofol," said Seth. "It's a sedative. We use it when we're working on large animals. It's also a really good drug to put down dogs. Our vet puts it in EpiPens. It makes them easier to carry around and use. The animals don't see it coming. And you're less likely to stick yourself."

Cody asked a question he already knew the answer to, "Why are you giving it to me?"

"Just in case you and Sweetie want to do it yourselves. That's my preference for my own pets. Been doing that since I was twelve. It makes it more personal for you and them… well, at least for me. When you take them to the vet, animals know. Better when you do it."

Cody knew his friend was right, and he immediately started crying. After a moment, he regained his composure and hugged his friend. "Thanks, man," said Cody.

Seth chuckled a little while gently pushing him away, holding the EpiPen in his other hand. "You gotta' be careful with these," he said in a cautioning tone. This dose will put down a horse. It'll kill a dog, four or five Pedros, and maybe a person if you give them the full dose. Probably, actually. It just takes a second to work. This is badass shit, brother. Be careful." Then he added an afterthought, "This is the shit that killed Michael Jackson."

Cody took it from him and put it sideways into the right lower hip pocket of his L.L.Bean cargo pants; it lay perfectly horizontal in the bottom of the pocket. Cody patted it twice before looking at Seth again and hugging him again. "You're the best, Seth. Thanks."

"Hey, careful. You'll prick me," Seth kidded. "The EpiPen." Cody just shook his head. 'Ever the joker,' he thought. "But you're welcome," said Seth. "Very welcome. Take your time, but don't let her suffer, that's all."

"Will do," Cody replied.

"And take care of Sweetie." Cody stared back, trying to hold it together, hoping not to come completely undone. "And say goodbye to Pedro for me, okay?"

With that, Cody started to lose it again, holding up his hand and choking out another "Thanks" before pivoting and hustling back to the house.

When Cody returned to the house, he did not tell Sweetie about the EpiPen, not wanting to burden Sweetie anymore with what everyone knew was imminent. Seth had given them a great gift to share, and his benevolence began to sink into Cody by the moment. He was a wonderfully kind and good friend, regardless of their politics.

"Let's take the pooch out for a pee, and then let's go sit outside."

"Okay," Sweetie said softly.

Pedro rallied for a couple of minutes, sniffing for the right spot before squatting feebly, wobbling some, almost falling over, but then peeing.

"She's so weak," said Cody. Sweetie just nodded.

Still, it was obvious that Pedro was where she wanted to be. After she finished, she wandered for a minute, sniffing to see where she had been before and if any other dogs or critters had been there recently. She was still doing her job checking out the perimeter. At some point, she looked up, giving Cody and Sweetie a halfhearted yap before approaching them. Sweetie picked her up and cradled her, Pedro content.

"Why don't you go put Pedro in her bed," Cody offered. "I'll get us a couple of beers and meet you outside."

After Sweetie returned, they talked for another couple of hours until dusk began to set in. Sweetie's folks were gone until Saturday night. She had asked Cody earlier if he would stay, and he had said yes, texting his mom about his plans and asking her to cover for him with his father. He had a group to guide on Sunday for five days, so as far as his father knew, he would return later Saturday from one before leaving for another the next day.

They went to bed early, and Cody and Sweetie both gave the dog some love before getting in bed. Pedro opened her eyes slightly, just enough to acknowledge their caresses and words of affection before falling asleep. Not wanting to hurt her unnecessarily, they opted to leave her be. If she peed during the night, no worries. Cody figured they could spend some time with her in the morning and then discuss putting her down. When Cody got up, he was careful not to disturb Sweetie, who had tossed and turned all night. He glanced over toward Pedro's bed and saw her curled up in a ball, so he peed, went to the kitchen, and put on a pot of coffee. When he returned to the bedroom and knelt to pet the dog, his hand recoiled when he touched her; her body was stiff and cool. Pedro had died in her sleep sometime during the night.

***

White Houses

Early August

By the end of July, the total Covid U.S. death toll was barely below one hundred fifty thousand. By the end of August, almost thirty thousand more would die. The pandemic had a global presence. It was national news for all nations every night. But to the world's surprise, the U.S. had become the epicenter for the disease. Still, most conservatives thought that the disease was either a hoax or was being blown out of proportion by liberal news media, a perspective mostly created and maintained by far-right communication channels. A benefit for all, however, was that medicine was quick to improve on treatments of patients, and initial mortality rates had come down some. Several conspiracy theory treatments were being circulated, some promoted by POTUS himself, who kept characterizing the disease as a nasty case of the flu. A common question asked over the summer was: Do you know anyone who died from Covid? Throughout the Midwest, the answer has commonly been 'No.' But that began to change by mid-August. People were not dying as rapidly, but the disease was spreading and getting worse in scope and scale. There was no doubt about that, and many of the president's supporters who lived politically near the center began to question the administration's management of the disease.

At one time, Emma had considered strategist Marlin Drove and wordsmith Larry Funtz as the go-to archetypes of conservative game plan development. While they had many notable victories over almost thirty years, conservatives had decreased as a percentage of all voters. Yeah, gerrymandering had kept the number of conservatives at the state legislature levels disproportionately high in many states. Still, the jig was up for it as a tool to maintain the same leads in the House. Same with the Senate. States were turning blue or, at least, blue-ish. Florida was always close, and Texas was becoming inundated with Californians, who were younger liberal ones. It seemed only a matter of time before the conservatives might irreversibly become the minority national party. Conservatives could keep cheating for a while, wait for all the gerrymandering to unravel, which would take years, and suppress the votes of minorities in the red states that could maintain them through their state legislatures for a while. It was hard work, though. A split in the conservative party might well be on the way, with the Tea Party at one extreme and the old guard at the other.

But while that might be bad for the conservative's power base, if that happened to them, it would also likely occur to the liberals, as well. That would likely be best for the country since all factions would have to start making deals with one another, but that would likely mean a whole new set of political power brokers, both politically and in industry.

Well, 'fuck that,' Emma had decided. 'Not on my watch.' Keep the riff going, and keep it wide. It did not matter who was in charge or if a few people got shot. America would be fine. It had the most potent military. It would be fine. POTUS was right. The only important thing was to retain power... by whatever means. POC-man and POR-man and all the other P-men? They did not need money. Most had plenty of that. They had power. And power's value? Priceless.

One of Emma's proposed strategies, politicizing the disease in general by questioning its presence and virulence as well as associating the wearing of masks as an overreach of government control, had done an excellent job of dividing the country even further with two new catalysts: Conservatives maintained the liberals were using the pandemic to ruin the economy and take away the fabric of the country's liberties and freedoms; Liberals perpetuated conservatives and the White House were chaos incarnate run amuck, a group bent on destroying the America's democratic form of government in favor of a fascist state. So, what to do next? Double down on what was still working.

***

Mid-August

Vancouver

It had been five days since he had met with his friends. He had just over two weeks before he was to leave. What would he tell Ali? The shop was doing wonderfully. The money was fine, but Ali was having fun for the first time in many years. It was as if he were young again and building a successful business with Balil's father. Youth begets energy and life. And what would he tell Layla? It had been almost three months since they had been together, and he knew he was falling in love if he had not already gotten there. And he knew she was, too. Part of him wished every day that the three would be forgotten by those who pulled the strings on these matters from wherever they were. He was never sure. But he did not have to go very far in the back of his mind to see that was not likely to happen. A lot of effort and money had been expended to get the three of them here. By all accounts, they had not been discovered. That made them very valuable… and dangerous.

Balil knew there was only one way out for him and his two friends. Ali suspected nothing. But Layla could sense something was on his mind immediately after the meeting. For all the time she had known him, he had not been aloof but, on specific topics, unapproachable. At times, he appeared to have a secret he could not share or did not want to. His interest in her, which she had grown accustomed to and relished, was suddenly absent.

It was a Sunday afternoon, and her parents had gone to a service. He had been over the night before, and they had all had dinner. Often, Mohammed and Mira went to Whistler to give the two lovers space, or Balil and Layla would go for alone time. Layla's parents were more liberal around such things, remembering what it was like to be young and in love. And they liked Balil, finding him a refreshing amalgam of traditional Muslim social conduct and their daughter's more nuevo genre. The two were a good balance for one another. Layla had not had a boyfriend for almost three years. People were still mostly isolated, so they were not concerned about what their friends and family might think and these particular specifics since nobody saw them. They had just finished lunch. Balil, who always helped her clean up, had gone to the living room and turned on the television to watch the news. After finishing cleaning, she went to the television, turned it off, and sat on the couch next to him.

"Something seems to be on your mind," she said. He just looked ahead without moving. "Do you want to talk about it?"

She waited for a response until he had to say something in return. He turned and looked at her for a moment, fearful his face was sagging as a great sadness began beating in his heart.

"I, I… I," he said, trying to get something out, unsure what it might be.

"Yes?" she said, faintly smiling.

His eyes turned down. Finally, he looked at her directly and said, "I have to leave at the end of the month. The 25th, actually."

She was not sure what she had expected to hear, but that was not it.

"What?" she said, shaking her head like she had just woken up. "Why?"

"I'm, uh," he said, sucking in a breath of air, "have some work to do in the East, and then I'm going back to Iraq. I have some things I need to do there."

"What things?" Layla asked calmly. "And who in the East? You haven't mentioned working with any contacts there."

"Well," he said deliberately, "Ali has identified some new retail outlets we can supply. Plus, I need to meet with my suppliers in Iraq. Maybe make some new ones." He paused for a moment. "We're doing very well… thanks to you."

She frowned, looking pensive. "That makes no sense."

"Why not?"

"Why all of a sudden now?"

"I told you. We need to secure more supplies. Many others want to sell our products. We can wholesale, too. You've made us too successful. The word is out."

She did not respond immediately, again considering carefully what he had just said, and she looked serious. But then, suddenly, a look of resignation filled her face. "Okay. So what about us?"

"What about us?" Balil asked rhetorically.

She was crushed. "That stings." She waited. "Are you coming back?"

"I hope so," he lied.

"When."

"I'm not sure."

"Balil," she said seriously.

"Yes?"

She stared at him long enough that he knew his time was up. "I'm going to have your baby—a boy. I was going to tell you next weekend after I shared it with my parents first. If they were to disown me, I thought I had better tell you that, too, but this changes things entirely. Now I'm not even sure what to tell them," she said confusedly before breaking into tears.

"How did this happen?" he asked, bewildered, then suddenly recognizing the absurdity of what he had just said. Layla's eyes widened, but before she could respond, he said, "I mean, aren't you on a contraceptive or something? Isn't that what women do in this country?"

"Short answer: no. I," she said stammering, "I guess it was wishful thinking we'd be lucky, or maybe down deep, I didn't care. I mean, I haven't had anyone in my life like you for some time, someone like you never, and I think, I mean, I knew I had fallen in love with you. I thought you loved me, too, and that you, we, would be happy." At that, she started crying again.

More than a little conflicted, he knew he had to think about what exactly to say, given the gravity of Layla's news. He shook his head pensively. It was only five more days until he left. He stood up and said, "I must leave now. We can talk about this later, perhaps. I will call you tomorrow. I'm sorry, Layla, but I cannot process this now. I'm sorry. I have to think." With that, he stood up and left. She thought about yelling and running to stop him, but something told her that was not a good idea.

***

Mid-August

Winthrop

It wasn't often that one of Sweetie's parents was home when he came by late afternoon. Sweetie's mom, Chirine, had parked her lime green MINI Cooper in the driveway. Rather than just walking in, Cody stopped to knock on the door, opened it just a little, and called in.

"Hi, Mrs. McManus. You there? It's me, Cody."

"Hi, Cody. I'm by the pool," she yelled back. "Come on out. Bring a beer if you'd like."

"You want one, too?" he yelled back.

"No thanks," she said. "I'm good."

Cody exited the sliding glass door and saw Chirine in the shaded area of two awnings covering a portion of the patio next to the swimming pool. She was stretched out in a lawn chair, relaxing and reading a magazine. Cody sat a few feet away in the sun, where The Squad usually sat, having turned the chair to face her. She and Sweetie looked alike; they were slender, had long legs, and were both very pretty, except Chirine was five inches taller. She closed the magazine as he approached, directing her attention to him.

"Hi, Cody."

"Hey. Mrs. McManus."

"We've talked about that," she said kiddingly.

Cody had always gotten along with the McManus.' He called Bill by his first name but did not always feel comfortable doing so with

Chirine, as her name in Arabic referred to something sweet and unique, effectively Sweetie. It would never have mattered if he had not been told that, but for some reason, it just did.

"Yeah, sorry," he said a little sheepishly. "Hi, Chirine."

"What's been happening?" She laughed. "It's been like a month or so, hasn't it? How do Bill and I keep not running into you in the Pasayten? We were just in there again last week."

"That's what Sweetie said," Cody replied, his brow furrowing in faked puzzlement. "It's our schedules, I guess. You guys have been in like four or five times this summer, haven't you?"

"Yes, I think that's about right. There are lots of trails, though. Lots of places to camp."

"Yeah, our paths just haven't crossed. One of these days."

"Well, you go in further than we do. Big area. We're just weekenders. Short hikes, mostly. Some overnighters. We like Lake Chelan with the boat. That's nice. Easy to get away from people… and you don't have to walk so much."

"You know, I've never done that, gotta try it."

"You should. You and Sweetie can use the boat."

"Thank you. I'll think about that."

"No school this fall, I hear."

"Nope. They're still shut down at the U."

"Are you going to do online classes?"

"Not this next term. Working too much. That and the folks want us kids to do a ride in for old time's sake the middle of next month."

"That should be fun," she said, her look and tone making it more of a question.

"I guess," Cody said. "All three kids haven't been in the house simultaneously for quite a while. Marie only comes home once a year, maybe. She's got her own life in Seattle."

Chirine was about to ask what Marie and Little Jimmy had been doing when Sweetie, who they had not heard drive up, yelled out, "Hey, you two."

"Hi, Honey," said Chirine.

Cody wanted to say the same but merely smiled and gave a one-shake wave. They all talked for another thirty minutes, getting caught up on family, friends, and work before Chirine stood and said, "I'd better go help your dad close. He's probably wondering what's happened to me. It was nice to get some reading time in. Nice to see you, Cody."

"Nice to see you, too, Mrs.," then catching himself, "uh, Chirine."

"There you go," she said with a smile as she walked into the house. "You all have fun."

"I'm gonna put my suit on," said Sweetie. "I'll be right back."

Shortly after Sweetie returned, Cody heard what he knew was Chris' car. But Seth must have been following him closely because the roar of Seth's behemoth almost immediately muffled Chris.' Sweetie caught up with the two in the house, and the three came through the back door together.

"Dope," Cody said, beaming. "I was hoping you'd both make it today. Sup?"

"Same-oh," said Chris, sitting down next to him.

"Same here," Seth said, leaving the empty seat to the right of Cody for Sweetie while grabbing the next one. "You?"

"Nadda mucho," Cody said. "Getting ready for another tour de' Pasayten this Monday."

"Where'd you just come from," Chris asked.

"Horseshoe Basin. We're going to Buckskin Ridge this coming week."

"Whoa, big one. How many days?" asked Seth.

"Five, I think," said Cody.

"You be doin' some hoofing, man," said Chris, chuckling.

"No cap dat," said Cody. "I think that's where the old man is talking about taking us."

"When's that?" Seth asked.

"Middle of September," said Cody.

"Not cool?" Seth asked, reading the look on Cody's face.

"I don't know. It's okay, I guess. How about you? Plans? Summer's almost done."

Seth squirmed in his seat a little, knowing what he was going to say would not go over very well. "Well, I guess the Freedom Fighters are talking about a counter-demonstration sometime around the end of the month, on a Saturday. I'm not sure of the date. But there are BLM demonstrations every night in Portland. Just a little kickback and show of support for the admin."

"The friend I told you about a couple of months ago who lives in Portland said the demonstrations have gotten a lot worse, actually," said Cody. "More violent.

"That's what we hope to influence," said Seth. "Just get 'em to stand down."

"Guns?" asked Sweetie, picking up the last pieces of the conversation as she joined the men.

"Sure," replied Seth, looking a little uncomfortable. "I'm sure plenty of guys will be carrying."

"You?" said Chris.

"I don't know. Maybe," Seth said, sounding reluctant. "I want to show face, but I don't want to provoke anyone. I worry about things dissolving into…" Seth's mind ran through a list of appropriate words, but he could not find one at the moment that satisfied him.

"Into shit," said Chris. "Be careful, man. There are crazies on both sides. Don't get in the middle of something you can't get out of."

"Yeah," said Seth. "I will. Makes me a little nervous, too, so that you know."

The four sat and talked for another thirty minutes, drinking beer and telling their most current dirty jokes. Seth, as usual, was the first to leave.

"Daylight comes early," he said, finally. "I gotta' go home, do a little work, and get to bed. We're tagging calves in the a.m., and there's more hay to deal with."

After Seth left, Chris turned to Cody and Sweetie and said, "Shit, guys, I'm really concerned." Chris had gone to the Yakima rally in June and had decided he wanted no part of the Freedom Fighters. "I'm telling you, they're fucking crazy. Mean motherfuckers. Lots of 'em are ex-military that did too many tours of duty in Iraq and Afghanistan. I don't know what Seth sees in Kent Des Moines. Fucking guy is a maniac. Really. A real troublemaker." Chris' eyes moved to Sweetie. "He hates women. Can't stop going on about LGBTQs. Really wants to run into one in the restroom. I'm telling you, that fucker is gonna' shoot someone."

"I hate hearing that," said Sweetie. "Worries me."

"Me, too," said Cody.

"And that other tool from the Seattle area, Charlie, what's his name... Charlie Chase. He's a crazy motherfucker, too. They're not down on anything brown, baby, I'm tellin' you. Those are racist, crazy, dangerous ass wipes. BLM? Their t-shirts say 'Because Law Matters' and 'Better Law Management.' They say they are the law. Guns, guns, guns. Looking for a fight." Chris shook his head. "They're going to kill someone."

"Well, I'm staying out of it," said Cody. "Seth's going to do what Seth wants to do. If I didn't love the big shit so much, it would be a lot easier to deal with."

"True dat," said Sweetie. Chris nodded in agreement.

The three, worried about their friend, exchanged ideas about how they might help him, but in the end, they all agreed that Seth was best left alone to follow his own course and reach his own conclusion. After about twenty minutes, Chris left, leaving Sweetie and Cody to discuss it further in private.

"What do you think," asked Sweetie, "… about Seth?"

"I don't know what to tell him, Baby. He's a big boy. I don't want to get into another morality thing like we've done before. I don't want to tell him how to live. It makes me feel selfish. Funny. I don't want to be selfish… or righteous. Even though I feel we're right." Cody said, with a glance to Sweetie. "He's a good guy. He'd do anything for all of us. Better to leave him alone and let Seth be Seth."

"Mmm," Sweetie concurred, her voice reflective and her face concerned.

***

White House

Mid-August

"Jesus Christ," POTUS yelled at Hoffman and Emma from behind his desk. The two sat at opposite corners of his desk, which put them eight to nine feet apart, an acceptable separation for social distancing. However, Emma distanced herself from Hoffman for reasons entirely unrelated to social matters. "Have you two seen the polls? We're fucking losing this race."

"Depends on which ones you're reading, sir," Emma countered.

"Emma's right, of course, Mr. President, but there are a couple that are worrisome, nonetheless," said the VP.

"Gimme examples," he demanded.

"Well, Monmouth and Reuters have a tie, as I recall, but the libs with a slight lead nonetheless." Hoffman always understated the leads to keep POTUS from going into a harangue that too often, as far as Hoffman was concerned, included bits of how stupid POTUS thought he was. "Monmouth has it a dead tie," he said somewhat enthusiastically. "I'm afraid Fox has you down three points."

"That motherfucking Aussie bastard," growled the president.

"Shit," said Emma. "That's not good."

"Well, it's a statistical tie," said the Veep, trying to be politically correct to the crowd. "Maybe just a mistake in the… uh… data collection," he said tepidly.

The President was fond of throwing a particular paperweight from his desk, one with the seal of the United States. Maryann kept a supply of them on her desk. He tended to break them when he threw them, so Maryann's collection were replacements. Three so far this month had not survived a toss, and there were still two months left. It looked as though, for a moment, he was reaching for it, and the two instinctively leaned away from the center so he would have plenty of unimpeded space up the middle if he decided to throw. They were both stealthily immobile. Suddenly he started to do a series of 360s in his chair before stopping suddenly, directly looking at them, and said, "Let's start bashing the wetbacks in the news."

"YES," said Emma, with a little fist shake, as if Megan Rapinoe had just kicked a winning penalty shot.

"And," he said, "fire up those hackers in Russia that help us. Let's get a Black Lives Matter riot going. Where's a good place to hold one?"

"Portland?" asked Emma.

"I don't know," POTUS said, "People are burning out on Portland. They have a riot there every fucking night. It's old news."

"We could send in the Freedom Fighters to one of them." Swiping her hand from left to right as though pointing to a building headline in Times Square, Emma said, "That'd be a great 'POTUS supports patriots on taking law and order into their own hands' pitch. The media would eat it up. Portland is easy, but it's already in the liberal bag. We need a riot in a swing state, too, where it might sway the direction of the vote."

"That's actually a very good idea," the President said, looking pleased. "Jack? What do you think?"

Hoffman nodded yes, though weakly, his face looking as though he had just bitten into a turd. POTUS read that as a 'Fuck, yeah,' but the VP was mentally questioning the wisdom and morality of sending in a radical militia, like the Freedom Fighters, to calm or manage any demonstration.

"Good," said Emma. "It's unanimous, then. I'll get right on it. I'll shoot for two weeks out. So, where else? Let's have one the following week. Missouri, Wisconsin, Ohio, Pennsylvania? Those are all necessary tossups." She looked around the room to the other two for feedback.

"I," began Hoffman, intending to say something like, 'I'm not sure that's a good thing to do' before POTUS cut him off.

"I think Missouri," said the President. "Those are gun-crazy, mask-hating dimwits. They'll be all over some BLM riot, especially on the heels of what could happen in Portland. You two pick the city and make it happen. No less than two weeks after Portland. That gives you three to four weeks to get it together."

"We're on it," said Emma, relishing it was really all on her.

Hoffman recognized it was all Emma, too, but if a link could be traced back to this encounter, he'd be discarded faster than a plastic bag of shit at the local dog park. He was convinced that if he could, the President would have yelled 'JACK, YOU'RE FIRED' several times already. The only thing that kept him from repeatedly doing it was his inability to do it.

Hoffman was first out the door, Emma on his heels. Just as she reached the door, the President called her back. "Hey. Emma. Come back and sit for a minute."

"Yes, sir?" she asked after going back and sitting in her chair.

"You're gonna keep Jack out of this, right?" he asked.

"Of course, sir."

"I was just including him to be nice. Make him think he's part of the team."

"I thought as much, sir."

"He's like a bad cold that won't go away." 'Or virus,' thought Emma. "How's your plan?" he asked surreptitiously, glancing left and right as if someone might be listening, even though they were alone.

"We're good, sir. Derek coordinates through his Middle Eastern connections. Assets should be in place right after Labor Day."

"Prices are going up, sir," she said. "What can we say about that?"

"We have to pay them more?" he asked.

"No, Sir," she said. "Prices in the stores. Food, gas."

"Shit. I told Jack to take care of that. Blame it on the immigrants coming into the country, rising costs from the riots, and the Chinks," he said. "Stay on message. It's *them*, never us."

"Copy that. Bart Simpson all the way, sir."

"Huh?" he said.

"Never mind, sir. TV show reference."

"So, whatever it takes. Right?" He gave her a thumbs up.

She smiled. "Whatever it takes, sir." She gave him two.

***

End of August

Vancouver

He was leaving tomorrow. As far as Ali knew, he was renting a car with Farhan and Odion and driving across the country. It made sense to him when he asked Balil why they were not flying, that they would not be able to buy an airline ticket as they were in the country illegally, and that such an action could get some or all of them in trouble. The same concerns apply to a train trip. A drive across the country would only take a few days, and they would be able to see the country. After they finish business in the East, Canada would be happy to see them fly out. Balil told him that he had made a reservation for a rental car and that an Uber driver would be picking them all up in the morning and taking them to get the car. But Ali was less concerned about the details of his departure than he was about his departure. Until the last minute, Balil expected him to plead for him to stay, which he did.

Getting Layla to believe that same story proved far more problematic. Why didn't he go to seek assistance from the consulate? Didn't he have a passport documenting his entry from the U.S.? What car rental company were they renting from? Could she please give him or them a ride there? Why couldn't she see him one more time and say goodbye?

After more than a twenty-minute grilling on the phone, she finally, in complete frustration, blurted out, "There is something up with you, Balil. I know it."

"Look, Layla," he replied stoically, "I'm sorry. But here is the unfortunate truth. I am sorry you are having a baby, but I do not want it, and I do not love you."

"I don't believe you, Balil. The rope of lying is short, my love," she said calmly and hung up.

***

He had packed a minimal amount of clothes and a small bag of bathroom supplies in a small bag, which he had stored under the bed. In the morning, he showered while it was still dark to watch the sun rise one last time. Shortly after daylight, he heard Ali stirring in the kitchen, making coffee as he did daily. When confident his presentation was complete, Balil got up and entered the kitchen.

"Shalom," he said.

"Shalom, my son," Ali replied meekly. After several seconds of uncomfortable silence, he said, "I got a call from Layla's dad last night." He paused but kept moving about the kitchen.

"Yes?" Balil said.

Ali looked him in the eye, his heart breaking, and said, "My son. You cannot leave her like this. She loves you." His eyes were watering, and his tone was shaky. "You love her. I know you do. Why are you doing this, my son? What is the matter? This is not you." On that, he broke down completely.

It was all Balil could do to maintain his composure. Reaching deep and not into his best place, he said, "Uncle. I know this is hard. I am so, so sorry for the pain and humiliation I have brought on you, but…"

"Humiliation?" said Ali with considerable disbelief. "I am so proud of you, Balil, as if you were my own. Look at all you've done. And Layla? You're in love. We're not in Iraq, my boy. It is not the end of the world here. It is the beginning."

"You're not ashamed of me? You don't worry about the scandal?"

"Scandal? Far from it. Scandal is just crazy talk gossip that tries to make interesting by attaching morals they think are important to others who don't even follow themselves. Don't be silly, my son. What I don't understand," he said with heartfelt concern, "is how you can leave the woman you love. What is up with you? There is something wrong in your life. I just know it."

Balil said nothing and finished his coffee, doing his best to enjoy his last croissant. As soon as he was done, he stood and hugged Ali one last time.

"I'm sorry, Uncle, but I must go. Thank you so much for all you've done."

"To'oborni," Ali whispered.

Then Balil grabbed his bag and walked out the door, wondering if what he once thought was a fair and reasonable judgment was now nothing more than his expressway to perdition.

***

Winthrop

Late August

It was a Wednesday. Cody was leaving tomorrow on a six-day trek, due to come out on the following Tuesday, the first day of September, and then leave again the next day with a Boise family he was taking back into Horseshoe through the upcoming Labor Day weekend. After that, he was to have a few days off before prepping for his family's seven-day trip into the Buckskin Ridge. They knew they could turn where the trail tied into the Pacific Coast Trail and ride further north or turn and go back the way they came, depending on foot traffic, which typically tapered off noticeably a few days after Labor Day weekend. He wanted to enjoy an afternoon with Sweetie and had texted her that he would meet her at her house around four. She beat him there by thirty minutes. Her folks had covered for her a little earlier than usual, knowing that she and Cody would not have much to any 'together time' over the next two to three weeks.

He loved her name, that it was a fitting double entendre.

"Hey, Sweetie," he said as he came out of the back of the house, his face beaming with happiness.

As usual, she was stretched out in a lawn chair, toning her naturally light brown skin to its gorgeous, dramatic olive shade.

"Hi, Honey," she said and waved.

"Looking good, baby," he said, as his eyes moved left and right, head to toe.

"Working on it. I have a tan line that I wanted to work on," she said seductively, "but I wasn't sure if you'd texted Chris or Seth to come, too."

"Not a peep," he said, smiling.

"Well, then I don't need these," she said as she sat up and removed the top and bottoms of her bikini before stretching back out.

Cody pulled up a chair beside her and laid back, looking at her eye level. "I can't stay long," he said.

"I know. You want to go in?" she asked with a slight but devilish grin.

He nodded, "Let's just sit for a couple of minutes so I can unwind a little. You can heat up."

"I get any hotter, honey, I'll slip off this chair," she said in her sexiest voice, a sultry hybrid of Mae West, Marilyn Monroe, Bernadette Peters, Sharon Stone, and Charlize Theron. Timeless yet timely.

"Rascal bitch."

"Yes. I am, aren't I?"

He got up, pulled her up, keeping hold of her hand, grabbed her bikini pieces, and led her into the house.

***

White House

End of August

Hoffman had waited fifteen minutes to be called into the President's office. The president was talking to Emma, a concoction that always made him nervous. He was sure, and usually correct, they would be talking about him.

"So how is Portland shaping up?" the President asked.

"Great. I talked to Antonio, and everything is a go. They have done a Facebook promo, and he thinks they could have anywhere from twenty-five hundred to five thousand shows. Maybe a few more than that."

"Whoa, five thousand would be incredible. That's a show of force. "Ratings, Baby," he said joyfully.

"And he's got a couple of nasty bastards leading the local chapters there. Bound to be trouble," Emma said, smiling. "TV Stations across the country will be paying attention to this one.

"I keep forgetting his name is Antonio," said the President. "Is he one of ours? I thought all those guys were one of us."

Emma was sure he wanted to ask, 'Wap or Spick?' "He's fine, sir," she said. "Portland is going to feel the pain."

"Bring it," he said impishly.

"I guess we'd better get Jack in here before he shits himself worrying about whether or not we're talking about him."

"He's a dipshit."

"Worse."

"Hey, how's the other item?"

"It's good, sir."

"Do we have a name for it?"

"Yep. Northern Exposure."

"Ohhhh, nice. I like it."

"Before this ends, people will want a wall between us and Canada."

"And we'll make them pay for it," said the President, slapping his thigh, and the two began to laugh loudly.

***

It was Monday, the last day of August, and Cody was due to lead his group out the next day, a six-hour walk back to the vehicles. The Boise family he was escorting included the parents, two kids, a boy and a girl around thirteen and fifteen, respectively, and another girl, a daughter's classmate. Cody had made them breakfast and was getting ready to take them on a two-mile hike to a small lake nestled up against a nearby mountain. The last half mile of the hike was downhill to the lake, and the views were spectacular, even by teenagers' standards. Cody had told them there were small fish in the lake, so the son and father were excited about doing a little fishing and perhaps catching dinner.

It was about 10:30 in the morning when Cody first heard the horse approaching. The rider, Bobby James, was a young scribe who worked for Steve. He had helped Cody on several occasions handling larger groups, but he mostly helped the guides, like Cody, prep for trips and then unload and clean up after they returned to the office.

Cody knew he had been running him a bit by the horse's looks. The horse, Brick, a reddish-colored gelding, was sweating freely and frothing a little around the mouth.

"Hey, Bobby," said Cody, with a confused look. "What's up, man?"

"Hey, Cody," Bobby replied a little sheepishly. "How's it going?"

"What are you doing here?" Cody asked.

Bobby got down, looked at Cody, and said, "Uh, Steve needs you to come back right away, Cody."

"Why?"

"I'm not sure exactly, but he told me to tell you that he has a problem and that you're the one to help him with it," Bobby said.

"Me?" he asked, looking confused. "Why me? How'd he even know I was here for sure?"

"I don't know, dude. He just said to tell you to come back right away. I guess he made a good guess about where you were. You guys follow a route, pretty much. I don't know. You know Steve. Seems to always know where everyone is. Your global turned on?"

"Yeah, that's probably it," Cody said, wondering at the same time when he last turned on his global phone. Guides were told to do it every evening before dark so that Steve could locate them, but they didn't always remember, and Cody was not sure he had done it the night before.

"He said you should ride Brick out. I'll help these people walk out, no worries." Bobby smiled and handed the horse's reins to Cody. "Here's the keys to the truck and trailer."

Cody took the reins in one hand and the keys in the other. He then slipped the keys in one pocket, pulled out the keys to his own vehicle from the other, and passed them to Bobby. Then he passed the reins back and said, "Wait a minute. I have to grab my things and say goodbye to Mr. and Mrs. Daniels."

"Well," said Bobby, "just grab what you absolutely need, and don't worry about the Daniels. I'll explain things to them," he said, smiling warmly. You need to get going, Cody."

Cody went to his tent and grabbed his knapsack. The Daniels were about a hundred yards off in the distance, looking at flowers in the meadow. Just a few feet away, Bobby stared at him uncomfortably, fidgeting all the while, so much so that Cody decided to leave the goodbyes in Bobby's hands as directed and get back to town. This had never happened to him before, and a sense of foreboding began to wash over him. He jumped on the horse and headed back to Winthrop.

***

Even riding a horse back to the truck, Cody still took five hours to return to town. He pulled up to the Winthrop Outfitters on the north end of town, and Steve was out the door to greet him before Cody made it out of the truck.

"Hey, buddy," said Steve, seeming just a little solemn.

"Hey, Steve. What's up?"

"I want you to go over to Sweeties right away," he said. "There's people there waiting for you."

"WHAT HAPPENED. IS SWEETIE ALRIGHT?" Cody was panicked.

"Hey, take it easy, brother. Yeah, Sweetie is fine," Steve said in a not-very-convincing voice.

"What is it, then? What's the matter?"

"Cody," Steve said, putting his hand on Cody's shoulder, "go to Sweetie's. They're waiting for you."

"Who?" he said, his tone still somewhat panicked but, at this point, more desperate.

Steve wanted to hug, comfort, and tell him what he knew. But he knew he was not the one to do it.

"Cody," he said firmly. "Go."

***

It was not more than a five-minute drive to Sweetie's house. Cody knew something important was happening because of the number of cars at the house, including his mother and father. Most he did not recognize. There was Chris.' He walked into the living room, where several kids were sitting on the furniture and floor, and a couple of adults were talking, people he knew but with whom he did not want to engage at the moment. He wanted to talk to Sweetie. One of the individuals eyeing him from the corner of the room must have read his mind, pointed toward the backyard, and said, "They're outside, son."

Cody walked through the kitchen past several people he would generally have acknowledged. When he got outside, he saw Bill and Chirine, his parents, Seth's parents, Chris, and Sweetie standing in a circle talking, and he began walking in that direction. Sweetie's back was turned away; Chris was facing him, and Cody saw his lips say, 'he's here.' Sweetie turned and began to run to him while Chris followed more slowly behind her. The group members watched them leave and stayed where they were.

Sweetie ran up to him and threw her arms around his chest.

"What's going on?" he said. "What's wrong."

"Cody," she said in a whisper. "It's Seth. He got shot."

"What?" he said in shock. Then, "What?" in complete disbelief. "When? Where?"

"In Portland. Saturday night. During the demonstration."

"Where is he? Is he alright?" Neither said anything. Sweetie just began sobbing, and Chris, looking at Cody, shook his head.

Cody, at this point, realized everyone was looking at him; he yelled, "NO," before breaking into tears himself. Chris came closer, and the three remaining members of The Squad began crying and holding one another while others from around the pool slowly made their way toward the trio to touch them, hug them, and offer condolences.

***

Seth's service was set for the next day. Steve personally covered Cody's upcoming trip.

"Don't worry, man, I got your back," he had said. "I have some things I want to check at some of the campsites anyway."

Cody assumed he would check whether pistols and ammo at some campgrounds were still there. He usually did it in early to mid-October, but Steve likely saw this as a chance to get a jump on it. Snowfalls in October or sooner were common in the high country, and Steve regularly got shut out of covering all the caches by the middle of the month. Steve allowed each guide to carry a sidearm and a small rifle. All pistols were Colt 45 revolvers carried by the guides in a Western-style holster. All rifles for his guides were Browning lever action, open site 243 calibers, housed in a saddle scabbard if they were on horses or in one attached to their backpacks if they were hiking. Holsters and scabbards were always leather; Steve thought they gave the guides a more realistic cowboy/outback look.

While optics were important, Steve was a realist. He had several related questions of concern: What if a guide forgot, misplaced, or lost a gun? What if they met unsavory characters, such as drug smugglers, alien runners, hikers turned rapists, etc.? Or what if they encountered critters their firearms were not adequate to impact? Grizzly bears were a real threat in large parts of the Pasayten, especially campgrounds in the area abutting Canada.

Over time, he had hidden Browning 9mm's at several campgrounds where the guides were directed to camp. Usually, he left three clips or magazines, each able to hold eleven shells apiece, with every pistol. He also included a 44 Magnum with 18 shells and three loads at three campgrounds in the far north areas. And just in case the situation turned especially bad, such as a sudden change of weather, he also included a skinning knife and a sealed set of matches. All the guides were given maps and directed to locate each piece for each campground to ensure they were there. While there was the risk someone might find them and an accident occur, Steve thought that their value outweighed the risk to the guides in an emergency, and so far, they had not lost any of the firearms in the eight years since the company was started.

Cody drove to Sweetie's house, where they piled into Bill and Chirine's Ford Explorer and went to Seth's service. There were seats for about sixty people at the open-air ceremony. Sweetie, Chris, and Cody sat in the front row with his parents, other family members, and their close friends. Another three hundred or so were standing around the sides and back of the chairs. Seth's dad and mom had had him cremated, and his ashes sat in a silver urn atop a small, short table that was placed in front of a picture of him posed atop his favorite horse. About eight people, including Chris and Cody, gave brief eulogies of him before the group began to disband.

Chris saw him first and pointed him out. "That's Kent Des Moines," he said to Sweetie and Cody."

"Where?" asked Cody.

"Over there," Chris said, pointing toward Seth's father, Angus Johannsen.

Des Moines was standing in a line of thirty or so to offer condolences to Mr. Johannsen, and Des Moines was currently number four. He was accompanied by two individuals that Cody recognized as having been involved in high school sports. One, Dan Christian, as he recalled, was from Tonasket, and the other, Cal Kirby, was, he thought, from Omak, both towns about seventy-five miles Northwest of Winthrop. Cody had the feeling, based on their glances, that these two recognized him as well and that they had communicated that to Des Moines. Once they had finished talking to Seth's dad, they made their way off to Chris, Sweetie, and Cody.

"Hi, Chris," Des Moines said, extending his hand.

Chris returned the shake but wore his lack of enthusiasm on his sleeve and face. "Hey," was all he said.

He scanned all three squad members and picked Sweetie to approach first.

"Hi, I'm Kent Des Moines. You must be Sweetie. Seth talked about you." Before she could respond, he moved on to Cody. "And you're Cody. Seth talked about you as well. So did these two," he said.

Des Moines had extended his hand to Cody, but Cody hesitated noticeably before returning the gesture. "Hey guys," he said to Kirby and Christian with a nod. They both smiled and nodded back.

"I'm really sorry for your loss," Des Moines said. "I don't know if you all know it, but Seth saved my life. He stepped in front of a fellow that was coming after me, an Antifa, and he got shot in the process."

"That's what we heard," said Chris.

"Quite a loss," Des Moines said.

"Especially when you consider the tradeoff," Sweetie said softly.

Des Moines tried hard to restrain a smirk, but a little twitch found its way to the left side of his upper lip. "You all should come to our next meeting. We're having a demonstration for law and order in Wenatchee," he said. "We'll be mourning the loss of one of our soldiers."

"He wasn't a soldier," Cody said quickly, looking at all three. "None of you are. You're weekend pretenders. Word is that several of you fuckers were packing and were about ready to shoot an Antifa. It was like Seth doing what he did, trying to break things up. He just got in the way."

Standing about five feet from Cody, Des Moines stepped forward and stared at him menacingly. He was about three inches taller than Cody and outweighed him by a good thirty pounds, which Cody assumed was muscle. He had a natural intimidating presence. He looked as ominous as Chris had described, and Cody was certain that if a fight broke out, Kent would kick his ass, an assumption Des Moines almost certainly shared. At the same time, Cody was sure Des Moines was not dumb enough to pick a fight today, so he spoke his mind.

"He was a hero," said Des Moines.

"No, he wasn't," Cody said defiantly and with frustration. "Sorry to say, he was a patsy just trying to do the right thing. You two are patsies, too," he continued, looking at Cal and Dan. "This guy doesn't care about either of you. He just used the shit going on in the country now to carve out his little fifteen minutes of fame."

Des Moines just grinned, showing no apparent irritation with the verbal assault. "Cody, you're just the liberal pussy, Seth, and these two said you are."

Kirby and Christian exchanged a quick glance, and Cody could tell by their faces that they had not said what their leader was representing. He was confident Seth would never disparage his close friends like that, either.

"Easy, shitbird," said Chris, who was closer to Des Moines' size but probably would still suffer Cody's likely fate.

Des Moines turned to Sweetie. "Seth was right about you, too. Mmmm, mmmm. But what's a cute little piece like you hanging out with two losers like these pussies? I definitely don't understand women."

"And you never will, fuck face," Sweetie shot back. "Assholes like you never do. You don't know how to love people for who they are as people. I'm not a piece. The four of us are friends; we love each other."

"Ohhhhh. Sexy, then."

"Jesus. You're a pig." She shook her head, her face showing more disgust than if she had just stepped in dogshit in bare feet. "Less than two minutes, and you've offended all three of Seth's best friends," said Sweetie. "Did your mommy teach you your manners, boy?"

Des Moines looked bored. "Look, Cody. As I said, if you and Chris want to come to a meeting, you're welcome to. You'll open your eyes to what's going on in America."

"I think we're getting a pretty good picture here," said Sweetie.

Des Moines ignored the jab. "Bring her," he said, looking at Sweetie with disdain. "You're all welcome as *friends* of Seth's. But we're taking back this country, whether you folks like it or not. You can be part of it, or you can be roadkill."

"I thought we lived in a democracy," said Cody.

"Well, we do… kind of… most of the time," said Des Moines, matter-of-factly. "But sometimes the courageous have to nudge it back in the right direction to ensure it stays on track. In the direction it was intended to go… Right?"

"Is that out of the Timothy McVeigh manifesto?" Cody said. "Sounds that way."

Chris and Sweetie gave each other a nod in support.

Des Moines scanned all three, a disgusted sneer on his face. "We didn't start the fire, but we'll fan the flames and take down names."

"Something like that," scoffed Sweetie.

Almost whispering as he leaned in, Des Moines said, "Watch yourselves, now. People are going to get hurt,"

"Wow. That sounds like a warning," said Sweetie.

"Maybe a threat?" Cody said suggestively. "Well, I carry," he said, referring to firearms, "just like you do, Kent. If you or any of your guys ever stop me on the road or anywhere else and try to tell me, you're the sheriff of the moment… you boys like to do that, don't you? That's what got Seth killed. Well, do it to me. I'll assume the Civil War you A-holes like to talk about is ON."

"Ditto," Chris said.

"Well, gosh, I look forward to seeing you again, then," Kent said, unflustered. "Come on, guys."

Dan and Cal followed him, but Cody felt they were unsure what had just happened or were entirely copacetic with the message.

"Asshole," said Chris. "Total asshole."

"No shit," Sweetie added. "What a loss. Seth saved a turd sandwich."

"I have a feeling we'll be seeing that dickhead again," said Cody. Chris and Sweetie said nothing but nodded in agreement.

***

White House

Monday, the Last Day of August

Emma and the President seemed genuinely excited when Hoffman walked into the office. "Hey, Jack, get in here. Have a seat."

"Hi, Sir. Hi, Emma," said Hoffman as he scuttled across the floor to an empty chair furthest away from Emma. He had been summoned earlier in the morning in a call from Mary. "Everything okay?"

"Oh, yeah," said the President. "Have you seen the news on what happened in Portland Saturday night?"

"Yes, Sir," Hoffman said solemnly. "Someone got killed."

"Yeah," the President responded happily. "A Freedom Fighter got killed. By an Antifa. God, we couldn't script this shit any better than that."

Emma nodded, and her face showed delight.

"I'm confused, Sir," said Hoffman. "Someone got killed. Aren't you a supporter of the Freedom Fighters, correct? How can that be good?"

"Well, I'm very sad, Jack," the President said unconcernedly. "Of course I am. But the optics. Shit, Jack, they're so awesome for us," his voice now reflecting giddy excitement. "Our core and a buttload of the independents and even some libs will be pissed beyond words… I hope. I mean, the press is going to eat this shit up, man. This will be great for the polls. God, the kid who got shot was only twenty-two. And a ranch kid from a small rural town. It's our base. By the end of the week, BOOM, we'll be up ten fucking points. You wait. This is going to make the Antifas and the whole BLM bunch thing look like the shitheads that they are. The Bible Belt must have prayin' overtime for me, baby, because this is a Godsend."

Emma knew how Jack felt about all this, so she let the President talk. Hoffman would not counter him, but he had to be upset that his kind would be accused of praying for someone's death. Well, except for that '*anybody but*' person. But not for one of their own. She knew the Vice President was trying to find the words that would fit this situation, to frame his concerns in a manner that did not conflict with the President's position but somehow captured his true feelings.

Finally, he said, "Are you going to call the parents of the young man who was shot?"

By the look on the President's face, he had not yet considered such an action. "Do you think it would help?" he said, looking toward Emma.

"Might add a point of two to the polls, Mr. President," she said. "Might be good if Jack called them, Mr. President. Elevates it to a tragedy but doesn't necessarily 'take sides' as might be if you made the call."

"Hmm," said the POTUS thoughtfully. "What do you think, Jack?"

Emma's asshole turned one complete turn tighter as she waited for Hoffman's response.

"I'd be honored, sir. Thank you for the opportunity."

"Very well then," said the President, agreeably. "Emma?" he asked.

Emma held up her right thumb and offered a cautious, weak smile. The guy was a complete doofus in her book, but she had to admit, somewhere in a small section of her tiny black heart, that he did have some redeeming values. Unfortunately, they did not jibe with good marketing and the realities of politics. Hoffman stood and left, wanting to say more but knowing that there was little he could impact. His best would be to provide some solace to the family who had just lost a loved one.

As soon as Hoffman was out the door, the President went back to his analysis of the Portland slaying.

"I know Hoffman doesn't see it like we do, Emma. Did you see his face when I said the Bible Belt thing? Hah."

"Yes. But no, sir. I doubt he sees it as we do."

"Candy ass," said the President. "Too bad about the kid, but hey, we're all terminal, right? I can't wait to see The Five this morning and see what they say about it. They and the radios in the heartland will be roasting that Antifa dude."

"I think you should call in, sir. Surprise them and their viewers. They'll love it."

"GOOD IDEA," he exclaimed. "Can you set that up? We'll do it like last time, like it was spontaneous. A big surprise. Viewers eat that up."

"Good thinking. Will do," said Emma. "Be thinking about what you'll say. This is a terrible example of the breakdown of law and order. Antifa is the real problem. You know the drill."

"God, this'll just be GREAT," he said. "This'll be all over right-wing and left-wing outlets. Let's see CNN, try to spin this positively." He pointed to the top of the far wall as if headlines were written on it. "Antifa shoots patriot peacekeeper! Libs fucked. The local media and national news will all have a field day with this. Social media will go nuts!"

For a moment, she was convinced he would stand up and start dancing. "They should. And if they don't now, they sure will in two weeks," replied Emma.

***

Somewhere in Canada

Early September

The man who picked up the three men did not immediately give his name. "Better, for the moment," he said, "we don't give any names, locations… just in case we get caught together. I'm just giving you three a ride east. You know the drill. If you need to call me something, call me Driver."

The driver appeared to be an early forty-something. His name was Bill Rogers. He had picked up the three in a van provided by his boss, Buck Carpenter, who he worked for regularly on numerous similar excursions for over twelve years.

They had been picked up at 10:30 in the morning, which gave them plenty of time to eat and perform any bathroom functions. Elements of the van had been modified to prevent the three men from knowing precisely where they were being taken. Carpenter had installed a thick, translucent, green plexiglass divider that let some light through but precluded anyone in the back from clearly seeing what was out front of the vehicle. The wall did not run flush to the van's ceiling but instead just to the top of the sides where the ceiling section arced up, leaving three or so inches open to some additional light at the top of the wall. The windows on the two rear doors were covered with dark plastic that let in minimal light while preventing the three passengers from seeing out the back, leaving them figuratively and somewhat literally in the dark. A five-gallon plastic container, which Driver called Honey Bucket and Odion dubbed 'the restroom,' was left in a back corner if anyone needed it for the four-hour ride to the east.

The three men were told there would be no stops. Still, they laughed at the facilities and accommodations amongst themselves, just the same, raving this was an incredible four-hour inconvenience compared to what they had gone through several months ago. Rogers played music they could hear from a Sirius station, and though none particularly cared for Country Western, nobody considered it especially torturous. They spoke in detail in Arabic about where they might be and what they might be doing, assuming all the while that the driver could not hear them and not knowing all the while their conversations were being taped.

"We're almost there," Bill announced to his three passengers a few hours later as they entered the outskirts of Princeton.

Still catching up on their sleep, Odion and Farhan dozed for most of the last hour while Balil, having no idea where they were, fidgeted nervously in his seat.

As the van pulled into the garage, Balil asked, "Where are we?"

"I can't tell you exactly," said Bill, "but I can tell you that you'll see some great country soon enough. You won't have a chauffeur. You'll be hiking, and it's a trek. We'll get you settled in here first. Make sure you get a little exercise, not that you need it," he said, looking at Odion. "In a few days, we'll get you headed to where you're off to."

"That will be a treat," said Odion. "I think we will all appreciate that, Mr. Driver."

"How long will we be here?" asked Balil. "How much is a few days?"

"Well, I'm not certain exactly," Rogers said. "You'll have to ask my boss. But I expect it's more like seven or eight. You'll like the apartment, though, I think. You'll have to stay inside, but you can watch TV and work out if you like."

Rogers dropped them off at a nondescript building owned by Carpenter that functioned as the office for his guide service and as a small apartment for him and employees when necessary. There was also a separate garage space that shared a doored wall with the east side of the building, the only way in or out of it being through the garage itself. In the back of the garage was a door hidden behind a pivoting shelf that led to a basement apartment under the garage and part of the main building. It was a spacious, open area with a bathroom shower, kitchenette, three cots, and a TV that could only be heard if one used one of two headsets attached by fifteen-foot cords. There were no windows but ample lighting. The men were escorted downstairs by Rogers, who showed them the premises and emphasized the need to be very quiet lest anyone upstairs, not knowing they were there, hear them. He noted that this was particularly true of running water and talking.

The fridge contained food, a water heater for tea and instant coffee, and a microwave for warming certain foods. Though their accommodations had varied in Vancouver, they were all happy to see the sensitive collection of confections, bread, cheeses, and hummus. Rogers noted that Buck would meet with them soon to discuss their trek's details. Finally, he advised them not to smoke and to be very careful about starting fires, as they were essentially locked in the space.

The men made themselves at home and began the wait.

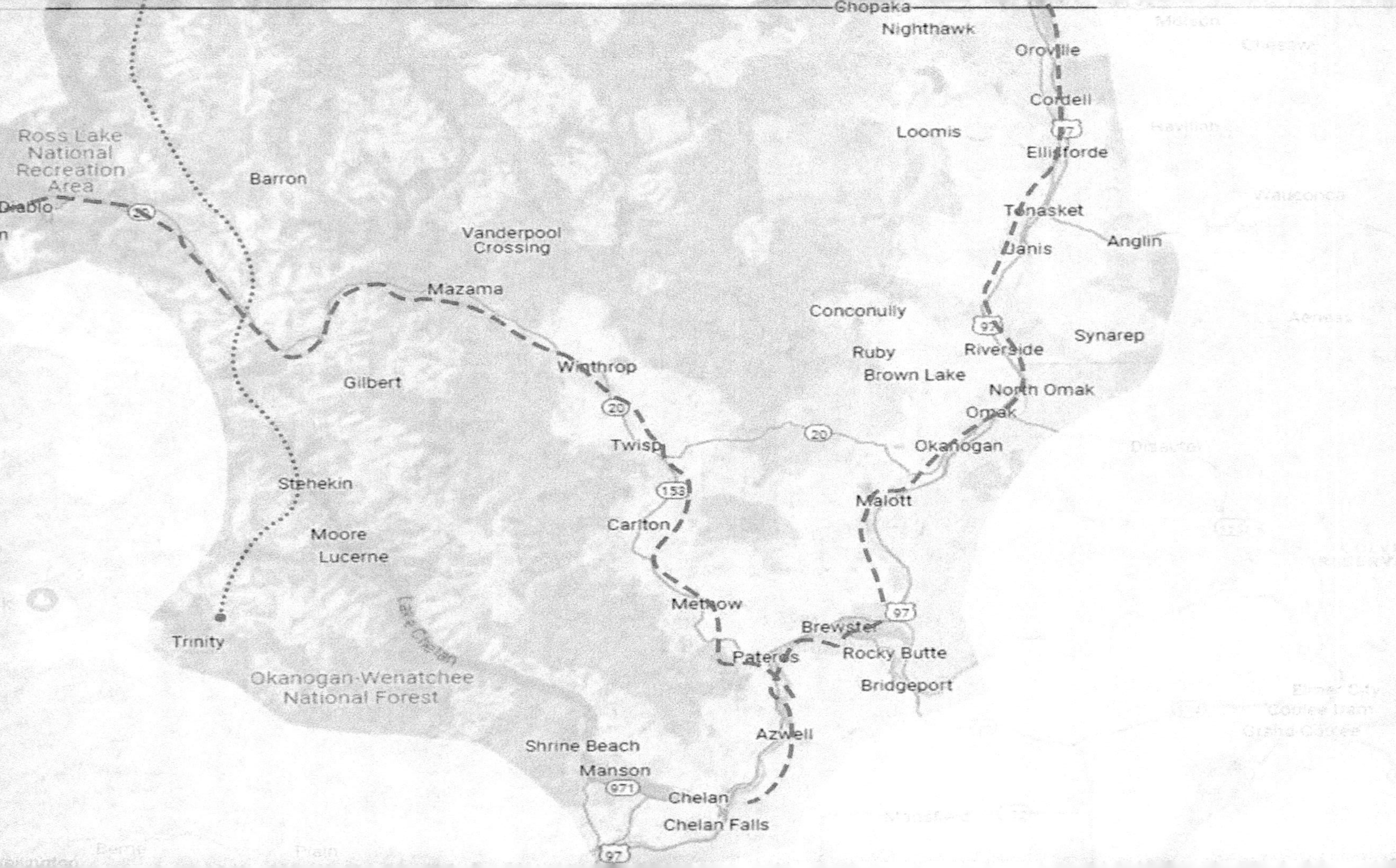

Ross Lake National Recreation Area
Diablo
Barron
Chopaka
Nighthawk
Oroville
Coldell
Loomis
Ellisforde
Tonasket
Danis
Anglin
Vanderpool Crossing
Mazama
Gilbert
Winthrop
Conconully
Ruby
Brown Lake
Riverside
Synarep
North Omak
Omak
Okanogan
Stehekin
Moore
Lucerne
Twisp
Carlton
Malott
Methow
Brewster
Rocky Butte
Bridgeport
Pateros
Azwell
Trinity
Okanogan-Wenatchee National Forest
Shrine Beach
Manson
Chelan
Chelan Falls
20
153
97
971
92

Part II –
Northern Exposure

Near Princeton, Canada

Two days after their arrival, Buck Carpenter came by mid-morning to meet the men for whom he would be responsible for the next two weeks. He brought a six-pack of beer for which Balil thanked him but noted they did not drink, much to Odion's unspoken dismay. Carpenter said they would have to spend five more days in the basement before he returned with supplies and equipment for their upcoming trek into the United States. He explained that their entire trip would be through the wilderness and take about three to five days. They would meet a guide on the other side that would lead them to their primary interim destinations on the other side. The men said okay, and Buck left.

Carpenter's real name was Avery Hanson, an American conscientious objector who had defected to Canada in the early 1970s to avoid being drafted into the Vietnam conflict. He now ran a guide service for hikers in the wilderness areas around Princeton. Only a few people still knew him as Avery Hanson, and those were all on the American side of the border. He had grown up in Omak and Oroville. When Buck was very young, his grandfather took him to Horseshoe Basin in the summer to visit a friend who was a sheepherder. On numerous occasions, he and his grandfather witnessed groups of illegal Chinese immigrants being smuggled into the U.S. from Canada. The eventual presence of hikers and campers compromised immigrant smuggling as a going concern in the region. But the trips with his grandfather had familiarized Buck with the area and, most notably, the myriad trails used in these ventures. When he received notice in 1970 from his local draft board that his presence was required in Vietnam, Buck, then Avery, decided to leave and flee to

Canada. For Buck, it was just another wonderful four-day hike. Once in Canada, it was less than another ten miles to Canadian Highway 3, where he hitched a ride to Penticton. As requested, the driver dropped him off at a cheap motel, whose owners then called the authorities with Buck's address. Soon after his arrival, Carpenter was arrested by two uniformed Mounties.

Rather than being sent back, Buck was put under house arrest. Two FBI and one CIA agent came to his jail early the following day, took him into custody, and then drove him to a safehouse in Vancouver. For three days, he was grilled about his knowledge of the Pasayten and was eventually offered an alternative way to serve his country. He would, they explained, smuggle people of value from other countries into the United States through the same wilderness trails used for the Chinese groups. These persons included foreign politicians, dignitaries, engineers, scientists, foreign spies, and even MIA soldiers who would become spies. Most of these people came voluntarily, but not all. This was just one of many ways to secretly transport people into the United States before reinventing them and moving them to nondescript locations with new identities.

Avery also got a new identity. He would bring people, he referred to them as 'tourists,' in and be paid for the person's import per each transport. As a cover, he could also do some genuine guiding of Canadian tourists. Carpenter quickly realized he had entered an extremely profitable 'contract' with a ready-made supply of customers, courtesy of the U.S. government. Over subsequent decades, he brought in scores of persons, including wives and children. He never felt threatened by his employer, always got paid on time, never had to pay taxes, and rarely questioned the character of those he was guiding. Over the years, he had never really met anyone he disliked. Until the three he had just met. And there was something especially odious about the two Iraqis in particular.

After leaving, Carpenter returned to his home in Kelowna. On the way, he first stopped at another property in Penticton that he used as a staging area to pick up the information and supplies he would usually give to those he was leading. He could have started this trek in the next couple of days. But something about how it had been set up bothered him, and he wanted to review aspects of the operation before he left. First, he had never worked with the contact who delivered the supplies he was told to share with the tourists. When Buck asked if he was CIA, he said no. FBI? No. When Buck asked who, he was told it was not his business. Second, the man offered no details about the tourists other than they had been spies for the U.S. working in their respective countries. What countries? None of his business. Finally, he was given a manila envelope that he was to give to the man in the group named Balil, and Buck was not to open the envelope. It was the first time Buck was ordered not to read any written documents accompanying a project.

The next morning, Buck opened the envelope. The complete document was written in what he guessed to be Arabic. Typically, such documents were in English and shared between himself and those he was taking in, so there was a common understanding of the upcoming details of the trek. However, for this group, he was not told their ultimate destinations, only to leave them at Rainy Pass, and other parties would pick them up. Who? Never mind. They were each to receive a backpack in which they could carry a limited amount of personal items as well as a briefcase, which was provided, that had IDs, cash, and some gold to get them started in their new locations.

Curious, Buck picked up one of the metal briefcases. "Shit," he said aloud to himself. "These must be forty pounds. A buttload of gold, if that's what it is. These boys have some work cut out for 'em carrying these in."

For all the time that Buck had done this, his clients were primarily Asian and Middle Eastern, with a smattering of Eastern Europeans, including Russian. They collectively represented over thirty-five countries with at least that many languages. Over time, he met eight individuals in Vancouver who read or spoke most of the languages, and Buck used them to help him customize communications when the tourists did not speak English. That included preparing written instructions to go with a particular map or audio to explain where they were going and what they might be seeing. These were particularly comforting to women and children.

He knew three people in Vancouver who read and spoke Arabic, his favorite being a woman professor in Vancouver named Adaj. Buck had called her and cryptically conveyed he had some documents for her to review and needed her to tell him what they said as quickly as possible. Buck told her that Rogers would be in Vancouver in a few days to pick up his cargo and drop the material at her office. She was to call Buck back on the matter after she had reviewed them. He gave her two phone numbers: his cell phone and Inmarsat 2 global satellite phone, which could reach him anywhere in the wilderness. Because he was leaving with the men in a few days, time, he had told her, was of the essence.

***

It had been three days since he had met the tourists, and it was time to get them delivered. But Buck still had not heard from Adaj, so he called.

"I haven't seen an envelope yet, Buck," Adaj said.

"Wtf," Buck had said. "Bill should have dropped that off when he was in Vancouver… days ago. Shit."

"Haven't seen anything, my friend," she repeated.

Buck immediately called Bill, who happened to be in Princeton, to find out what had happened to the envelope. "Oh shit, Buck," he said. "I forgot to leave it. I'd put it under the seat and just forgot… I blanked on it, man. I'm so, so sorry."

For all the time Bill had worked for Buck, almost twelve years now, he had never made a mistake, at least not one that mattered. Upset, Buck, nonetheless, reminded himself of the adage: a rose does not a bouquet make. "Shit happens, partner," he said. "No harm, no foul. Just get it there a.s.a.p. and then haul ass back to Princeton. I'm taking them in tomorrow."

Late that evening Bill made it to Vancouver and dropped a large envelope inside the slot in Adaj's office door before driving back to Princeton. Buck arrived in Princeton at about 9:00 a.m.; Bill was waiting for him. Rogers moved the van out of the garage, and Carpenter loaded the packs the three would carry. Though he had been assured that this operation was being coordinated by the highest levels of the U.S. government and that he had nothing to worry about, his internal radar said there was something wrong with this assignment. These three were definitely not diplomats or scientists or anything of any political or national value that was evident to Buck. He had been told they were spies for Americans that were 'likely receiving some kind of witness protection like refuge,' and he had nothing to worry about. Buck's plan at that moment was to accompany them, as he did presently on all such assignments, to just over the border and then let his usual contact there take them to the highway where they would be picked up and taken to their respective relocation destinations. Sometimes, tourists destined for Seattle were delivered for pickup near Ross Dam. In contrast, others hiked another 20 miles or so south before cutting east to connect to the north end of Lake Chelan, where a boat would pick them up and carry them back to the town of Chelan at the lake's south end. Most of Buck's *tourists* ended up relocating within a 300-400 mile semicircle to the west, east, and south of Chelan.

The drive from Princeton to the trailhead at E.C. Manning Provincial Park was only about thirty minutes. Rogers dropped them off where the four of them would hike about six or seven miles through the park into the U.S. that day and then camp at the End of the Line Campground until Buck's American guide showed up, which should be anytime over the next three or so days. The three would then be led down the Pacific Crest Trail to Washington Highway 20 at Rainy Pass, about a thirty-five-mile hike, which typically took three or four days, weather permitting.

Balil had read the instructions in detail. Inside each of their packs were briefcase-sized bombs that they were to detonate at three separate locations. The bombs had been 'laced' with radioactive material. One of the men, Odion, would detonate his device at the nearby Ross Lake Dam. The other two would be driven to Seattle, where they would detonate their devices simultaneously, one in the Kirkland tech area and the other near Fort Lewis in Tacoma. A detailed description of the two vehicles that would pick them up at Highway 20 was also given. Also included in the pack were a sleeping bag, a one-man tent, and some clothes, including a light jacket for cooler weather, gloves, pants, warm socks, and a pair of Timberland waterproof hiking shoes. There was also a butane lighter and a sheathed Gerber five-inch blade knife. When Buck's contact arrived, they were to kill both men and hide their bodies. Any other campers in the area might well have to be disposed of as well, though they were advised to wait, if possible, until such a situation was minimalized. Because, though, visitors were only allowed on a 'by permit only' basis, that possibility was not likely. Afterward, they would follow the included maps down the Pacific Crest Trail to the Rainy Pass trailhead to meet their contacts in the parking area, who would take them to their destinations.

***

Mid-September

Winthrop

Cody was leaving with his family tomorrow, and he had stopped by to see Sweetie one last time before they left. Chris had stopped by earlier, and the two were talking by the pool when Cody walked in.

"Hey, baby," Sweetie said, beaming.

Chris flashed the peace sign and smiled welcomingly. "Dude," he yelled.

Cody gave a slight nod, his face unenthusiastic. After making his way over, he gave Sweetie a peck on the cheek and sat down next to her. Looking around as if he might be missing something, he said, "No Pedro, no Seth."

He had not been by for two days; he was busy, she knew, getting ready for his family's trip. "Are Marie and Little Jimmy back?" Sweetie asked, trying to change the subject to something less solemn.

"Yeah," Cody said, exhaustedly. "She came in two days ago. Jimmy's been back for three."

"He missed Seth's service?" Chris said, bewilderingly.

"You know LJ's priorities," was all Cody could think of saying.

Cody's older sister, Marie, was five years older than him, having graduated from college at the University of Washington the spring before he started school there. After graduation, she went to work for Nordstrom at their corporate headquarters in Seattle. As a buyer of several fashion lines carried by the store, Marie traveled regularly to New York, China, Japan, and Thailand to negotiate and follow the contracting and manufacturing of several brands. Sweetie did not really know Marie well, though she had met her a couple of times, but she had never spent much time getting to know her.

"Really. Well, that's cool," she said, surprised. "I haven't seen LJ around town at all. So what's he been doing?"

Little Jimmy, Cody noted, was back in town, two days deep into a two-week leave. "Same old Jimmy," Cody said, "Watching Mickey Mouse Club reruns." Cody paused. "Actually, he's got a pretty good gig as an intern with Cong Agra in Kent this summer. He should have a job when he graduates if he wants."

Little Jimmy, aka LJ, was James Donald Dickson, Jr., the namesake for their father, known locally as Big Jim, BJ for short, despite his 5'7" height. Little Jimmy was only thirteen months older than Cody, which was the root of much consternation between the two growing up. They were both bright, both good athletes, Cody, though with an edge. The most significant difference was that Cody was a social extrovert when he wanted to be, and LJ was an incurable introvert. LJ had not dated much in high school. In fact, he had only dated one girl, Lisa Johnson, a classmate of Cody's, and she had asked him out first to a Sadie Hawkins dance. And that was toward the end of his senior year. The relationship held on through Lisa's last year of high school based on the allure of her dating a college man. But Lisa had dumped him by Christmas into her first year of college. Little Jimmy had gone to Washington State University in Pullman, majoring in Food Science, while Lisa had gone to Gonzaga in Spokane on a track scholarship as a pole vaulter. Though only eighty miles between schools, the distance ultimately proved too big a chasm for the duo to curve, at least not to Lisa's liking. Devastated, Little Jimmy eventually asked out Judy Peterson, Lisa's best friend and a convenient local who was also attending WSU. They had been an item ever since.

The left corner of Sweetie's mouth raised slightly into an Elvis grin. "Does he still watch that shit?" she asked, shaking her head.

"Oh yeah. He had it on the other day when I got home."

"What fucking channel is that on, anyway?" asked Chris.

"Shit if I know," said Cody. "Disney?"

"Is he still dating Judy?" Sweetie asked.

"Yeah," said Chris. "They were at the drive-in in Twisp earlier this afternoon. She looks good."

"Yeah," Cody said stoically. "Apparently, she's been staying with LJ in Auburn most of the summer. They're actually staying with her folks now. I guess he comes by our place to watch cartoons and talk to Marie. Mom tells me they're getting along pretty well. I thought she'd have dumped his ass by now, but hey."

"Well, it'll be fine," Sweetie replied unconvincingly. "One last chance for the fam to have a great adventure. I'm sure your Mom is looking forward to it. And you've got someone to talk to besides your father."

"When are your folks coming back?" Chris asked Sweetie.

"In a few days. Maybe next Monday or Tuesday, I think," she answered. "They've got some friends to see in Friday Harbor before hitting Costco and buying the store."

"Man, they get around. So, you're in charge for like another week?" he asked.

Sweetie held up her arms, hands above her shoulders, waving her palms away from her face while panning the grounds. "I'm in charge," she said, smiling mischievously.

Cody started laughing. "For a whole week. And me out of town."

"I know," she said, grinning. "What's a girl to do, right?"

***

Pasayten Wilderness

End of the Line Campground, Canada/U.S. Border

Day 1

At the End of the Line campground, Buck stopped to adjust his pack and take a drink of water. Twice, they had passed some individual hikers coming out, but there was no one besides themselves at the campground. In both cases, Buck, who led the group, expressed salutations, while the three simply smiled and said, 'Hi.' No Mounties on the Canadian side, and hopefully, no Forest Rangers tomorrow on the American side. Buck had distributed hiking permits to the three required on both sides of the border, lest the group run into any authorities. He was impressed at the hiking ability of all three tourists. Had they known his age, seventy, they might likely have been equally impressed, perhaps more so, as he could easily pass for someone in their early sixties. He was never one to hide his age; however, he always attributed his physical conditioning to 'good genes, good air, and clean living,' a verbal claim he usually followed with a toast with his favorite spirit, the fifteen-year-old McCallan scotch.

"Hey! HEY!!," Farhan yelled at Buck, who came up from behind. "Is this where we are camping?"

"No," said Buck. "We're camping on the U.S. side just past the border."

"How much longer before we get to the border?" Farhan's voice began to show a little exasperation.

"Relax! It's only another half mile or so. Less than half an hour."

"I hope so. Are you sure we can still be in Seattle by Monday?"

"I think so. Shouldn't be a problem. But we can only do what we can do. Your escort won't be here for another day or two. Besides, it's good to camp for a couple of days, anyway. People see you in that context, and that's what they remember. You're on vacation. Relax. Enjoy the scenery."

They arrived at the campsite shortly thereafter, and Carpenter announced, "This is it," and pointed to an open area near the lakeside. It was about five in the afternoon, and sunset was just another forty or so minutes away. Buck helped each of the three set up their individual tents and then took out what he intended to prepare for dinner: a package of instant soup for four and four fresh bagels. He had packed enough food for four or five lite meals for maybe three days, figuring that there was plenty of fish in the two small lakes, each a short hundred-yard walk from their camp, to supplant his supplies.

"Who's up for some fishing?" Buck asked.

Odion quickly raised his hand while the others dropped their eyes, shook their heads, weakly waved hands, and wandered off together in the opposite direction, quietly mumbling under their breaths to one another.

"Suit yourself, boys, but the fishin' here is great." Not sure they were listening, he shouted, "Say, can you two get some firewood?"

Hearing no response, Buck proceeded to get ready for fishing. In less than five minutes, he had fetched two poles, joined up the sections, attached the reels, threaded the line, tied on two swivels, grabbed his bait box, found what he knew were two winning lures, and headed up the shore with Odion toward the closest of one of several favorite spots.

"Man. A couple of real dicks," he muttered out loud to himself. "Out here in the middle of the wilderness, and they can't take two minutes to enjoy it."

"What is a dick, Mr. Carpenter?" asked Odion.

"Just another name for Richard," said Buck. "Shorter version." Odion looked confused as the context of the explanation did not seem to fit the application. "Okay, so someone named Richard can also be called Dick." Odion nodded but clearly waited for an explanation. "It also can be a slang term. You know the term 'slang'?"

Odion nodded and said, "Yes, I know that term."

"Well, dick can also imply, uh, uh, someone important. Maybe a good leader. Those two seem like they could be good leaders, yeah. Are they?" Buck asked Odion, his face convincingly inquisitive.

Odion's face was quizzical as he considered the question, then hunching his shoulders nonchalantly before casting out his line, he said, "I think Balil is dick. Farhan… maybe."

"Looks like you've done that before," Carpenter said of his casting.

"Yes, Nigeria. We fished to catch food to eat."

"So, you like fish?"

"I like *to* fish," said Odion. "I got tired of eating fish, however, long ago. But it has been a while since I last ate one that I caught."

At that point, the two had caught five or six fish each. "Well, let's clean these and cook 'em. Personally, I'm hungry."

Buck quickly gutted those they had caught, throwing the innards as far as he could and in the opposite direction of camp and then handing them back to Odion to rinse. "I probably should have walked another hundred yards," he said. "Don't want the bears bothering us."

"There are bears here?" asked Odion.

"Oh yeah. Black bears, mostly. Sometimes grizzlies. And mountain lions."

"Lions? Like our lions?"

"Well, not as big as your lions. Yours are big. Like three hundred plus pounds, I think, for a big lioness. Ours are called cougars. They're probably a little bigger than cheetahs. A big male might break two hundred pounds."

"Hmm. Cougar in Vancouver means something about some of the women there. I think some of them were dangerous, too," Odion added with a reflective chuckle.

"Hah," said Buck. "Good one. Yeah, lots of words in English can have two meanings. Lots. Especially names. And yeah, I've seen both types of cougars, and you're right; they can both be dangerous. Did you meet some cougars in Vancouver, Odion?"

"A couple, yes," he said, smiling.

"And?"

"I might have tamed a couple," Odion said mischievously. "I certainly did my best."

"Yeah? Good for you." Buck was starting to like this guy a little.

"Are the bears big?" Odion asked.

"Is the Pope Catholic?"

Odion momentarily pondered the question before saying, "I think so." His face was pensive as he paused another second before saying, "Yes, I am certain that he is."

Carpenter chuckled and then said, "Well, yeah. Those bears can be big, too. Let's get back to camp and fix these things."

Suddenly, Odion saw the connection between Buck's question and his own and began to laugh. "I see," he said to Carpenter. "The answer is yes to your question, so yes in both cases. That is funny. I've never seen a bear. So, which is bigger, lions or bears?"

"Bears. The Grizzlies can be huge, like males can be seventeen hundred pounds or so. A big black bear would only be six hundred to six hundred and fifty pounds."

"Oh my. Then they are more dangerous than lions… or cougars."

"Well, they both can kill you. A cougar kills like a lion. They snap your spine at the neck. Nice and clean. Bears, well, since they fight each other with their mouths, they attack your face. Instinctively. So, if they kill a human, they'll rip up your face and upper body quite a bit. Makes a bit of a mess. You don't want the last thing you see to be a grizzly staring you in the face. Very different than a cougar."

"Sounds really frightening," said Odion, concernedly as he nonchalantly began panning the area.

"I'm sure," said Buck. "But it doesn't happen very often. A few times a year, maybe, in Canada and Alaska. Once in a while around here."

When they returned to the campground, Balil and Farhan were sitting on a log near the site's fire pit, next to which they had piled, to his surprise, a nice heap of limbs for firewood. Carpenter quickly built a fire and put a small pot of water on the pit's grate. A few minutes later, he had hot water for tea and instant soup. At the same time, he was heating the water and began frying the fish Odion and he had caught. Less than thirty minutes later, he delivered a meal of hot soup, fresh fish, warmed bagels, and hot tea. Despite his stated opinion of fish, Odion, like the other two, cleaned his plate.

"What do you think, Odion? Were they worth the effort?" Carpenter asked.

"Does Mel Gibson hate Jews?" he replied, grinning like the Cheshire Cat. The other two looked at Odion dumbfoundedly. Buck, laughing, gave him a thumbs up. "Thank you, Mr. Carpenter. They're very good."

"Thanks," said Buck. "Thought you might like them. Why don't you guys clean up, if you don't mind, while I ring up my contact."

Buck walked off down the trail into the darkness. When satisfied he was out of hearing range, he hurriedly phoned his contact.

"Oscar here," said a voice. "That you, Big Turd?"

"Big Turd," Buck half spoke, half laughed in return. "That's choice."

"Where are you?"

"We're at the lake."

"How's the fishing?"

"Great. Caught enough for dinner."

"How many mouths are you feeding?"

"Three plus me."

"Just like planned, huh?'

"Yep. You cool with that?"

"Yeah, that's fine. I should be there the day after tomorrow."

"Christ, man," said Buck. "These guys are really giving me the creeps. I've brought some real shitbirds across the border, but these guys really weird me out. Two really seem to have some attitude."

"Well," said the voice, "it'll be over soon enough. Take them fishing tomorrow; show 'em the sites."

"Shit, kid, these guys could care less. I've got a bad feeling about them. Still waiting to hear back from my Vancouver translator on some communications they were given that I copied. I want to hear from her before you actually come into camp."

"Copy that. Leave your phone on for two hours in the morning, say eight to ten and two hours in the afternoon, maybe four to six? We can catch those windows if necessary."

"Sounds good," said Buck.

"Okay. Well, hang in there. I'll try and make it sooner, but it's not likely. If the weather turns shitty, it could be two and a half."

"Fuck, I hope not," said Carpenter.

Carpenter clicked off the phone and walked back to camp, where he reached inside his tent and tossed the phone onto his sleeping bag in disgust. He did not want to spend another night with these three… well, two of the three, anyway. He sensed they were dangerous and had an odd sense of foreboding in his belly. He was so caught up in his fears that he didn't hear the three coming up from behind.

"Did you speak with your contact?" Balil asked.

"Yeah, he's good. Should be here in two days. Might be some weather coming in, though. That could add a day if it's really bad. But right now, it looks fine."

Balil stirred nervously.

"No, no. Nothing to worry about," said Buck, struggling to sound convincing. "It's a minor glitch. You should still make your meeting in Seattle."

Odion pondered this inconvenience momentarily before asking, "Mr. Buck, we have been lucky not to run into anyone yet. Is there a greater likelihood we will see anyone on holiday when we cross the border? What about police?"

"Well, we've crossed the border," he replied. "We're in America. Maybe just over a hundred yards in. There's no Mounties now. We might see a forest ranger or two, but just show them your hiking permit. They might ask for more, but I'm told you have U.S. passports. Is that correct?"

They all nodded affirmatively.

"Well, there you go. They likely won't ask, but if they do, you have one, right? Nobody up here gives a shit what anyone else is doing for the most part. Mostly, they're concerned with where you've been, where you're headed, and whether or not you've been leaving a clean camp. We need to pick up our trash and not leave stuff lying around. Leave your personals, your packs and such, in your tents. Use the outhouses when you have to poop, okay? My contact will be here soon; then it's a two-day walk out of here for you three to the highway. From there, it's a couple hours' drive to Seattle. Piece of cake. Like I said earlier, you'll be in Seattle by Monday, likely sooner. Maybe Sunday," he said, smiling.

***

"Rise and shine," Grace said, melodically.

"Move your asses, you two. Get with it," Big Jim yelled as he shook the boy's tent. "Get the fucking horses saddled. Daylight's already a wastin.'"

"Do what your dad says, boys," Grace said, encouragingly. "Breakfast in twenty."

Little Jimmie climbed out of his bag first, with Cody right behind him. Both slipped out of their sweatpants and into their Levi's, grabbed their sweaters, and crawled out of the tent into the crisp morning air. Cody figured it couldn't be any later than 6:30. This was his favorite time of the day, at least when he could pull himself out of bed early enough to appreciate it; a predawn fall day. The sun had a couple hours to go before it would make the climb over the ridgeline, but the sky was bright enough to clearly see where you were going and what you were doing. If they had not been in the mountain valley, the sun would have been up already. A pinkish hue colored the thin layer of clouds that peppered the eastern horizon, gradually fading west into a pale aqua. Big Jim had started a fire, and Grace had been preparing to fix breakfast.

Cody proceeded to saddle the five horses as his mom finished cooking. Marie, with direction from Grace, prepared sandwiches for lunch. The smoke from the campfire began drifting around the campsite, mixing itself with the smells of frying bacon, scrambled eggs, coffee, and the early morning odors of the forest. As he finished saddling the last horse, Cody paused, closed his eyes, and took a deep breath, acutely isolating each smell in the amalgam of aromas permeating the camp.

"Mmmmm," he half voiced out loud. Only in the forest was he able to experience nature like this, and he savored it like the last bite of a far too-small serving of your favorite ice cream. His connection, however, was quickly unplugged by his father's voice.

"Come on, Cody," yelled Big Jim. "Move it already, kid. Come and eat."

"On it," Cody mumbled.

Shortly after breakfast, the men disassembled the tents and repacked the two cases that carried their supplies. Besides the five horses, the group had one pack animal, a mule, to carry their tents, bedding, and other related supplies. Stomachs full of breakfast, the family stuck their lunches into their respective saddle bags and set off to the north. They had left from the trailhead the day before in the early afternoon and ridden about ten miles. Their destination today, End of the Line Campground and its two adjacent lakes, was another fifteen miles up the trail, which they should have no problem reaching by three or four in the afternoon, arriving with plenty of time to set up camp before dark and maybe even get in some fishing.

The first mile was easy, but then the trail began zigzagging up the side of Grouse Mountain. The subsequent four miles, though not terribly difficult terrain, still tested the resilience of the human ass' extended interface with a constantly repositioning saddle. Except for the last one and a half mile, the horses trudged laboriously uphill, their heads bobbing rhythmically with each step forward, the rider's crotch stretched apart like wishbones, rocking back and forth in the saddles.

Occasionally one would lift its tail and fart three or four times with each forward pull of each step, the trail of flatulence temporarily gagging the rider behind. Little Jimmy laughed out loud with each fart, touting the decibel level of each one. "Good one," he'd say, or "Whoa, that's a nine and a half!!" And with each exclamation, he would look at Cody for comic affirmation.

The family rode in a line, each about two horse lengths behind the one in front of them. Their order in the line mirrored their ages: Big Jim in front leading the mule, Grace next, then Marie, Little Jimmy, and Cody. Most of Cody's trips were walk-ins, but there was something wonderfully cathartic for him about riding a horse. Cody bent forward, putting both hands atop the other onto the saddle horn. He pulled in his elbows and leaned his upper body's weight onto his palms. The posture allowed him to relax while riding, even stretch a little, and enjoy the rhythmic motion of the horse's slow, methodical gate better. Riding in the back was his favorite position, as he only had to keep up with the rest of the group. When he was leading a group, he had to look back constantly to ensure that everyone was keeping pace, accounted for, and sufficiently entertained. In this position, he could just enjoy the scenery.

As a guide, one had to be a coach, instructor, referee, nurse, historian, botanist, geologist, storyteller, and gopher. He pondered that perhaps that was why his father was constantly complaining and seemingly unhappy, that he simply did not enjoy wearing such hats and did not want to be responsible for, or bothered by, anyone else's wellbeing. That was probably why he had not stayed in the military and why he pursued a profession that allowed him to spend long stints alone in the forest, at least when he was younger. When the boys were little, he would often take LJ on camping trips at several different lakes, and the two would be gone for a week or more to fish, everyday-all day. However, Cody usually stayed at home to spend time with friends, which was why he assumed that his dad did not seem to like him much. If you did not like how BJ did things or saw the world as he did, he did not have much interest in, or patience for, you.

They arrived at the campground around 3:30 that afternoon. Around noon they had passed one party of hikers heading south, two married couples on their way home. After Labor Day, trekkers' numbers dropped considerably as summer officially ended. The weather very quickly became more unpredictable, and the evenings and early mornings became noticeably colder. Cody was then surprised to see a group of four men set up in Camp #1, which was at the northwest limits of the grounds. There were three tents near each other on the west side of the fire pit and a lone one just a little removed on the opposite side, nearer the trail. There were no other campers set up in the area. The trail ran north to south through the center of the campground, which was divided into two sections, with five campsites on each side of the trail.

The Dicksons, to be closer to the lakes, set up on the eastern side of the trail in Camp #6, about one hundred fifty feet from the neighboring group. Most of the larger of the two lakes sat on the Canadian side while the smaller lake was completely in the U.S. LJ and Cody shared a tent, Marie had her own, and BJ and Grace shared a third. The tents formed an equidistant triangle around the fire pit, with the boys' and Marie's tents on the north side closest to the other campers. After setting up the campsite, Big Jim and Little Jimmy organized the fishing gear and immediately headed off to fish. Cody decided to take a walk up the trail and visit the neighbors.

***

"Where's the package, Emma? Do we know?" asked the President.

"No, Sir, not exactly," she responded. It may still be in Canada or has just crossed the border into Washington State. Our sources are tracking the guide's phone location and whether he makes any calls. They say he doesn't always turn it on, and when it's not, the locating function doesn't work."

POTUS bit his lower lip and pensively stared toward the far corner of the room. Reflexively, he fidgeted with the hair flowing backward over the top of his right ear.

"Well, this'll either be a savior or a shitstorm for the election. I'm glad we're connected to some intel regularly so we can direct the response going forward."

In a pleased voice, he looked back at her and said, "That's good news. Now it's all about when and how to inform the country and the Democrats."

"Trust me," Emma Grant cooed, "it'll be fine, sir. If things go south, you can always declare a national emergency. Delay the elections. The key is to not let this get tied back to us, and I'm comfortable that's not going to happen."

POTUS smiled at that. "Yeah," he said, nodding, "it is a bit of a win/win, isn't it? I'm a hero if I stop it or a great leader if I just take control." He gave an unconscious, Mussolini-style touch on his coat lapel as he stared toward the ceiling before adding, "This is just what

172

we needed, Emma. This election is mine. Fuck the polls." Then he gave her an admiring look and added, "You've done great, Emma."

Grant, however, had serious concerns about the outcome of this event, knowing better than to keep them all to herself, at least at this point. The plan had taken the better part of the administration's first three years in office to put together, one that would rally the country around them, in case they needed it, over the critical sixty to ninety days leading up to the election. Americans had the attention span of a teenage boy viewing porn sites online. Normally, such distractions of this magnitude were ultimately delivered outside the country to avoid U.S. citizen casualties or at least keep them to a bare minimum. That also minimized the American press' interest. Ones like 9-11, however, that brought the carnage home, both angered and frightened the masses. The challenge when covertly funding terrorist groups like this, one could never entirely guarantee what they might have morphed by the time of a project's execution.

"Well, we need it, sir," she replied very seriously. "The virus has been going on for six months now. People aren't happy with how it's been handled, and they're becoming more fearful. Some hysterical. Everyone in the country is frustrated. Deaths seem to be on the rise, and the experts seem to think it'll get worse in the Fall. The lockdowns are killing the economy. Eighty percent of the people are doing fine financially, but it's in the crapper for the other twenty. And ninety percent of those are our core."

"So, tell me some of the details again, Emma," said POTUS, "of what you and Derek have working."

This was the third time in as many days that he had asked for a briefing, and it was everything she could do to hold back saying,

'How many fucking times do we have to do this?' It was like teaching an atheist dyslexic to spell dog. NSA and the CIA both had likely bugged this office and the rest of the building. On the other hand, what could they do without showing... well, their hand? If they did know, that is. This President had stealthily degraded their credibility as reliable information sources in the public's mind, and any such accusations would be seen as politically motivated fake news. He had watched how POC, POR, and a dozen other despots from around the globe had dismantled their governments' constitutions over the last several years and had become rulers for life. POTUS wanted that, as well, and Emma wanted to help.

Emma gave a quick, five-minute review of the details. Almost four years ago, Derek, while in Qatar working on a family hotel deal, was approached by an ex-KGB spy from Ukraine who was working there on a contract to help Russia keep the Eastern side of the country destabilized. He told Derek that during the sixties and early seventies, he said, the Soviets had developed a small nuclear bomb that could fit into a briefcase. This complemented, Derek learned later, a 1997 *Sixty Minute* episode that had claimed that around two hundred fifty such devices had been 'misplaced' during the fall of the Soviet Union. The man claimed that about half of the bombs had been spread around the globe in key countries and housed by Soviet agents or civilians still loyal to Russia. Several were in Canada near military bases, at least initially, and at least two dozen in the United States, either near bases or in key metropolitan areas, including Washington, D.C., Los Angeles, New York, and Seattle. Over the years, some had literally been lost as politics changed and people guarding them died. The ex-agent, however, had information where a half dozen or so of the bombs in Canada were being kept. If Derek's father, the President, saw some value in knowing where they were, then he could take possession of them. For example, exposing their existence and location might be valuable for both him and Russia's current president.

Though POTUS realized their value in that respect, he also saw their potential value in other regards. The idea of him alone having their very own, albeit small, arsenal of nuclear weapons made him more anxious than a five-year-old being told 'wait just a minute' before being let loose to open their Christmas presents. She had heard the question before more than once. She answered it in detail every time, but he asked it again anyway. "And what are we going to do with them?"

Derek, Emma went on, had worked with an intermediate supplier of U.S. weapons to the Middle East region to funnel money to identify, train, and smuggle three Al-Qaeda operatives into Canada under the pretext that they were double agents bringing in key information on the organization's administrative structure and tactical plans. However, once in Canada, they would each be given a bomb. Because the original Russian suitcase bombs were, in reality, not that small, the plutonium from the few found was parceled into three lead-lined briefcase-size containers that also contained sizable charges of plastic explosives. The product was three *dirty bombs*. The entire process had taken the better part of three years to piece together. The three Al-Qaeda operatives were in Vancouver and were to be smuggled in by an ex-American through a wilderness area in north-central Washington state. They believed they were on a jihad and that their missions were to explode the three small nuclear devices, one behind Ross Dam because of its easy access and a source of drinking water and power for Seattle, and two in Seattle, one near Fort Lewis, Tacoma and the other in Kirkland, a key U.S. tech area. There could be real damage and disruptions by the weapons, but the real defilement would be the debasement to the country's military and overall perceived sense of security.

All of this, however, was strictly hypothetical if the terrorists were not intercepted as planned. In fact, a local chapter of the Freedom Fighters had been told to stand by, that they would be asked, in confidence, to perform a patriotic deed for the President that could involve terrorists with explosives coming in from Canada. The press for the President and the militia would be epic. They would engage them at a predetermined pickup point, kill them, and seize their weapons of mass destruction. All the concerns of the country's vulnerability, safety, and security would still be an issue, just as had been the case with 9-11. A national emergency would be proclaimed, and the militia would be given further policing powers, in effect, a private militia for the President going forward.

"But what happens if they kill some of the militia or set off one or more of the bombs where they're intercepted?" asked POTUS.

"Well," said Emma, "the bombs are small. If they're set off at the point of interception, they're at the edge of a wilderness area. They'll mostly kill themselves and a few of the militia… maybe a few unlucky others in the immediate area. And if they happened to get to a target, well, again, shit happens. I'm told Ross Dam won't collapse, but operations could be affected for some time. It could affect Seattle's electricity for a while… operations, anyway. The immediate area and the water quality will also be compromised. The impacts of radiation on the army base and the Kirkland region would be significant, at both a practical and psychological level."

"Wow," said POTUS. "Now that'll be an excuse to postpone the elections if there ever was one. Nobody is going to argue with that."

"Yep," said Emma, nodding her head. "Nobody. Not even the Libs. They'd be too worried about blowback from their voters on that one."

***

End of the Line Campground

Pasayten Wilderness, USA

Day 2

Farhan was the first to see someone coming up the trail. Buck had gone for a bathroom break, and it was just the three of them in camp. "We have a visitor," he said.

Balil and Odion had been stretched out, napping in their respective tents. They had seen the family arrive almost two hours before and had anticipated a visitation. There were five of them plus their horses and pack mule, they had noted. Assuming a possible brawl, the three tourists would be against a slightly older man and two young adult males. The two women were not of concern. The three discussed the horses in detail, even planning for which one each wanted to ride, excited that they might have a much faster alternative to get to their transportation at the highway. If they left at daybreak on a given day, they thought they might make the distance in a single day. While Farhan and Balil had ridden horses in Hawaii and Iraq, Odion had not.

Cody walked into the campsite as Balil and Odion were exiting their tents. "Hi, I'm Cody Dickson," he said, extending his hand to the closest, Farhan.

"Hello, I'm Farhan," he said, shaking back.

Cody sized up three of the men unconsciously. Farhan and Balil were about the same size, just slightly shorter and smaller than himself, while Odion was perhaps an inch taller but far bulkier and muscular. Cody repeated Farhan's name back twice to make sure he was pronouncing it correctly, and then he repeated the process with Balil and Odion. "Where are you folks from?" he said.

Balil answered for all three. "We are from Canada. From Calgary."

"Okay. Cool. Well, what brings you here?" he said inquisitively.

"My uncle has a business there. We were visiting him on business, but the pandemic marooned us."

"Bummer. Calgary is a pretty good city, though," Cody said. "I went there a couple of summers ago for the stampede." They all looked at him quizzically when he said stampede. "The rodeo? They have a big one. Probably canceled last summer because of the pandemic."

"Yes, yes," the three men said agreeingly in unison.

"You drove here from Calgary?"

"No," said Balil. "We drove to Vancouver, and our guide picked us up there."

"So, are you here just to see the area?"

"Yes," said Balil. "It is very beautiful. Stunning. Our friends told us that. 'You must see the wilderness,' they said."

"You know this is the United States, don't you?"

"Hi, there," Cody heard a voice behind him say. He turned around to see a tall, lean, maybe early to mid-sixties man. "I'm Buck Carpenter. I'm these fellas' Guide."

"Hi, Buck," Cody said with genuine pleasure. "I'm Cody Dickson."

"You related to Jim Dickson, the ranger in Winthrop?" asked Buck.

"Yes sir, I am. I'm his youngest."

"You don't say. I've heard a couple of things about you."

"Really?"

"Yeah, you guide up here yourself, I understand."

"You understand correctly. I do," Cody said, smiling widely.

"I heard you ask these guys if they knew if they were in the United States. They do. I take responsibility for it. Your dad around?"

"Yeah, he's here. Whole family. We're down in campsite six."

"Well, I bring groups down here often, and we sometimes camp on this side, just so they can say they did it. It's a novelty for some. Haven't done a statistical analysis on it, but I'm pretty sure it results in bigger tips," he said, winking. "But's never been a problem."

"Oh. Okay, yeah, I know some groups from both sides do that. I don't care, personally. Just curious. I'm sure dad feels the same,"

Cody replied.

Buck went on. "They're businessmen from the Middle East. Iraq, I think. Right guys?" They all nodded their heads. "What's your business again?"

"Rugs and textiles," said Balil.

"Yeah," Buck repeated. "Rugs and textiles. They came to visit and make some contacts, and they got caught here by that pesky Covid pandemic a few months back. They're just killing some time now. Wanted to visit the wilderness, so a friend of theirs called me. We just came in through Manning and will leave in a day or two. Depends on the weather reports. But just letting these guys do some sightseeing and a little fishing." Cody nodded in interest. "What about you, Cody? What brings you folks here?"

"Oh, the family is on a trip. Probably the last one we'll make together like this… as a family. We were all in the area, so Mom and Dad requested we all do one more ride in for old time's sake."

"Excellent," said Buck. "How'd you come up?"

"Well, we were going to come up Buckskin Ridgeway and go back down the Pacific Coast Trail, but we got started late yesterday, so we're doing just the opposite. Dad wants to stay here for a couple of days and then ride back down the Buckskin Ridge trail. Take our time."

"Wow, you made it up here pretty quick then. That'll be a nice ride."

"Hey, Buck," said a voice off to their right. Big Jim had walked up quietly with LJ.

"Hey there, Jim," said Buck, once he recognized him. "How you doing?"

"Good. How you doin'?" said Big Jim, extending his hand.

"Making a living," Buck said, returning the shake.

"Same oh, same oh?" BJ asked, looking at the three men.

"Pretty much," said Buck.

Over the next several minutes, BJ introduced himself and LJ to Buck and his tourists and heard the story of who they were and how they had gotten there.

Finally, BJ asked, "What are you all doin' for dinner tonight?"

"Instant soup and maybe a couple of two-day-old rolls," said Buck. "And maybe another fish or two, if I can get these guys to eat a couple."

The three, smiling, all shook their heads no. "No fish," said Odion.

"Well," said Big Jim, "Grace has been cooking a lamb roast in the Dutch Oven. I think it's getting close to done. You all want to come over for some dinner in thirty minutes or so? I think she probably has some instant potatoes to go with that. It'd be nice to meet some international travelers."

Buck looked at the three. They all nodded heartily, and Odion added two thumbs up. "Well," Buck said, " I believe it's unanimous. Thanks, Jim. We'll see you soon."

***

"Who are they?" asked Grace.

181

"Well, Buck's a spook for the government," Jim began.

"The black guy works for the government? I thought Buck was the white guy," said LJ.

"What? No, the black guy is from Africa or something. Buck is a spook. A spy. Different kind of spook," said Big Jim.

"Good grief, dad," said Marie, shaking her head in disbelief. "You're both so bad. How do you even survive in the city, LJ?"

"He brings in defectors and spies and shit like that. Smuggles them into the country for asylum. He knows I know. We're directed to make sure he's left alone and don't acknowledge to anyone you know or talk to shit about it. Do not question any documents they have. You know, just let 'em camp on this side, no big thing. I'm sure he hands 'em off to someone on this side. Truthfully, that's all I want to know. They're harmless. DON'T say anything about it," Big Jim said in a low, farcical whisper. "I should not have told you, really. Don't want him to think he has to have me kill you or anything."

"How many are there?" said Grace, worried about the extras she would have to make and how much time she had to do so.

"There's four," said Big Jim. "Buck and his three *tourists*. That's what *he* calls them. One from Africa. The other two are from Iraq, my old stomping grounds. Should be fun. Boys? Get some wood for the fire. Could be a late night."

***

"Hi. Welcome, welcome," said Grace cheerfully. "Come sit down. My name is Grace."

Holding a six-ounce cup full of Jack Daniels that he had just refilled, Big Jim stepped up and commenced introducing Grace and Marie to the four guests, beginning with Buck Carpenter.

"Hi, Mr. Carpenter. We've heard so much about you," Grace said warmly.

Knowing that could mean many things, coming from her husband, he said, "Well, I hope I'm more interesting and not nearly as homely." Turning to Marie, he put out his hand and said, "Hi, Marie. Nice to meet you. You're as pretty as your mom. Not that your dad ain't pretty, but you chose the right genes on looks, my dear."

All six men were making mental notes on good lines for introductions as Buck continued to introduce his three tourists. He told the Dicksons who each was, where they were from, and why they were there, a story that engendered real interest on the part of the family in the guests. It was not common for residents from the area to talk to foreign visitors from these regions, let alone see them in the middle of a wilderness area.

"You guys want a drink?" he asked Buck and his guests.

"We don't drink, thank you, Mr. Jim," said Balil.

Buck shook his head. "I'm good, Jim, thanks."

Grace and Marie had prepared a fine dinner of roast leg of lamb, rice, fried tomatoes, and some fruit wedges of apples and oranges. By dinner, dusk had settled, and darkness had taken over, laying out a pitch-black blanket on which a bazillion constellations slowly began presenting themselves as an unfolding display of celestial brilliance. Starry nights in the wilderness took the breath of the most hardened of hearts. Cody and LJ had gathered a mound of good firewood pieces, and there were already two large, longer logs positioned near the pit that looked as though they had been there a while, each of which could seat a few people.

"You folks are welcome to sit around the fire for a bit," offered Big Jim. "Starting to get a little cold, and we already have a good one going."

"And I have some desserts," said Grace. "Some pastries" amounted to some small, wrapped cakes from Costco. Happy to have this good of a meal freshly prepared after so many days of mostly junk food, the four guests offered no resistance.

Cody led the way in scraping his plate with leftovers into a plastic bag and then throwing the paper plates into the fire. The three tourists left their plastic utensils on their plates, and when they threw them into the fire, a small amount of caustic black smoke with a common acrid stench from burning plastic. There was a slight breeze, so everyone repositioned on the logs to avoid being in the smoke's path. Not wasting any time, Marie zeroed in on Farhan. Cody saw it immediately for what it was and was bemused, as Farhan was several years older than her, given she usually hit on boys around Cody's age. More recently, she had asked about Seth when she was in town, apparently having given up Chris after repeatedly hitting on him while he was still a senior in high school.

Getting as close as she could without touching, but not so far that a hamburger bun would comfortably fit between them, she asked, "Have you been to New York?" He looked a little taken aback, uncertain where the conversation might end. "New York City." His look of puzzlement dangled on his face like a poor-fitting mask.

"Your t-shirt." She pointed at it. "It says 'I 'heart' NYC.' I love New York City."

"Oh no. I mean, yes, that is what it says. But no, I have not been there. I would like to, though, someday."

"It's wonderful. I've been there many times," she said, leaning into him just a bit. "Wonderful city. You should go. I *love* New York." With this last piece of information, she leaned in a little more heavily, reached across her breasts, and lightly touched his forearm.

"Marie," Grace said, "tell Farring what you do. What your job is."

Marie gave Farhan a three-minute thumbnail sketch of her job, the wonderful cities she traveled to, and all the famous brands she dealt with.

"Have you been to the Middle East?" asked Balil.

"No, but I really want to go to Dubai," she said.

"You should come to Iraq," said Balil.

"Are there any five-star hotels?" she asked.

"Oh, we have some very nice, almost five-star hotels, but they're not as grand as what you can find in Dubai."

"Well, I'm a bit of a luxury girl. Love Hong Kong. Singapore is great. Bangkok. Wow. They know how to treat you there. I used to love China, but they're not like the French anymore. You get out of the hotel, and they're all like, 'We're Chinese,'" she said, flapping her hands.

"I see," Balil said, bemused. There had been a couple of other side conversations, but the others were now silent, and their attention had shifted to this one. "So, what do you expect them to be like?" he asked almost playfully, his curiosity purportedly sincere.

"Well, I don't know," she said, thoughtfully considering an answer. "They just don't have to be so full of themselves, is all."

"So… less Chinese, then," said Balil.

"Yeah, well, kind of." Suddenly, Marie felt cornered. Check. Everybody there anticipated Balil's next question.

"Should they be more, say, American? Speak English. Eat American food?" he asked.

"They kinda already do like American food, don't they?" asked Cody rhetorically. "I mean… they're already loaded with American burgers, chicken, coffee. That's pretty American. Apple's big, and more of them speak English than in this country."

Big Jim looked at his youngest and just shook his head. "Oh, come on," said Big Jim, coming to his daughter's rescue. "You know what she means," he said to Balil, with a hardly noticeable slur.

"Actually, I believe I do, my friend," said Balil.

Big Jim was suddenly uncomfortable with the term 'my friend.' It sounded a little patronizing, and he did not like to be talked down to, especially by someone whose country he helped liberate from the rule of a tyrant. "What do you think she means, then?" he asked.

"As I suggested, perhaps she would have been more comfortable had they been more American."

"Is that so bad?" asked Big Jim, refilling his cup with his now third ample serving of Jack Daniels.

"That depends on who you ask, Mr. Jim," said Farhan. Odion looked confidently at BJ and smiled.

"What do you mean by that?" Big Jim replied. "Give me an example."

Buck, who had been listening nervously to the exchange, had begun to worry about the timber change in the men's voices. "Let me take a stab at this, if you don't mind," he interjected in the direction of Farhan. "America gives money and aid to countries all over the world. We give food and medical supplies. We also bomb the living shit out of lots of places and kill tens of thousands annually. Maybe more. Probably more. Somebody is certainly counting, but the numbers don't make it to our free presses."

"Aren't you Canadian now," asked LJ?

Big Jim smiled at his son and then Carpenter. "Good question," he said.

"I'm both," said Buck, unflustered. "I still love my home, America, but I have issues with her politics."

"Love it or leave it, man," said LJ, thinking he was on a roll. "I guess you left it."

"Oh, I don't buy that logic for a second, MJ," said Buck politely.

"LJ," said Little Jimmy. Buck looked at him blankly. "Little Jim… LJ."

"Oh," said Buck. "Oh. Little. I thought it was… never mind, sorry. Anyway, America and its allies, including Canada, sent soldiers to fight in other countries so that those people would have the same liberties and freedoms that we do, at least in theory, like speaking your mind openly and freely. Being constructively critical, heck, maybe just critical, without fear of retribution. You start to question those fundamental freedoms by packaging their prohibition as being patriotic here," he said while pointing to the ground he was standing on, "well, it demeans the very basis of our sending soldiers elsewhere. Doesn't it?" He punctuated his question with a shake of his head and an enquiring face directed to Big Jim.

The look on LJ's face suggested he was thinking about the question Buck had posed. Before he responded, Grace offered, "Well, our intentions are generally good, I believe. Don't you think so, Mr. Carpenter?"

"Yours or the people that require your sons and daughters to go there under some pretense? I believe the values of American citizens are fundamentally good, very good. But they're naive to think those giving them the orders always necessarily share the same objectives they're touting or even the same values. When you get toward the top of the decision-making pyramid, I think self-serving... self-preservation options become the ones more commonly considered."

"So, our leaders have bad intentions?" asked Grace innocently.

"Sometimes," said Buck, matter-of-factly. "Vietnam started out with good intentions... maybe. But it just turned into a pissing match where we didn't want to say we were losing, killing too many innocents on the other side and too many of our own for no good reason other than selling more military hardware. Don't forget McNamara also worked for Ford Motor for a while before becoming the Secretary of Defense. If there's one thing the military needs, it's vehicles of one kind or another. A lot of companies made a lot of money on that war. Heck, Chaney was CEO of Halliburton. Shucks, they got some great contracts in the Second Gulf War. War is good for business. But a lot of young men died for nothing, in my opinion." He paused and looked directly at Grace. "So, Grace, we just need to regularly check to make sure our rhetoric is in step with our values and stated objectives."

"I think that perspective is shared by people in both Afghanistan and Iraq," said Odion. Farhan and Balil nodded in agreement.

"Oh, come on, man," Big Jim said exhaustedly. "We got rid of the Tally-bans and Hussein. The people were liberated. Gawd. We did a great service." BJ shook his head. The liquor was slowing his cognitive abilities, and he buried his head in his hands for a moment and then added, "We saved your folks' bacon," he said almost joyfully, looking directly at the tourists. "Sorry for some casualties, gentlemen. Shit happens, right? Even with good things."

The three tourists began to sit more rigidly. "We don't eat bacon, sir," said Odion.

Big Jim laughed, amused at the misinterpretation. "Sorry. We saved your asses," he corrected. "How's that?"

"Our asses?" said Odion, still confused.

"Your lives. Your well-being," said BJ, sounding a little patronizing.

"Ah, our asses. You saved our asses?" responded Balil, his tone a little haughty.

"Yep," said Big Jim.

"But you killed our goats, my friend," which brought a chuckle from his two friends and most of the family. "And many of our sheep, cows, and horses. Those losses ruined the lives of many."

From the look on Big Jim's face, it was obvious that his mind could not process the responses to his comments as fast as they were being delivered, so Buck jumped in. "It depends on how you frame things, Jim. What's the difference between a liberation and an invasion, a great victory or a massacre? A casualty or a victim. Answer?" He looked around momentarily, everyone waiting for his answer. "Which side of the line you're on. It's all relative, man."

"Is that 'The Carpenter's Theory of Relativity'?" Cody asked lightheartedly.

"Mmmm," said Buck, catching the religious association juxtaposed with his physics reference. "Nice one. It does support 'turn the other cheek,' don't you think?"

"Well, Mr. Buck," Odion said, "turning the other cheek is fine when dealing with someone reasonable. However, how reasonable is someone who keeps smacking your newest cheek? It is not always a virtue to stay down. That's why some dogs decide to bite back, and a compassionate human will support the dog's response to abusive owners."

"It's easy to say to turn the other cheek when it's not *your* cheek under discussion," said Farhan.

"That's true," said Cody, nodding.

"We have a saying in Africa," Odion said. "The lion doesn't turn around when the small dog barks."

"What's that mean, Mr. Obi-wan?" asked Grace politely.

"It sounds like it means don't bother with people that are giving you shit who don't matter," said Cody.

"Yes, Mr. Cody," said Odion. "It does mean that. Mostly. But one can assume from it, I believe, that if it is a *big dog* barking, you can smack its cheek. You can pay attention."

"Say," said LJ, trying to turn the conversation to something more interesting for himself, "is it true that the Tally-ban or Al Kay-duh are putting together a Corn Hole team for the Olympics? Thought I read that on Zero Hedge... somewhere online."

The three tourists looked confused, sharing perplexed looks with one another, while everyone else remained completely silent for a moment, uncertain how to respond.

Looking at Farhan, Cody asked, "Did you or Balil lose any family?" trying to avoid LJ's barb.

Balil turned and looked at Farhan. "My family was his family," said Farhan. "His losses are my losses."

"My father died not long after the invasion, and my wife and two children died about five years ago," said Balil.

"I'm so sorry," said Marie. The rest of the family looked down, hanging their heads in sudden, awkward silence. "What happened to your family, if you don't mind me asking."

"My father's story is a long one," Balil said. "My wife and children were killed by a roadside explosion."

Big Jim downed his third cup and was considering pouring a fourth. "Theirs or ours," asked Big Jim solemnly.

Balil paused, his face reflective as he considered the question. In a microsecond, visions of the grizzly scene he was forced to scrutinize for identifications leaked in from the past like a cold wind suddenly blowing through a door left partially closed. When he arrived at the explosion, the three inhabitants had been burned to a crisp, save a few body parts that had been blown outside the car. An intact hand with a wedding ring still attached. A shoe belonging to his daughter. And a piece of skull full of his son's unique curly, light-reddish hair. Finally, he said, "I really don't know, sir. But it doesn't matter. Either way, they're dead."

"Well, let's pray for peace there," said Grace magnanimously.

"I do not think your country can afford peace, madam," said Odion in an almost sympathetic tone.

"What do you mean, Mr. Obi-Wan?" asked Grace.

"Mom, it's O-dee-on," said Cody, slowly sounding out each syllable. "Obi-Wan lives in a galaxy far, far away."

Grace smiled, though visibly annoyed with the correction. "The names just sound funny to me," she said. "I'm sorry. Wasn't I close enough?"

"Only if Grass is close enough, Mom," said Marie, not entirely kindly, leaning into Farhan and touching his forearm again.

"Not to worry, Mrs. Dickson," Odion said graciously. "I knew you were talking to me."

Big Jim, visibly annoyed by the exchange, brought it back to the topic. "So, what's wrong this time?" he asked, exhaustedly looking at the three tourists. "It's not like we like war. Or do you think we ask for it?"

"Well, Mr. Jim," Farhan said, doing his best to inch away from Marie. "Most people in our region believe your Mr. Dick wanted our oil. The boy, George, I'm not so certain. Second, there are just a lot of American weapons in the country. Some Russian and Chinese, as well, but not as many, even though they are cheaper."

"So," LJ said, trying for one more vapid lampoon, "are you saying that the boy, George, didn't really know Dick?"

"Yes," said Odion seriously, looking at Buck for concurrence. "And he was not a good leader."

"I think he's got you there. When this country began, we had to deal with King George. More recently, we had to deal with Boy George. That had to have been one of, if not the, dumbest fuckers we ever elected… until now," said Buck. "Though I think 'the boy' was a good guy. His father was excellent. This guy now?" Buck said, shaking his head with a face of disrespect.

"Bush was a great president. This one, now? Probably another Lincoln," said Big Jim.

"True dat," said LJ loudly.

"You know," Cody said, "I've always wondered if some of the terrorist activity wasn't funded by our military or, more probably, industry. Just marketing promotional dollars."

"God, Cody," said his father, annoyed. "What side are you on?"

"Well, that's what Eisenhower talked about, the military-industrial complex," Buck replied. "Great business model."

"You're not actually suggesting that our government or American companies would intentionally slip money to terrorists just to sell more jets and arms and shit, are you?" Grace asked incredulously.

"I think that's been the business model for quite some time," said Buck. "Pretty effective, if so. I mean, there'd be a lot of unemployment in America if peace broke out." Buck said. "So funnel some money to support a terrorist group or activity, sell billions of dollars of arms. Get your citizens to believe you're just keeping them more secure. Make the soldiers into heroes. Maybe even fund some video games about war to get young men and women immune, even excited, about killing. I mean… if you're the one pulling the strings, how do you turn the rest into puppets?"

"That is one motherfucking cynical perspective," said Big Jim, beginning to sound ominously defensive. "America is the greatest country in the world," he said, disdain permeating from his voice. "We're the greatest country in the world," BJ repeated in a pensive, reflective, finality voice. "And our military is the best of this country, second to none. Nothin's better than our men and women in uniform. If they can't fix the problem, nobody can. Gotta have peace and stability before you start sending in our civilians." BJ looked proud with his comeback. "Yeah, man, we're the greatest," his tone clearly daring. "You got a problem with that?"

Buck tried to regain control of the narrative. "What is it, Jim, that makes America so great? By what measure? I'm not trying to be cynical, really. Isn't there just a hint of propaganda in that?"

Big Jim was immediately flummoxed by Buck's question. 'We are the greatest' was a common idiom he had heard growing up hundreds of times in different contexts; he had said it many times himself. It was a truism… that he had never had to explain nor had ever questioned. It was understood as a given by all Americans who said it.

"Well," he said pensively, "well, we're generous, you know. We… we help people." He paused, then went on. "Yeah, we help countries… countries and their people."

"What countries?" asked Buck gently.

Again, Big Jim was a little taken aback. Believing the best offense was a good defense, he pressed on like a Boeing C-17 transport, dropping flares on takeoff to confuse any heat-seeking missiles in the area.

"Well, for starters, their lovely country. Iraq," he said. "I was there in the first Gulf War. Operation 'Let's Kick that Crazy Fucker's Ass.' And why am I telling you this? Shit, you're just a cowardly, draft dodging… whatever."

Buck kept his cool, having heard of Big Jim's temperamental mood swings, especially when he had been drinking. "How did we fair from that invasion? How did it benefit the people?" he asked.

"Well, it helped Kuwait. And it put Saddam on notice."

"And what about the second time? How did that help us?"

"Well, that one was 'We got rid of the crazy fucker that was running your shithole country.'"

"And that was it? What was the objective of the operation?"

"Find WMDs," said Little Jimmie.

"Did you find any?" asked Farhan.

"Not sure," LJ said, his tone mendacious.

"No, you did not," said Buck, shaking his head. "But we left many dead and years of war. We accomplished nothing good. Nothing."

"Quit saying we," said Big Jim. "You're Canadian."

"Lots of Canadians and Brits died, too," said Buck.

"Australians, too," Cody added supportively.

"Yeah, that's another thing this country does. Make it sound like our adventures are just ours. That nobody else suffers for *our freedoms*. I'm mostly Canadian now, but I've served my country, my original country, America, over the years and at a personal sacrifice," Buck said emphatically.

"Oh, now you're a great patriot because you bring people into the country?" scoffed BJ.

"Dad," offered Cody calmly. "Dad. We're just talking."

Big Jim looked at his youngest son with seething contempt. In private, his reflexive response would be his standard bollocking M.O. to regain control of the narrative. But there was an audience, so he simply shook his head in disgust. Nobody else said a word. Big Jim's stare panned to the three tourists, who remained silent. BJ's face broadcast total anger while the three tourists remained stoic.

Big Jim offered his two most common invective calumnies for his youngest son. "Our youngest daughter," he said, gesturing an open hand toward Cody while his eyes panned those around. "Still not sure who the father of this one is."

Grace hung her head, eyes closed. LJ looked down, eyes open, a faint smile on his face. Marie gasped a little but remained silent. The three tourists' faces showed confusion, unsure of Big Jim's point, while Buck's face extolled immediate, restrained amazement at the odious comments.

"You know what I like most about this country?" said Balil, his voice soothingly genuine. "What I most look forward to?"

Big Jim's leer said skepticism, but his voice suggested a possible respite. "What?"

"Freedom of speech, Mr. Jim. I know I can speak my mind here without fear of penalty. Even when some do not like hearing what I'm saying," said Balil, sounding sincere and respectful. "We didn't have that privilege in Iraq, my friend. I'm looking forward to enjoying the First Amendment and its many benefits."

Too drunk at this point to think clearly, Big Jim was not certain of the meaning and intent of Balil's comment. Finally, Big Jim's body rigidity deflated noticeably, and he said, "Well, thank you for that. Y'all seemed a bit negative." He laughed a little. "I can't speak for our leaders, who I believe are generally good, but I know the U.S. soldiers were trying to help. I'm not sure what else we could have done."

Taking Jim's comment seriously, Odian offered a waggish riposte. "You could have given five thousand doctors."

"What?" said Jim, sounding confused.

"And ten thousand more teachers, Mr. Jim. Those would have helped." Farhan said with a broad smile. "Maybe some engineers, a couple thousand more perhaps. Roads and bridges like the ones you have throughout your country are nice to have, you know. Oh, yes, and some nurses and hospitals to go with those doctors. Fresh water and electricity. They're all not as plentiful as before."

"Maybe some venture capital to help with some new businesses, you know," added Balil, his voice playful. "It's not like everyone wants to grow opium, my friend. Sorry. Mr. Jim. It's very hard work, and compared to the prices I've been told that you get for drugs in America, well, I can tell you that not much trickles down into our economy."

Big Jim slumped forward, putting his hand to his forehead and looking defeated. He looked up, smiled, and said, "Okay, give it to me. Don't hold back, fellas."

"I thought education was one of the important accomplishments in Afghanistan," said Cody, cautiously, the initial chagrin of his father's comment about him still stinging but beginning to fade, his father having done it at least a dozen times over the last six or so years, when introducing Cody to strangers and always when drunk. "There are more doctors and engineers. Isn't that right.?" Balil started to respond, but Cody continued before he could cut in. "Women and girls have been major recipients. There's been construction, entrepreneurship, jobs… isn't that right?"

"That's partially true, Mr. Cody," said Odion enthusiastically, glad at having a real conversation. "But at what cost and to what ends? Many Americans have died and many, many more wounded." Big Jim moved his head slowly up and down, eyes closed, as if considering every word being spoken. "Kabul faired the best. But the rural areas did not do as well, I believe." He looked to his friends for confirmation. Both shared slight nods. "Your country has been there almost twenty years, and no real industries, such as mining, have emerged. Unfortunately, your presence there does not seem sustainable across the country. Too much of the wealth goes to dishonest rulers, corrupt politicians, and warlords."

"That's because your rulers are fucked," said Big Jim. "Right?" Not our fault."

"Put in by your American government," Balil quickly added. "Russia and America both do that when they invade. People want to choose their own leaders."

"That makes sense. I can understand that. We value our elections," said Grace.

"You have an interesting system, though," said Balil. "The one with the most votes doesn't always win. Your minority party seems to have rules that help keep it in power even when it is clearly not the most popular choice. Yet you still say you are a democracy."

"Let's don't go there, folks," Buck chimed in suddenly. "The night's not long enough. This has been great, though," he said, standing. "Thank you so much. But I've got to make a call and then get to bed. These three, too. They'll most likely have to do some walking tomorrow." Buck's three tourists looked up at him expectantly. "I'm hoping you three get to journey on tomorrow, boys," he said to them directly, "so let's get to bed."

With that, Buck's three followers stood and began the process of thanking the family for dinner before following Buck, with a flashlight in hand, up the trail back to their camp. As soon as the four were out of earshot, the family began a muffled review of their company.

"Man," said LJ, "those are three weird dudes."

"I don't know," Marie said, "they're okay. Interesting perspectives. Just different."

"Interesting?" said her father. "I think they're dangerous. Why are they here, anyway?"

"They're businessmen coming here to relocate," said Cody. "Buck said they helped us in Iraq. Why else would they be let in?"

"I don't think that's the case," said Big Jim. "They sound like they hate America."

"They just have different cultures," Cody said. "Like Marie said, different perspectives. Balil said he traveled all over the country to find villages where he could buy rugs. He probably knows lots of valuable information about helping the military."

"What about the other two?" said Big Jim, not convinced.

"Well, Farhan is his lifelong friend. They work together now," said Marie. "I don't know about the other guy. Probably from a poor country, Nigeria, wasn't it, who went to Iraq to get work or something."

"Well, they definitely weren't very respectful," said Grace. "And that one with the yellowish eyes. Bazil?" she said questioningly. "He looks like the devil. Sounds like one, too."

"His name is Balil, mom, not Bazil," said Cody.

"I don't care," said his mother. "He's creepy. And their names are all fucked up. They might as well just change them to American names. They'll get along better here that way."

"Whoa, Mom," Marie said, smiling, impressed with her mom's sudden panache.

"They do speak American pretty good," said LJ nonchalantly.

"English," said Cody.

"What?" said LJ.

"English. The language is English."

"Whatever," LJ replied.

"Well, I thought they were fine. And Farhan was *very* nice," said Marie a little defiantly. The rest of the family stared at her with various facial expressions, not all of which were entirely positive. "Well, he was," she responded defensively.

"I'm glad if they're leaving tomorrow," said Big Jim. "They seem especially suspicious. I don't know what Buck is up to with these three, but they're not the profile of the typical characters he brings in, as I understand it. They don't seem to have any constructive interest in coming here, either. Nobody said they felt lucky or appreciative. Nobody seemed excited."

"That's not true," said Cody. "Balil said he was looking forward to free speech."

"And then they went into more complaints about what's wrong with us. They just seemed argumentative," said Big Jim. He paused a moment, then glanced back and forth between Marie and Cody. "And

I don't want to hear any more shit from either of you two about their perspectives."

"Amen," added Grace, standing and picking at various items left on the ground to throw into the fire.

"We should be up by daylight. Time to hit the hay," said BJ and the family began moving to get ready for bed.

***

When the four returned to camp, Buck began briefing the three about what to expect over the next couple of days.

"Hope you all enjoyed dinner," he began. The three all nodded passively. "Nice family."

"What about tomorrow, Mr. Buck?" asked Odion.

"So, my aide should arrive around 10:30 or 11:00. You'll need to be ready to go by the time he shows up. We'll want to get up early, say 7:30, eat breakfast, and break down our camp."

"Break down camp?" said Odion, confused.

"Yeah, eat, get packed up, clean up our site here, and be ready to go. If we can get out absolutely no later than noon, you'll be able to get to the trailhead sometime in daylight the following day. You all will be in Seattle later that night or early the following morning. How's that sound."

"Good," they all mumbled in unison.

"In the morning, I'll walk down the trail to meet the man to guide you out. That's how we do it. He'll want to know everything is okay and who's here before he comes in. It's best to keep his identity secret from the locals. I'm going to walk up the trail now, just a bit and call him just to make sure everything is okay. If there's an issue, I'll let you know. Okay? Questions?" They all remained silent. "Good. Now, get to bed.

They all wagged their heads, and Buck headed up the trail. As soon as he was gone, the three huddled into a muted conversation in Arabic.

"So, we leave tomorrow," said Balil.

"And we kill the family, correct?" asked Farhan.

"Yes."

"Good," Farhan replied. "They're all ignorant infidels. The young girl is a whore. I swear, if she had touched me one more time, I would have had to either take a bath immediately or cut off my arm and leg."

Balil and Odion both chuckled. "And the mother, praise Ala, listen to our names, madam," said Balil. Another muffled laugh from the other two.

"Good lamb roast, though," said Odion, to which the others nodded their heads in agreement. "If the family leaves first, can they be spared?"

This was a decision Balil might otherwise have put to a vote for ethical deliberation, but not this time. "No," he said. "They must all die, including Mr. Buck and his aide. No witnesses. Those are our orders. We must wait until his aide arrives."

"We're not going to let him lead us out?" asked Farhan.

"No. Our directives say to kill him, Mr. Buck, and any other witnesses that might be in the camp at the time."

"How do we find our way out, then?" Farhan said.

"We are on the main trail. It should remain dominant. There will be trail signs along the way to keep us oriented. And we have a map. The mountains run north and south. Follow the mountain ridges. It's just a matter of continuing south until we get to the highway. With their horses, we may get there by dark tomorrow. A car should be there that matches a set of keys, either the family's or the aide's. The boy said the family parked there as well and rode horses in. We will take all keys, find a car they match, and then drive to Seattle."

"We will have to kill them all at once," said Farhan. "How do we do that? They will all need to be together. We have no guns."

"That's true," said Balil. "I've been thinking about that. Mr. Jim wears a revolver sometimes. I believe he will have it on in the morning. Both boys also have guns. We can visit them in the morning before the guide arrives, take their guns, hold them until the guide arrives with Mr. Buck, and then kill them all. We can finalize a plan in the morning when we see where everyone is."

"I'm sorry, but I wish there were another way we could avoid killing this family," said Odion remorsefully.

"Do you think Big Jim would hesitate to kill your family if ordered to do so?" asked Farhan.

"Probably not. But doesn't our prophet Mohammed, peace upon him, tell us to treat others as we *want* to be treated?"

"No. That's bullshit Christians tell themselves to do and then ignore. And this is not a time for a religious discussion," Balil said. "It is done. Let's get to bed."

***

Day 3:

End of the Line Campground

Cody got up early and gathered his fishing gear. Later, his father would almost certainly ask where he had been and why, and his intended cover story was that he just wanted to catch some fish for breakfast. BJ and LJ would likely be headed to fish by themselves, regardless. Cody assumed his father would say the ones he caught were too small. He could care less about his father's opinion of the fish. But he did not want to rehash their dinner from the night before with Buck's tourists. Though they seemed a bit suspicious and extremely negative about the United States, that did not bother him. The discussions themselves were interesting and insightful, if one was interested, to begin with. His family, well, not Marie so much, seemed ensconced in their same old ethnocentric silos. The tourists offered an alternative reality, that of the residents of countries that find themselves occupied by a foreign power. Wouldn't they have different views on our presence and our behaviors in their country than us? Still, their seeming inability to identify at least some positive aspects of his country bothered him. Why were they coming here if they found it so negative?

To get to the upper trail that wrapped around the north side of the lake, Cody had to pass the camp of the three tourists. A fire was burning, and Balil, dropping sticks into the flame, was standing alone, appearing to be trying to heat some water.

205

"Good morning," Cody yelled out.

Balil looked up, waved slightly, and smiled. "Good morning, Cody. Come join me for a coffee?"

"Sure," he said and veered toward the offer. "Where's Odion and Farhan?"

"They're gathering firewood. We're a little colder than we planned for," said Balil.

"Yeah, the mornings are nippy. Should be the high fifties, maybe even low sixties, by noon or soon thereafter, I think."

"I hope so. We begin walking out today. It would be nice if it were warm."

"Where's Buck?"

"Oh, he walked down to meet our guide. So he knows all is well, and it is safe to come into camp."

"Makes sense."

"Are you off to fish?"

"Yeah, I thought I would catch lunch. I'm sure mom is worried now about having enough food for the rest of the trip. Fish is always a good substitute."

"Ah, we caused problems?"

"No, no. It was fun. Just trying to help mom worry a little less."

"Come sit, Cody." Cody moved to one of the large, empty logs near the first and sat. Balil had made a full pot, poured Cody a cup, and handed it to him.

Cody sat down and took the cup. "Where are you all headed today?" he asked.

"It's my understanding that when the guide arrives, we will head to the Highway 20 trailhead. We will camp tonight and then go on tomorrow. After we get there, we will be taken to Seattle and delivered to our respective new homes."

"Cool, cool," Cody said. "Are you looking forward to it?"

"Oh yes," said Balil. "Why wouldn't we?"

"Well, actually, you all didn't seem too positive on America."

"Oh, really? No, we are all very excited. Very excited." Balil paused, knowing he had to choose his words carefully. "I think you may have mistakenly missed the catalysts behind our comments, that being our excitement for being able to speak out on our opinions in a safe environment." Cody watched him, his face serious. "The wonderful thing about your country," he said, then corrected to "our country, is that we can identify both the good and the bad policies of a government. Freedom. Free speech. We simply hope our advice can help your country craft better, more responsive, successful international political policies going forward."

Balil's voice was casual and matter-of-fact. Cody considered his words and deemed them honest. "That makes sense," he said. He took a sip and said, "This coffee is amazing. Did you know that? Where'd you get it?"

"It's my uncle's favorite?"

"Where's is he?"

"He's in Vancouver. We got to spend a couple of days there before Mr. Buck picked us up and brought us here."

"It's wonderful."

"Well, after breakfast, I'll walk over to where you are fishing to make sure you get another cup before we leave and give you its name and his address so you can ask him to send you some. Tell him you met me, and I told you to do so. He will honor that."

"Thank you," Cody said sincerely. "I will. Not sure when I'll get to Vancouver next time, but if I do, I'll go see him."

Just then, Odion and Farhan returned, each carrying a load of firewood in their arms.

"Good morning, Mr. Cody," they both said in unison.

"Morning, guys. That'll last you awhile."

The two sat their loads down, and Farhan threw two of his pieces on the fire. "Yes, it's very cold," he said, rubbing his hands together. "But it is a nice day, so I hope it's warm."

"Should be," said Cody. "You two ready to leave?"

"Yes," replied Farhan. "As soon as the guide arrives. It's beautiful here, but I'm looking forward to a bed."

"Well, I'm going to do a little fishing. Not sure when you're leaving exactly, but if I don't make it back before you leave, nice to meet you and good luck," he said, stood, and shook the hands of all three, all three responding with similar farewells and best wishes.

When Cody was out of earshot, Balil turned to the others and said, "It's eight o'clock. If he is still out there in two hours, I will go there first and kill him first."

***

Cody had been fishing for about an hour. He watched as his family got up and seemingly ate breakfast. BJ and LJ had led all the horses to the edge of the lake to allow them to drink, then had moved them to an area with more grass but still near the camp. As Forest Service horses, the six animals were familiar with people generally and the routine of riding into wilderness areas, camping, grazing, and then going home. The animals found comfort in the presence of one another, and though they were tied up at night, they commonly roamed untethered during the day to graze. They were workhorses, always approachable. And, when the people were ready to go to work, so were they.

At about 9:15, Cody noted that Marie was walking in his direction, having taken the southern trail. He was at the far side of the two hundred yards long lake. About ten minutes later, when she arrived, he realized she was carrying his rifle and scabbard on her back.

"Fish biting?" she asked gleefully.

Cody loved his sister's energy, her mettle key to her weathering growing up in their family, a sharp contrast to their feckless brother.

"Got a few," he said, motioning his head to his right toward a V-shaped stick, one side of which was threaded through the gills of six small rainbow trout. "What's with the gun?" he said.

209

"Dad said to shoot a small deer if you see one," she said as she leaned the scabbard up against the back of the log on which Cody was sitting. "Mom is worried about running out of meat. The roast was supposed to last a couple of days."

"Why doesn't he or LJ?"

"I think Dad wants to move camp tomorrow. He and LJ are taking a little ride to scout the Canadian side. He said the scenery is better and that there's a couple of lakes that don't get a lot of traffic, the fishing is better, and the fish are bigger. He wants to find a good camp spot, but he doesn't want to take a chance to shoot anything in there, if it is avoidable."

"He probably doesn't want another Penny episode," Cody scoffed, referencing the horse his father had lost the year before while hunting. BJ's story was that he had laid his rifle across the saddle to take a shot at an elk, and the horse, spooked by the noise, ran off. Cody suspected his father was beating the animal again for 'who knows what.' Either way, the animal trotted off and was never seen again. "Not many rangers would go into Canada like that."

"He says 'fuck it,' that Buck does it here. Plus, nobody's around. He's waiting for Buck to get back, to get some guidance… and make sure his tourists are gone."

"Did he say anything about the company last night?" asked Cody, hoping for signs Marie did not share a concern for their perfidy.

"Oh, he's convinced they're up to no good. That Mr. Carpenter has gone to the dark side."

"Really. What do you think?"

"I think they're okay," she said cautiously. "They were a little assertive in their positions. But I've traveled a lot. America has really lost some of its credibility the last couple of years, and people are just more comfortable and confident about speaking their minds about things they're not happy that America is doing around the world."

"Hmm. You liked Farhan?"

"Yeah. He's cute. Balil was cute, but I'm with Mom. His eyes creeped me out. Too intense."

Just then, the pole began signaling a fish was biting. "You want this one?" asked Cody.

Marie did not answer. Instead, she picked up the pole and waited for the tip to dip before flipping it up. The attempt was successful. She hooked a fish that immediately began jumping to shake the hook from its mouth. Two minutes later, she had hauled in a nice, twelve-inch rainbow.

"Nice one," said Cody as he netted the catch.

"Mom wants these for lunch. Maybe dinner, so I'm taking them back," she said. You gonna be long?"

"I'll stay another half hour or so. See if a couple of deer come in for a drink. I can probably get a small one."

"Okay," said Marie, and she began walking back on the northern trail.

***

211

As Marie got to the tourists' campground, she saw the three men had constellated near the fire and made her way toward them to say hello.

"Hi," she said, waving. "How are you all today?" Only Odion smiled and returned the greeting. Farhan and Balil stood silent, stoic. Undaunted, she continued to the edge of the campsite. She stopped there and said, "It was wonderful meeting all of you last night."

With that, the other two smiled but still said nothing while Odion added, "It was very nice meeting you and your family as well, Miss Marie. That was most enjoyable."

"Thank you. Are you all leaving soon?"

"We hope so," said Balil.

In the meantime, Big Jim noticed that Marie was just up the trail talking to the tourists. He shook his head and said, "Why the fuck is she talking to those assholes. Come on, LJ, let's go see what's up there. Get your horse."

The men saddled two of the horses while Marie and Cody were talking and waiting for Grace to finish making lunch so they could take on their ride to locate a nearby campsite on the Canadian side. Grabbing the reins of their horses, they began leading the horses up the trail.

Seeing the two coming, Balil instinctively began coxing Marie to come closer. "Come," he said, smiling and pointing to a spot on the log next to Farhan. "Please sit over here and try this coffee. Your brother loved it."

Marie walked over next to the log, sat beside Farhan, and took the cup of coffee Balil poured for her. After blowing some and taking a sip, she said, "Mmmm. This *is* good."

Expecting that Big Jim would move closer when invited, Balil moved toward the trail several feet on the fire's south side. The log where Farhan sat next to Marie was to the west, and Odion had been standing near the tents, which were to the north and opposite Balil's position. If one or both men moved much toward the fire, they would automatically be largely flanked.

When Big Jim arrived, he stopped and handed his horse's reins to LJ, walking toward the fire and into the semicircle of men. He stopped directly between Odion and Balil. "Morning, gentlemen," he said, his tone formal.

Farhan and Odion each smiled and mumbled an appropriate greeting, but Balil took a slight step forward and said, "Hello, Mr. Jim."

"You folks leaving soon?" Big Jim asked.

"Yes, we are, sir. We expect Mr. Carpenter back at any moment with the guide, and when they arrive, we intend to leave immediately."

BJ pondered that for a moment and then said, "Where did you say you folks are headed?"

"Seattle."

"And the guide is taking you?"

"Yes, sir."

Big Jim looked at the tourists' three packs they had carried in that sat neatly on the ground in front of one of the tents. "What's in the packs?"

"Supplies for our trip," said Balil.

"Not taking the tents?"

"No, Mr. Buck is taking those back with him. I'm assuming our guide has a tent for us."

Big Jim began to sidle the few feet to packs, which sat to Odion's left, just slightly behind him, all the while panning his view of the three tourists. He grabbed one of the packs and tugged it up slightly. "Whoa," he exclaimed. "Heavy." He tugged up on another and said the same. "Feels like they're about the same. Mind if I look inside?" he asked.

"Yes, sir, we do," said Balil politely.

"Well, I am a Forest Ranger. An employee of the Federal Government. He patted the Glock semiautomatic pistol on his side, and I'm sorry, but I have the authority to search these, buddy."

Balil glanced casually at Farhan and Odion, looked back at Big Jim, and said, "Pardon me, my friend. Please help yourself." Balil glanced again at Farhan. As if cued, Farhan casually stood, moved behind Marie, took out his knife from his belt behind him and squatted behind her. He had put his left hand on her shoulder, and as he crouched, he quietly hissed, "Shhhhhh," putting the point of the knife against her neck. Big Jim and LJ's attention was both focused on BJ's inspection of the packs. He lifted and held the pack's flap in his right hand as he began to move items near the top with his left. But Marie's whimper made him glance in her direction.

When he saw the knife, Big Jim stood and yelled at Farhan, "What the… Leave her alone!" He yelled it loud enough that Grace heard it, and she quickly began walking toward the tourists' campsite.

LJ began reaching for his pistol, but Balil halted him with, "Easy, son."

Grace had covered about half of the one hundred feet to the campsite when she saw Marie and the knife, now to her throat. "Stop," she implored. "Don't hurt her. Please."

Big Jim's hand began slowly moving toward his firearm, and Odion reached out, touched his arm, and kindly requested, "Please don't do that, sir." Big Jim eased his motion but held his hand at the ready a few inches from the handle of the pistol. "I'm going to take the gun, sir," said Odion. "You'll be fine. Please stop." Odion reached down, eased the pistol from the holster, and took two steps away from BJ.

Grace had arrived at the campsite and stood next to LJ. "Oh my god. Oh my god," she cried. "Please don't hurt us. Please."

Balil walked over to Odion and took BJ's gun, as Odion moved to retrieve Little Jimmy's. Balil inspected it conspicuously, turning it left and right, pulling back on the slide slightly to check if the chamber held a live shell; it did. He turned to view the left side of the gun again and flicked off the safety.

"What are you doing in our country?" said Big Jim defiantly.

"What are you doing in mine?" Balil replied sharply.

"Don't hurt us. Please," Grace repeated. "We didn't do anything to you."

"We didn't do anything to you… or your family," Big Jim said, his voice beginning to stammer a little.

"Somebody did," Balil said.

"It's not our fault," said Big Jim.

"Then whose fault is it, my friend?" said Balil with no compassion in his voice. Big Jim remained silent.

"You're here to seek revenge. Right? You're not immigrants; you're terrorists," said Big Jim solemnly.

"We're soldiers, freedom fighters, my friend. Like you," Balil said mockingly. "We're just on different sides, my friend."

"Bullshit. You're a terrorist, a fucking animal. A fucking coward who kills innocent people. This is our home, and you don't belong here. And I'm not your friend, buddy."

"You are correct, sir. We should not be in your country. And you do not belong in ours. It is very simple. Just think of us as Navy Seals." He paused. "Just not from your navy." Big Jim just stared, tense, like a cat about to lurch. "You know what I think, Mr. Jim?" queried Balil patiently.

"What's that?" Big Jim said defiantly.

Balil hesitated momentarily, weighing the gravity of what he was about to say. He knew he had to immediately de-escalate this confrontation for just a little longer until Carpenter got back or figured out how to kill them all without firing a gun. "Mr. Jim, you have made it very clear that you are not my friend, and I am certain I am not your buddy. But I am sorry, you have demonstrated an extreme ignorance…"

Before Balil could finish, Big Jim cut in, his temerity clearly beginning to get the best of him. His posture stiffened, his shoulders went back, and he took a half step forward and growled, "Now wait just a minute, you fucking rag-headed motherfucker…"

But Balil cut him off as he stuck out his arm in the manner of a traffic monitor in a cross-section directing traffic to halt. "*Mr. Jim, stop right there!*" Balil said firmly, raising the pistol he was holding to a more ominous position.

Big Jim stopped. Defiant, he said, "Nobody, especially a shithole foreigner in my own country, calls me stupid."

"I did not call you stupid, Mr. Jim. I called you ignorant," Balil said, sounding annoyed.

"Like there's a difference," replied Big Jim contemptuously

It was too late for Balil to retain his attempt at reason or restrain his own contempt. He stared at Jim Dickson, appalled at himself for even trying to reason with yet another American who only viewed the world through their own narrow lens. "Mr. Jim, your lack of knowledge of my country, its culture, and the damage your country has done to it, and even to me personally, demonstrates your ignorance. Not knowing the difference in meaning between the two words in your own language demonstrates your stupidity, which I am certain, my friend, transcends all international borders."

That did it. "I'm not your fucking friend," Big Jim yelled as he rushed forward. Balil raised the pistol enough to shoot Big Jim squarely in the center of his forehead. Looking to his right, Balil saw Grace, who was now screaming in horror, waiting to see if there was any life in her husband's body. There was not.

LJ immediately pissed himself. "You motherfucker," he muttered, dropping the reins of the two horses. Balil swept the barrel toward Little Jimmie and shot once. The bullet caught the boy just below his lower lip at a slight upward angle, exiting near the juxtaposition of his skull and spine, hitting the high end of the saddle's seat of one of the horses behind him after painting a red line across the saddle that led to its exit. LJ's eyeballs rolled up, and he fell to his knees and slumped dead, his head next to his father's shoes. Grace never even heard the second crack of the Glock. Instead, she only felt the sting of pieces of her son's skull that splattered across the right side of her face. Brains clouded her right eye, and she wiped it reflexively. Her husband and son lay in front of her, their faces buried in the ground. This time, Grace did not scream but fainted on the ground.

Big Jim's horse jumped sideways from the simultaneous jolt of the bullet hitting the saddle and the noise of the gunshot and began trotting up the trail. The other horse backed several feet away from the commotion, turned south and started to walk away like a bystander at the edge of a brawl who had just assessed the brouhaha and was getting just a little too close to them for comfort. The remaining four animals, sensing danger, commenced trotting south down the trail for a hundred yards or so before morphing into a zealous walk toward home.

Balil stood in front of Marie, raised his gun and pointed it at her forehead. But Odion grabbed the muzzle suddenly and pushed the barrel toward the ground, shaking his head from side to side.

"What?" asked Balil.

"That's enough, Balil," Odion said calmly, going to Marie's side and facing him. "We don't have to kill them all. We can tie them up.

They're a family. Mr. Jim is… was right. They've done nothing to us."

"It is our directive," Balil responded calmly. "There cannot be any witnesses. None."

Suddenly, Marie yelled, "Cody, run. Run!" and Cody saw the simultaneous realization of the three's awareness that he was still alive as all turned in unison and looked across the lake in his direction.

Farhan glared at Odion. "They're pigs," he yelled. "American pigs. They care about nothing but themselves, and this bitch is a fucking whore."

Grabbing a handful of Marie's hair, he yanked her head back, stabbed his knife into the side of her neck to the handle and then forced the entire blade out the front. Half of her neck had been sliced in two. She fell to the ground, dead in seconds. Balil then walked over to Grace, still passed out, and shot her in the back of the head.

"The boy," said Farhan, pointing. "He is on the other side of the lake. What should we do?"

"Leave him, go," said Odion. "Let us get the horses and get out of here."

"There are three of us and six animals," said Farhan, annoyed. "He can ride out."

"Then kill the other three," said Odion. "Better and easier to kill them than him."

There was something about Cody that had appealed to Balil on a personal level. It was easy to see the angst the boy felt around his father. Big Jim had generally terrorized his family; he had gathered, especially his wife and youngest son. Balil was happy to have killed him. One less tyrant, he had thought. And this was business.

"The trail circles the lake," Balil said. "Each of you, go around one side and see if you can find him. If you find him, kill him. Be back in thirty minutes, regardless. We must leave immediately. Two horses are already saddled."

"But one has run up the trail," said Farhan. "And the others have run down the trail."

"I'll see if I can get the one that ran up first. Then we can all go look for the other four. They're going in the same direction that we are. Hopefully, they will stick together."

***

From afar, Cody had been watching what he could view of the group, largely obscured by LJ and the two horses he was holding. He had heard a couple of voices, but from a distance, what he could see and hear, the people appeared to be talking amicably. Suddenly, there were screams and gunshots. When the horses bolted, he got an unimpeded view of the campsite. His father, mother, and brother all lay on the ground. The three terrorists began yelling at one another, and instinctively, he jumped behind the dead, downed tree from which he had been fishing and against which his rifle lay.

Quickly collecting himself, he rolled onto his stomach and peeked toward the camp between a space between two of the dead trees. Completely out of sight, he watched as the three men, about one hundred and fifty to two hundred yards away, began assessing their own situation, arguing to some extent, it seemed by their voices, about what to do next. Odion seemed somewhat at odds with the other two, but he could not say what, as they were yelling in Arabic. Farhan was holding Marie by the hair, and then he abruptly cut her throat. Then, an instant later, Balil walked to where his mother was lying and shot her in the back of the head. Numb, Cody struggled to process what had just happened. It was surreal; his family, all of them, were dead.

None of the men, he hoped, had seen Marie leave earlier in the morning to the opposite side of the lake where Cody had been fishing. If so, none saw the scabbard holding his rifle strapped to her back. When she got there and told him his father had wanted him to shoot a deer, he removed the rifle and leaned the 243 Browning against the pile of fallen trees he was now hiding behind. He reached over and grabbed the rifle, pulling it toward him. Certain they had not seen his movements, he pulled it toward him while watching the three to see their next move. He had stuck one magazine into the rifle before leaving camp, giving him just five rounds of ammunition.

The rifle had open sites, which included a round bead sitting atop a short post at the front of the barrels and a blade of metal towards the back, sitting horizontally on the barrel with a small V cut into the middle. When aimed properly, the bead at the front would visually sit in this nook as the shooter pointed the barrel at the target. Cody was especially accurate with this sight inside of a hundred and fifty yards or so. As a target moved further away, however, the smaller it would appear to the naked eye, the more the site itself covered the target rather than a particular area of it when the target was nearer. That was the value of a scope, i.e., bringing the detail of a viewed object seemingly much closer and in focus, while the crosshairs could define the exact spot the shooter would hit with nuanced gun movements. With open sites at long distances, such adjustments were far more difficult to gauge and at greater distances, all but impossible.

Cody moved the lever of the 243 and chambered a round. Then, staying on his stomach, out of site, he stuck the rifle between the opening of two logs, pulled the butt of the stock tight to his shoulder, and laid the combined sites onto Odion's back. Knowing that at two hundred yards, a 243 bullet would fall about 3.5 inches before impact, he sat the front bead between Odion's shoulders at the bottom of his neck, took a deep breath, and held it. All of a sudden, both Odion and Farhan moved, each walking in opposite directions. Cody realized they were coming toward him. Suddenly, Odion stopped, turned back toward Balil, and began yelling something in Arabic.

As they spoke, Cody drew down again on Odion, who was till the most visible, the other two slightly obscured by trees.

"This is a waste of time," Odion said, his tone somewhat seditious.

"Just go," Balil said angrily.

Cody quickly re-aimed and shot. Although he had aimed at the top middle of Odion's back, his shot was slightly rushed, and the shot pulled slightly to his left, which was a fortunate mistake for Cody and an unfortunate one for Odion. Balil had just finished speaking when the area just below Odion's heart exploded toward him. Killed instantly, his body fell onto Grace's.

"Go get him," Balil commanded, now with concern. "I'll get the horses."

Because the lake's southern trail went through a continuous stand of lodgepole pine, it provided much more cover than the northern trail. But Farhan would have had to cross an exposed open area where Odion had just been killed, leaving him exposed for at least thirty yards. Cody had just shot his comrade from almost two hundred yards, so he opted for the much closer northern trail, which provided good cover for at least the next fifty yards.

***

Balil began to work his way south from one tree to another toward the saddled horse that LJ had intended to ride. Balil had grabbed LJ's pistol just after shooting Grace and tossed it to Farhan after Odion was shot. After picking up the pistol, another Glock, Farhan made his way stealthily to the first clearing of vulnerability. Cody would have just a few seconds as Farhan covered the thirty feet of clearing to get to the next clump of trees, to get a shot off. He would have to lead him perfectly, shooting to where the prey was running, a difficult task with a scope. Cody aimed about three feet to his left of the tree to where Farhan would be running, looking for a motion to the left of where he had his sight focused. He estimated he had to lead him by about three or four feet. But which? There was no room for error. Farhan actually tripped as he left the cover before getting up and sprinting toward the next mass of trees.

Had Farhan not tripped, Cody might have hit him, but he reflexively moved his rifle back toward a fallen Farhan, but by the time he readjusted, Farhan was sprinting forward again. As soon as Cody pulled the trigger, he guessed he had missed. He was right. As was the case with Odion, he pulled slightly left. This time, however, that was enough to miss, his shot falling just behind his target. It was close enough, though, for Farhan to hear the bullet hiss past his head before the noise of the shot itself. The next clearing, which was forty-five feet across, was about another sixty feet away. Had Farhan known the area a little better, his best bet would have been to keep running as fast as he could from where he was until he reached and ran through the next clearing, not giving time for the shooter to

223

prepare physically or mentally. But he dove to his stomach ten or so feet into the stand of trees, caught his breath, and thanked Allah several times to be alive.

Farhan would be a little less than halfway to the end of the lake after crossing the next clear. As a target, he knew he was getting larger. Easier to see and easier to shoot. He sat on the edge of the clearing, pumping himself up to make the leap. Cody took another deep breath, trying to calm himself down. He was not shaking terribly, but it affected his ability to hold the rifle steady. Cody aligned the barrel to a place two-thirds of the way through the clearing, the bead sitting neatly in the V of the rear blade, and waited, waited for Farhan to run into the bullet he was about to deliver. He continued three deep breaths. 'When Farhan gets to that place,' Cody thought, 'I will pull the trigger. This time, Farhan gave three blood-curdling screams to distract Cody, and just after starting the third, he started running. His distraction worked. The scream deflected Cody's focus just long enough to momentarily divert his attention away from holding his aim steady. When Cody pulled the trigger, he was a little late again, and the bullet went just behind Farhan. Three shots remaining.

Again, Farhan threw himself to the ground, thanking Allah. He was about seventy percent of the way through the trail, another sixty yards and another hundred feet. There were only two more clearings. Cody was at the far edge of the second. His only cover would be about a dozen trees that separated the next clearing from where Cody was hiding at the far end of the second clearing. If he could get to the absolute edge of that group of trees, he would still have a challenging shot at that distance, maybe sixty to eighty feet, with a pistol. He checked the magazine in his Glock. He surmised it was close to full, somewhere between ten and the max, fifteen.

Farhan was getting dangerously close, and Cody knew he would have to hit him soon. Cody decided to hold his fire until Farhan ran to the next group of trees. At that point, he would be much closer and more head-on as a target, needing to face Cody directly. Cody had, then, to align himself about ninety degrees to where he had been aiming, and his cover now was a standing tree he was hiding behind, though he was still prone. Staying as calm as possible, he waited. Farhan screamed again before he ran, running shortly after he began his wail. As soon as Farhan got to the small stand of trees, he commenced shuffling from tree to tree to get as close to the edge of the clearing as possible and the shortest shot available at Cody. The last tree was just big enough to hide behind, and shortly after getting there, he poked his head out just enough to see where Cody was. On spotting him, he collected himself before leaning his head and half his torso out and firing two quick shots.

Cody had anticipated Farhan's ploy and was aiming toward the left edge of the tree. Cody had never been shot at before, and at least one of Farhan's shots hit the tree he was hiding behind. He reflexively flinched, but as Farhan was turning his body back in for cover, Cody fired. It barely caught the edge of the tree and sprayed wood shrapnel into Farhan's barely hidden face.

"You are dead, boy," yelled Farhan.

"You killed my family, you fucker," Cody screamed back.

"Yes, I did. And I enjoyed it. Especially cutting that bitch, whore of a sister's throat."

With that, Farhan spun out, almost completely exposed, and fired three quick shots in Cody's direction. Cody, unfazed by the burst of bullets, held his aim steady, pulled the trigger, and hit Farhan about three inches in from the edge of his waste. Farhan twirled back behind the tree and yelped in pain.

"Aaahhhh. Fuck you, you little bastard. I will kill you," Farhan yelled, stepped out fully exposed, and charged, firing about every other step. Clearly wounded, it was more of a labored hurried walk than a full running charge.

Cody immediately cocked the rifle to chamber a shell, aimed directly at Farhan's breastbone and pulled the trigger. Farhan, who was fully expecting to die, heard the click, slowed for one second, and then picked up his disabled pace and began yelling again. Believing Cody was out of ammunition, he stopped firing, intending to empty what remained in the magazine into the boy's body. Cody was in disbelief as he gazed at the empty chamber. Had he counted wrong? There should have been five shells. His mind raced, and as he looked up at his new nemesis, he realized that he had fired one shell two days earlier during the first day of his family's trip. Big Jim and LJ had decided to do some target practice with their Glocks and had chided Cody into taking a shot at a crow in a tree about one hundred yards away. "I'll bet you five dollars you can't hit it," his brother had said. Not wanting to kill the bird, Cody said he would shoot the branch it was standing on instead. LJ agreed, and Cody took the shot, hitting the six-inch Ponderosa Pine branch and happily pocketing the five dollars he insisted his brother pay up.

When Farhan was about twenty feet away, he slowed to a much slower, deliberate pace. He raised the pistol to a far more menacing position and said, "I told you I would kill you, you little…"

Before he could finish his sentence, the right side of his jaw detached from the rest of his head. Cody had never seen anyone shot before, just game animals and varmints, such as gophers, that he, Seth, and Chris occasionally shot for target practice in ranchers' fields for fun. He had given up shooting both types of prey a few years earlier, as he grew to consider killing other animals for fun too cruel. Farhan fell to his knees, perhaps trying to say something but producing just an unsettling, gurgling sound, like what Cody had heard deer make when they were shot in the neck. Farhan's body tilted to what seemed to be the beginning of a slow-motion fall forward when another round hit him in the neck, knocking him to his right and to the ground.

"Get up," someone said. "We have to get out of here."

***

Buck had been waiting for his guide to show at their predetermined meeting place, a fork in the trail about two miles from the End of the Line campground. The Pacific Crest's main trail continued straight to the south, while the other branched a hard right leading to the far northern end of Ross Lake. On their previous phone call, he had told the guide that he had yet to hear from his Arab contact in Vancouver about the copy of the directive he had provided his three tourists at the beginning of their trek. Buck had reached the meeting point early, per his initial estimation of when the aide would show. The tourists expected him back at around eleven. He had left as soon as daylight allowed, and it had taken him about an hour to hike to where he was from the campground. It was eight-thirty. His guide needed to be there no later than nine forty-five if Buck were to have adequate time to brief him and get back to camp on time. About ten minutes after he sat down, his global phone rang.

"Buck here," he said.

"Buck?" the woman on the phone said.

"Yes, it's me."

"Buck, you're alive," she whimpered in happiness. "Oh, my god, Buck. Praise Allah. You're okay."

"Adaj? What's the matter?"

"They're going to kill you. All of you," she said frantically

"What are you talking about? Adaj? Slow down. Take a breath. Who is killing who?"

"Your tourists. They're terrorists. Your government, some agency, or someone else has sent them in. They are supposed to kill everyone in the area, you, your aide, and anyone else who is there at the time, as soon as your aide arrives. They want no witnesses."

"Oh, boy," said Buck, mostly to himself, as he considered the situation for what he feared it was all along. "I knew they were bad news. I just really didn't know what to do. The U.S. government is definitely involved somehow?"

"Yes. Absolutely. Is anyone else there?" she asked.

"Yes," he said solemnly. "A family. Five of them."

"Oh no. Do they have weapons? Do you?"

"I do," he said. Then he realized he did not. "Oh shit, I don't have it with me. They do... the family. Shit, shit, shit, I knew these fellas were up to no good. They're on a mission for certain. They're just waiting for me to get back to them with their guide. Jesus, I hope they haven't already done it."

"Oh, Buck. I'm so sorry. I don't know what to tell you. Help them? Save yourself? Oh my god, this is terrible."

"Hey, Adaj, I'm going to get off the line. I don't think it's safe. Thanks for your help. Talk later," and Buck hit the phone's off button before she had time to answer.

"Holy shit," he said out loud before sitting down to wait. "What a clusterfuck."

At about nine, his contact whistled out from about a hundred feet away. When Buck looked up and saw him, panic exuded from his face. The guide's smile quickly turned to concern.

"What's up, man?" he asked.

"I was right. Those three are trouble. I've got to get back to camp as soon as possible."

"Talk to me."

"Those three are terrorists," said Buck. "Adaj from Vancouver, my friend, just called. I'd sent her a copy of material that had been with their equipment. Did I tell you that?" The guide nodded affirmatively. "It was written in Arabic. Anyway, they're supposed to kill everyone. You, too. The Dicksons are there. Now. I've got to get back."

"Oh shit. I'll go with you."

"No, Bill. Get out of here. You've got to get back to town. Immediately. We'll need help."

"Cops?"

"No. Call me tonight in Penticton. Same number. Call me every thirty minutes beginning at 8:30, say, until you get me. Call until midnight. We'll figure out our next moves. Turn your global off now.

Hide it at the trailhead where you can get it later in case someone is trying to track you."

"You really going to try and make it out? This late?"

"I'm gonna try," Buck said. "You have to make it out, too, kid. You may have to send someone in, especially if there are injured survivors… or any survivors. I'll know more later. Don't do anything, though, until we talk."

"You aren't packing?"

"Actually, no. I forgot. I'm getting too old, I guess."

"Here, take mine. It's a 44 Magnum."

"Very Dirty Harry, man. I like it," said Buck. "Afraid of bears?" Buck mused.

"Exactly. Lighter than a rifle but does the job."

"No," said Buck. "You keep it. I know where Steve's stash is. I think I can get to it without being seen. I'll take the cutoff trail. I just hope there's time."

"Sounds good. Good luck, and be careful."

The two hugged briefly. "I will. Talk later," Buck said and turned and hustled away.

Buck was just over a quarter mile away from the campground when he heard the first gunshots. Those were followed by periodic screams and shouts that made their way down the valley toward him. The fight was on. He began to run as much as his seventy-one-year-old legs and knees would allow, his gate more of a quick hustle than a run. He estimated that he could be there in another ten minutes or so, the trail being reasonably flat and completely clear of any fallen materials all the way to the camp. His primary concern was his visibility; he would be seen for the last hundred fifty yards as he approached the camp from the primary trial. There was a lesser-used trail that forked to the northeast off the main trail a little less about an eighth of a mile from camp. It went through the woods and came out at the far end of the lake. Not warn like the main trail, Buck supposed it had been created by more seasoned hikers who knew from experience and information sharing they could camp there, as an alternative to the regular campground. It also led to the best fishing spots on the lake. The rangers technically frowned upon the trail's use, though the most they could do was to ask groups camping there to move to the main campground. Buck figured that he could view the camp while surreptitiously assessing the situation by going in that direction. But more importantly, he knew that about fifty feet off the east side of the trail, just before it broke out of the trees, was Steve's cache of firearms for that camp.

Just before he turned up the fork in the trail, two horses and a mule hastened into view and scuttled past him. It was just less than a four-minute walk through the woods, and as he approached the lake, the periodic gunshots grew progressively louder and nearer. He heard screams that seemed to come from someone running along the north trail, who periodically came into view. Shots were coming from a place near him at the lake's far end and appeared directed toward the screaming runner. Buck had easily located Steve's gun cache, which was inside a dirt-covered box buried just under the ground immediately left of a noticeably tall lodgepole pine. Buck immediately saw the red string that protruded from the ground and pulled it, which immediately lifted the lid of the metal box just underneath the surface of the soil. Giving the matter no thought, he grabbed a Colt 45 and one extra clip. Making his way back toward the trail but staying just inside the tree line, he crept up to a log near the edge of the clearing, where he saw Cody lying on the ground near the lake, shielding himself behind a tree from someone coming from the north. When the individual ran to the last clump of trees, Buck recognized who it was. Farhan.

The two were exchanging gunfire, and Cody appeared to have the advantage. But that changed quickly when his gun either jammed, misfired, or ran out of ammunition, and Farhan realized it. As he began walking quickly toward Cody, Farhan kept his eyes forward, fixed on Cody, not paying attention to what was going on around him. Buck stayed crouched behind his log. When Farhan walked directly in front of him, he was only a mere twenty feet away. Buck let him take another step and a half so that he was a touch behind his line-of-sight, aimed, and shot, hitting Farhan directly in the left side of his face. While the terrorist fell to his knees, Buck shot him again, leaving Farhan with all but nothing left to think with.

***

Had the shots gotten louder? Cody was not certain. He had recoiled when his gun did not fire, and shots started ringing out and bullets landing around him. What the hell had happened to Farhan? Keeping his arms over his head, he peeked up.

"I said GET UP," Buck said firmly, lifting him by the arm. "We have to get out of here."

"Buck? Where'd you come from? What… what happened?"

"Well, that little shit was going to kill you. Hate to make a big deal out of it, but I think I got here just in time," Buck said with a smile.

"My family… they're all dead."

"I'm sorry, Cody," Buck said solemnly. "But you need to get out of here. Maybe we can get you a horse. If not, you have to start walking. Who knows what other kinds of shit are going on around here. We're alive, and we're not supposed to be. Someone is about to execute a Plan B. We gotta move."

Cody stared blankly across the lake. "Balil," he said. "He's still alive."

"I know," said Buck. "I saw him get on the horse and skedaddle as soon as his friend here went down. I saw some of the other horses down the trail, too. Maybe you can catch one, but you need to get going regardless."

"Who are these people? You brought them in," Cody said in bewilderment. "What's going on?"

"Cody," Buck said seriously, "I don't know what this is about. The government arranged to have them come in. The United States government. Your government. I did what I was told. My gut told me something else, but I didn't know who to complain to. Look, I'll take care of your family. Don't go look," Buck implored, assuming an abattoir. "Get some supplies and some warm clothes. You need to get back to town. I'll have some people meet you along the way or at the trailhead. Just get going. You'll be okay." Buck stuck out his hand for Cody to shake. When he did, Buck pulled him close into an awkward hug. "Sorry, man. We'll get this figured out. I promise. Now go."

Buck headed toward the north trail back to his campsite, and Cody, struggling to stay focused, took the south. It was about twenty-two miles to the trailhead. He had a few hours of daylight left. The trail and terrain were too dangerous to try and traverse at night. If he could make ten or more miles today, he might be able to get to Winthrop by two or three o'clock tomorrow. Cody went to his tent to change clothes. He would need a sweater, pants, a sleeping bag, energy bars, matches, and some water. Cody had brought a day pack for short hikes. All his items fit inside, though some of the sleeping bag stuck out the top. While his father had mocked him on the first night of their trip for having brought the items he had, their collective presence was suddenly felicitous.

He had been wearing his cargo shorts and began patting down the pockets to see if there were added items to take. Pocket knife, his Tough Tesla lighter, Seth's EpiPen. He had forgotten about the pen. When his mother washed his clothes, she always put the items she found back into the same pockets they were in so that Cody would never forget them. They were always there when he might need them, and he never had to worry about remembering or forgetting them. He studied the pen and shook his head in bewilderment. This piece of Seth had stuck with him, and its presence, in concert with all that had happened in the last hour, suddenly overwhelmed and comforted him simultaneously.

"I miss you, man," he said to the pen. "I need your help, buddy." He started crying. "They killed my fucking family, Seth. They killed my family. First you. Now this. What the fuck is going on?"

Cody had always considered himself a strong person, but his limits had been exceeded. He did not know if it came from inside his head or if he heard an actual voice, but something told him, "Cody, get hold of yourself. Get a grip. Get moving. Get help. It's not safe here." The last warning shook him. It was not safe. Buck had said it, too. Grabbing his belt, he fed it through his shorts, attached his hunting knife toward the back, and then attached the holster for his Browning 9mm at his right side. He also had a Berretta 9mm, smaller in size than the Browning, that he slipped into one of the backpack's side pockets. Then he strapped the scabbard to his back, put a fresh clip in the rifle, holstered the rifle in the scabbard, hoisted the backpack into place, took one last look up the trail at the carnage, said goodbye to his family, and started running down the trail. His L.L.Bean trail hiking boots were for hiking, not running, but simply walking was out of the question.

***

Buck checked the family to make sure they were all dead. They were. When he saw Odion, he stopped and said farewell. "Sad to see this way, man," he muttered. "I was hoping for something better for you."

If he started now, Carpenter believed he could make it out by six or seven, the last couple of hours having to be in the dark. However, after he had walked two hundred yards up the trail, he saw one of the Dickson's horses, a roan gelding named Dusty, standing in the middle of the trail looking back in his direction, trying to decide, Buck surmised, whether to keep heading north or go south toward home. The horse stood firm as Buck approached, happy to see a live human who could attend to him, comfort him, and help make sense of what was going on. Buck saw immediately that the saddle was smattered with a streak of blood, hair and brains, the streak ending in a bullet hole at the apex of the seat. Checking the saddlebags, Buck found some paper towels and a sandwich someone had prepared earlier for lunch. After pouring some bottled water that was also in the bag, he wiped off the saddle. Then he grabbed the reins, tied Dusty to a nearby skinny tree, and sat down to call Rodgers.

"Hey, man," he said as soon as Rodgers picked up. "We need a cleanup on Isle One. You need to bring in three horses. One for yourself and the other to haul out four collaterals."

"Holy shit, boss. What happened?"

"No time to explain. They're at the End of the Line. It's a family. Two tourists, too."

"Holy shit," Rodgers repeated.

"Call me after you get here. We'll have to figure out what to do with the tourists, but be sure to bring a shovel."

"I'm on it."

"Hey, call my niece, too, will you? Jody. Tell her you don't know all the details yet, but if she thinks maybe we can get a helicopter in here to haul them out. What do you think? That'd be a better alternative, if we can arrange that."

"Might work. I'll call her."

"Well, if that doesn't work, I've collared a horse, so you might pass me on the way in. If I beat you there, well, the horse will be tied up. You figure out what to do later."

"Will do. Talk later."

Buck pressed his off button and pondered his next move for a few minutes as he ate the tuna fish sandwich he had found. After a few minutes, he hopped on Dusty and began the ride out. Dusty was ready to get home, even if the home was new, so the horse amiably provided the quickened gate Carpenter desired as he kicked his hills into the horse's ribs. Two hours later, he was at the trailhead. Rodgers had not arrived, so he tied the horse's halter rope tight to the handle of one of the cars parked in the area, hoping the car's owner would take care of it if necessary. As it turned out, he arrived forty-five minutes later. Having arranged for a helicopter in lieu of having to use horses, Rodgers climbed back on Dusty and made his way back to the End of the Line.

By the time Buck drove to Penticton, dusk was setting in. He went immediately to the payphone he used to call his aide, who received or made such calls from or to his father in Mazama, a small, unincorporated community just off Highway 20, about 14 miles north of Winthrop. The two used these phones as potentially secure ways to briefly engage with one another at predetermined time periods. After transferring 'cargo,' they would normally talk two nights later at 11:00 p.m. The phone was to ring three times before someone answered. If it rang a fourth, the caller would hang up and wait five minutes because it was possible that the recipient could be on another phone. The recipient could call the primary contact number exactly five minutes after the hour, hang up after three rings, wait thirty seconds, repeat, and then call in another thirty seconds. If the process was repeated three times, the original caller could answer on the third ring of the third call, knowing the initiator was not calling from their 'home base' location. This also gave the intended recipient a chance to be five minutes late.

If no connection was not made that night, the two would duplicate the effort at 10:00 a.m. the next morning, Buck from a pay phone in Penticton while Bill would take or make a call from a pay phone in

Twisp, just down the road from Winthrop. Thanks to the NSA, no systems were completely secure anymore. Still, if they kept the calls short, they assumed, they could stay ahead of a traced interception or at least make it difficult for any agency, Canadian or American, to cull through related information that would track the calls directly or even indirectly back to them. If the organization or similar agencies were to listen in, it would most likely have to be a preplanned effort, which was unlikely.

Buck had called the Mazama phone at precisely 11:00 p.m. No answer. It was 11:04 when the phone rang. He let it ring three times once, then a second time. About thirty seconds after the second time, it rang again. On the third time, he answered it.

"Hello."

"I'm not in Mazama."

"Location two?"

"Yes."

"Major damage. Four collaterals dead. Two tourists."

"Oh god, is…?" Bill wanted to say his name but knew better.

"The boy survived."

"Thank God. But shit or dear. Where is he?"

"He needs someone to go in and get him. He's probably on his way out."

"I got it."

"Good. Call me tomorrow. If we miss tomorrow, the day after until we connect," said Buck and hung up.

***

Cody had no idea how much time had passed before he stopped to catch his breath. He knew the trail very well and all its many landmarks by which he measured his progress in distance rather than the number of hours on his watch. He figured dusk was about thirty minutes away and knew he had gone about ten miles. Glancing at his watch, he saw he had been running a good portion of the last four hours. Balil, he was certain, had come this way as the tracks of his horse had remained visible since he left the campground. From the placement of the hoofprints, it was obvious that he trotted and ran some when the terrain allowed it. Having no idea where he might be, he decided; nonetheless, it was best to keep out of sight for the evening. He decided to go another twenty minutes or so to a location where he knew the trail cut through a stand of thick lodgepole pines where he could cut across an easy hundred yards and make his way to a clearing where he could camp without being seen from the trail itself or any approaching hikers coming from either the north or south.

When he got to the clearing, Cody went directly to the stream and ran through it. He drank from such streams regularly, which were usually clearer than many municipal sources. He first looked up and down the stream for any dead animals and, seeing none, fell to his knees and drank. Darkness was only about twenty minutes away, so he began gathering twigs for a bed covering and some larger pieces for a fire. With the fire burning, he arranged his bed for the evening, sleeping just inside the trees about ten feet from his fire.

For an hour, he reflected on the day. His family was dead. He had killed a man. What else could go wrong? What would he do when he got home? In the morning, he would walk out. 'Shit,' he thought, realizing he had forgotten to get the car keys. Better to flag a car down than to have had to get them from his dad if he even had them on him. A car would stop for him, he was sure. He just hoped he had the strength to get there as quickly as possible.

***

Somewhere in the Pasayten Wilderness

Day 4

Kent Des Moines, dressed in full camo, carrying his new Colt M4 LE assault rifle with his Glock pistol strapped to his hip, had been waiting impatiently in the trailhead parking area for the three terrorists as he and his two comrades had been directed to engage per his contact. Dan Christen and Cal Kirby were waiting with him, also in camo and fully armed. Originally, they were to intercept and kill the men. The estimated time of arrival (ETA) for the three men was sometime late yesterday, and Des Moines was getting nervous. It was about two that afternoon when he received a call saying there had been a gunfight at the End of the Line Campground and that two of the terrorists were dead, as well as a Forest Service family from Winthrop that had been camping there. The youngest son, Cody Dickson, had apparently participated with the terrorists in killing his family. The surviving terrorist and the son might be together or split up. Des Moines' team was to kill them, either together or separately.

Des Moines was suddenly excited to near arousal. He did not want to wait. He was going in. "Get your shit together, fellas," he barked. "That was a heads up from the White House," said Kent. He related the story of the family and three terrorists as he had heard it. "They're on their way out. Let's find a good place to give them a proper welcome. That asshole Dickson is all mine."

"That doesn't sound like Cody," said Cal. "You sure you heard that, right?"

"Yeah," said Dan, agreeing. "Makes no sense. They must have got it wrong."

"Ours is not to reason why," Des Moines said gleefully. "Ours is but to make them die."

Along with a small amount of gear and short-term supplies, Dan and Cal put on their holster belts, strapped on their assault rifles, and headed up the trail where they had been advised the terrorists would come out. Kent noted that there were two four-horse trailers connected to two Forest Service pickups on the other side of the lot. They would be coming right to them, he concluded.

***

Cody had gotten up three times that night to feed the fire. He had slept lightly and woke in spurts. Fortunately, he had brought a sweater, as the nights had been getting noticeably colder. And without the tent, it felt even colder. When he got up in the morning, there was frost on the ground. There were still a few embers in the fire from the last time he fed it, so he quickly gathered up some pine needles and twigs and got the fire going again. For twenty minutes or so, he warmed up, waiting for it to get a little lighter. He had tossed a tin cup in his bag, which he filled with stream water. Shivering, he moved the cup next to the fire to heat, sat on his haunches, and waited. When the water finally began to steam heavily, he dumped in a packet of

Starbucks instant coffee he had included. After he drank it, it had its effect: the urge to purge and accompanying surge within a couple of minutes.

Assuming he would make it out before sunset, Cody moved to simplify his load and reduce the weight of his backpack to a minimum. He decided to leave his sleeping bag in which he bundled some nonessentials that he would not immediately need and placed the bunch under several needle-filled branches that he gathered. He would get them next spring… hopefully. Within fifteen minutes of finishing his coffee and preparations, he headed south toward the trailhead.

After about three miles, Cody noticed the horse tracks he had been watching veered west, following another trail that he knew ended near the center of Ross Lake. It was definitely Balil. He thought momentarily about whether to follow it but knew there was no way he could realistically catch him. His only hope was getting to Highway 27 and returning to town to get help. For a moment, he sat and thought about all that had transpired over the last few weeks. His life had pivoted faster and as tragically as Ned Beatty's character, Bobby Trippe in *Deliverance*, from dork to pork. Pedro, Seth, and his family. Growing up, he had never really known death, and now it seemed to mock him from every angle.

Cody was sitting at the edge of a stand of trees far off to the east of the ridgeline's apex. From where he sat, he could see two people, through his Leupold 8X binoculars, riding horses in his direction, the one in the rear leading a third horse. They were about a mile and a half away, he guessed. About another half mile ahead of them were three hikers, also headed in his direction. The two on horseback were moving at a crisp rate and looked like they might be Sweetie and

Chris. The three walking in front of them were not so familiar to him that he recognized them, though there was something familiar about them. 'I should have bought the 12X,' Cody thought to himself. The two groups were likely unaware of the other, obscured by stands of trees and bends in the trail, but Cody estimated that the duo would overtake the trio in another half to three-quarters of a mile. He decided to stay where he was until both groups passed. Going back up the trail to the fork, he proceeded west for about a hundred and fifty feet before jutting into the trees, where he nestled himself behind a clump of logs that would shield him from either group. Removing his backpack and scabbard, he lay prone behind the clump, wishing he had brought his sleeping bag for a moment, and sat his binoculars and rifle on the ground next to him, waiting.

About thirty minutes later, the group of three arrived. He swallowed hard when he realized who it was, Kent Des Moines with Dan and Cal in tow. All three were carrying assault rifles, Auburn with his in his right hand while Dan and Cal had strapped theirs horizontally, from left shoulder to right hip, across their backs. When they arrived at the fork in the trail, they began talking loudly about what to do next. In the thin, cool mountain air, Cody could hear them clearly.

"Which way?" asked Dan. "Looks like someone came from the north and turned here toward the lake."

"Yeah, looks like there's been some footprints here, too," said Cal. "They also go that way. Should we follow them?"

Kent Des Moines sounded vexed. "Good question. I'm not sure. My concern is that if they haven't come this way yet, we'd be screwed if we go that way. What do you guys think?"

"I'd say we follow those tracks," said Cal. "It's either Cody after one of them on horseback or one of the terrorists is walking, and one is riding."

"Probably the first," said Dan. "If it's two terrorists, one is holding up the other. Why wouldn't they double up on the horse?"

"Maybe neither ride that much," said Des Moines.

"Did you hear that?" asked Cal, looking back down the trail. "Sounded like a horse whinnying."

"Yeah," the other two said in unison as the sound suddenly repeated itself.

"That's a horse, alright," said Des Moines. "Quick, let's hide in the trees. If they've got horses, we can take them… confiscate them for security reasons. We've been deputized by the White House. That gives us liberties."

Dan and Cal nodded positively, and the three hustled into trees for cover on the opposite side of the main trail where Cody was positioned. Several minutes later, two riders came into view. It was Chris and Sweetie. The third horse, which Chris was leading, had gotten close enough to bump the one he was riding, which had dozed off a little after they had slowed down, with its nose. That elicited a half kick from his horse, warning the one behind to back off, who in turn had vocalized his disapproval. When the two reached the fork in the trail, they halted, both noticing the horse tracks leading west to their left.

"What do you think?" Chris asked Sweetie as he rode up next to her.

"I think you should get down off your horses, nice and easy," said a voice from behind them

Chris and Sweetie both turned around to see Des Moines walking just ahead of Dan and Cal, coming up the trail just a little behind them.

"Oh fuck," said Chris, followed by Sweetie saying, "Shit."

Des Moines now had his rifle hanging off his right shoulder; the other two still had theirs slung on their backs. Chris and Sweetie had both gotten off their horses and had turned to face Kent.

"We'll be taking those horses, guys," said Des Moines, then adding, while looking directly at Sweetie, "Sorry, I mean folks. Gotta keep it PC. Right, sweetheart?"

"Fuck you, asshole. You're not taking these horses. They're ours," said Sweetie, patting Apple's neck. "Besides, she doesn't like worms crawling on her, anyway,"

"Listen, bitch," he said purposefully, quickly slinging his rifle more securely and taking out his pistol in his right hand. "We're operating as deputized Federal Marshalls by the White House itself." He raised his Glock in the air and fired it once, causing all three horses to flinch and fidget skittishly. The third horse's movements caused Dan and Cal to take a step back nervously to a safer distance. Instinctively, they distanced themselves from the horses, one moving right, the other left, both just modestly while keeping their eyes keenly glued to the horses' actions.

"The third horse for your boyfriend? Wow. It's even saddled." Chris and Sweetie said nothing. "You know he's a wanted man," said Des Moines.

"Bullshit," said Chris. "For what?"

"Helping some terrorists get into the country. Even did nothing when they killed his parents. Didn't even try and stop them," Des Moines said, prodding them. "What do you think of that?"

"We think you're full of shit. How many times do I have to tell you that?" said Sweetie. "You're as dumb as you are deaf."

"I got it from a pretty good source," Des Moines said chidingly. "Your boy's in trouble. We've been sent in to get him, and we need your horses. And we're taking them."

"Let 'em alone, Kent," someone said, their voice coming from Chris' right. Cody had come out of the trees and moved up to Chris' right, arms out at his sides and hands palms up. After Cody was about three feet from Chris, he turned toward Des Moines and then took three steps forward at an angle to his left so that when he stopped, he was directly in front of Chris, as if shielding him.

"Well, well, look who's here, boys. It's Benedict Arnold himself." Cody eyed the other two, who were still concerned, it seemed, with the actions of the horses in front of them than him. "Where's your guns?" asked Des Moines.

Before he had come out, Cody had moved his knife on his belt to be more visible to his right side to where it was just behind his holstered Browning 9MM and stuck the smaller Baretta 9MM behind him in the space between his jeans and spine; draped under his t-shirt. "It's what you see. My rifle's over there with my pack," he said, motioning in that direction with his head. He had sat both items in front of the logs behind which he was hiding, now clearly visible to Des Moines. "You can see the pistol. I'm not gonna point it out."

"Smart. You know, you're wanted dead or alive, dingus. Mostly dead, I'm thinkin,'" Des Moines said tauntingly. "What do you think, boys?" Cal and Dan remained silent. "Take off your belt and let the sidearm and knife fall to the ground."

Cody did as instructed, moving slowly to undo the belt buckle before pulling the belt's left side with his right hand. As he pulled the belt, the right side snaked back around him, allowing his holster and knife to fall to the ground. Gradually, the entire belt came free, and Cody dropped it, hoping his optics would satisfy Des Moines. For the moment, at least, that appeared to be the case. "That's it," he said, raising his arms to where his elbows were about as high as the center of his ears.

Dan and Cal said nothing, looking back and forth, clearly not entirely on board with killing any of the people present.

Des Moines kept staring straight ahead, his eyes locked on Cody. "Hmm. I'm kinda liking the notion of pulling you out of here behind one of these horses for the twelve miles or so back to the trailhead. What do you think of that, slick?"

"Do what you have to do, Kent. Just leave these two alone," said Cody.

"We'll see," Des Moines said causally. "Kick that holster and knife this way." Cody did as ordered. "Now, empty your pockets, one hand at a time, left side first. Keep the right hand up. High."

Cody raised his right hand again, turned his left hip just slightly forward, slowly lowered his left arm, and patted his rear left-hand pocket to show there was nothing in it. "Matches," he announced, nodding toward his left before slowly reaching into his left pocket and pulling out a small plastic cylinder with four matches. Des Moines stepped forward and held out his left hand to take the object, pulling the pistol back somewhat with his right so that it was a shade out of Cody's reach. Cody dropped the object into Kent's hand and studied it briefly before putting it in his pocket.

"Now the right," commanded Des Moines.

Cody raised his left arm slowly to as high as the right, completed the process with the right side, lowered his right, and began with his right rear pocket, emptying it before moving to the front. "I have a pocketknife, Kent," said Cody as he slowly removed it. When his hand came out of the pocket, he was holding it so that a bit was sticking out beyond his thumb, making it evident that it was a pocketknife. He slowly rotated his hand to palm up before unfolding his fist and showing the knife.

"Give it to me," said Des Moines as he reached and took it from Cody's hand. He studied it quickly and then squinted at a slight but noticeable bulge in the bottom of Cody's front, the lower right thigh-high pocket of his Cargo Shorts. "What's that?" Des Moines said, pointing.

"Allergy medicine."

"Give it to me."

Cody kept his eyes fixed on Kent as he slowly stuck it back in and then retrieved the EpiPen. Cody held it out in the flat of his palm with the plunger nearest his thumb.

"What's it for?" asked Des Moines.

"I've got allergies. Bees. It's epinephrine."

"Give it to me," Des Moines said again, sounding slightly annoyed and sticking out his left hand a little further than before.

"Sure, man," said Cody, matter-of-factly. "You can see it. But I'd like it back if you don't mind."

"We'll see, puss," said Des Moines. "No bees up here right now. Too cold. You must be a real chickenshit, Dickson."

When Cody reached out to drop it in Des Moines' hand, he made an imperceptible lean toward him, all the while looking at him, and rather than pass off the pen, he plunged the tip into Kent's wrist.

The impact of the drug on Des Moines was immediate. For Des Moines, it suddenly felt like things were running in slow motion and that his cognitive and physiological processes were suddenly disconnected. Under normal circumstances, upon feeling the prick of the pen on his wrist, he would have immediately shot Cody. Before he could assess what had happened, he felt a tingling wave begin running through him. His brain fogged. His gun. He had wanted to pull the trigger. Had he done it? Teetering, Des Moines was able to say, "What the?" before he slumped to the ground and dreamland.

As Des Moines' attention had shifted, for just a moment, to the prick in his wrist, Cody moved forward and grabbed the pistol with his left hand, pushing it toward the ground, causing the gun to go off, shooting harmlessly into the ground just outside Kent Des Moines' right foot. Simultaneously, Chris moved up to take the Beretta from Cody's belt, which he had seen the first time Cody raised his arms above ear level, which had lifted his t-shirt, exposing the gun. The horses whinnied and moved nervously again for a moment, reacting to the gunshot. Before Kent hit the ground, both boys had pistols aimed at Dan and Cal, whose attention, up to that moment, had remained on staying out of the way of the horse in the rear.

"Don't move, fellas," said Cody as he and Chris walked toward them, their guns pointing at the two.

"Don't shoot," said Dan. "We didn't want to hurt you, folks. But Kent was certain you'd helped some terrorists?"

"Not true. You think I'd kill my parents, my family, Cal?" asked Cody. "Help a fucking terrorist?"

"I'm Dan."

"Dude, I don't give a shit. Fuck. Why are you two here with this asswipe anyway?"

"Shit," said Cal, "That's what he told us. Said the White House said so. We heard him talking on the phone to someone he said was there. What happened?"

"Some asshole brought them in from Canada. Long story. Fuck it. I don't want to talk about it now. I didn't kill my family. That's dogshit. I think I know where he's headed, and I need to get back to town. So, here's what's gonna happen, you two. We're gonna ride outta here, and you're going to stay in front of us. You're going to pick up the pace. Trot. If you can't stay ahead, I'm going to shoot you. Got it?" They both nodded earnestly. "Now, slowly take off your guns, drop them on the ground and take five steps back. You first, Dan, and then Cal." Both obeyed as directed. "Now lay face down on the trail, put your face in the dirt, and put your hands behind your head." After they had complied, Cody turned to Chris, pointed to the rifles, and said, "Take those up the trail and throw them in the brush." Then he turned to Sweetie, pulled her to him, and kissed her.

They enjoyed a quick embrace as Cody held her with his left arm and kept his gun aimed at Dan and Cal. "I'm so happy to see you, "she said. "And so hot," she added, with mock suggestiveness.

"God, I love you," he whispered before briefly kissing her again. "Let's get going."

"What about him," Sweetie asked, pointing to Des Moines, who had not moved since the injection. "Is he dead?"

"Let's just shoot the fucker," said Chris as he returned. "I hate when they just don't do that in books or the movies."

"Probably should," said Cody. "Otherwise, he'll just keep coming at us."

"What did you give him?" asked Sweetie.

"Propofol. It's the stuff that killed Michael Jackson."

"How'd you get it?" she asked admiringly.

"Seth. They use it to sedate large animals they're treating or to put down small ones. Gave it to me for Pedro. Pedro died first."

"Sweet," said Sweetie affectionately. "Seems to work on big pieces of shit, too. Do you think he's dead?"

"I'm not sure," said Cody.

"Hope so," said Chris, picking up Kent's rifle and slinging it on his back.

"Gimme' his pistol," said Cody, who took it, made sure the safety was on, and stuck it into the front of his jeans.

"His eyes are open. So weird. Maybe he can hear us," Sweetie said, sounding like a child who was about to play a prank. She squatted down near him, picked up a stick, and poked him in the cheek and lips a few times. "Fuck you," she said with each poke. "You like that, Kent, you asshole?"

"I'm not really sure how much of a dose I gave him." Cody picked up the EpiPen and examined it. "Shit," he said. "I can't tell how much of it I have left. Can't see inside." He took a deep breath, exhaled, and said, "Over the lips, past the gums, fuck you, Kent, here it comes," he said softly as he squatted onto his haunches and stabbed the rest of the contents into Des Moines' neck.

"Dope," said Sweetie wickedly.

Chris nodded agreeably. "Literal. Will *that* kill him?"

"I don't know," Cody replied unemotionally. "I don't care. He'll be out for a couple of hours anyway… I think. Or out for good. Whatever." He motioned a momentary huddle with Chris and Sweetie so Dan and Cal could not hear. "Let's just take these two dipshits three or four miles down the trail, then we can ride on," he whispered. "They can either keep walking out from there or come back and get fuckface here. They'll either be out tomorrow morning sometime or late tomorrow afternoon. We can just leave the horses in the trailer and be back in town by night. Steve'll send someone out to get them tomorrow morning. Sound good?" The two each gave him a thumbs up.

"I gotta pee before we go," said Chris.

"Me, too," said Sweetie, and both jaunted off in different directions to do their business.

"Grab my rifle, too, Chris, will you please? I'll watch these two."
Chris gave a right thumb up. Cody watched Dan and Cal, and when
Sweetie and Chris had returned, he mounted the horse they had
brought for him and said, "Okay, let's get out of here."

***

An hour later, Dan and Cal were exhausted, having had to
fluctuate between trotting and speed walking to keep pace with the
horses.

"Okay, you two. Hold up," said Cody. "Here's the deal. You can
either keep walking behind us at your own pace, or you're welcome
to go back and get Kent. Your call."

"You gonna' leave us out here without a firearm?" asked Cal.

"No, Dan," said Cody. "I dropped a fully loaded magazine about
two hundred yards back in the middle of the trail. Here's Kent's
pistol." He handed it to Cal handle first.

"I'm not… uh, I'm…" stammered Cal.

"What is it?" Cody said loudly, sounding irritated.

"I'm grateful," said Cal, taking the gun. "Thank you. Sorry for the
hassle, Cody. No hard feelings?"

"Lots of hard feelings, Dan. I still don't get why you guys are
here, man. You don't seem to be that into this shit."

"We're just trying to keep our homes and our values the way they
are," said Dan. He hesitated a little, reluctant to continue, but then
added, "Man, all the rich fucks, the blacks, the fags are moving in
here."

253

"Change happens," said Sweetie.

"Yeah, but they don't just come in here on weekends anymore. With the pandemic, they're working at home, and they're around all the time," Cal said. "I hate fags, man."

"What do your dads do?" asked Chris.

"Mine's a rancher," said Cal.

"Mine's a cop. Retired," said Dan.

"That explains it," said Chris matter-of-factly to Sweetie and Cody.

"Half the Freedom Fighters are cops or ex-military," said Cal, sounding somewhere between apologetic and obvious.

"I believe you," said Cody.

"Look what's happened to Winthrop," Cal went on.

"What's happened to Winthrop?" Chris asked.

"Shit, there's Seattleites everywhere. All summer. Everyday. Used to be a great, little town."

"Still is, Cal. That's why people come." Chris said. "My dad's a mechanic. Those people are the only reason he's still in business. There's not enough local business for us to make a go of it. That's why most kids leave town to get jobs or go to school. Same as where you guys come from. If your dad doesn't already have a business, you're kinda fucked. Unless the business is dying... like my dad's."

"Same with our deli," said Sweetie. "Without those tourists from the Westside, we'd be just another little turd operation trying to get by in a community that can't support us on its own."

"You know," Chris said, "when I was younger, I said the same things my old man did about blacks, gays, you name it. But I like what's happened to Winthrop. It'd be just another Eastern Washington, dying shithole without them. You can't make it farming or ranching anymore unless you do it as a hobby."

"I'll give you that," said Cal, nodding. "But all the LGTQ-bs, or whatever it is? We don't want that here."

"Fellas," said Sweetie, laughing, "they've been here forever. For as long as there's people, they've been here. They've just been too scared to come out because assholes like Des Moines, and it sounds like your dads, and now you, would kick their asses or worse. It's about time we got used to it. They're just people, boys. You guys just want things to stay white, macho white. Old white guys in charge."

"You make it sound like we're a bunch of racists and homophobes," said Dan. "But we just don't want all this change crammed down our throats."

"Oh, Dan," she said. "Come on. What change are you talking about, boy?"

"Country values," he said.

"You have a cell phone?"

"Of course. Everyone does," he said, though suddenly sensing a trap.

"Email?"

"Yeah," said both.

"Facebook?"

"Some," said Dan. "Mostly Instagram."

"Those aren't headquartered in Orville. You text?" Both nodded yes. "You smoke pot?" Sweetie asked. Neither said yes nor made any indication they did not. "Do meth?" Sweetie asked.

"Of course not," Dan replied, sounding somewhere between insulted and annoyed.

"Know anyone who has," asked Chris.

"Yeah."

"The curse of country folks, right?" said Chris, pryingly.

"You still round up your cows with just horses?" asked Cody.

Cal shook his head. "Not so much anymore," he said.

"Quads?" said Cody.

"Yeah, and helicopters," said Cal, smiling. "When we can."

"Whoa. That's big time," Cody said. "Well, you still got the boots and hats, right."

"You a gamer?" Chris said. Both boys' heads indicated yes. "Xbox?"

"Play Station," the two said in chorus.

"Favorite game?" asked Cody.

"Call of Duty," said Cal.

"Me, too," said Chris.

"Zombie Army," said Dan, smiling at his friend.

"Either of you in the military?" asked Cody.

Both said, "No."

"The call wasn't that loud for me either," said Chris.

"My older brother was killed in Iraq," Cal said.

"Sorry to hear that, man," Chris replied. "That brings it home. Thanks for his service."

"And thanks for his sacrifice for our service stations," mocked Sweetie.

"Harsh, baby," said Cody.

"Too soon?" said Sweetie, quickly. "Where are my manners?"

"Some truth, though, to that," said Cody, making a sympathetic glance at Cal. "Sorry, man."

"Hip Hop or Country?" Sweetie asked, her tone now kind.

"Depends on the party," said Dan, smiling. "But both of those are American. Right? What's your point?"

"Shit, boy, you ever been anywhere besides your own berg? Seattle don't count," she said. "And neither does Spokane. Where the fuck is Keith Urban from, dude?" They both stood silent, unsure what to say, though their faces said they knew the answer. "Okay, yeah, you know. Australia. He's white, so it's okay, right? Ever heard of Charlie Rich?"

Feeling they were not likely to be shot by these three, the two began to open up more confidently. "No," both said in unison.

"Black. In the seventies. All the black country singers went to hip-hop. More money," said Sweetie. Everyone smiled. "What's wrong with Blacks?" she asked. Silence. "You like Travis Scott, right?" Both nodded. "When's the last time you dated a black girl?" No answers. "What's wrong with Muslims?"

"They hate us for our freedom," said Dan with confidence.

"Yes, the world would be a better place if we could just get rid of *those* people," Sweetie said theatrically while shaking her fist. "Both extremes, right and left, say the same thing."

"Yeah," said Cal, "well, they hate the infidels. They want us all dead."

"Like Hakeem Olajuwon or Rudy Tomjanovich?" said Cody. "Aqib Talib? Ahmad Rashād? Right. They want you dead. Dangerous, right?"

"I don't know who all of them are," said Cal.

"Well, you should. You ever talked to a Muslim... a Muslim woman? You actually believe you know what they're like or what they're thinking because you read something on the web or listened to some dumbshit, right-wing radio host like Rush Limbaugh or Alex fucking Jones tell you what they're like or what they think? You want to meet a cool Muslim? Do you?" Both boys simply hunched their shoulders. "Come meet my mom." She paused. Everyone was silent. "You ever talk to a gay?" she went on. They both hunched their shoulders in uncertainty. "I mean, actually talk to one, instead of threatening them or calling them names?" They continued shaking their heads. "You have, fellas, believe me. They just didn't want to tell you. *OR*, maybe you just didn't pay attention. Maybe you couldn't tell, you know, just because they weren't wearing that T-shirt with a red F or G on it. Shit, Seth was gay." Both Chris and Cody looked at her, mouths a little agape. She looked back at them and nodded. "Yeah, he asked me to stop trying to set him up. Said it embarrassed him."

"No fucking way," said Chris. However, it explained a lot of Seth's behavior, which they had seen and discussed over the years in a different context. "Damn, that makes some sense. He's never really had any girlfriends, really, even at college.

"Why was he even in the Freedom Fighters, then?" said Cody.

"I think he was just trying to figure things out," Sweetie said. "You know the day he came early before he went to Portland?" Cody nodded. "Said he was conflicted about going, given *all* he knew they stood for. I think his initial interest really came from a sense of guilt… at first. He wanted all around him to think he was a tough guy. Us. His folks. Later, he said he wanted to protect some of the people on the other side when he was out there. He was all bluster and bullshit on the surface about conservative values. But Seth wasn't a hater. He was a protector."

"Holy crap," said Cody. "I don't know what to say. I had no idea."

"Well," Sweetie said, "I think he wanted to believe he was a good conservative, like his dad and grandfather. To show them. He wasn't, you know, gay."

"No doubt his dad and grandfather would have disowned him," said Cody.

"Major," said Chris. "His old man would never have given him the ranch had he known that. Shit. God, poor Seth."

"Can't believe he never told us, though," said Cody, realizing he never completely knew his friend, never knew what he might have been going through, and how he might have been able to offer support, to help.

"Well, like I said. He was trying to figure things out. But he loved you guys. That's why he'd never said anything. He didn't want it to ruin our friendships," Sweetie said.

"Why did he tell you and not us, too, do you think?" Cody asked, still bewildered.

"I don't know. Maybe my thing with Pedro. I was safe to him, I suppose. I really don't know. He was curious, though, when he finally talked. Wanted to know things about Pedro. What happened. How I saw him."

Cody looked at Dan and Cal and said, "And there you have it, fellas," his voice cracking a little. "Sometimes you have no idea who's who and what's up with them, even when they're best friends. Even family. So what, though, right? Why do we give a shit about stuff like that, anyway? I mean, if they're a good person, they're a good person, and Seth was the best." Cody was suddenly overcome with emotion at the moment, tearing up a little, his voice cracking noticeably. He just wished he had had the opportunity to tell the friend he loved that it did not matter. "It's their fucking business," he said decisively. "Don't you have other things to worry about than what people do on their own time, in their own homes? Would it have changed how you felt about Seth if you'd known he was gay?" The two said nothing, just hanging their heads. "Probably. And that's sad if so. But that makes no sense, right? You wouldn't have gotten to know him, and that would be on you. Right? Same guy, right, Dan?" he said, looking at Cal. "Kent and his friends? They guilt people they think are weak, that they can pick on, and then they punk other people into believing those people's behaviors somehow infringe on their lives. And people love to gang on and bully, don't they? Especially when there are fewer of them," he said, slowly shaking his head.

"And they do it around race. And gender," said Sweetie. "Only a man can turn the word '*pussy*' into a bad thing," she said, shaking her head. "Every guy wants some. Nobody wants to be one." Reluctant to respond, the boys' silence began making Sweetie uncomfortable. So she quickly added, with a little snicker, "And the best pussies can take a pounding. Go figure."

The four boys began laughing loudly. But wanting to keep the conversation focused and serious, Cody collected himself and said, "Hey, you two get the fuck out of here before I change my mind. I don't want to talk to you anymore." Dan and Cal, saying nothing more, turned on their heels and began walking back from where they had just come.

When they were comfortably out of earshot, Sweetie said, "That was Cal, you know."

"I know," said Cody purposefully.

Sweetie looked at Chris and said, "You were starting to sound a little lib there, partner."

"Well, I guess I've just been hanging around you two, too long." He shrugged. "I feel safe with you two. We all talk freely, no harm, no foul. The world's a big place. I'm still evolving, I guess," said Chris, smiling. "Glad you two are in my life."

"I hear you, brother," said Cody. "We're all evolving. As long as we keep talking and being a little open-minded. That was true for Seth, too, I believe. I just really wish he'd, we all, had gotten the chance to share more."

Chris and Sweetie both nodded. "True dat," said Sweetie. "And I hate Call of Duty, just so you know." Looking at Cody, she said, "I'm so glad you don't play it. But I love you both," she added, looking back and smiling at Chris.

Chris smiled, gave a thumb up, and the three rode on.

***

Kent Des Moines had no idea how long he had been out. His mind was foggy as his eyes began to focus. He might have been unconscious for another couple of hours had he not been prompted into awareness by a hot, smelly breath on his face. His eyes had been open the entire time he was out, and they were dry and sore. His vision was fuzzy. Blinking slowly and painfully at first and then rapidly, tears began to moisten Kent's eyes, and they slowly came back into focus in spurts. Suddenly, he realized a creature was staring at him in the face. Des Moines' mouth opened a little, and his lips quivered, but he was otherwise paralyzed, unable to move, unable to make a sound other than a low groan, which was the best scream he could muster. His mouth opened wider, and his lips tightened a little, but all the animal in his face saw, was a set of menacing teeth growling at him.

***

When they found the pistol's magazine, Dan picked it up and handed it to Cal. "What are we going to do?" he asked.

Cal loaded the pistol and slipped it behind his belt in the back of his jeans. "Don't you think we should go get him?"

"I suppose. God, Kent would shit a brick, though, if he'd known Seth was gay," said Dan, smirking. "It explains, though, why he put himself between Kent and the guy with the Gay Pride t-shirt. It was more than just getting in the way of the moment. He really was protecting him."

"I'm done with this shit, dude," said Cal. "Cody didn't kill his folks, and he's no terrorist. He's a lib-tard, but he's still one of us."

"Agreed. This BS has gotten way out of control. We shouldn't be fighting with one another like this. They're right; there are no 'others,' there's just us. We should be talking, especially with those we know are our neighbors, even if we don't agree with them."

Dan gave Cal a thumbs up in agreement, and they started walking back to get Des Moines. "It's gonna' be cold tonight," said Cal.

"Well," Dan said smiling, "Kent's got some matches. "Our packs are there. Maybe we can find something to eat."

***

Cody, Sweetie, and Chris let the horses rest for a moment, watching Dan and Cal pick up the magazine and then head in Des Moines' direction. While they waited, Sweetie and Chris informed him that the local news stations had indeed reported that terrorists had killed his family and that he may not have been, that his body had not been located and that if alive, he might still be in the Pasayten or even Canada.

"Fuck," said Cody, "Where is that news coming from? Carpenter must have told them that. Besides him, Balil, the leader, was the only one there."

"Buck Carpenter?" asked Sweetie.

"Yeah."

"Do you know him?" Cody asked. "He brought them in."

"He's my grandfather," she said. "And he's a great guy."

"What…?" said Cody, stammering in confusion. "How… I thought your grandfather…"

"He's my bio grandfather. Dad was adopted. Sort of. Buck got my gramma pregnant just before both got out of high school. He didn't have the money to go to college and knew he'd get drafted immediately. But he didn't want to go to Vietnam, so he went to Canada… along with thirty thousand other Americans. His real name is Avery Hanson. Gramma married my grandpa, and they raised my dad. Seven or so years ago, my dad sent in a 23 & Me spit sample for the heck of it, and before you know it, he got a notification asking him if he'd like to meet his real dad. Buck had sent one in, too. Dad got the notification on his birthday."

"Cool," said Chris.

"That is cool," Cody said. "Gramma must have had some 'splainen' to do."

"Yeah, she did," said Sweetie, chuckling. "Dad had no idea he was adopted. My grandpa, the fellow who raised him, died ten years ago, so Gramma was fine to have Dad meet up with Buck. They met up at the End of the Line on one of Buck's trips into the U.S. side. Mom went in, too. Turns out Buck was helping immigrants and asked Mom and Dad if they wanted to help."

"Is that why your folks are gone so much?" asked Chris.

"Yep. They've all been working together for the last five or so years, bringing people in from Canada and helping to place them in the area. Government spy helpers."

"That's so dope," said Chris. "I'll have to start calling your dad, Mr. Bond."

"Grandpa pays 'em good, and they get to do liberal-related stuff that makes 'em feel good," said Sweetie. "'Doing good for good people,' mom says. I guess these weren't good people."

"He told me he'd fucked this one up," said Cody, "and that he was really sorry. He headed back for Canada, said he'd try and get some help, and that someone 'in his loop' must have been involved in this in a bad way. He said he was not going to use his satellite phone for now and that I shouldn't either. Probably, 'they' might be hacking our calls or trying to pinpoint our locations. I didn't know whether to listen to him or blow him off."

"He's a good guy. Did you use your phone?" Sweetie said.

"No," said Cody.

"Where's your phone?" asked Sweetie.

"I've got it in my pack."

"Turned off?"

"Yeah."

"Well, glad you did what he said. When dad got back home last night, he said this whole thing had gone to hell," said Sweetie. "He said you were in trouble. That's why Chris and I are here. Buck had told dad that according to his Canadian agent, his usual go-between on these things, he thought the guy on the American side orchestrating this operation was some new State Department fellow working directly at the direction of the White House. Buck's guy was keeping him updated, per Buck's updates. But he said the guy didn't appear to be a typical diplomat. He wasn't a lifer, just a temp. The guy was an appointee of some kind and seemed to be working directly with the President or a close aide. His codename was Eldest. Buck said he thought Klingon was probably more appropriate."

***

Balil sat atop his horse and gazed down at Ross Lake reservoir in the distance. This was supposed to be Odion's target, based on their individual decisions after reading their instructions. He preferred minimizing deaths, opting instead for creating severe inconvenience and discomfort. Had everything gone correctly, they could command Buck's aide's car at the trailhead and drive here. But the aide had never appeared, Buck had disappeared, and his colleagues were all dead, as was the Forest Service family, except for the youngest, who was likely pursuing him.

Balil shot two of the horses after he secured his, and the other three ran off. Cody may have captured one of them, but he had not yet seen him. Currently, his goal was to make it down to the reservoir and then somehow to the dam. From where he sat, the terrain looked steep.

His map indicated a trail running along the edge on the east side, but he could not tell from where he stood. There were some boats on the water; he could see a few. If he could find one near shore, either moored or at a campsite, he could possibly hijack it and drive it to the dam.

The idea was Farhan's, having remembered a Nova episode he had watched one evening while the boys were students in Hawaii about Barnes Wallis, a British engineer who developed a way to effectively bomb German dams during WWII. The specially made bombs would skip along the water when dropped behind the dams. When they exploded, the force of the displaced water moving in the direction of the dam created by the plane's speed, as opposed to a direct hit by any bomb on concrete, would fracture the dam. The method worked extremely well in destroying German dams, well enough to earn Wallis a knighthood, though the mortality rate for the pilots flying the missions was especially high. The pontoons for the planes replaced the need for a skipping bomb, and none of the three terrorists were planning on going home.

With map in hand, Balil had made his way west to Ross Lake, presuming that a speeding boat, if he could find one, would be every bit as effective as a skipping bomb or floating plane. If he could not find a boat, his plan was to get as close as possible to the dam and jump into the water, sink until he could not hold his breath any longer, and then detonate the bomb. While hopeful of inflicting real damage, he did not care. The 9-11 soldiers had shown the disruptive value of such attacks in inflicting severe fear on America's social fabric. However, the psychological impact of the act on the United States was only half the value. Executing an event in Seattle would be far more dramatic and with more deaths, but setting off a bomb near a primary power and drinking water source would be a definite win as well. He would be an inspiration, his story and name spoken by those in his country fighting the American occupancy. His mission would be complete.

As he neared the lake, Balil realized that the trail he was on, Devil's Dome, ran downhill and eventually intersected Ross Lake near its center at the East Bank Trail, which ran about half the total length of the reservoir which ran due north from Ross Dam. The two trails intersected near the Devil's Creek Campground on the lake. There appeared to be a couple of other campgrounds to the north and several to the south on the way to the dam, which Balil estimated to be a five- or six-mile trek south. If he was lucky, he could hijack a boat at Devil's Creek or at one of those to the south. Otherwise, he could simply continue riding the horse. However, a motorized boat would make the trip quickly, and he could get much closer to the dam without attracting much attention. He knew the longer he stayed on the trail and the closer he got to the highway to where the East Bank led, the greater the chance he might be intercepted.

Balil spotted two groups of campers from the low bluff as he approached the Devil's Creek campground. There was only one craft, a fifteen or so foot boat with a sizable outboard motor that looked equipped for fishing, anchored in shallow water just offshore. He dismounted his horse, who he had named 'Ruhan,' or spirit, sat down his pack, positioned the horse to head back up the trail, thanked him, took off the bridle and saddle, and slapped him on the butt. Knowing home was back up the hill, the horse, having taken every opportunity to try and turn back that direction ever since they had taken the fork in the trail westward, began trotting up the hill toward home.

His plan was simple enough. He would stagger into the campground near one of the camps, cry for help, and then collapse. If it went as planned, both groups would come to help. He was correct. Both did.

The two campers that owned the boat were two brothers, Ed and Tod Franulovich, both in their fifties and from a nearby town, Sedro Woolley, further down the river. The other two were a thirty-something couple, Mike and Candy Wright from Seattle, who had hiked to the campground from the East Bank trailhead off Highway 20. While the hike in from the south was ten or so miles, a boat trip back south toward the dam was only around seven miles, which Balil guessed could be made in thirty-five minutes or less.

Still smattered in dried blood from the murders at the End of the Line, Balil clearly looked like an injured hiker, and when both groups, who were about equidistant from where he was, rushed to help him, they arrived at about the same time. Lying on his stomach, he had kept careful account of how the four were approaching. The two brothers arrived first. As they came closer, he rose to a crouched, 'all fours' position, keeping his right hand near his knee, his Glock stuck in front of his belt near his navel. His right arm supported him near his knee. Under his palm was the knife handle, the blade covered by his knee. Tod arrived first. Balil looked up and reached out with his left arm as if reaching for help. Seeing this, Tod went to his left side.

Balil looked up pleadingly. "Please help me," he said. "My wife and child were hurt. You must help me get them."

Tod leaned in, his knees bent slightly so he could reach Balil's left elbow. "Take it easy, man," he said. "What happened?"

Ed was about five feet directly in front of Balil. Mike and Candy arrived a couple of seconds later, directly to Ed's right.

"What happened?" asked Candy.

"He okay?" Mike asked concernedly.

Ed had a bewildered look on his face and merely pointed to Balil. "No idea," he said softly.

"My wife and boy. Please help me up," and with that, he began to stand but appeared weak.

"Easy," Tod said as he gently grabbed Balil's elbow and wrist with his two hands to help him up. As Balil rose, he grabbed Tod's shirt in the middle of his chest for apparent support. Between Balil pulling down on his shirt and Tod's real attempt to lift him, Tod had been thrown slightly off balance. At this point, Tod's back was to the other three. As Balil stood, he kept the knife in his hand, blade pointing down, tight against the back of his leg. As Tod wavered a little with Balil's shifting weight, Balil turned Tod ninety degrees so his right and Tod's right sides faced the other three. Ed had begun moving toward his brother but halted, waiting for the two men to stabilize. But before he could move again, Balil plunged the knife two times through Tod's rib cage, just below his armpit, and into his heart. Tod gave a moan that was so low the others thought it was associated with his effort to raise the stranger. As he pulled the knife from Tod's heart with his right hand, Balil reached with his left to grab the Glock tucked in his belt just in front of his navel.

As Tod slumped to the ground, blood spurting from his wound, Balil pointed the gun at the three. "Don't move," he warned them loudly.

Candy screamed.

"What are you doing?" cried Mike.

"What the fuck?" bawled Ed.

Gun pointed, Balil calmly said, "Stay back." Ed flinched in a forward motion, and Balil cautioned him to "Stay back" in a far more ominous tone.

"Don't hurt us," Candy pleaded.

"Shut up," said Balil sternly. He had scanned the two brothers' campsite when he first arrived, but now he was considering the two more closely. The brother had a larger tent, one, that would probably sleep at least four and was tall enough for him and probably the others to stand up. Waving his gun in the direction of the tent, he said, "Go to that tent."

Ed led the way while the other two filed behind him, Candy in the middle. "Don't hurt us," she wailed.

"I said shut up," he reminded her. "I won't tell you again."

"Okay, I'm sorry," she said.

'Women,' thought Balil to himself. 'The curse of mankind.' His mind went to Maya and his wife, Janan. 'Well,' he amended the thought, 'mankind's most enigmatic creature.' Curse or gift? He was not sure.

***

Balil had directed the three to the brothers' tent. "Get in," he commanded. They filed in as directed, Bill leading the way. Balil stood in the doorway. "You get over there," he directed Ed, who moved to Balil's left. "You there," he told Candy, pointing to the middle, "and you there," he said to Mike, motioning to his right. "Throw me that sleeping bag," he said to Ed, standing in front of what appeared to be a lightweight, insulated bag on a cot. Ed reached behind him, grabbed a piece of it in his hand, and threw it toward Balil's. "That your boat?" asked Balil.

"Yes," Ed said.

"How do you start it?"

"It's hooked to a battery. You just turn the key and push the start button next to it. It's blue. It's easy. Just take it."

Looking down, Candy stood limply, looking as if she were wilting, sniffling quietly as if she were watching a sad movie in a theatre, holding it back as best she could, not wanting anyone to hear. "Please don't hurt us," she whimpered.

"What did I tell you about talking?" said Balil. Looking at Mike, he said firmly, "Sir, please keep your wife quiet." Mike nodded silently but understandingly. "Please lay down while I try and figure out how to secure you."

Assuming the best, the three quickly all laid down on their stomachs, faces to the ground and about three feet.

"There's some rope just in front of me to my right," Ed said into the ground.

"Thank you. I appreciate that." Balil then walked over in front of Candy and draped the sleeping bag over each side of his hand, covering the gun. Knowing there were several campgrounds a half mile to the north, per his map, he was concerned about muffling the sound of the gun.

The gun covered, he shot in the direction of Ed and Mike, once each, and Candy, who did not even scream, once in the back of the head. Both men were moving, Mike groaning, so he quickly went to each, Mike first, and stuck his knife twice into their necks. Candy had been clearly hit in the base of her skull and was motionless, but he stabbed her five times as well, in concert with an admonishment for her, "I told… you… to… shut… up… madam."

***

About two miles north of Mazama, Chris slowed down and took a sharp left off the highway onto a semi-worn, two-lane trail into the woods.

"Where we headed?" Cody asked.

"A friend's cabin," said Sweetie.

"Aren't we on Forest Service land?" said Cody.

"There's a private parcel up here in another hundred yards or so on the river."

"Whose? I thought I knew most of the cabins out here."

At that point, they drove over a cattle guard, and though dark, Cody could see that a chain link fence ran in both directions of the guard, and there was an open gate that could swing shut and presumably lock. Cody could read a very large sign on the gate that, when closed, would clearly tell all who had driven in that far that this was:

Private Property
Do Not Enter
Trespassers Will Be Prosecuted
Or Worse

"You know the owner. They might be here," said Sweetie.

A couple of minutes later, a small log cabin came into view. It was probably about sixty years old but seemed well-maintained. The lights were on, and a new Ford 150 was parked outside.

"That looks like Steve's truck," Cody said.

"It is," responded Sweetie.

"This is his?"

"Yep."

"I didn't know he owned this out here," said Cody.

"I didn't either," said Chris, "until we stopped on the way up."

"For what?" asked Cody.

"Steve will explain," said Sweetie.

The three piled out of the truck and went to the door. Sweetie knocked twice but walked in immediately after, not waiting for anyone to answer.

"There you are," said Steve, as they came through the door. He was sitting on the couch with his computer in his lap. "God, I'm glad to see you all." He set the computer aside, stood, and walked over to Cody. Cody thought he would be shaking his hand for a moment, but when Steve got to him, he hugged him. Cody responded in part, still wondering why they were here. "Really glad to see you, man," said Steve. "You all hungry?"

"Famished," said Sweetie.

"Yeah," said Cody and Chris in tandem.

Briefly after sharing a rotisserie chicken from the Winthrop market and some chips, the four sat down in the living room.

"How long you had this?" asked Cody.

"Wow, for a while," said Steve.

"You never mentioned it," said Cody. "How come."

"Good question, Cody. Short answer is there was no good reason to tell you. Longer answer is it was best that you didn't know. This property has been in my family for a while, but I have spent some time shuffling it through different companies and aliases over the last fifteen years or so to obscure any ties to me. Right now, the owner is some company in the Cayman Islands."

"Why?" said Cody.

"To keep it off the grid. So, we have a place whose history is hard to track on paper, giving us a convenient, off-the-grid place, just like this one, in case we have a problem, just like the one you have, and you need a place just like this." Like a seasoned real estate agent who just finished their closing pitch, Steve held his arms out, palms up, with a body language that said 'voila' and an expression on his face that said 'easy-peasy.'

Cody shook his head, bewildered. "What else don't I know about you?"

"Well, let's talk about that. I'm going to share some things with you folks and show you some things that will be hard to watch. But at the very least, you need to know they exist, particularly you, Cody, and that they are essential to keeping you safe, in the short term and in the long term. That depends in part on who's in charge, but who you believe is in charge is not always the case. So, when you can, it is best to have some materials that'll protect you from the obvious and the not-so-obvious. Knowing some of this information actually puts you in danger but, at the same time, puts you in a position of strength. You just have to understand the difference and play your hands accordingly."

Steve's story began with a quick overview of his history in surveillance with Boeing. Most of them had assumed that this history ended with a decision to dial down the stress in his life and run a guide service in Winthrop that capitalized on the community's juxtaposition with the massive Pasayten Wilderness, a sizable chunk, almost fifteen percent, of the state of Washington's land mass. Clusters in its north central region, the area had a history of illegal immigration for decades, but more recently, it had become a favored route to covertly hike in immigrants of status from other countries. But others of not necessarily favored status were coming in, too, though in small numbers. To those ends and for those reasons, the area was on the 'watch list' of several federal agencies. However, overtly watching what went on at key crossing points would not only impact the security of those being brought into the country by showcasing their presence but also run afoul of conservation groups' positions on how to best maintain the sanctity of the wilderness experience.

One way to address all issues would be to outsource low-impact but highly effective security measures to complementary cover businesses like Steve's. Steve's experience and understanding of surveillance technologies were a perfect fit for a government hell-bent on watching their citizens in all places under the assertion of keeping them safe. Satellites and drones were effective means under limited circumstances. However, inclement weather and heavy vegetation in many areas provided unique challenges in the remote regions of the Pasayten. With government-funded efforts, however, Steve's operations were able to distribute and maintain various security devices in key locations to keep an eye on human traffic going into, through, and out of key routes in the region.

"I made the NSA, FBI, and CIA a proposal none refused," he told his three listeners. "It was the CIA that put me in touch with Buck Carpenter about seven years ago. He was bringing in his tourists, I call them transplants, more and more 'til he was up to a dozen or more a season. The government wanted to pick them up with cameras at the End of the Line or a point or two in between and then see them passed off at the trailheads. I put in cameras at a couple of other locations as security for campers and hikers, too, but mostly for our customers, since I already had a system in place. I figured the cameras might come in handy if any of my guides got into trouble or maybe made trouble. Just like the guns."

"So, you watch us?" Cody asked in amazement.

"Yep."

He considered it a moment and then said, "Is that why you said you *knew* I was telling the truth when that girl claimed I was coming on to her?"

"What?" said Sweetie.

"Yep," said Steve. Then he turned to Sweetie, adding, "Some girl accused Cody of trying to feel her up. Said they'd been making out while her folks were out hiking, and he tried to take it further. Cody said she came on to him and had just ignored her. I had it all on tape." Sweetie just smiled. "The whole woman scorned vengeance thing. I didn't say anything because I didn't want you to know about the system."

"Then you'd have had to kill him?" said Chris, jesting.

Steve smiled with a minor raise in his eyebrows but said nothing. "It's one of those pieces of information best known by as few as possible."

"So, Buck knows all that's there?" Cody asked.

"Yep. Pretty much just Buck and me and a few people who work for the government. I wouldn't be surprised if Buck has shared it with a couple of his contacts on the Canada side, just in case."

"In case what?" asked Chris.

"In case something were to happen to him, or untrue claims were made by some on either side of the border. Depending on what it was and where it happened, he might have some helpful backup evidence."

"Wow. Well, until all this shit came down, I'd have called bullshit on that. But now that it has…" Cody said, his voice trailing off. "I have a feeling I know, then, what some things are that you said I'll never want to see," he said solemnly.

"Yeah," said Steve quietly. "I'm afraid so."

"Give me the bad news, then."

"It's not all bad, at least for you. Some is helpful."

"Like what?"

"Well, the bad news first, you guessed it. I have what happened to your parents on tape. The angle was such that we could also see what was going on across the lake. We can blow it up for detail, and though a little of the clarity is lost, it's clear you were not in the camp when they were killed, that you shot one, and that one tried to kill you, but Buck got to him first. It's quite a showdown. We also picked up some of the conversations that the three Freedom Fighters were having at the trailhead. One of them, the leader, was talking to someone on his global phone."

"Kent Des Moines," Sweetie and Chris said in unison.

"He said your name out loud while he was talking to the other person on the phone," Steve said to Cody.

"Who was it, do you think?" Sweetie said.

"Not sure, but he… Des Moines, you said… was bragging that he was dealing directly with the White House. That means the White House has probably gone rogue, outside normal channels. They're giving directives directly to militia groups. I don't believe the military would be cooperating with them or regular law enforcement, and if they are, at least at the federal level, we're fucked. Local level? Who knows? There's lots of cowboys out there that would like a direct connection with the White House."

"Holy shit," said Chris.

"Exactly," said Steve.

"Shouldn't someone tell the CIA or FBI or someone?" Chris said.

"I'm sure they already know," Steve said, "but you can bet they'll be talking to Buck… and probably me soon enough."

"Why don't they do something now?" said Sweetie.

"What can they do?" said Cody coldly, begging to understand the gravity of the situation.

"Bingo," said Steve. "I mean, the whole system, though corrupt in so many ways, assumes that all the players will still operate within certain boundaries. The whole checks and balances thing. Different parties are responsible for different things. Some, like the CIA and NSA, go to extremes, no doubt, but we assume for the greater good. These clowns just do anything they want. If intelligence speaks up, they're admitting they're listening… watching. Then it's a discussion around who's really in charge."

"That's what J. Edger did, isn't it?" said Cody. "Got so much dirt on everyone that nobody could touch him. The FBI was pretty corrupt, at least in that regard."

"Yeah. That's a pretty good comparison," said Steve. "It's a bit of a game about who's got what on whom and how they can craft a story that'll best sell to the public. Sex is always a good one. People love dirt on sex. That was J. Edger's primary focus. If you were heard plotting to overthrow the country, you were in trouble. If you were heard screwing your secretary or a page, you were notified. POTUS has also discredited or questioned the accuracy or integrity of all the major spy agencies. Says he knows more than them. The public doesn't know who to believe anymore. And some ridiculous stories are ending up on social media. The public is watching and listening to the wildest social media conspiracies, thinking they know everything and mostly know nothing. It's a problem."

"Crazy," said Sweetie.

"So, what do we do?" asked Chris.

"We do what they do. We play by our own rules," said Steve.

"What's that include?" asked Cody.

"Well, first, we get you out of here, out of the country. You need to get to Canada. From there, Buck can figure out where to house you safely… with help from their and our agencies. Second, we need to go mining."

"Mining? Mining what?" said Cody.

"For dirt," said Steve. "We need to figure out who Des Moines was talking to and then study them. And POTUS, too, but he's more problematic. I'll figure it out. In the short term, though, I need to copy the information we have, encrypt it, and get it out to three or four safe locations. I think they'll try to pin all this on you, Cody, at least initially. But we can defend you with the truth, which we have on video. I'm certain they don't know it exists, unless they have a mole in the NSA. That's who I work for. Them and the CIA. They both inform the FBI about what I do to the extent they feel they need to. I've got contacts in all three that I can talk to. But their contacts only run so deep. The White House will have moles in all three on the lookout for such information, but most of them will probably be easy to spot. They'll be appointees by this administration and their hires post-election, most likely."

"Aren't there people in those agencies that support the president politically?" Chris asked.

"Sure," said Steve. "But most are lifers that stay out of such details and drama. They want to protect their jobs. And most, actually, believe they're serving a higher purpose."

"Not that many Snowdens then?" asked Chris.

"Well, that's a different type altogether, but no. Most of these folks are just putting in their time for the country's benefit. For all the right reasons." He paused and then added, "Most of them."

"What about you?" asked Chris. "What's your story."

Steve looked at him, a little taken aback by the question, not sure exactly where he might be coming from. "Well," he said, "I used to be a cog in the machine, like I've told you. It paid well. I thought I was doing good for the country and the world. I got a little bored pretty fast by it all, though. Originally, after I left, I just wanted to do the guide thing. Change of pace, you know. But they found me and asked if I wanted to do this added service. It had, has… some positive features, it seemed, and the pay was good, so I said sure. I think I was right about it doing some good."

"How's that?" said Cody. "It does run contrary to the whole wilderness experience thing, not to mention some privacy matters."

"Well, here we are. Right?" he said, opening his arms in a welcoming manner, while panning the faces of all three. "If we didn't have that equipment in place, you'd be knee-deep in shit. Probably dead."

Cody nodded, agreeingly. "True dat, boss, but I might be knee-deep anyway."

"Maybe, but we've got some pretty good shovels to help deal with that," Steve said, holding up a flash drive. "It'll be interesting to see what they come up with and how they'll walk it back after they know we have these. Because whatever it is they say, they almost certainly will have to walk it back. Otherwise, about their only other play would be, 'Yeah, we did it, so what, let's start the next Civil War.' I guess that would have some appeal to many in their base. But they gotta' win. Otherwise, it could turn into trying to start an uprising that doesn't go anywhere."

"Sounds pretty extreme," said Chris. "Surreal, actually. You don't think they'd actually try and do something like that, do you?"

"Like Mel Brooks said in *The History of the World*, 'It's nice to be the king.' It can be hard to let go of that kind of power, not just by the king but all those around them. These folks seem to be willing to do anything, even if it means burning down the country."

"So, Civil War, you think?" said Sweetie.

"I think as big an issue," Steve said, "is how other countries will see us when they realize we're this divided. It makes us look weak. Hell, it makes us weak. What's going on is B-A-D. I'd say regardless of who wins the next election, the other big guys like Russia and China will start muscling into being number one. They'll be testing us for sure. Just wait."

"While we argue if 'the elites' are drinking the blood of and fucking young kids," said Sweetie.

"Or if masks violate our freedoms," said Cody, shaking his head. "All that crucial shit."

"So, here's the plan, Cody," Steve said. "Tomorrow before sunrise, I will get you back to the Windy Peak trailhead. I have a battery-powered trail bike in the back of my truck. I'll drop you off, and you'll ride it into Canada. Buck will meet you at their trailhead. It's only five or six miles beyond the border. The whole trip is thirty miles or so. You should just make it. But, with the hills and such, you might run out of juice, so there's another battery on the back."

"What if someone sees me," asked Cody. "There may still be hikers in there that'll see me. They'll go apeshit if they see a motorized vehicle on the trail, won't they?"

"Maybe, but it's an electric bike. They won't hear you, which is ninety-five percent of the issue. You'll be in Forest Ranger attire. If someone sees you, and it's a big if, just tell them you're conducting an emergency run for an injured hiker further up the trail, like a serious sprain, who called in on their global phone. I've put a visible, big ass first aid kit on the back for optics… or if *you* end up needing it."

"What if the batteries still don't get him there?" asked Chris.

"Then just move it off the trail and start hoofing it. We'll get it later. We've given them an ETA of between 2:00-3:00 p.m. That's aggressive, but we want to get you in before dark. Sun goes down earlier as you go further north."

"What happens when I get to Canada?" Cody said.

"Buck will take care of that. And I think getting you up there via the trail is a good idea. He'll get you into hiding. They'll be banging on doors here looking for you. And it would only be a matter of time before they found you here.”

“Who’s they, if the agencies are all on our side?” asked Chris.

“Militias. Some local law enforcement. Whoever the White House is tapped into. And it’s obvious they have some contacts who’ll do their bidding. Buck’s in good graces with the CIA and CSIS, Canada’s version. You’ll find a good interim home until this thing sorts out. But those responsible for bringing in those three will be on the lookout, too. Whoever his contact was on this calamity is tainted.”

“When do we leave?” said Cody.

“Four a.m.,” said Steve. “That’ll get us to the trailhead a good hour or so before daybreak. We can see if there are any other cars and get an idea of whether or not someone might be in there, and if so, who it might be. I doubt they’re thinking of you going back in, and if they are, I don’t think they can cover every trailhead at this point.”

“Unless they’ve rallied that many of their militiamen,” said Sweetie.

“Possibly, but again, they only have so many to deploy without raising some serious red flags around the area, so I’d guess, well, I am guessing, their attention will be in Winthrop or Twisp. They’ll definitely be watching your homes. Hoping one of you will show up with him. So, after we leave in the morning, Cody, you two go home,” Steve said, looking at Chris and Sweetie. “Be visible, like nothing ever happened.”

“Cool,” said Chris.

Sweetie nodded, though her face expressed worry. She walked over to Cody and hugged him. He returned her hug, though tentatively. "You'll be okay," she said.

"I know," he said, somewhat uncertainly.

"Fix him something to eat," Steve said to nobody. "He could be on the trail awhile, especially if the weather is bad."

"I'll fix some sandwiches," Sweetie said.

"I'll help," said Chris.

"When you're done, you two get back to town. Don't turn on your lights leaving here until you get to the highway. Don't turn them on until you're sure no cars are coming from either direction. Last person to unload, park your car in the garage, if possible. Let's try to keep them guessing what we might be doing as long as possible."

Sweetie and Chris both nodded, understandingly. When they had finished fixing Cody's sandwiches, they said their goodbyes to Cody. All three cried openly, not knowing when they would see one another again.

"Take care of yourself, and I'll see you soon. I love you," Sweetie choked out while giving him a long, warm hug, before she and Chris got in the car and headed home.

***

Day 5

White House

"What the fuck happened?" yelled POTUS. "This is a shitstorm to challenge all shitstorms, Emma" He picked up a paperweight and threw it at the bulletproof window behind his desk, a favorite POTUS antic, as he knew it would just bounce off. But the optics were unsettling to viewers in the room, especially new ones, who had not yet grown accustomed to a one or two-pound brass object being tossed at what otherwise seemed a normal glass window. Great optics for disarming the bystanders and getting everyone else's full attention. "We have to find that kid and kill the little fucker," he screamed.

He crouched deep into his chair, arms crossed, looking angry, all if in tandem with his trademark complementary pouty face that would have surely garnered most elementary school children extra detention.

"Sir," Emma said sternly, "Calm down. Please. We can't lose our composure here."

He had swiveled the chair and was facing out the window, arms still crossed. For a brief few seconds, he stamped his feet, saying nothing. "Don't talk to me like that," he demanded. "I'm not a fucking child."

'Bullshit,' she thought. "Take a deep breath, sir," she said. He did. "Let it out slowly." He did. "We have this under control."

He swung the chair and made a half turn back to where he was facing his desk. Glaring at her menacingly, he said, "Emma. You promised this would be okay." His coloring was odd, a hint of angry flushed red with a touch of his normal orange. Pinkish? "You promised." His words were beginning to sound pleading.

"Hey," she said, trying to sound matter-of-factly. "They didn't kill everybody they were supposed to. The guide got away, and the kid got away."

"And the guide's aide," the president reminded her quietly.

"Yeah, and the aide," she said. "We're getting Canada to arrest the guide and the kid to return them here. The guide's a deserter anyway. Nobody will believe his shit. He's easy to discredit."

"Should we send in some Navy seals?"

"No, we can't do that. Not without asking Canada, and they'll say no. They're still trying to figure out what exactly is going on and who orchestrated it. They know it wasn't CIA or FBI."

"We can tell them it was. I'm their boss. They'll believe me."

"Well, that might result in some mass resignations. That'd generate the need for some serious explaining."

"He's worked with the State Department for almost fifty years," said POTUS, raising his voice just a bit. "That's gonna get out, don't you think? He's more than just a draft dodger."

'Yeah, he walked to Canada,' she thought. 'He definitely couldn't claim bone spurs.' "Look," she said out loud, "we'll control that information with the press and the narrative. Not to worry, sir. Haven't had a chance to tell you. Guess who the guide's aide is?"

"Nancy Pelosi?" he said, smiling.

"Better. His son… and he's married to a Lebanese. How's that?" Emma said with glee.

"No shit," said the president, now getting upbeat.

Emma continued wagging her head in a 'yeah, yeah' manner. "And, the kid we'll say killed the Freedom Fighter? It's getting better. His girlfriend is the aide's daughter." The president's face said,

'Huh?' as he tried to track the connections. "Sooo," Emma continued, slowing down the presentation so he could keep up, "the Canadian guide is a Vietnam War protest-deserter. His son, who helps him smuggle in aliens, is married to a Lebanese. Their daughter is the girlfriend of the boy whose family was killed. And that boy killed the Freedom Fighter. Mother fucking fucker," she ballyhooed, "you couldn't write a book and make this shit up any better. This ties together perfectly. Diversity's Achille's heel." Emma gave a shiver of satisfaction, pivoted, and looked directly at him with glee. "This shit is really going to piss off our base and the public in general. There's so many spins in here." She held up her hands as if framing a newspaper headline. "Kid helps terrorists get into the country. Subtext kills his parents and patriots trying to protect our citizens. Great story for the press."

"That might be a tough one to keep together," said the president skeptically. "The liberal press will be looking into this one for months. Probably years. Conservatives, too. Lots of questions to answer, Emma. Hard to contain the truth on something like this."

"Well, the truth is what we tell them is the truth," Emma said. "Unless, of course, we have to change some facts. Then that's the truth," she said matter-of-factly. "Shit, our core... your core," she said, as if actually correcting herself, "will believe anything you tell them. How many times have they never questioned you on a flipflop?" The president's face said, 'Yeah, you gotta point there.' "You just say, nah, that's not what I said or meant, the liberal press got it wrong or took it out of context trying to make it into something else, and voila, it's yesterday's news that nobody gives a shit about anymore."

He continued with tiny nods as he looked pensively. "What about the two that found the Freedom Fighter, Ken Demon? Who did they talk to?"

"They just redialed the last number of the dead guy's global phone."

"Who'd they get?" POTUS asked.

"Me," said Emma. "They won't say anything," said Emma. "I scared the crap out of them. Based on what they said, I think we've got a kidnapping case against the kid and his two friends for making them walk with them. And murder, of course. FBI will be all over it."

"Where are they now?"

"I told them to drag their buddy into the woods, cover him up as best they could, and walk out with all the guns, phones, etc. Then, I arranged for a Freedom Fighters' vehicle to pick them up at the trailhead and put them in hiding. They're at some home in a little turd town called Conconully."

"Well, they didn't kill the guy, right? So, no murder, right?"

"Yeah, a bear got him, but indications are he was drugged. The boys witnessed it. Serious manslaughter, anyway, at the least. Shit, he was still alive when his two minions got there. Sort of alive. His face was kind of… gone, they said. I guess he bled out. The boy on the phone was crying like a little bitch. Said his name was Dan or Cal. I can't remember."

"Whoa. What kind of bear?" asked POTUS.

Emma thought about saying Panda just to see what he would say. "Probably a black bear, the kid said. He said too bad it wasn't a grizzly. Then he'd have been dead a lot faster."

"Wow. That's gross."

"No shit," said Emma.

"Kinda cool, though, yeah?" said POTUS, smiling, holding back a laugh.

"Yeah, kind of," said Emma, nodding fervently, eyes wide. "Nature, right?"

"What's next?" asked POTUS.

"Find those two," said Emma, resolutely. "We're pretty sure they went back to their little town and are hiding out somewhere. We'll get 'em before they can talk to the media."

"Then what?"

"Make sure they stay quiet. Keep 'em in jail if necessary. Maybe forever. Gotta control the narrative and information pipeline. Most of the metro media in Seattle and Portland are pretty liberal. We're leaking out some details to right-wing radio stations in the Northwest, their complementary websites, and Facebook and Twitter accounts so we can begin orchestrating how we want the story to morph. When it's ready for TV, we can give an exclusive to Fox in Spokane. From the Cascades to Chicago, it is all red. But get those folks worked up and believe what we want them to first; it won't really matter what shows up on television."

"Yeah, you'll have a good time developing a storyline around the players you've disguised," said POTUS. "What about the terrorist that got away?"

"Yeah, he's not the biggest problem," Emma said. "One way or another, he'll be dead soon. You know what they say about terrorists," she said quizzically. POTUS' eyebrows lifted. "Hard to find. Even harder to interrogate."

POTUS grinned broadly. "I like it. What if he detonates the bomb?"

"I hope he does. Like I just said." POTUS shared his 'Like' with two thumbs up. "And, if he does," Emma went on, "all this other shit won't matter. It's 9-11 all over again, baby. The focus will be on the act of terrorism, and the public will believe everything we say about the guide and the kid. They'll want a lynching."

"Shit, maybe they'll want us to nuke Iraq… or Iran.? That's what happened with 9-11."

"Maybe even Canada!" Emma said with mock enthusiasm.

"That'd fix that Canuck bastard." the president said, suddenly appearing somewhat thoughtful, referring to the Prime Minister. "I think he wanted to fuck my wife, you know." Then he turned to Emma with a grin bigger than a tickled hyena, "Good luck, mister hotshot Prime Minister. I can't even get her to fuck me." Then he added, with concern, "What about our security agencies? They'll be onto us sooner or later. Communications without Canadian contact have gone cold."

"I'm sure they've already picked up pieces of it, but since it's not 'theirs,' it'll be another day, two max, before they figure out how we put it together."

"Then?"

"Then?" She smiled broadly. "Then fuck them. What are they going to do? Tell the world the President of the United States set up a plan to bring in three terrorists to execute an attack on the country? They can't do that. That'd make them and the country look like an even bigger shitshow. And they can't claim credit for it. They gotta stay quiet on this until they figure out a response. The only reasonable explanation is to blame another country and punish them."

"Canada?" said POTUS.

"No."

"Can our agencies claim ignorance?"

"That makes them look even more incompetent. No, this is a completely new approach by the White House, and they're fucked. They're not in charge anymore. You are. We have them by the balls."

With that, POTUS gave her a high five and eyed Emma with admiration. 'This is a great woman,' POTUS thought to himself. Emma had a very cute face and looked a little like Emma Watson with a short haircut. Her hair was black, and she commonly wore blazers and jeans, which were a perfect way to complement her 5'4 slight frame. 'Loyal to the bone,' he knew. 'She'd probably be a great little fuck if she just wasn't so damn dikey,' he thought to himself.

Emma smiled back. 'Such a clown, a fat orange one, at that,' she thought. 'So easy. Men just love to believe they're in charge. They'll always follow their dick, so you just must help them point it in the desired direction. I wonder if he's heard his wife's favorite Secret Service guard is fucking her?'

It was not that the POTUS was a great strategist. He just didn't respect safeguards as being safeguards or rules that had been in place for, well, always, had anything to do with him. Democracies are used by those in power to bend the rules. But he simply ignored the rules. Nobody had done that, out loud and in full public view with no fear of retaliation. If he had a strategy at all, it was one of *strategic indifference*. He was president; he could do and say what he wanted, and many people loved that he did just that. He would have your back if you were loyal or if he was not hurt or threatened. Nonetheless, Emma knew one had to make sure they always had a plan B, C, and D because if the water were to get too rough and he had to cut somebody loose, she was confident he would drop you faster than Prince Andrew's pants at a Jeffry Epstein camp for high school cheerleaders.

***

It had only taken Emma about eight minutes to bring the Vice President up to speed on their attempt to bring three terrorists into the country to create an optics diversion from the pandemic to one of national security. The country was growing weary of the 'invasion' at the southern border. It was losing its cache with most states north of Arizona and Texas, even with some of their most ardent core. Concerns were rapidly shifting to the pandemic, Emma had acknowledged, its worsening, and whether there would be a need for further security measures to be enforced on businesses, measures that would be stifling the country's economy even further. They could lose the election simply because of a failing economy, the catalyst for

294

which was beyond their control. Their choices of action either produced more deaths and pandemonium from loser restrictions on business or better control of the pandemic at the expense of many, many jobs. Regardless of their choice, she argued, they would be judged by the negative outcome of either choice. "Damned if we do, damned if we don't," she had said near the end of her overview. "This diversion will be a great diversion back to something that we can show leadership and action on that will have appeal to the majority of the country."

"Mr. President," said Jack, "this is highly irregular, sir. I... I don't... I don't like this. I don't like this at all."

"What don't you like about it, Jack?" asked POTUS.

"Well, it's illegal." He paused before cautiously adding, "It's treasonous."

"Come on, Jack," POTUS goaded. "Don't be such a pussy, man. All's fair in love, war, and politics, right? It's not like our CIA and others don't pull this sort of shit all the time for their own benefits in countries around the world."

"For the good of the country, sir?" the Vice President said firmly. "This is for *your* benefit,"

"What's the difference, Jack? He's the president," said Emma. "He's the boss; he is the country. Everyone in the executive and military branches works for him, for Christ's sake. You want your job to go on for another four years, don't you? This is for all our goddamn benefits."

Obviously upset, Hoffman's voice took the numinous tone of a softcore evangelical. "I am Mr. Vice President to you, madam, and please don't use the Lord's name in vain like that when I'm here."

Emma and the president looked at one another briefly before simultaneously erupting into a guffaw. The president even slapped his knee twice.

"God, that was great, Jack. Just great. Made me want to stand at attention and salute you, man. I'm going to start calling you the Snowman. You're so cool, man." Hoffman's face turned quizzical when POTUS said 'Snowman,' keenly aware of the man's propensity for sardonic nicknames. Sensing his disconnect, POTUS explained. "Snowman. You're so white. The hair. Your skin. Your demeanor. I'm getting you a top hat for Christmas. *The Snowman* in front. Abominable," POTUS' tone turning the word to an ugly dig, "on the back."

Hoffman stood, fists clenched, but for just a little. He stayed cool, not letting his anger get the best of him. "What you're doing, what you have done, it's wrong."

"That's a matter of perspective. It's a great move. Game winner," said POTUS. "Guaranteed to scare the shit of people on both sides of the fence before the election. We can't lose. Shit, we can cancel the election, and nobody would say a word. Not Speaker Polaski. Not Speaker Mac-colon or Senator Shyster. This will be a bigger rallying call than 9-11. The country will not want to shift leaders with this crisis in place."

"Sir, you open the door for more Middle East conflict."

"Yeah. And?"

"Russia and China will both have a green light to begin making incursions into who knows where, as we figure out who we're going to declare war on this time. If all our energies and focus are directed at keeping our business in order at home, then others will try and take advantage of the situation to advance their own agendas, regionally and internally."

"And blah, blah, blah, Jack. I suppose Mexico and Canada will be after our goodies, too, huh? Jesus, you're such a fucking downer. I don't think I can count on you, Jack. I don't think you'll be there for me when I need you most, man."

"Nobody has been a bigger supporter of you from the very beginning, Mr. President. I don't know how you can say that. But this," he said, waving his hand in an arc across the room that included Grant, "this is bovine feces."

"OMG, Jack. You can't even say bullshit? Go figure out how that vaccine stuff is going, will you please," POTUS said, waving the back of his hand toward the door. "You were supposed to have fixed that. Have you? No, you haven't. And that, my friend, is why we're in the mess we're in in the polls. This is your fault, loser. All yours," POTUS almost shouted while pointing his finger angrily at Hoffman. "You are why we're having to do what we're doing." Before the Vice President could respond, POTUS said, "*Now go*. Get out of here, Mr. Snowman. I mean it. Goddamn abominable."

When he got there, Hoffman stood and walked to the door, turning and said, "This isn't how a democracy works, sir. We're a nation of laws. This is illegal. We'll all go to jail."

"Nation of laws? Are you fucking kidding me? We're a nation of lawyers. All ready to sell their souls for the right price, and tell themselves they're making sure everyone gets a fair trial. The really good ones keep people like us from ever going to jail… no, no matter what we do. Especially someone at this level. The rest of 'em? They pretend to take care of the people that don't matter." Emma loved extreme applications of power to control, and the president's tirade was starting to make her tingle a little down there. "Did Nixon go to jail? You remember that one? Fuck no, he didn't. This? Shit, man, I'm just doing my job, and a big part of my job is just keeping my job."

Dumbstruck, Hoffman looked down for a moment, then said, "And your nickname by historians, Mr. President?"

The president shrugged his shoulders, raised his hands high, palms turned to the sky, and said, "Enlighten me, Snowman."

"Pogo."

POTUS closed his eyes, shook his head, and waved his hands back toward the exit. The Vice President, his face looking scornful, opened the door and, like a small child sent to their room for time out, sulked away.

"Pogo?" POTUS mused vexingly after Hoffman had left.

Not wanting to explain, Emma said, "Snowman? Where did that come from?"

"Should have changed it to icicle dick and bounced that one off his wife."

"What do you think he'll do?" she asked.

"Nothing," she said. Then, borrowing a line from the song High Noon, she added, "He's *a craven coward.*"

Can you imagine a president like that?" POTUS said. "Putin would roll over him like a Goddamn…" Then, catching himself, he added, "Oh, and I just said another no-no. Saw-wee," he said mockingly while making a bungled cross on his stomach.

Emma laughed politely but was worried, underneath, what Hoffman might do. He was a loyalist at heart. Not only to the president, but far more so to the country. She had been reluctant to tell him of their plot, but it was hard for them to pull it off without him in the fold, especially if things got more complicated than they already were. However, if he did not go public immediately or leak it, which she was certain he would not, then he was complicit via inaction. How the next few days would unfold was critical in that regard. He had contacts, friends, at all the law enforcement and security agencies. Involving them could complicate things. But that, too, was unlikely. What could they do? He was the president. He represented the country, and what would such a plot, fostered by the president, say about the country.

It was likely, Emma thought, that she and the president might have to personally involve Canada to assist them in dealing with some of these issues. The three terrorists had taken care of themselves in Canada for the time they were there. It would take a little time, a week if they were lucky, two weeks if they were really lucky. But, in this world of covert actions and information, almost anything could be purchased for the right amount of money. Say what they might about the negative aspects of capitalism; even communists and terrorists loved money. And the American government had plenty. In the meantime, she would have to monitor the Snowman's behavior and make sure he did not start a hailstorm.

"What if the press gets wind of this?"

"I'm on the press, sir. There's only a very few people who know the complete genesis of this thing. It's really just Derek, his contact, and us who know all the details. Now, Jack, too, but he lacks some of the details in the beginning. I do worry some, though, about the Vice President."

"Snowman?" The president stood, did a pivot, and looked out the window. "He can't do anything. Really, what can he do? This country isn't set up to handle this kind of shit. It's one of its greatest weaknesses." He turned back and looked at Emma. If Darth Vader had been smiling behind that helmet, POTUS would likely have made a perfect impression. "I'll fix that." Even Emma felt a slight, momentary chill from the tone in his voice. "Where's the kid?" he said.

"He's gotta' be in or near his hometown."

"Find him."

"A top priority, sir. We're hoping to be able to track his phone."

"And tell our boys it's time to get ready to stop standing down. Time to stand up."

"I'm on it, sir. He's a dead kid walking."

"The militias will be bragging this up. About helping us."

"Yeah, but again, they don't know the whole story. They think they're doing a great service to the country."

The president immediately interjected, "They are."

Emma continued her thoughts. "We can always just deny any direct connections. It's a myth of the Freedom Fighters. Fake news by a liberal media."

"Seems to work every time."

"At least with the ones who count."

"Exactly," said POTUS.

***

Balil woke suddenly to the sound of two voices outside of the tent. Sheila and Paul Donnelly had begun their walk out from the next campground a mile up the trail and had stopped to use the restroom. Sheila was the one in need, and Paul, curious, walked toward the tent where Balil was sleeping.

Balil had arranged himself at the end of the four cadavers, having pulled Mike's body to the tent shortly after killing the other three, positioning himself so that at first glance, he might possibly be confused as a fifth victim by anyone happening on the campsite. In the morning, he intended to say prayers, the first time he would have done so in almost a week, eat something, get in the boat, speed down the lake, and blow up his bomb near Ross Dam… and himself in the process. Balil was not about being a martyr. Nor was he interested in more virgins than he was able to comprehend in one location, let alone having sex with all of them. He just wanted to be with his family. Unbeknownst to him, news had broken early in the morning on local and national news that:

A psychologically disturbed male immigrant, originally from Iraq, entered the country through a remote region in North Central Washington state at the Canadian border, possibly led in by a guide who, when younger, was a Vietnam deserter. As they entered the country, the men encountered an American family from a small nearby town that were camping. An altercation apparently broke out between the intruder and at least four members of the family. The guide escaped back into Canada. The fifth family member may have been killed or wounded, may still be in the Pasayten, or may have escaped into Canada with the guide.

"Hello? Hello? Anybody in there?" Paul said, his voice friendly.

At first, Paul thought that whoever was camping there might have gone fishing. They had noticed a boat three days before when they had walked in. The tent and general setup were the same as he had noticed earlier, except the camp was a bit more messy. The table, which had been neat and organized, now had opened packages of different kinds of food strewn across the entire tabletop. Curious, Paul decided to peek inside the tent.

"Knock. Knock," he said, then paused. "Coming in." The first two bodies were right before him and laid out left to right. There were five in all. The two in front of him were covered in dried blood. "Fuck! Fuck!" he screamed.

"What is it?" yelled Sheila, now coming out of the toilet.

Paul turned, standing in the tent's entry, and yelled back, "There's dead bodies in here! Run! Run!" he said, holding his arm up and waving his hand to the south. "I'm right..." His last words were suddenly cut short.

Balil, seeing Paul had turned his back, quickly snuck up behind him and put his hand over his mouth as he simultaneously stuck the blade of his knife into the middle of the right side of Paul's rib cage.

He quickly pulled out the knife and then aggressively pulled the blade across the length of Paul's throat. Blood gushed from the wound, and Paul quickly collapsed to his knees and then forward onto his face. Seeing it all, Sheila turned and began running down the trail to the south, screaming manically and yelling 'Help!' at least for the first two hundred feet.

Having no idea who else might be in the immediate area and hearing the commotion, Balil grabbed his backpack and began heading to the lake's edge to board the boat. There was no time for prayers, no time for a snack. He had to get out of there. It was his time.

Balil had no idea how deep the two brothers had in their boat. When he got to the edge, he lifted the pack above his head and slowly walked in. The boat was no more than twenty feet from shore. As he began to wade in, he was surprised at how quickly the shoreline began to drop off. In just about five feet, the water was up to his crotch. Worried he would be over his head by the time he got to the boat and how he would get the pack in, he slowed his walk, cautiously inching forward. But, by the time he got to the boat, the height of the water was only up to his pecs. He raised the pack as high as he could and dumped it up and over into the craft. Moving slowly to the boat's aft, he grabbed a ladder that hung from the side well into the water. Pulling himself up, he climbed into the boat Balil and, lifted the ladder and dropped into the lake. Then, he grabbed a white rope that he correctly guessed to be the anchor, raised it, and dropped it at the bottom of the boat. Moving to the front of the boat, he turned the key to the right and pushed the blue button to its left. It started on the third try. After waiting a moment for it to warm up, Balil pushed the throttle to his right forward. The boat began moving forward, and Balil, who had wanted to say his prayers before he left, felt a surge of relief that the effort of starting the boat had gone as easily as it had.

***

As soon as daylight allowed, which was about forty minutes after Steve had dropped him off, Cody began to make his way up the trail. In the beginning, he kept his speed very low. Having walked and ridden horseback into this particular area many times, he knew the first mile or so by heart. But being on a vehicle that went this fast when it was still darkish while at the same time trying to keep his balance proved more challenging than he had expected, a challenge exacerbated by the pack on his back. Besides a change of clothes and some toiletries, Steve had given him three thousand dollars, which was at least twice what he was owed for outstanding wages. But everything else he owned was being left behind. This was a complete *life do-over*.

As daylight continued to increase in intensity and as he grew more accustomed to his pack, Cody was able to pick up speed. Over the next few hours, he could vary his progress on the Ebike Fat Tire anywhere from six or seven miles per hour up to ten for sustained periods with occasional bursts to twenty-five across the flats. At some of the highest elevations, there was a couple of inches of snow in areas with sustained degrees of shade. Given the great variation in terrain, his battery expired about two-thirds of the way through, and he had to replace it with the spare Steve had given him.

Not long after noon, he reached the U.S.-Canadian border. Fortunately, for the entire period, he had not seen any hikers. However, seeing one car parked at the trailhead left him assuming the owners had probably taken one of the several tangential trails that broke off along the main route as it meandered its way north. A wilderness purist, he would have resisted using such vehicles in this setting, had he ever heard of such a proposed use, considering them a standard, noisy, obnoxious off-road vehicle. But after experiencing their value on this adventure, he knew he would actively consider one as an option where they were legally allowed. And if he were running an actual search and rescue or research effort, these would be incredibly efficient.

As Steve had suggested before he left, he decided to walk in the last quarter to a half mile so that he could reconnoiter the trailhead before committing to walk into the area. Guessing out how far he was from the end, based on signs along the way and his bike's odometer, he ended up walking only the last quarter or three-eighths-mile. After walking the bike behind a huge Douglas fir, he slowly began walking toward the trail's end. When he caught a glimpse of a car through the trees, he ducked about twenty feet into the trees, obscuring himself to get a better look. After checking to make sure his 9mm pistol was tucked securely in the back of his pants, he crouched down and slowly began moving forward, darting from tree to tree, trying to keep out of site.

As he approached the edge of the parking lot, he saw a total of three vehicles, two cars and a pickup truck. About fifty feet to his left sat a stone restroom with a women-only stall on one side and a men's stall on the opposite side. Two cars were in front of him, one directly, the other five stalls to the right. The truck, which was in the row behind the two cars, was about eight stalls away from the passenger side of the one in front of Cody. It had an emblem on its side that Cody could not make out. Using the car in front of him as cover, he began to move closer toward its rear end, intending to peek around to get a better look. Crouched down, out of sight, sitting on his haunches, he stuck his head around the taillight. While the details of the emblem itself were unclear, the letters to its left, RCMP, and right, GRC, were clear. He knew what RCMP meant, Royal Canadian Mounted Police. Thin blue, red, and yellow lines ran from the front to the rear of the vehicle. Above the front tire read Police.

"Shit," Cody said softly out loud to himself. "Fucking cops."

"Do you know what the GRC stands for?" a voice behind him asked.

Cody jumped in surprise, turning to face the voice. A pleasant-looking Canadian Mounty in full uniform, female, probably in her mid-to-late thirties, stood about twenty feet away, hands on her hips, her right one next to her pistol. She had come out of the restroom and had quietly walked up behind him as he peered around the car.

"Are you Cody," she asked.

"Yes," he said quietly while nodding.

"I'm Officer Hanson. I have something for you," she said, reaching with her right hand.

Cody began to move his right hand behind him reflexively.

Officer Hanson immediately stuck her arms straight out, palms up. "Whoa, Cody. Wait. I'm not reaching for my gun. With that, she slowly moved her right hand past her pistol and into her right pocket. She pulled out a set of car keys. "These go to the Prius. The red one," she said and then tossed them. "Nice catch," she said.

"Good toss," he said, smiling, unsure what was happening.

"Sorry for not introducing myself differently. I was just enjoying seeing you sneak around the car. Sorry. I'm Buck's niece, by the way. He asked me to meet you here and get you going."

"Going where?"

"Follow the GPS. It's all set up in the car. Just hit go, and it'll guide you to where you're headed. There's also a cell phone in the driver's seat. It's disposable. Don't make any calls. Only take calls. Buck or someone else will call you later. For now, just get on the road."

"Will Buck be there?"

"Cody, just get out of here," she said firmly, the tone in her voice shifting from affable to concerned. "You need to get into hiding. People will be looking for you. Probably already are, I'm sure. There'll be more once they start to put the pieces of all this together. For now, throw your shit in the car and get out of here. Go. Buck will contact you, don't worry."

"Steve's bike…" he began to say, pointing toward the woods.

"Don't worry. We'll find it. No worries."

Cody loaded up his items, hit 'start' on the GPS, and rolled down the window. "Bike's a quarter or three eights mile up the trail. On the left. Laying down behind a huge Douglas Fir."

"Got it."

"Thanks," he said.

"Glad to help."

"What's it mean?"

"What does what mean?" she asked.

"GRC."

"Ah. Gendarmerie Royale du Canada. RMPC is for French speakers on the east side of the country. Don't want to have to shoot anyone because they don't speak English. Right?" she said lightheartedly.

Cody gave her a thumbs up. "Thank you, Officer Hanson."

"My pleasure, Cody. Take care and good luck. Oh yeah," she said. "And we've never met. This," she said, wagging her finger rapidly around parts of the parking lot, "this never happened. You got that?" Her face was amiable but serious.

Cody gave her another thumb up, smiled, rolled up the window, and drove off.

***

Balil was surprised at the speed of the small vessel. From his map, he knew he only had a few miles to go to get to the dam. The dam should be visible on his right about where the lake took a hard left toward a trailhead. He knew he could reach the trailhead in the boat, but it appeared to be almost another couple of miles past the dam to the east.

Unbeknownst to him, Sheila had made the run to the next campsite in about twelve minutes, where she had encountered a ranger who had radioed to a colleague that a man had killed some people and her husband at the next campground up the lake and was commandeering a red fishing boat that was headed south. The ranger who had taken the call was at the trailhead. Equipped with a sidearm,

State Ranger Katherine Keiser fired up her police boat and proceeded, along with another ranger, Officer Katherine Yamamoto, also armed, to intercept the killer.

When he had waded into the lake, Balil was running on adrenalin, almost completely ignoring the near-freezing water. Fortunately, he had slept in a sweater. But after about ten minutes on the water, the wind blowing in his face, and the comforting realization he was almost at the end of his journey, his adrenalin rush had largely worn off, and he began to shiver. To be able to put his backpack on, he slowed the boat down a little to easily maintain a straight line without someone at the wheel. Before hefting the pack on, he took out the detonator to begin the bomb's countdown. The count, the instructions had said, was short, just sixty seconds. 'I guess they don't want the wearer to have too much time to think about it,' he mused.

As Ross Dam came into full view, Balil's shiver abated some, and he began to feel warmer rather than colder. 'Probably Allah welcoming me,' he thought. To create the forward motion of the blast, as the British had done in WWII to the German dams, he planned to stop about two hundred yards or so from the dam, push the detonation button, let the timer run down about forty-five seconds, and then hit the accelerator full throttle so the boat was going full speed when the bomb exploded. A very short distance away, he saw a line of floats tethered from one shoreline to the other behind the dam. This nonetheless penetrable boundary meekly kept boats from getting any closer to the dam. As he approached it, he cut the engine and hit the lever that raised the motor's propellor.

After the craft had finished gliding over the line, Balil lowered the motor, estimating that he could initiate his countdown in about another one hundred fifty yards. Just behind him, three quick gunshots and an immediate accompanying bullhorn announcement jolted him. It was a woman's voice.

"Don't move. This is the police. You are under arrest. Put your hands in the air and stay where you are, or we *will* shoot."

If Balil started the timer now, he would crash into the dam before the bomb exploded. He could start it now but would have to avoid them for at least thirty seconds or more. They were close, close enough that they might hit him if they began firing. He had one more option that might retain some of the boat's inertia when the bomb exploded.

"*You* stop," he yelled. "You see this on my back. *I have a bomb!* Stop right there." Barely idling, they came to a complete stop. They were about a hundred feet away. "Stay there. If you come closer, I will kill us all. I promise. Let me think. Please." He did not need to think. He knew exactly what he was going to do. Balil waited ten seconds and then surreptitiously pressed the detonator.

"Sir," said Officer Keiser, "stay calm. But stay still. *Do not* move."

Balil looked back and saw that the two officers had drawn their guns and were aiming at him. Both had their arms resting on the windshield of their craft. Although the boat had stopped, it still rocked somewhat from the waves on the lake. And for revolvers, they were not that close. They could shoot, but it would be a lucky shot if they hit him. He turned and dove toward the throttle. Landing on his stomach, he stretched out his right arm and pushed the throttle fully forward.

The boat lurched ahead, and Officer Yamamoto yelled, "Bonsai, motherfucker," firing four quick shots in Balil's direction. "He's got a fucking bomb!" Kaiser yelled. Stop shooting, you fucking idiot. Let's get out of here." Keiser then jammed her own throttle forward before jutting sharply to the left, almost throwing Yamamoto into the lake.

Despite the distance, Yamamoto's second shot had pierced Balil's boat windshield, and the third one had hit the motor. 'Nice shot,' he had thought, surprised. The boat had turned right somewhat, and he had to slow it down and direct it back toward the dam. Uncertain of his distance from the dam, he looked at the clock on the boat's dash. He guessed he had about fifteen seconds or less left. The motor was beginning to sputter, smoke began to trail from its sides, and though it still had power, the power was noticeably waning. Unsure whether he was going fast enough that his speed would adequately provide the desired consequence, he stood up to a crouch, took as deep a breath as best he could, and threw himself into the water. This was it.

The weight of the pack took Balil down much faster than he had expected. He could feel the rapid change in the water's pressure on his skull. Still lucid enough to reason, his mind flashed that the deeper he went, the greater the extent of water displacement by the blast. His lungs began to burn. He desperately wanted to take a breath but held out. 'How much time has passed?' he wondered. 'Just a little longer,' he told himself as a final conviction. Finally, he could no longer maintain and inhaled deeply. Then, a state of exaltation. And then, the great hereafter.

***

Cody followed the GPS for over four hours before reaching its programmed destination, a home just outside the northern edge of Penticton. He pulled in cautiously to a long driveway that meandered across a pasture for about a hundred yards to a stand of trees. Not positive if he was in the right location, he proceeded slowly, stopping at the edge of the tree line. Suddenly, the phone that Officer Hanson had given him rang. It rang three more times before he mustered the courage to answer it.

"Hello?"

"Hey buddy," said a voice.

"Buck?"

"Yeah, it's me, man. That you coming in?"

"Yeah. I wasn't sure whether to go any further. It's dark here. I can't see shit. How'd you even know someone was out here?"

"Don't worry about it. You're on TV. There's a camera, about seventy-five feet to your right, up in a tree that's watching you."

"Fuck."

"Yeah, don't worry. Just keep coming. You'll see the lights of the house in another hundred yards or so. The garage door will be up. Just pull in."

"Okay."

Cody made his way slowly up the road and into the woods. He had not gone far when he began catching flickers of lights through the trees. The house lights became clear as he approached the edge of the trees where the land opened into another pasture. As soon as he emerged out of the trees, the inside lights of the garage came on, as well as several peripheral lights, which highlighted what appeared to be a nice-sized, seventies-era home. He sped up to cover the remaining eighty feet or so of the driveway before pulling the auto into the structure. As soon as he stopped, the garage door began to close behind him, and just as a single door leading into the house in front of the car opened, Buck appeared.

"Hey, man," Buck said enthusiastically.

Cody, who still had limited exposure to Buck, most of it overly experiential, to say the least, guardedly replied, "Hey."

"Come on in. You need help with anything?"

"No, thanks," said Cody. "I just have a couple of things."

Once inside, Buck directed Cody to one of the bedrooms with a bathroom and told him to come out when ready and talk to him in the living room. A few minutes later, Cody returned and found that Buck had set a plate of finger foods on the coffee table.

"Thanks," he said before digging in.

"No worries. Hungry?"

"Yes, sir. I'm pretty hungry. Just had a sandwich earlier today. This your place?" Cody asked after the second handful of fries and chicken sticks.

"Actually, no. This place belongs to a friend. I have a place on the other side of town. But I spend most of my time in Kelowna. I have a condo there."

"The owners here?"

"No, they just headed to a place they own in Phoenix for the winter. I have a key, and we trade out places with one another when we have a need. It's just you and me."

The two made small talk for a little longer, Buck filling in Cody a little more on what he had been doing for the last forty-plus years besides smuggling government-sponsored aliens into the United States. When Buck was in his mid-twenties, he married and had two children, a boy and a girl. His wife had passed away from breast cancer when they were both forty-two, leaving Buck as a single parent to finish raising the children, the girl, Summer, fifteen at the time and the boy, Matt, seventeen.

"Matt was fine," he said. "Summer, though, had a really tough time. It wasn't until she had kids of her own that she began to really forgive me for some of the struggles I put her through," Buck related. "I didn't do a very good job of meeting her needs and helping her with what she was going through. Boys have a different struggle, plus Matt was seventeen. So it was easier for us to support one another. Girls really need their moms, especially at that age. They just have a ton of shit to deal with that boys don't, most of it, ironically, having directly or indirectly to do with boys. We got it good, Cody, compared to them. Trust me."

For a moment, the conversation lapsed, so Cody took the opportunity to bring the topic back to himself. "What's going to happen to me, Buck?" he said, his tone and demeanor downcast.

"Fair question, Cody," he replied. "I don't have a good answer at the moment. Things are still unfolding. We've got to see how things go over the next few days. It's still hard to tell what exactly is going on, who orchestrated this shit, and who is in the know. My contacts in Canada and a couple in the U.S. are still trying to answer those questions.”

“What about my family. Where are they.”

For the next five minutes, Buck recounted the events of the previous day. Buck’s employee, Bill Rodgers, had planned on taking out all six bodies, but before he got to the campground, Buck had arranged for a helicopter from Vancouver to pick up all six bodies inside Canada. Rodgers just had to move them all north to a nearby meadow a couple hundred yards away. All six were taken to a Canadian military base just outside Vancouver. There was considerable interest in identifying the two terrorists, although only one had an unrecognizable head. The family’s bodies would be held pending discussions with the American government, discussions that were being intentionally delayed until trusted American military and/or government associates could be contacted to determine precisely what had taken place, who was involved, and what should be done next.

“So, you’ll stay here for the next couple of days, if that sounds okay to you,” said Buck. “I’m having a friend pick me up soon. Then I’m going home. I don’t think I’m being watched yet, but you never know. I’m sure I will be by sometime tomorrow.”

“Who’ll be watching you?” said Cody.

“Someone on the American’s payroll. Whoever is responsible for this will want to know where the survivors are. I can guarantee you we weren’t supposed to survive.”

“Why did you take them in, to begin with? Didn’t you think they were terrorists?”

"Yeah, I suspected it. But I was thinking, shit, I've been doing this for almost forty years. I've never had a problem or reason to question what I was asked to do. Was I missing something? Who were these guys? I suspected their packs had bombs, but for all I knew, I thought maybe they were bringing evidence of some kind or secret stuff. Shit, I didn't know… at least in the beginning. But they acted so weirdly, I became suspicious."

"Well, one got away. What happens if he detonates it?"

"I got a chance before we passed out their packs to inspect them closely, an ex-military friend of mine and me. He confirmed they were clearly bombs. We took the batteries out of the detonators. I figured it really shouldn't matter whether they worked or not if they were good guys bringing them in. Right? Before we set them up to pack in at the trailhead, I put the detonators back in their packs. Figured I could always convey that to them at the border, directly or indirectly, if they turned out to be alright. That didn't happen."

"So, the guy can't detonate it?"

"Nope. He just be pushin' that button to no avail," said Buck, pumping his thumb to make the point. "Glad I did it."

"Whoa, no shit," Cody said.

"I don't know why those clowns that put this whole thing together thought they could pull something like that off and not raise a red flag or two. I mean, those guys were walking red flags themselves, man."

"I don't know. I thought they seemed okay that first night. I was open-minded. Or maybe I just thought I should be PC."

"Ah, I don't know. I say always assume the best. I believe the vast majority of immigrants are just fine. And not just immigrants but people in general. I mean, Canada and America both have their share of homegrown assholes. The vast majority of Muslims in both countries are good people, just trying to make a living and provide a better life for their kids than what they had. Same with Christians. And there's tons of success stories. We only hear about the exceptions."

"Funny, though. I was sympathetic when I heard their stories that first night. Now I'm glad they're dead."

"Well, being sympathetic or empathetic means you're open-minded and willing to help. You're open to understanding and talking. It doesn't mean you're open to they're killing you or your family in retribution. It means you want to understand their motivation better, but it doesn't mean you condone whatever response they deem appropriate."

"Yeah, they came and killed my family. Hard to be liberal, let me tell you."

"I hear you. But someone along the way has to say, 'Hey, I don't want to do this anymore. I want to work it out.'"

"But the other side has to listen."

"And the side wanting the other side to listen has to be patient and listen as well."

"Is the U.S. just fucked up, Buck?"

"Oh, we're better than most, by far. But you're not the best just because you say you are. It's a position that's earned. Every day. Our intentions aren't always evident. Like with some of our wars. Some have just been wrong. And dark prisons. With some other issues, though, like Biolabs, it's not necessarily as clear. Bad countries are producing bad shit. So, we have to produce some, too, so we have vaccines. You just hope our intentions are good and that they stay that way. It's a lot like being a good parent. Most parents are good people, yet they fuck up all the time. They do really irresponsible things. I know I did. But if you care about your actions, you'll probably do good on balance. You just have to fess up when you make a mistake. Wear it. Same with a country. The U.S. doesn't always do a good job of that. Politicians on both sides."

"That's for sure," said Cody. "Most will justify their bad behavior because someone else had done it, too."

"Yep," Buck agreed. "Parents will try that, too. 'Well, Neighbor John cheated on his wife, so why are you so pissed at me?'" Buck purposefully whined out the last several words. "Look, this had the support of someone in the States because that's where they were headed. Probably someone in the government. Maybe even the White House itself. Otherwise, I wouldn't be involved. Only someone with real government contacts knows about me and what I do."

"They'll be wanting to kill you for sure."

"Yep. And you, too. We're the only ones that know what happened… besides the ones that organized this clusterfuck. We've got to protect ourselves and those close to us and make these fuckers pay."

"Am I safe here?" asked Cody.

"Well, again, for a day or two. This house has a lot of surveillance and high-tech stuff. The owner is ex-military. If people come in from any direction, there's alarms that'll go off." Cody remained silent as he processed all the information Buck had just passed on. Buck paused for a few moments. When Cody said nothing, he went on. "There's no alcohol in the house. I'd love to offer you a beer, but you need to stay sharp."

"Understood," said Cody.

"There's actually a safe room in the house that you can sleep in. It's got an escape hatch in the floor that leads to a tunnel that'll take you to an exit about a hundred fifty feet in the woods. Several screens for the different cameras. And I've got you a Glock with four loaded magazines, just in case."

"You heard anything about Sweetie and Chris?"

"Yeah, I gotta' call from Bill today. They made it home this morning. They're good. I probably won't be able to talk to him for a couple days until this mess sorts out. Too dangerous."

"Okay."

"Hey, time for me to go and for you to get some sleep. I'll be back in the morning, probably around ten-ish. I believe I have a couple of ways to get in and out of here without being seen. I'll call this phone first." Buck handed him a disposable phone. "I'll call once; let it ring three times. Twenty or thirty seconds, I'll call again, let it ring once, and hang up. That means it's me, and I'm here. Don't answer either one. I'll come through the front door."

"Sounds good... I guess."

"Hey, hang in there, kid. This'll be over soon enough. See you tomorrow. I'll have some news, I'm sure."

Cody gave a weak wave of agreement as Buck exited the front door. Buck went around the house and found the trail that led to a stand of trees that bordered the east side of the property. He followed it for about five minutes until it exited into a Walmart parking lot. Waiting for him was a friend who drove him to a convenience store five blocks from his home. He noted the cars in the lot before going in, wandering for a couple of minutes, and then buying a cheap bottle of wine. Then he exited, reviewed the cars again, and, seeing nothing noteworthy, walked home.

***

Day 6

White House.

"I knew this was wrong," Hoffman said firmly. "I told you that. I told you."

"Would you please shut the fuck up, you fucking tweak," yelled POTUS. "What the fuck happened, Emma? What do we know?"

If still waters were an indication of depth, most would have guessed Emma at twenty thousand leagues. Though calm in appearance, Emma's stomach was knotting on the inside. Rarely one to fluster, when she did, she never showed it. Knowing the current situation might certainly get worse before it got better, keeping her cool, or at least appearing to do so, was critical. They had broken more than a few mores, norms, rules, and, this time, laws. POTUS believed that crazy always trumped smarts, a philosophy to which she also ascribed. History was replete with leaders who probably were not all

320

that bright but had the balls to do the unexpected, the unsanctioned, and the unacceptable. They had to be willing to 'push the button' to be successful, but they also needed a few people enthusiastically volunteering to push it for them. And there almost always was. Usually plenty.

The Founding Fathers had created an organization and set of behaviors to keep someone from ruling as a king. But what happens when someone decides to rule like a king. The key was to load your top positions with people who will do what you tell them to, your bidding. Then, their underlings have been trained culturally and organizationally in so many ways and at so many levels to do what they are told to do, whether they like it or not. That is the model of most organizations. If someone will not follow your orders, especially at the top, get rid of them and replace them with someone who will. If they are not at the top, who cares? Fuck protocol. Be indifferent. But be *strategically indifferent*.

What are the options for a country from a freely elected president who wants to be a self-appointed despot? They could lose the election. But then, results could always be challenged and contested. The USPS was more fucked up than a Three Stooges skit. Seeds were being planted, watered, and nurtured, and if POTUS lost, it was because the other side cheated. Call fraud. They had stacked the federal courts with conservative appointees. Although POTUS was sure they would do his bidding, Emma was not so sure on this one, however. A few high-level military personnel might be sympathetic enough to cause some trouble, but that was not a path any of them had been trained to consider, let alone take. No, their ace-in-the-hole were their militias standing by, on call. If they lost the election, simply cry fraud and thousands with guns would be ready to act. It can't happen here? Says who?

Emma had pushed the envelope with this most recent event, however. Trying to get a militia to kill a couple of their own to keep POTUS safe had not gone well. The two boys survived the attempt to get rid of them, and now the FBI was involved. Fortunately, some far-right-wing sources aside, the press was unaware of the associations between recent, seemingly disparate events. It would be game over if they win the election; they would be safe. Continued stories around such a 'plot' would likely be seen as harassment by a public tired of partisan bickering. However, any credible stories over the short term of any White House involvement could affect the election outcome. If the actual truth began to leak out and supersede gossip or conjecture, they had their positions in place. POTUS could play the get-out-of-jail-free card, a presidential pardon. Could POTUS pardon himself? The courts would spend the rest of his life arguing that one. And what about everyone else he pardoned? They would be safe, though their lives in the United States would be miserable, most likely forever pestered with new charges for new issues, real or imagined, and closer scrutiny on their taxes than a dermatologist checking for melanomas. Or they could always move. Assassination? Perhaps, but the government had played most of its cards around that option when they killed Kennedy.

"I said, what the fuck happened?" repeated POTUS, clearly irritated.

Emma's mind snapped back to the moment. "We needed to get rid of those two boys. A small group from the west side of the state said they'd take care of it. It didn't go as planned. What can I say?"

"As planned?" scoffed POTUS. "That's an understatement," he said, dialing down his tenor a little.

"I didn't know one of the boys had an uncle who was a cop, and his father was at one time, too. The uncle is one of our heavies in the area, so he wasn't about to go along with the 'escort' back to Seattle that group was pushing," said Emma. "I'm not exactly sure what they said to concern the local group, but I guess their insistence sort of compounded the discussion."

"Fuck," said the president.

"Sir, if I might," said Hoffman.

"If you might what?" POTUS sneered back. Hoffman hesitated. "Well? What?"

He had intended to offer some recommendations about the involvement of the FBI, but something in the president's voice, his attitude and treatment toward him, finally got the best of him. "You know, Mr. President, I was one of your first supporters. That's why I'm here." The president nodded and waved his hand irritably, motioning for the VP to get to the point. Hoffman smiled and pointed at the president, shaking his head just a little. "Gosh, I'm sick of that, sir," Hoffman smiled. The look on the president's face changed abruptly from a sneer of disdain to complete shock.

"What did you say?" asked POTUS, disbelievingly.

Sensing further admonishments if he backed off, Hoffman held his ground. "I said I'm sick of how you talk to me."

"Jack, you should…" Emma began, cautiously.

"Fuck you, Emma," said Hoffman. "I'm talking to the president. If I have something to say to you, I'll call you by your name… bitch."

It was unclear whether he was calling her a bitch or whether that would be his name for her going forward. The president was about to ask but was cut off by Emma.

"I know you're upset, Mr. Vice President," she said calmly.

Hoffman would have none of it. "Did I call your name? Did I, Emma?" he said. That clarified it for the president. Hoffman had called her a bitch. Emma said nothing. "What you two have done is so incredibly egregious, I… I can't believe it. You've brought in terrorists to commit acts against citizens of the United States and attempted to have two young men killed, all so you can win an election."

"So, we can win. We, Jack," said POTUS soothingly, circling his hand while panning his eyes back and forth to signify all three as inclusionaries.

"You know, Mr. President, and you, too, Emma, I won't help you with this monstrosity you have created. It is such a travesty. I want nothing to do with you from here on out. I have the worst feeling in my gut that you'll continue to keep asking me to cover your asses, wanting me to take the fall for your own sad, pathetic decisions. Not going to do it," said Hoffman, looking down momentarily before looking up and continuing. "I'm going to keep working with our pharmas, and it's pharmas, not pharmacies," he said, shaking his head and looking directly at POTUS, "to find a vaccine. That's it. For the country, not for you two miserable dipshits. You're traitors."

"Listen, mister," said POTUS, but Hoffman was not listening. His long-committed fealty to the president had finally expired.

Hoffman headed for the exit and, on his way out, held up his middle finger before slamming the door. Neither laughed at him this time.

"Wow," said POTUS. "I didn't expect that."

Emma did not immediately respond as her mind raced to consider and evaluate the myriad tangents to where this moment might lead. They needed the VP. To his credit, he was dedicated and dependable. To date, he had remained steadfastly loyal. Sure, he was a bit of a dweeb. But he was also a great gopher, a reliable 'go to' point man, even when he did not volunteer, agree or support the effort. That had made him, on occasion, a great scapegoat, a role. Perhaps he had tired of playing. POTUS at times had called him The Pincushion, explaining he could 'take a prick with the best of them.' But she was worried that they had lost him completely, that he might be inclined to prick them in return. And he was certainly capable of giving them a prick that might well bring them to their knees.

"Yeah, that was a bit of a surprise," Emma responded after a few moments of reflection. The Vice President was not as craven as she had considered. "Jack seems to have suddenly grown a pair. Admirable, but it worries me."

"It's a problem, isn't it?" said POTUS.

"Could be. Or he could just be sounding off. I'm not convinced, though, that there is much he can do. I'm sure he'll be talking to his contacts in the CIA and FBI. Their bosses and a lot of their appointed underlings still work for you, though. You're the boss. So, they can't do anything too drastic. It's the lifer underlings we have to worry about. Most of them can't be so easily fired. Anyway, we'll see."

"We've got to get a headline out before the agencies do, don't you think?" POTUS said.

"Yes, definitely," she said quietly, still thinking. "The two militia kids are in custody. They've done some talking, for sure. So, the FBI and CIA will be starting to put this together. But they won't let anything out of the bottle until they know the whole story. Even then."

"What about the kid whose family got killed?"

"Same. We won't be finding him anytime soon. Let's let them come to us. They probably won't right away. They'll watch us. In the meantime, let's get control of the narrative." The FBI will give out some information on the one who killed the campers and the two militias that clashed in that small town in Washington. We'll offer condolences to the campers' families and take credit for the FBI being in on the search for the culprit's body."

"What if they find it?"

"They won't. Similar with the boys. Believe me, they're probably not even in the country. We don't want them to talk to the press, but the feds won't. We'll say we're on it and that we abhor violence; the boys are under government protection, which they are, yadda yadda. The country itself will back us. Virtually none will suspect we had anything to do with it."

"What about the people you've been working with on this?"

"Well, one of them is dead; no worries, there. The other will do what I say. He'll clam up those around him, too. He's ex-military police and a cop, so he's got some control over this."

"Cool. Counting on you, Emma," said POTUS.

"I'm going to go home and think about this, sir. I'll figure out where this is and how to keep it on track or turn it around, whichever."

"I have no doubt you will. Say hi to Max for me?"

"Yeah. Call me if you need me. I'll be in early in the morning."

The president gave a weak one-hand-up, and Emma left.

***

When Emma got home, she sent a secured message to Derek asking if they could possibly find 'the boy' using his cell. Derek messaged back, saying they were working on that. As Emma sat on the couch before her laptop, Max came in from the kitchen, sat beside her, and cuddled in. She put her arm around his shoulder and leaned into him. "I'm so glad I have you," she cooed. "I love you so much. You're my best buddy."

Canada, Outside Penticton

Cody's eyes opened wide on the phone's first ring. There were no windows in the safe room, so it had remained black, even into the daylight hours. The disposable phone had no screen, and he scrambled to find his pants to reflexively find his own phone. As his head cleared, however, he remembered Steve had made him leave it with him, knowing that the device could lead others to his location. Unbeknownst to Cody, after dropping him off at the trailhead, Steve had left the boy's phone on his way back to town, just off the northeast side of the highway near a twenty-foot cliff that bordered the Methow River, a move that generated a thirty-six-hour search for Cody's body in the area after searchers located the phone via its GPS signal.

Remembering the direction of the door, Cody fumbled his way to its handle and opened it just after the third ring. With the room now lit, he grabbed his clothes and quickly got dressed. He finished shortly after one more ring and headed to the front door to wait, after first picking up the Glock he had kept under his pillow the night before. Three minutes later, he heard the front door deadbolt turn. He was seated in a living room chair that faced it. The Glock was tucked between his thigh and the chair, the barrel stuck down into the space between the cushion and chair arm so that just the handle protruded, which he held tightly.

As the door opened, he heard an unfamiliar voice talking. Almost immediately, an unfamiliar crop of hair began to come into view. Cody stood and aimed the gun at the door. As the rest of the person's head came into view, their eyes turned to Cody. Having no idea who it was, Cody pulled the trigger three times.

Seeing Cody's motions, the head immediately disappeared, slamming the door, while a voice yelled, "Fuck, he's got a gun."

"Cody, it's me, Buck. Stop. Don't shoot."

Cody looked at his finger on the trigger, realizing that the gun had not fired. Fortunately for the man owning the crop of hair, Cody had not pushed the magazine entirely into the gun's handle, so there was no bullet in the chamber.

"Cody, Cody. It's me, Buck. Don't shoot." All were silent. Cody stood, aiming at the door, but realized it was Buck's voice. "You okay?" Buck called.

"Yeah, I'm okay. Who was that?" Cody asked with agitation.

"It's a friend. A good friend… for both of us. Don't shoot. I should have called out. Our bad. My bad. Sorry. Put the gun down," Buck said, chuckling a little. "You sure you're alright?"

"Yeah."

"Okay, we're coming in. Me first."

Buck opened the door, peeked around the door cautiously, and, after making eye contact with Cody, smiled, opened the door slowly, and walked in.

"That was close," said Buck.

"You have no idea," said Cody.

Buck was followed by two men, one in his late forties and the other younger, probably in his mid-thirties. The three made their way to the living room where Cody had been seated, where Buck introduced them. The older one was an American FBI agent named Dick Denesen, and the other, Terry Randal, was with the Canadian Security Intelligence Service, or CSIS, the country's version of the CIA.

"Sleep well?" Buck asked.

"Not bad," Cody answered. "Your phone woke me up, actually. I guess I was pretty tired. Sorry, I almost shot you," said Cody, realizing it was Denesen's greying crop that was the one coming through the door.

"No worries. You've been through a lot the last few days," responded Denesen, sounding genuinely sympathetic.

"Why don't you tell us what you know about the fellows you ran into at the campground," said Randal.

"Not much to say," said Cody. "I know less than Buck. We met 'em at the campground and spent a little time that night. They seemed okay. A little edgy. Said they were being relocated to Seattle."

"Did they say where they had been in Canada?"

"Not really... well, Calgary, then a few days in Vancouver. One had an uncle there.

"Did he say the name?" asked Randal.

"No, not that I recall."

"Did they all live at the same location?"

"No idea," said Cody.

Randal asked a few more questions about where they said they were from, where they may have lived, how they got there, their names, and so on. Other than their first names, Cody provided no helpful information, he assumed. Denesen then asked some questions about Kent Des Moines, whose name they had gotten from Sweetie and Chris, who, along with Steve and Bill, had all been questioned by the FBI earlier in the day. Again, Cody said he really did not know much about the man, having only met him at Seth's funeral and then on the trail. He explained how he had gotten the Propofol from Seth and how he used it to drug Des Moines and escape from his two colleagues.

"Wow. Great story. You're lucky. What do you know about them, the two guys with him?" Randal asked.

"Not much, really," said Cody. "I recognized them from high school sports, was all. Basketball and football. They didn't really seem to be into the whole Freedom Fighters thing that much," said Cody, "but they were there, nonetheless. Des Moines was definitely calling the shots. They sorta seemed to be caught up in it all."

"Well, it didn't turn out so well for all three," Agent Randal said.

"How so?" Cody asked.

"The one you drugged?" he said quizzically. Cody nodded. "A bear killed him. Ate his face off." Cody's eyes widened in disbelief but with no sign of remorse. "The other two found him. They hit *69 on Des Moines' global phone, apparently the last number that had called him when they were at the trailhead. They told us all this yesterday. Anyway, it turns out the person who answered, the person giving Des Moines orders, works in the White House."

"Do you know who?" asked Cody.

"Yeah, we know who. One of the president's aides. They thought Des Moines called them when they saw the incoming number. When the kid asked who they were talking to, the aide told him something like, 'It's me, stupid.' The kid calling in then told the aide what had happened and who they were. So, the aide told them to get the body off the trail and walk out. Turns out, though, that while they were taking care of Des Moines' body, a couple of horses wandered by. Apparently, two of your family's. They rode them out. Before that, though, one used Des Moines phone to call an uncle to meet them at the trailhead. Probably a good thing for them because they probably would not have fared so well, as things turned out later, had they waited for the ones the aide was arranging from the west side. Took them to some little town called Conconully. Heard of it?"

"Yeah, I've been there. Not many people. Tiny, in fact."

"Well, it's a bastion of POTUS supporters and a favorite hangout on weekends for some of the FF-ers. We've been keeping an eye on it for the last few years, actually. There's a couple of local militias that like to call it home base. So, anyway, the White House contact decides these two young fellas with Des Moines, can't remember their names…"

"Dan and Cal."

"Yes, that's right, Dan and Cal. She… well, the White House person, decides they know too much and tells the FF-ers who are keeping them to turn them over to their group from Seattle. Except one of the guys' uncles is a cop and an FF-er and says no way. A fight breaks out when those fellas show up, and a couple of people on both sides start shooting at each other. There was a standoff for a couple of hours before police from a couple of the nearby towns, and the FBI was called in and broke it up."

"The boys are okay?" Cody asked.

"One got shot, but he'll be alright," Randal said.

"Which one?" asked Cody.

"Not sure," said Randal. "The cop's nephew, maybe."

"Tell him what happened to the tourist. Balil. Remember him? The one with the creepy eyes?" asked Buck, looking at Cody.

"Tourist," said Denesen with a broad smile. "Great euphemism."

"Oh, right. Sure," said Randal. "Well, he made it to Ross Lake on horseback. Well, we're pretty sure it was him. Killed four or five campers, stole a boat, and drove it to Ross Dam, presumably to blow it up. Based on what we were told by a couple of state park rangers who tried to intercept him. He told them he had a bomb or what could have been one. He had it on his back. Anyway, they took off to get away, and he jumped in the lake. Must have gone straight to the bottom." Randal shook his head in wonderment. "Must have blown his mind when he realized the bomb wasn't going off."

"Buck tell you he deactivated the detonators?" Randal asked. Cody nodded yes.

"One for Buck," said Denesen, turning to Carpenter and giving him a gentle fist bump.

"What now?" asked Cody.

"Good question," said Denesen. "I think you and the two boys will end up in witness protection if Canada has you. Those discussions are underway. We'll move the boys out of the country in the next couple of days. Right now, they're in an FBI safehouse. Can't leave them in the U.S. while Dingus is president. We're pretty sure the three weren't in Calgary. They likely were held up in Vancouver. We'll figure out where and with whom soon enough. They may have come through there and got held up coincidentally because of Covid. My guess is nobody there at this point in time knows they were killed in the Pasayten or who the crazy was that killed a few people before drowning himself somewhere in the lake. But as details about all this leak out, somebody will figure out it was someone they knew and come forward."

"Will they find his body?" asked Cody. "If they do, won't they be able to identify him?"

"Hell, that lake is almost five hundred feet deep behind the dam. The plan is to play down his exact location and fake a search. He's gone. He's nobody now. We'll figure out who it was by other means… I think."

"What about the gunfight in Conconully?" asked Cody.

"Well, there's already some conspiracy theories floating around the far-right websites about some militia boys trying to intercept some terrorists coming in from Canada but tying that thread somehow to why two dipshit militias in Conconully are shooting at each other is kinda problematic. Especially with the FBI and the White House all saying they know nothing about any such terrorists or conversations with any militias. And all the militias know POTUS loves his militias, so they'll quiet down and follow his lead soon enough. And if a few have a change of heart and want to talk to the media, few to none will buy a story like that without some proof. Nobody but you and your family saw all three terrorists together… sorry, Buck… tourists. And well, you know…" Denesen's voice trailed off as he intuited from Cody's face what he was about to ask.

"What will happen to my family?"

"We'll have to figure that out later, Cody," said Randal, his voice choking a little. "Try to be patient, though, on that if you can. We're sensitive to your feelings, son."

"Holy shit," said Cody. "Am I ever going to get to go home, then?"

"Not anytime soon, I'm afraid," said Denesen. "Like I said, very few people know anything other than a piece or two of the whole story… except the White House. We've put most of the pieces together but have a bit more to go. If those responsible for this remain where they are, in power, nobody who's privy to even a piece, is safe. There's some in Vancouver who are yet to be identified. But presently? You, Buck, Bill, your girlfriend, your friend, Chris, the two fellas that were with Des Moines, you're all at risk. Collectively, you know enough to bring those lunatics down. But not while they're in office."

"Why?" asked Cody.

"Too many people wouldn't believe it. Too many of his supporters don't care. And even if everyone believed it, the country would be so discredited they'd never recover its international standing. It's a Mexican standoff… and Mexico isn't even involved for a change," Randal said jokingly. "You have to stay in hiding until other powers-that-be can figure out how to best deal with this thing *and* the people who did it. The powers include POTUS and crew and agencies like us," he said, pointing at himself and Denesen, "We have to figure out our next moves. With Buck's help, we'll have a plan."

"Sounds like they're going to get away with this," said Cody, lamentingly.

"No. They won't," said Randal pensively, his eyes shifting to somewhere on the ceiling momentarily. "No, they'll probably never go to trial for reasons I've already explained. But we'll figure out some appropriate punishments for all of them. They'll all be fucked for the rest of their lives, believe me."

"What happens if he gets reelected?" asked Cody.

"Yeah, well, I think that's one of the first things we'll be looking to influence, if necessary. There's lots of other truths about these people that will likely be discussed in public. It may take a while to convince some of the president's hardliners to see who and what he is."

"Cluster fuck," said Cody.

"Yep," said Buck. "The White House went crazy rogue. We've had some doozies as president… Nixon was my least favorite, oh my god, but this one and his crew take the cake. Worse than Nixon's shit by a mile. I can tell you this, Cody, for me, it will be business as usual. I live in Canada. I'm probably done bringing people in for the U.S. anymore. Too old, anyway. But I have enough friends in high places that I'm not worried about them sending in anyone to mess with me. It's you folks I worry about. But collectively, we are one another's insurance policies. As agent Randal explained, different people know different things. They'd have eliminated us all at the same time to keep the entire story quiet if they could have."

"Yep, but like I said before, too, even if POTUS loses the election, America doesn't ever want you to tell this story," Randal said. "Not that they'd kill you or anything, but instead of helping you, they can sure make your life miserable if you were to break an agreement and discredit you to the point you won't believe yourself and who you are and what happened."

Cody said nothing, but his face showed his concern for and grasp of the extent to which this matter contravened the very nature of the values on which a true democracy functioned.

"So, Cody," said Buck, "I've got a place where we'll keep you for the next few months. Only I will know where you are. I'll get you there in the next few days. Randal brought enough cash to last you for the next several months while we all try and figure out what to do long term based on how the near term and the election plays out."

"What about Sweetie?" Cody asked sadly.

"You and I can talk about that later. Write her a letter tonight. I'll make sure she gets it. Tomorrow, we get you out of here."

The two agents thanked Cody for his input and pledged support to keep him safe. When the two agents left, he and Buck talked for another hour, Buck offering more support and confidence about where things were headed and how he was certain everything would turn out fine.

That night, Cody wrote a long letter to Sweetie. If there was one thing that this ordeal had done for him, it was to solidify in his mind and heart how he felt about her, a focus he clearly communicated to her. It was an especially lonely night as the gravity of how his life had changed so markedly weighed on him in its totality. It appeared that this would be a journey with many new ends and many new beginnings.

***

Day 7

Canada, Outside Penticton

Buck came to get him the next morning at 6:00 a.m., well before dawn. He brought Cody a breakfast Happy Meal from McDonald's, Buck said, to 'Make him happy.' As they got in the SUV, Buck added, "You'll like where we're going, Cody. It's not home, but you'll like it. It'll do for now."

***

The story that was beginning to coalesce was simple enough: a pandemic-crazed Iraqi living in Canada had tried to walk into the United States through a wilderness area in Northern Washington state and had encountered a local family that was camping. The father, a Forest Service ranger, accosted the man, who then commandeered his gun and killed the family. He then took one of the family's horses and made his way to Ross Lake, where he killed five other campers before having a shootout with two state park rangers near the dam. It's unknown whether the man, who said he had a bomb, had been shot and fell into the lake or jumped in. He was presumed to have drowned. A search for his body was underway. The FBI would be bringing in divers to look for the body, but given it was unclear exactly where he entered the water, the lake's depth, visibility, and water movement in that part of the lake, officials were not optimistic about locating the individual's body.

Winthrop

The town had been aghast for the last two days as details of the Dickson family's death became better known. Victims of a crazed individual that they had run into while camping in the most northern points of the Pasayten. All five members of the family, tragically, had been killed in Canada. They had seemingly crossed the border to fish at a nearby lake, where they had run into the killer. The youngest had

338

initially thought to have perhaps survived, but his body had been found later at the other end of the lake by searchers. Investigators believed he may have been the first one killed, at which time the intruder secured his firearm. The family's bodies had been flown to Vancouver, B.C., where they would be kept pending coordination with family members for their return to the States.

A string of supportive mourners had been paying their respects to Sweetie at her home as well as a few friends in the Twisp area to Chris.' An evening service was held at the local Forest Service ranger station to commemorate the family, where hundreds of candles were lit until the minister announced that they had to start putting some out at the request of staff because of concerns about starting a fire in the immediate shrubbery. There were whispers of terrorist connections but no substantive speculation around what had happened in Conconully.

Bill and Chirine had closed the deli for the next week. Sweetie had isolated and rejected numerous offers from girlfriends to get together. Chris continued to handle jobs for his father, and he and Sweetie spent an hour or two on separate occasions answering questions for the FBI and being instructed as to what to say to any inquisitive local law enforcement officers or the press. For now, though, Cody was a ghost to both. Bill had not spoken to Buck since their last communication a day after the shootings.

All everyone could do was hope for a sense of normalcy and be patient to see how events unfolded as best they could. A new era, however, seemed to be in full swing. The rift that had split the country now seemed wider than ever, and everyone appeared to be holding their breaths in anticipation of what would happen next. Like a gas stove whose handle had been turned on, the spark clicking was just a matter of time before the flame ignited. And the longer the pause, the bigger the burst.

White House

FBI Assistant Director Adams had just left the office and finished a twenty-minute visit with POTUS, Emma, and the Vice President. The assistant director had asked for the meeting to brief the group on the militia group confrontation in Washington State and its likely association with the terrorist that had killed the family in the Pasayten campground. He did not give up that the killings had technically occurred in the U.S. but rather implied Canada, saying the bodies would remain there pending discussions with family members to claim the bodies. Adams made no mention during the meeting of the other two terrorists but rather hoped either the president or Emma would inquire about them. Neither did, uncertain what the assistant director might already know, either from related informants or witnesses, including the vice president. For their part, all three attendants to Adam's requested meeting asked very few questions.

"What do you think he knows?" POTUS asked after Adams had left.

Emma looked squarely at Hoffman and said, "Well, everything. And probably more."

"Are you suggesting I have said anything, Emma?" Hoffman asked.

Emma's voice was more conciliatory than normal. "Why no, sir. Not at all. One for all and all for one. Right?" Emma knew full well he almost certainly had already.

"You know my feelings on this. You two are on your own. But I would agree. He seemed to be on a fact-finding mission. Putting the pieces together. Just trying to figure out what any or all of us know."

"I don't know," said POTUS. "Maybe he knows something. I doubt they know the whole story, though. He said the whole family was killed. We know that's not true. They're fishing. Hoping we'll slip up."

"Well," said Emma, "unless one of us has talked, you're probably right, at least to some extent. They don't know the whole story." She glanced again at Hoffman, who returned an unwavering, cold stare. "Yet."

"Well, none of us know all the dots," replied POTUS. It'll take them weeks, if not months, to track down these folks and how they got here. They'll run down some leads in Vancouver, but it's a long trail back to Mohammed-ville."

"Yeah, but they'll get there… eventually," said Emma. "Well, I have things to do. I'll be in my office."

As soon as Emma had left, Hoffman said, "I have things to do as well, sir."

"How's the vaccine program coming, Jack?" POTUS asked in a tone that almost sounded as if he were truly interested.

"They're close." Hoffman had focused on making a conscious effort not to call him 'sir' or 'Mr. President.' "They're days away from the DNA sequencing of the virus. Once they do, they'll have a vaccine at the same time."

"Wow. That's good. The polls say people are suspicious of them. Too much press, too, the whole pandemic thing being a hoax," said POTUS. "Hoax, hoax, hoax, says *The Five* on Fox News," he said, laughing.

"Well, people really are dying," said Hoffman. "It's going to get a lot worse before it gets better, I'm being told, by the medical experts." He almost ended, again, with sir.

"Well, I don't think that'll happen until the election is over if I understand Mr. Grouchy's predictions correctly. At that point, it doesn't matter to me anymore. If I'm here, we make the vaccines available. If I'm not, I don't give a shit. It's the next guy's problem."

Hoffman gave a weak grin that hid the sadness in his heart. "Let 'em eat cake. Right?"

"What's that mean?" POTUS replied.

"Nothing," said the vice president and left.

A few minutes after Hoffman left, POTUS heard a knock on his door. "Come in."

Emma peeked around the door, scanning the room. "Just wanted to make sure he was gone."

"What's up?"

She sat down, took a deep breath, and exhaled slowly. "We need to mix it up a little, sir."

"What are you talking about?"

"Let's have some shit at the southern border. We need a story there."

"Southern one, right?" he said, smiling.

"Right. Let's bomb some bad guys in Syria."

"Okay."

"And let's get you to the hospital."

"What?"

"I don't think you look so well."

"I'm fine. Whadda' you talking about?"

"No. You look a little sick." POTUS cocked his head to his left slightly, his look questioning. I think it's time for you to go to the hospital… and make a strong recovery. And you're strong. Healthy. Virulent. Right? And you're the president, goddamnit. A little scare… no, not a scare, a mild concern, for a day or two, and then we remind them who the fuck you are and this whole thing is a ruse."

POTUS sat up straight but said nothing, just wagging his head, understanding the narrative, smiling in agreement, and marveling at his sagacious management abilities. Nice deflection. Great, new story.

***

Over the next couple of days, the authorities continued to feed the press misinformation and disinformation about the man's identity and history, which placated the news sources and the public. In reality, his body had been found on day two. The search ended formally on day three. Pictures of his face would be shared in Vancouver to identify him. Until then, the FBI and RCMP would stick with their story with a couple added discoveries: he was an out-of-work immigrant from

Toronto who had gone into a deep depression and drove across Canada to the Manning Park trailhead off Canadian Highway 3, intending to walk into the U.S. to make it to Seattle and connect with family members. Law enforcement authorities believed the man tried to steal one of the family's horses and that a failed theft turned into a violent confrontation. They assured the public, however, that the man was very, very dead and that the public was quite safe. Other than some follow-up stories by local news outlets around funerals for some of the bereaved, the story was soon over, just another unfortunate example of gun violence in America at its border, this one, for a change, having seeped in from the north.

Part III –
Epilogue

Coming Full Circle

It was a little over a month away from the elections. The polls showed a dead heat. Emma and POTUS' talking point of the moment was that if they lost the election, it was because of fraud. Doubts about a fair election taking place had been planted in the 2016 election as a safeguard against explaining a possible loss. Unexpectantly, however, they had won. Suddenly, however, the accusation had relevance, and half the country initially ate it up like a six-month-old eating pablum. Much of what they were being fed did not really hit the mark, had no real sustenance, was spit up, and was generally messy, but a market hungry for anything other than the truth ate up concoction, nonetheless. Win or lose, the narrative had been set to contest the outcome, albeit good or bad. If they lost, it was a fraud. If they had won, they would have won more had there not been a fraud.

Almost immediately after states started sending out early mail-in ballots, stories of tossed ballots began coming directly out of the White House. There were never any details about where such ballots were found, how many there were, whether actual votes had been cast therein, or if there had been, for which candidates. There were only vague details to foment doubts about election legitimacy. Right-friendly websites began to water and fertilize the seeds of doubt, cautioning potential, likely riots by liberals if POTUS won while at the same time suggesting the need for retribution by conservatives, perhaps even militias, if there was any indication that the election was stolen.

POTUS had been hospitalized with a case of Covid. Initially, it looked as though he might be truly ill. But after two days of treatment at Bethesda Medical Hospital, he had recovered completely and was back to predicting an early end to a pandemic that, up to then, had only killed a couple hundred thousand people or so. 'Just a moderate case of the flu,' he told the public. 'Gone in a couple of days.'

By the end of October, however, the number of people in the summer who claimed to have not only not known anyone who had had Covid, let alone anyone who had died, had changed markedly. While cities felt the initial impact of the disease, many rural areas of the country had been largely spared from infections. However, those who experienced outbreaks often got hit especially fast and hard, many having ignored all the recommended CDC protocols, including masks and social distancing. The public had grown progressively suspicious of the administration's ability to assess the pandemic's severity and keep it in check. By the time the election took place in early November, a clear numerical majority of Americans were aligned with the Democratic candidate. Given the country's electoral college format, whether the party in control could retain it remained uncertain for almost two days. It would ultimately remain contested by POTUS and most of his most ardent followers in perpetuity.

***

Washington D.C.

It had been almost six full weeks since the election. Emma had not been outside her apartment since the end of the third week. Her predictions of a contested election proved accurate, and a substantial part of the country believed POTUS had won. At that point, it had been painfully obvious to her, at least, that they had lost. She suspected the president knew that as well but was not admitting it for a multitude of reasons. Knowing the man as she did, she expected him to eventually believe his lies were true, encouraged in large part by sycophants who genuinely thought the election might be reversed, those who did not care but just wanted to serve the power source, and those conservative politicians, many correctly, that believed, despite hating him, if they did not support him, they would not be reelected. Part of that included blaming others for what had happened, which included her. When she told him three weeks after the press finalized their opinions that they were accurate and that it was time to move on, time to start planning for a rerun in 2024, that was the day she was excommunicated from the White House.

Rex lay on his back on the bed, staring at Emma. "If there's one thing I wish we had done differently," she told him as she ran her fingers across his stomach, "it would have been giving more attention to promoting the vaccine. We waited too long. That success was enough to leverage into a win. Hoffman was right. But we let it become too political. Too decisive. Couldn't make the whole 'save the world from the terrorists' a story," she lamented. Then her tone turned matter-of-fact. "So, in the end, we didn't have a story. And there you have it. Just two pissed-off sides of the populace. All that shit for nothing."

Rex kept his excitement to himself, staring in adulation at his love, waiting for her next move.

***

Cody had spent the winter in a cabin outside of Prince George's owned by yet another friend of Buck. The cabin was about two miles outside Prince George's, about a half mile of which was a trail from the cabin to a maintained road that led to town. The cabin had been stocked with plenty of food in the freezer and pantry. Buck visited him three times, once in late October, another a few days before

Thanksgiving, and again in late March. Cody had otherwise been entirely alone, save for one attempted break into the cabin by a hungry black bear coming out of hibernation in early March. In fact, by late winter, the isolation and darkness had begun to weigh heavily on his psyche. He would say many times later that he knew what it was like to be kept in the dark for too long.

During his first two visits, Buck brought letters from Sweetie and initiated the delivery of several Cody had written. Agent Randal had given Buck fifteen thousand Canadian dollars for Cody to use, as necessary, for his stay in Prince George. Twice, he ventured into the town of seventy-five thousand people, the first a few days before Christmas and the second around the middle of January. Both times, he could not shake a feeling of being watched, though looking back later, he knew it was paranoia mixed with guilt. No one of any consequence knew he was here, and he knew that is how it should remain. At the same time, though, he yearned for someone to share the holidays with. He missed his family, even members with a penchant for ruining holidays. To fend off the boredom and loneliness, he focused on completing necessary tasks that took up his time while at the same time providing some sense of accomplishment. He watched television news, read the books he found in the cabin and the few Buck had left, took up drawing with a focus on real-life settings he saw out various windows of the cabin as well as its rooms and their contents, and split cords of wood for his wood stove. If *they* ever found him, it would be because someone had somehow followed Buck, and Buck was proficient at not being followed, having developed a broad network of friends on which he could rely for myriad favors.

Despite his efforts to pass his time productively, by February, the walls of the cabin seemed to have moved closer to one another. The once spacious living room seemed smaller, the copious number of animal heads hanging on the walls, seemingly watching his every move while casting menacing shadows that moved with the dancing flames of the fire that shined through the glass window of the large woodstove that now inhabited the fireplace. He had run out of new ways to stay busy and stay interested. By mid-December, Cody had to stop splitting wood altogether, as he began to fear not having a sufficient supply of pieces that would last him through April, which were big enough to burn through the night. He did, he surmised; however, he had enough kindling. As daylight began to noticeably lengthen in March, he took up snowshoeing for a couple of weeks, until he encountered a large bull moose, scourging near a pond that was as tall as him at the shoulder and seemed to smell him, as the animal first sniffed and then began to move purposefully in his direction. Cody, somewhat hidden from the animal by the trees in which he had been hiking, had not gotten far from the cabin but got an unforgettable workout slogging his way back home in record time.

Buck's visits were short, the first two days; each, just long enough to catch up on major news stories. Buck gave him his own inclined perspective of what was going on in the states and globally, the two talking into the early hours of the morning in November around America's recent presidential election results and where the country might be headed. Cody watched a local TV station that he received via an antenna connection, an entertaining, homey, yet limited filter through which to view the world. He had no internet, so Buck's filter on where the United States and the world were was Cody's. Cody understood this bias but fundamentally trusted Buck, nonetheless, as a reliable news source.

"So, do you think things will settle down a bit now that we're going to have a new president?" Cody had asked Buck.

"I don't know. This guy will do anything, I think, to hold onto power. And his believers are… such… such believers," Buck said. "Doesn't matter how much he lies. It's incredible. They believe him no matter what. They don't get just how desperate they are."

"Desperate?" said Cody.

"Yeah. I'm not sure for what, though. Desperate to be recognized, I guess. Acknowledged, maybe. Who knows? But that clown doesn't give two shits about his core. It's amazing. He's just one of the elites he encourages them to hate. Drain the swamp should be updated to flush the toilet. His whole group should go to jail. They're lucky most of them got a pardon."

"What about the person who talked to Dan and Cal? That organized that whole shitshow?"

"Oh, funny you should ask. Steve tells me someone did an Edward Snowden on her. Hacked her computer's camera and caught her giving a little 'handy' to her dog. A St. Bernard. Then they sent her an email with the video clip attached telling her to go find another job or else it'd be on Facebook."

"Holy shit," Cody said, laughing.

"Yeah. UFC, right? Yeah, POTUS may run again, but she's out."

Cody asked him whether he knew anything of Dan and Cal's fate. Buck told him that he was not sure but that Randal had told him that, in the short term, the two were probably being sent to Ukraine to tutor students in English at one of the universities on the west side of the country. It seems one of the two boys, he thought it was Cal, had a Russian grandmother who had taught him some Russian. Government officials thought the assignment would be safe for a year or so until they could figure out a long-term solution for each young man.

Cody's main interest, of course, was Sweetie. Buck brought letters with him on his first two visits, lots of them. Cody gave him many handwritten pages to take back. Buck counseled him on the second visit that the worst days were probably yet to come, and they were. December, January, and February were dark and dismal. The Northern Lights that danced in the sky from the end of October and the first week of November were replaced with beautiful starry nights, nights whose beauty matched the brilliance of the Pasayten but nights that went on for sixteen or so hours at their worst. As one who loved the early morning sunrises of summer, Cody's resolve and determination began to fade in December around Christmas and were almost completely upended by early March. But as the days began getting longer, the cabin warmed more quickly in the morning, held its heat longer between logs fed into the stove, and it took a little less fuel to maintain the temperature at night. Birds began showing themselves during the day and sharing their mating songs. Deer and elk ventured outside the cabin's front window, and sunrise had moved from 9:30 a.m. to almost three hours earlier. Cody's spirits heightened as he began to 'see the light.' When he saw the vehicle Buck used in his prior visit coming down his driveway, he was suddenly a blend of excited, happy, and hopeful. But all those emotions swelled by a factor of ten when he saw who was with him.

Neither Sweetie nor Cody hid their emotions. Cody hustled toward the car, almost slipping on the melting ice that encapsulated the stairs that led off the front porch. Sweetie vaulted from the SUV and scurried through the snow toward Cody, meeting him at the front of the car for a loving, kiss-filled embrace. Both cried and Buck, who sat in the car waiting, giving them a couple of minutes to themselves, momentarily teared up himself.

"I missed you so much, baby," Sweetie said, cupping his cheek with her right hand and leaning back slightly to see his face.

"I missed you, too," Cody choked out. "I… I just had no idea how much I love you. Does that sound weird? You're all I've thought about."

"No," she replied, shaking her head firmly. "No. It's not weird. I know exactly what you mean. I've missed you so much. I'm not whole when you're not with me. I want to be with you, which has become clearer by not being together."

After a couple of minutes, Buck exited the car and gave his greetings, advising the two to go in and get comfortable while he moved in his and Sweetie's luggage. When he went in, Sweetie and Cody sat on the couch, babbling, trying to find a starting place to get caught up on almost six months of lost time. Sweetie commented on the ten pounds Cody seemed to have lost, which did not come from surplus.

"You been taking care of yourself? Eating okay? Getting some exercise?" she asked concernedly.

"Yeah, I guess. Not really. Not like I should, I suppose. Started out okay. But honestly, the loneliness and the darkness finally got to me. I missed you so much. I'm really glad you got here when you did. I tell you, I was losing it," Cody said, his voice fragile. "Got tired of cooking and eating the same old shit. Elk meat and rice. Mmm. I miss my vegetables. Funny, huh?"

"I'll cook you something nice tonight, then," she said warmly, snuggling into his shoulder while snaking her arm under his chin, hooking her hand up behind his head and pulling it toward her where she planted a solid kiss on his cheek.

"I'll go into town and buy something for dinner," said Buck, having heard the exchange. "What do you want me to get, Sweetie?"

"We can all go," said Cody, excited about getting out of the cabin and doing something with other people.

Buck smiled, shaking his head slightly. "No," he said. That's not a good idea. I'll go. We all don't need to be seen together. Let's stay cautious… til we're positive, we're safe. That'll give you two some time alone, anyway. I'll be back in, uh, let's say, an hour. Probably a little more, but let's say an hour. Sound good?"

Sweetie and Cody nodded affirmatively. A minute after Buck began backing down the driveway, the two began making the most of the hour Buck had given them. Buck spent considerably far more time in the produce section than he needed to. But he also spent more time in the Dairy, Bakery, and Meat section than he needed to. The result, though, was a panoply of fresh fruits and vegetables that he knew Cody had not tasted for almost four months. Being single himself, Buck had not given much thought to the matter after leaving Cody the last two times. Sweetie, though, was now a welcomed catalyst for more attention to such details. Buck's shopping efforts paid dividends for the couple. When he returned, it was apparent Cody and Sweetie had, given the looks on their faces, had enough time to reconnect or at least enough time to start the process. Sweetie cooked a wonderful stir fry for dinner that both he and Cody savored appreciably.

The kids went to bed early that night; Buck sat and watched the fire burn through the woodstove, the room's lights turned off. As the fire lights flickered, the shadows moved, and expressionless dead animals stared at him blankly; it occurred to him that this was Cody's world for almost six months, a world of solitude, death, and darkness.

Buck was overcome with emotion, overwhelming empathy, and identification. Buck had his own severe moments of depression from loneliness in his life. Still, he had a plethora of friends and family, but most fortunately for him, a job that kept him moving, challenged, and engaged. Cody, the vibrant, caring, intelligent, and talented young man that he was, had none of these here. Buck was surprised at the feeling of guilt that suddenly rushed over him like a hot shower that, without explanation, suddenly turned ice cold. He had news about the couple's future that he would share with them tomorrow. Would Cody trust him again after having experienced what he had for the last several months? Buck was tired. That would help him. But he expected a long, restless night for himself.

***

Buck got up first, made coffee, and watched the morning news, careful to be quiet and not wake up Sweetie and Cody. He finally heard them stirring around 9:30 and moved back to the kitchen, put on a fresh pot of coffee, turned on the stove, and began cooking eight strips of bacon in a large frypan, hoping the aromas would coax them out of bed. Fifteen minutes later, the two walked in, looking refreshed and happy.

"Sleep well?" asked Buck.

"Yes, sir," Cody said. "Best rest in a long time."

Sweetie just made a nonverbal sound of affirmation while nodding and smiling sheepishly. She shuffled toward the coffee pot in oversized wool slippers she had coopted from the closet in their room. She poured herself and Cody a cup and came and sat down at the kitchen table where Buck and Cody were seated. Buck had presented a plate of freshly cooked bacon and a bowl of scrambled eggs.

"Mmmm. Looks great, Grandpa," said Sweetie. "Thank you."

Buck loved that moniker, and hearing it from Sweetie, with whom there were so many lost years, gave him goosebumps and a warm feeling in his heart. "My pleasure, sweetheart," he replied.

"So, I have some information for you two to consider. It's important for your short-term and long-term decisions."

"Let's hear it," said Cody. "I hope it involves getting out of here. It's nice here, don't get me wrong; I appreciate all you've done, Buck. But I don't want to stay here much over the near term, let alone the long term."

"Understood," said Buck.

With that, Buck laid out their choices, which, given Cody's announcement, were narrow. While Sweetie could stay in Winthrop, Cody could likely never go home. Presently, he was dead to the world. In early June, Buck told them, Cody would be relocated back to the Vancouver, B.C. area. Between now and then, Sweetie could stay here with him, meet him in Vancouver in June, or remain in Winthrop. The comprehensive decision, presumably, was something that they would both work out.

"Where he goes or stays, I'm there," interjected Sweetie.

"I like it," Cody immediately replied.

Buck continued. The terms of their witness protection were quite good. First, they would be given a free, clear condo north of the city. They would be responsible for associated expenses. To that end, they would be provided with a checking account with a million and a half Canadian dollars that would have to last them the rest of their lives. Cody would be able to finish his education at the University of British Columbia, and an academic scholarship would pay all expenses. Thereafter, he was guaranteed a job with the Canadian government if he could not find a good position in the private sector. Sweetie would be given a job to her liking if she was interested in working; she could also finish school. They were to be given new names and histories. Each would receive a Canadian driver's license and passport, although both could not enter the United States under any circumstances unless coordinated through a designated Canadian agency contact. His new name was Kiley Robinette, and hers was Christy Miller. Their accounts would be joint, though their records showed each to be legally single.

"So, you two better get along and trust one another," Buck said.

They would have to learn their 'histories' and work out their longer-term arrangements as a couple. Going forward, they would forever be Canadians, not Americans. While Cody had no close family, Sweetie, of course, did. And while she probably would not see her parents for at least the next couple of years, Buck said he was certain they could eventually visit, perhaps not in Vancouver, but likely closer to where he lived in the eastern part of the province. If one or the other got sick and needed to visit, something could be worked out.

Cody and Sweetie sat in silence, considering the option. Cody finally put his hand over hers and asked, "What do you think, Sweetie?"

She pondered the question for a moment and then said, "Oh, boy. Well, sometimes the worst things that happen to us can turn out for the best. Some of this shit that's gone down, well, I don't know how it could be any worse. But I have a lot of confidence in Cody and me. So, I think we can make something wonderful out of this opportunity," she said while looking at him and squeezing his hand, then adding, "As long as trying too hard doesn't get the best of us."

"I think I've heard something like that before," said Buck.

Sweetie just hunched her shoulders. "And I want to stay now. I don't want to go back and leave Cody here alone any longer."

"So, it's done then. You two will stay here until June. I'll come back and get you then. Be safe here. Go for hikes, but don't loiter in town. Ride in, ride out, but don't walk around. Sweetie, you do the shopping and wear a mask, and Cody, you wait outside. Stay safe."

"Got it," said Cody.

"I'll leave today," said Buck.

"Why so soon?" said Sweetie. "Can't you wait until tomorrow?"

"Oh, I checked the weather. There's a front moving in tomorrow. I want to get some miles behind me before it gets dark."

Fifty minutes later, Buck, having shat, showered, and shaved, was ready to go.

"You two take care and stay safe," he said.

"We love you, Grandpa," Sweetie said, as Cody nodded in agreement.

After giving each a hug, Buck squeezed into the driver's seat and, before shutting his door, added, "I'll see you both in June."

As Buck pulled away, Sweetie and Cody held one another at the waist and waved, watching Buck until the car was out of sight, before going back into the cabin, where they made their way to the living room, sat down, and began excitedly laying out their future.

***

Vancouver, Canada

Six months later, Early Fall

Buck had picked them up at the cabin and driven them to an Airbnb that had been reserved for Kiley Robinette in Vancouver. Over the next two months, they were shown different suburbs within the greater metro area. In addition, they spent considerable time online looking at different projects within the areas they were most interested in: condo projects and single-family homes within their established purchase budget to get a sense of what they could expect in different locations.

Cody and Sweetie, now Kiley and Christy, had enrolled for fall classes. Cody continued his marketing major in the business program at the University of British Columbia, and Sweetie took courses on interior design fundamentals at the British Columbia Institute of

Technology. In July, they found an upscale, two-bedroom townhouse in Richmond, allowing convenient metro transportation to their respective schools.

It was the third week of August, and their new townhouse unit was scheduled to close in early September, while classes for each were to start the third week of that month. They had not seen Buck since he delivered them to their Airbnb unit in mid-June. On the third weekend of August, he came to their unit for an unexpected meeting.

"Hi, Grandpa," said Sweetie, pleasantly surprised and joyful.

"Hi, Christy," he replied. "I give if I call you Sweetie, at least as a greeting, nobody will think anything about it… maybe."

"Come in," she said, giving him a warm, welcoming embrace. "It's been so hard getting used to a new name."

"Well, keep at it. Who was that Avery guy, anyway? Who am I now? I'm Buck Carpenter, god damnit," he said with farcical emphasis.

"I can't imagine," she said, chuckling, "but, yeah, I'll keep at it."

"Kiley here?"

"Yeah. He's peeing. Let's go sit in the living room. You want anything? Beer?" she asked.

"No, I'm good."

"Hi, Buck," said Cody excitedly. "What's up, man? How are you doing, anyway?"

Buck stood, and the two quickly embraced each other. Given their shared histories and long talks, Cody had come to like the man considerably. When he and Sweetie talked about him, he often longed for his company afterward. For Cody, Back was a valued source of opinion and perspectives around a complex world and life, a father figure he had wished he had growing up.

"I'm good. How you doing, Kiley?"

"I wish we could be who we really are," Cody replied.

"You are. You're Kiley, damnit."

Buck had been tracking their hunt for a residence through the real estate agent they had been assigned to work with, who believed 'Kiley and Christy,' as she had been told, to have moved to Vancouver recently from Florida following the death of Christy's grandmother, who had left her a moderately sized inheritance. The agent, in turn, had referred Buck to a local interior designer. They were to all meet tomorrow, Buck told them, at the unit. At his expense, as a gift to the two, Buck was offering a budget of $50,000 to furnish the unit. Whatever shortfall they might encounter beyond that for their desired furnishings, they would have to pay for themselves. T

***

Buck picked up Kiley and Christy mid-morning and drove them to the unit. Their new life was now in full swing and about to go to another level. They were greeted by their masked, COVID-protected real estate agent, Dusty Highland, who had left the door open.

"Hi, Kiley," he said. "Hi, Christy. How are you two doing?"

"We're good," they said in almost unison.

Dusty introduced himself to Buck, the two having talked on the phone but not having met until now.

361

"Hi, Dusty," said Buck, gently fist-bumping Mark's hand. "Nice to put a face to a name."

"Indeed," said Dusty. "Come meet my friend."

When they got to the living room, a woman facing the opposite direction was scanning the room, contemplating something.

"Mayla," said Dusty, "I'd like to introduce you to two new friends of mine.

When Mayla turned around, Dusty's new friends were all momentarily staggered, Mayla's beauty having left them momentarily breathless.

"Hi, I'm Christy," said Sweetie, now fully ensconced in her new identity.

"I'm Mayla."

The men quickly followed suit.

"Hi, I'm Kiley."

"Hi, Mayla. I'm Buck."

"Ah, you're the gentleman I spoke with," said Mayla graciously.

"That's correct," said Buck.

Mayla is a first-class interior decorator," said Dusty. Then quickly added, "World class. She'll help you find suppliers of whatever style you have in mind and probably show you some that you didn't. She's awesome."

"I'm so excited," said Christy. "I'm taking some classes this fall in interior design."

"That's wonderful," said Mayla. "We'll have a lot of fun with this, then. I'm also happy to have you come along on some other assignments. You can learn, and I'll have some company."

"That would be so awesome."

"Dusty tells me you've just located here," said Mayla.

"Yep. A new beginning," said Christy.

"How exciting," said Mayla. "New beginnings, new adventures."

"We hope so. And who is this?" asked Christy, pointing to a stroller that had collapsed to its bassinet function.

"This is Bodhi," replied Mayla.

"Wow. Look at those eyes. They're beautiful."

"Thank you. Yes, they are, aren't they?" Mayla said proudly.

"God, they're almost full-on green. Hazel. Right?"

"Yes. One of the two. Time will tell," Mayla said, smiling.

"Nice name, too. Bodhi." When Christy said the name, the child seemed to smile. "I saw that on a popular names list recently. It means 'the chosen one,' doesn't it?"

"Yes, it does."

"Hi, Bodhi," Christy said, gently reaching and tickling him with her index finger, eliciting a bright smile from the boy and a complementary baby coo. "Is he named after anyone in particular?"

"Well, his dad, sort of."

"His dad's name was Bodhi?"

"No… it's a long story. But no, not exactly. His dad wasn't the chosen one, that's for certain."

"Sounds like a story, alright."

"Yes. Well, it is. But not one that is worth hearing. Trust me…"

"Well, always nice to hear a good story," said Christy. "I'm really looking forward to working with you on this, Mayla. I've never done this from scratch. I'm so excited. This is going to be so much fun."

"Well, it's fun to have fun," replied Mayla, "So, let's get started."

Dusty Highland had pulled the men into the kitchen briefly, and they returned with a bottle of champagne, which he had bought, and five glasses that the remaining two men were carrying.

"I'll toast to that," said Highland as he quickly filled Kiley and Buck's glasses. They all followed his lead as he held up his glass.

"To new beginnings," offered Mayla.

"To friends and family," said Christy. "New and old."

"Peace and harmony," proposed Kiley.

"Good fortune and good health," Buck suggested.

"Oh wow," said Highland. "You guys got all the good ones. Uh… well, to a timely close. CHEERS!"

And they all laughed, clinked glasses, and in chorus whooped a resounding, "CHEERS!"